THE SINGHING DETECTIVE

Also by this author:

THE DEVIL'S TEARS
SILENT NIGHT

THE SINGHING DETECTIVE

M.C. DUTTON

This is a work of fiction.
Any similarity to persons
living or dead is merely coincidental.

Matador
5 Weir Road
Kibworth Beauchamp
Leicester LE8 0LQ, UK
Tel: (+44) 116 279 2299
Fax: (+44) 116 279 2277
Email: books@troubador.co.uk
Web: www.troubador.co.uk/matador

ISBN 978 1848767 218

British Library Cataloguing in Publication Data.
A catalogue record for this book is available from the British Library.

Printed and bound in the UK by TJ International, Padstow, Cornwall

Typeset in 11pt Stempel Garamond by Troubador Publishing Ltd, Leicester, UK

Matador is an imprint of Troubador Publishing Ltd

*I dedicate this book to Upkar Ghatta-Aureh
known as Uppy to his friends and colleagues.
Your Loyalty, enthusiasm and commitment to the job
has been an inspiration.*

I thank you for your friendship.

CHAPTER ONE

She watered her plant above the sink with a shaky hand. There were things that had to be done every day and in the right order. She had washed her breakfast things and before she dried up, she would water the miniature Azalea bush she had bought in Sainsbury's last month. It had beautiful mauve flowers that looked so cheery and pretty on her kitchen window ledge above the sink. When she had dried up she would have that cup of tea she had promised herself; her throat was gasping for a nice cuppa. She liked to sit and watch Jeremy Kyle with her cup of tea. He was such a good man trying to help those angry and sad people on his programme. Their tales of woe both shocked her and made her laugh to hear such shenanigans going on.

She was 85 years old and it was her birthday today. Tonight she would have a glass of special sherry. Harveys Bristol Cream was her favourite. With a piece of fresh salmon for her tea, she would have a meal fit for the queen. There was no one to visit her but she always had her imaginary friend, Cissie. Alice had a school friend called Cissie but they lost touch during the war. She was telling Cissie about her Freddie who had died 30 years ago. He had one of those heart attacks and just died. He had got up to go and tell next door's dog to shut up. It had been barking for hours, no one ever knew why this dog barked so much. She recalled how Freddie had gone puce with rage, and had startled her when he got out of his chair and stood so angrily. He had shouted at the door, saying how he was going to kick that dog up the arse until it choked on its balls.

"My Freddie was not a man to mess with," Alice told Cissie in a shaky dry voice. "He was not very tall but he was big built with a barrel chest that he puffed out proudly when he walked down the street." She smiled at the thought and wistfully recalled, "He would take my arm and we walked like a pair of toffs." She paused for a moment, remembering him arm in arm with her. The days had seemed sunny and bright all those years ago. With a sigh, she continued her story with her imaginary friend. "So Freddie was very angry now and said he was going to give the neighbours a piece of his mind. Apparently, he knocked at their house and when they came to the door to see who was there, Freddie opened his mouth, went bright red and keeled over. Of course they ran and got me but I could see he was dead when I got there". Alice paused for a moment, her eyes pricked remembering clearly that horrible day. "They took his false teeth out Cissie, and I don't know why they did that, he was dead after all. It made him look old without them and that was not how I wanted to remember him." Alice blinked and let go of the memory. She sighed; it was a long time ago and she had got used to being alone. He had never been much of a talker anyway, but it was nice to have someone to watch telly with. She had Nettie the cat but she didn't come in much these days. "Still," she added warmly, "I am pleased to have you here Cissie. We can sit and watch Jeremy Kyle together but you had better cover your ears, they say some very bad things." Alice smiled and thought oh yes, Cissie and her had some laughs together. It was time to put the kettle on.

Alice Watson had been quite happy living in her home of 59 years. She had moved in with Freddie after they got married and they had never moved. It needed a bit of paint now, but Alice wasn't too bothered. She had seen some changes over the years. Her road 59 years ago when they first moved in was so quiet and very nice and you hardly ever saw a car in those days. Now, when she looked outside, all the front gardens had been paved over and were full of cars and the street had cars up on the pavement as well. Newbury Park had been quite posh when they first moved in. It was very different from the East End. They came originally from Bow but Freddie had always liked Newbury Park. He had an aunt they used to visit when he was a child, who lived in Aldborough Road. He couldn't afford one of those big houses but Wards Road was close by and the houses, newly finished after the war, had upstairs bathrooms and toilets, which was very posh. It was quiet and sedate and they had been very happy there. Now it was noisy and car music could be heard late at night.

The first Indian family moved into the street just after Freddie died. They lived opposite her. Alice was upset that Freddie didn't meet them. Freddie had been somewhere near India during his time with the merchant navy and he just loved a curry. Alice could never make them. Freddie told Alice about his time in India and how different and wonderful it was. She had a wooden carved elephant he had brought back from one of his trips. He would have loved the Indian family, he always talked fondly about his time in India. She got talking to Amereen and Jaswinder and she watched little Jaswinder grow into a big lad. They could never get Alice to try a curry though. After many attempts to get her to try a spoonful, Alice had said, courteously begging their pardon for being so blunt, that she thought curry smelt like shit and there was no way she could eat that stuff. She always said her Freddie would have loved it though. This was accepted by the Singh family and never mentioned again.

Alice and Mr and Mrs Singh formed a close and warm friendship which lasted many years. Mr Singh had died 10 years ago and that was sad. Mrs Singh had died two years ago and Alice missed her. Little Jaswinder was big now and had left home a long time ago and joined the police force. Mr Singh lived long enough to see little Jaswinder join the police force and saw him rise through the ranks. They were very proud of their son. It was a great source of sadness to Amereen that Mr Singh died just before Jaswinder or Jazz as he was now known, became a Detective Sergeant. When Jazz came back for the funeral of his mother, Alice saw him looking taller and leaner than most of the other family members she saw go into the house. She was shocked to see he had shaved his head. He laughed when she asked why he had done that. As a boy, he had thick black hair with a beautiful wave through it. He had laughed off her comments and said it was the worry of having had two wives. Alice hoped he hadn't had them at the same time. He assured her that one wife at a time was enough for him. What he didn't tell her was the marriage break up, the pressure of the job and that time back in Ilford had caused his hair to fall out. He liked Alice, who he knew was a sweet, kind and naïve old lady from an era that had long since passed. She didn't need to know what was out there in the real world.

Strange things were happening in Alice's house. She had told Cissie about it but Cissie never had an opinion about anything. Alice had whispered that she thought she might be haunted. There were strange noises that happened like clockwork: in the morning, lunchtime, evening and in the middle of the night. The evening didn't seem so bad because the TV was on in her room but the strange noises in the middle of the night frightened her. Her walls in her living room were really hot. If someone had lived next door, she would have thought it was their heating but no one lived next door. It wasn't winter anyway so why would next door have their heating on? she wondered. It also occurred to her that her house was a bit warm too. It wasn't that hot outside and although she did like a bit of warmth, it wasn't right and it didn't make any sense. There could only be one reason, she concluded.

Alice listened, and thought, and what she eventually decided was that she wasn't haunted but next door was. It was very frightening. The noises she heard were not voices, more like moans. The walls adjoining next door were hot to touch. She knew it must be the devil in there. She had taken to getting all the crosses she had in her drawers out and putting them on and trying to put them near the wall next door. There was the crucifix her mother left her, another from a visit to a church in Kent and another which was for her to wear. She used to keep it in her jewellery box but now she had taken to wearing it all the time. She found an old bible in a cupboard and put that beside her bed.

Next door had been bought about six months ago. It was a Chinese family, she thought, well they looked kind of Chinese. Freddie would have told her off for saying that. To Alice, if you looked a bit oriental, you were Chinese. Freddie said there were lots of oriental people; some were Chinese but some were Japanese, or even Vietnamese. Alice remembered she used to say, "Well they all end with *ese* so Chinese will do." Freddie was much more worldly than she was. She did missed him. He would know what to do about the Chinese house next door; he always knew what was best. The Chinese people had done some work in the house but then they had stopped and left. Occasionally, she saw someone go back in for a few hours but no one lived there. It was the end house so sometimes a car would be driven down the sideway and she never saw who had come to visit.

Alice didn't know what to make of it all. She was frightened by the thought that all the noise and heat could be the devil's work. She had to do something and after considering everything, she had decided that when the Chinese persons next came to the house, she would knock and ask them if the house was haunted and whether that was why they didn't live there. She was going to suggest they had it exorcised. She had seen a programme about it on Jeremy Kyle and that sounded the best idea. She would watch every day so she didn't miss them arriving. The car going down the sideway meant no one went in the front door, they went in the side door and unless she was vigilant, she might miss them.

She watched Jeremy Kyle with her cup of tea and was amazed at how people spoke to each other on the TV. She would never have had words with Mr Watson in public. They had more pride. Sometimes Freddie would say something quite sharply and she would raise her eyebrows at him. That seemed to settle him down and that was about as bad as it got between them. He was a gentleman, and would never have raised his voice at her in private, let alone in public. People were different all those years ago. Today, she was shocked to see the woman hitting and shouting at a man on *The Jeremy Kyle Show.* Goodness me, she thought, whatever is the world coming to.

After Jeremy Kyle, Alice got up to start her daily chores. It was Monday so washing had to be done. She had a few personal bits to wash and the towels and bed linen would go in her washing machine. She had bought an automatic washing machine with Amereen about 15 years ago. They had both gone to the electricity shop and ordered it. Amereen had been such a good friend to her. The washing machine had changed her life. Up until then Alice had a washing machine that just washed. You had to take the clothes out at the top all soapy and rinse everything. There had been a wringer attached to the top of the washing machine and all the clothes were put through the wringer. It had been considered very posh when she first bought the Hoover washing machine, but as she got older, it was hard work, especially when washing sheets and the towels weighed so much when they were full of soapy water. Her arms and shoulders used to ache. Amereen had suggested an automatic machine. Well, Alice thought that as there was only her, it wasn't worth the money. But, goodness, was she glad she got it. It was now 15 years old and still going strong and there wasn't a scratch on it. Nothing wore out in her house, except herself of course. She laughed at that thought.

Yes, she missed Amereen very much. They would sit and chat, each hardly knowing what the other was saying. Amereen had a very confusing accent and her English was always a bit limited. Alice had a strong cockney accent that Amereen found hard to understand, but they laughed and chatted together and looked out for each other. When little Jaswinder left home to work away in Manchester, Amereen was very sad and lost. She had relatives who lived up north but their visits were rare these days. Alice visited every day for months, bringing Amereen's favourite chocolate digestives to have with a cup of tea. Eventually, Amereen felt better and was not so sad. When Alice had a fall and was bed bound for three weeks, Amereen made her a casserole, cooked her chicken, bought her fish and chips on a Friday and kept her company. Alice was very appreciative of Amereen's help and she didn't cook any of that foreign curry stuff for her to eat, which was very nice of her. Everyone she cared about seemed to have gone. Still, it would be her turn soon, she thought, and then they would all be together again.

Her washing was out on the line. She loved to see it blowing in the wind; it gave her so much pleasure. In fact, if it was a nice Monday, she would wash anything and everything so she could see it blowing on the line. Today was a lovely day to sit in the garden. When she had finished her chores, she would have her lunch in the garden and watch the birds. She was looking forward to her sherry tonight. Alice liked a sherry but confined herself to special occasions only. Her parents had been Methodists and didn't drink at all. Freddie liked his rum and said that the odd sherry would do no harm so Alice allowed herself such a delicious pleasure every now and then.

This little old lady, who had lived an uneventful life, was about to be responsible for starting a blood bath between gang members.

Today, Alice changed her routine. Instead of cleaning the bedroom, which was a Monday job, she decided to weed the front garden. She thought that next door might appear and she would notice more if she was outside. She remembered it was always on a Monday that the Chinese gentlemen usually appeared. Alice should have had her sherry at lunchtime, by teatime she would be dead.

CHAPTER TWO

Jaswinder Singh, or the Jazz Singer, and just Jazz to his friends and enemies, was packing up his desk. He got called into his Chief Super's office first thing Monday morning and told he was off to join the Met and he would be stationed in Ilford. "Look I know its not where you want to go Jazz," the Chief adopted a friendly tone and used his nickname. Jazz could lose it when antagonised and he didn't want a fuss in his office. The Chief also didn't want Jazz to go. He was a pain in the neck a lot of the time and he got a bit close to the edge most of the time, but a good Detective he was. Dedicated, sensible, enthusiastic and, at the same time, an absolute nightmare for his partners to work with. He had been stationed in Manchester for the past five years and now he was to return to the Met.

The past couple of years had been an experience Jazz would rather forget. His Chief Super had been a true friend to him and acted like the father he had lost. At times he was bollocked and at other times taken to the pub for a drink and some friendly advice. He had been on an insane merry go round. His wife, picked for him by his family, lasted barely a year. She was too stupid, too foreign and too lazy for him. His family had fled

Uganda in 1969 when he was just a baby and he became an East London boy. His second wife was English. A blonde beauty who, at the beginning made him laugh and at the end of their relationship made him cry. His family in Bradford were not happy at all but he didn't give a flying fuck what they thought. The arranged marriage had been organised by his uncle, who obviously didn't know what the fuck he wanted or needed so bollocks to them, he thought.

His second marriage to Linda was destined to fail. He was working every hour under the sun and only going home to sleep. The marriage was never going to last under this pressure, but finding time to argue and split up takes more hours than he spent at home. He worked hard for his money and she went out and spent it. It was opening the door to the bailiffs one morning that finally closed the door on his second marriage.

The mental breakdown had been a long time coming out but the build up could be tracked back to the stake out. There were many ingredients that vied for pole position. His first marriage was finished in a blasé way that belied the shame he felt for the loss of face he had brought on his family. Jazz had blustered but all the posturing, shouting and condemning of arranged marriages didn't stop the depression he felt for humiliating his family. He was born and brought up in England. He spoke like an East Ender, joked like a Londoner and ate like a westerner, but he was Sikh deep down in his heart and he knew what he had done was wrong.

Priya was a girl from the Punjab. She was 19 years old

and a sought-after bride. Priya was 16 years younger than Jazz and her experience of life was simplistic and protected. Her father was very respected and it was only because Jazz had such a good job and was in England that the marriage was agreed. She had been used to servants waiting on her and the sun had always shined on her. In Manchester, she knew very few people and it was dark and wet and she had to cook and clean. She was very unhappy. The community in Bradford knew she came from good stock and deserved more respect.

Through Jazz and Priya's marriage, the Singh family were now aligned to a very rich and well known family. The Singh's were Ugandan Sikhs, which meant they were not as strict in their religion as those from the Punjab. The marriage was seen as the pinnacle of the Singh family's rise in Sikh society. In Sikh culture marriage is not just between two people, it is the marriage of two families. Priya came to live in England and all the grandchildren would be English. Jazz had a very good job and it was known that he was going to do very well in the police force. The marriage was deemed perfect. The Singh family basked in the glory it brought them.

Looking back, Jazz realised why he had been railroaded into an arranged marriage he never wanted: The timing had been perfect. He had been sent away in disgrace to the Manchester Police force and his mind was tottering between either wiping away the events in Ilford or just going for a full blown breakdown. To be his family's saviour, he paraphrased his uncles words, by such a prestigious marriage, seemed a good idea at the time. He wanted to please someone. A big mistake.

The marriage was a disaster. Jazz found Priya spoilt, stupid and pathetic. It wasn't her fault, he conceded, but this is not how he saw his life turning out. They had nothing in common and couldn't talk about anything on similar grounds. She came from a culture very different from the life Jazz was living. Watching football, a beer in the pub, fish and chips on a Saturday night; none of this made sense to Priya. The sex had been interesting but not enough. They didn't love each other and very soon after their marriage, they couldn't tolerate being in the same room together. She wanted to go home. Jazz divorced Priya; something that was unthinkable in their class. The Singh family's dignity and prestige in the community was lost and this hurt them badly. Priya was taken in by Jazz's uncle and she lived in Bradford until Priya's family decided what they wanted to do. Jazz was told not to darken their door again. The humiliation was appeased by this estrangement and the Sikh society forgave the Singh family but they could not forgive Jazz. His mother prayed for him and forgave him. It had been a distressing time for her but she loved him. He was her only son and he could do no wrong.

CHAPTER THREE

After he moved to Manchester, Amereen didn't see Jazz very much. As she had told Alice, he was so important and busy he just didn't have the time. His first bride, Priya, was a good marriage. There was a big society wedding, which meant Amereen and her family in Bradford had to travel to India. It had been very many years since Amereen had travelled to India, or even been on a plane. One of her brothers came to get her and she travelled with him to India. Her brother acted as the elder of the family and spoke for Amereen and for Jazz. She stayed for several months in India and saw some of her family who lived there. She didn't want to come back but Jazz lived in England and she wanted to be in the same country as him. A visa was applied for and after quite a short time, Priya was able to travel to England with Jazz. She told Alice that she missed not being with her own family but her home was in Newbury Park. The wedding had been spectacular and the celebrations went on for days. Priya's family had made her very welcome.

Amereen had sat one afternoon and tried to explain to Alice what a Sikh wedding was like. She started by explaining when the marriage took place and about the holy shabads and the rituals but Amereen could see that Alice was finding it hard to grasp all the names and what the rituals meant so she cut it short and said the ceremony ended with the holy sweet pudding Karah Pasad, which was distributed to all present.

Alice had thought Gawd, all those confusing and strange names, it all sounds very complicated. But she could see that Amereen felt very proud and so she made her a cup of tea and brought out Amereen's favourite chocolate digestives. Alice was very pleased to see Amereen back. She had missed her and listened for hours to the strange and beautiful tales Amereen told her of the wedding and the reception.

Amereen had come home with a suitcase full of colourful saris bought as presents for her and gold bracelets on her arm. As the mother of the groom, she was paid a lot of attention and it was something she talked about for a long time. Alice could imagine all the colours of the saris and the flower petals and the music and the dancing. It sounded beautiful to her. Amereen bought Alice a necklace made of a bright gold. The necklace was so beautiful and Alice was overawed that such a fine piece of jewellery had been bought for her. She kept it in a jewellery box to be worn on special occasions. When Amereen died, Alice wore it for months, not wanting to take it off; it reminded her of Amereen and she felt she was close by when she wore the necklace.

CHAPTER FOUR

There were things Amereen hadn't told Alice, one of
which was how religious Priya's family were and that
they didn't drink so there were no drinks at the wedding
celebrations. Jazz had brought a secret stash for himself.
He was seen to slip out to his car often for a drink. This
was kept secret by Jazz's male relatives. It was when
Jazz took to the dance floor later in the evening that all
became apparent and very public. Jazz never wore a
turban, but as a mark of respect for his future family, he
arrived in the Punjab wearing traditional clothes and a
turban. He had decided that for his wedding day
celebrations he would drink whisky instead of beer. This
was a big mistake, which he later confessed to his
mother. The music had got livelier during the evening
and the five-piece band were enthusiastically banging
out a popular tune.

Jazz, fuelled up with an alcoholic confidence, strode
onto the dance floor to join in the Bangra dance; an
enthusiastic step in time to the music caused him to
slipped backwards in a grotesque display of Bangra gone
wrong. As he hit the floor face up, for a few moments of
disbelief, he lay still whilst his turban left his head and
slid three metres across the dance floor. The music

stopped and everyone present became mute with shock. It was, Amereen knew, the most disastrous and embarrassing moment for the groom's family. It would be said in Punjab circles for years that the wedding bode disaster for the marriage from that eventful moment.

Amereen had kept another secret from Alice. She never told her of the marriage break up with Priya. This was very painful and although she forgave Jazz, she would never live the shame of it down. She took to her grave the heartbreak and the rift in her family this had caused.

As the mother of Jaswinder Singh, Amereen carried much shame. The Singh family may not have visited her but the phone calls upset her greatly. With no man in the family to protect her, she was buffeted and bullied by her brother in law to disown Jazz as her son. Because the Singh family had publicly renounced Jazz as a member of the Singh family, they could not speak to him. They satisfied their need to vent their shame by terrorising Amereen. Her life was unhappy and she carried the mantle of shame across her buckling shoulders. Jazz never knew what the Singh family did to her. Alice was her one saving grace and her ignorance of these shameful events gave Amereen an oasis in her life. When Amereen died suddenly from an aneurism, no one took the blame of the stress that may have caused it.

At 38 years old, Jazz only became aware that he had no family to call on when his mother died. He inherited the family house in Newbury Park and spent a week clearing it out and accumulating bits and pieces of memorabilia. He missed the gentleness and uncompromising love of his mother. *If only* was added to the list of triggers that would cause the breakdown.

Jazz took Alice to his mother's funeral. She was the only person there talking to him. The Singh family arrived and left as soon as the funeral finished. They had fulfilled their obligation to Amereen and it was organised that the head of the family would collect the ashes after a suitable time and distribute them in flowing water as is the custom. They ignored Jazz, adding another side swipe to ensure he was fully aware of the ongoing rift he had caused in the Singh family. It phased Jazz out. He had hoped that his mother's funeral would bring him back into the family and they would forgive him as his mother had done.

After the funeral, Jazz spent the evening with Alice. He knew she was grieving badly for his mother and he hoped they could grieve together. He felt Alice's pain when she said, none too gently and actually incorrectly, "A bleeding heart attack has taken another loved person from me." She added defiantly, "How come he only takes the good ones? Bollocks to him and all the bleeding priests in the world." With that statement, Alice had cried for an hour. It was only after drinking the sherry Jazz poured her, in a desperate attempt to keep her from collapsing under so many tears, that Alice managed to regain her composure. He had always liked Alice, but in that moment he loved her with all his heart.

He cuddled her and joined her in having a sherry. After they finished the bottle, the stories began. Alice told Jazz all his mother's thoughts and how proud she was of *"her Jazz"* as his mother had always lovingly called him. They laughed when Alice told the story of teaching Amereen to do the Okey Kokey and the mess they got into trying to keep up with the music. He would remember it as the best funeral night he could have had for his mother. In years to come, his mother's love as felt through Alice, would keep him afloat.

After a week of packing up the house, he returned to Manchester, glad in some way to return to normality, whatever that was. He had spent every evening with Alice. The local Tesco was busy restocking their Harvey's Bristol Cream sherry. Alice had never been so tiddley so often as during that week. She giggled as she told Cissie how wonderful little Jaswinder had been. She was so sad to see him go but he had promised to keep in touch. Two years had passed since Amereen had died and little Jaswinder must have been very busy because he hadn't rung her yet. She told Cissie he would ring her when he had time.

CHAPTER FIVE

When Jazz had arrived back in Manchester, all the niggley little things that had caused him problems over the years intensified. He ignored all the symptoms as best he could; it was at Manchester Police Station, two months after his mother's funeral, that cracks started to show. He was interviewing a known *pain in the neck* domestic violence case. Jazz, having been here before, listened to this cocky lump of shit who knew his wife would withdraw her statement, even though he had beaten her so badly she needed stitches to her lip where he had punched her hard in the face. This skinny little woman's body had turned purple from the barrage of punches landed with a force that threw her across the room. As she lay on the floor, her husband continued to pummel her with huge fists. The exertion of it all left him sweating heavily and out of breath but the fucking bitch deserved more. The final kicks fractured two of her ribs. He was going to get away with it again!

Jazz sat opposite the fucking bastard in the custody suite interview room listening to the bastard baiting him. Jazz watched as this low life sitting there calmly smiling that *you cant touch me bastard* look which intensely annoyed Jazz. In the past, he could cover it with a professionalism that didn't allow the baiting to get to him. Today, he was getting seriously angry.

The fat, ugly tosser in front of Jazz knew he had got away with the charges. His Tracy knew what was good for her. She was nothing without him and she knew it, he had told her often enough. He could tell that the bastards were just trying to find another reason to keep him there. It was the fourth time that year she had called the police and they didn't want to let him go again. He would make sure she didn't call the police again; they said next time they would do a victimless prosecution on him. The bitch would lose her sodding mobile when he got out of here, he would take it from her and smash it to bits.

For now, he, Charlie Shaw, was in control. He controlled her, he could control the police because they had nothing they could use, and he controlled the Social Services. He liked the feeling of control. With no job and all his bills paid through children's allowance, dole money and a bit of disability money, he had no goals in life other than to be the biggest pain in the butt to anyone he came into contact with. Tracy looked after the three kids: Skye, Bart and Sumer. His kids were good. It meant Social Services got them a 42" flat screen HD TV, and the washing machine and tumble dryer were also given to them for the children. All the heating bills were paid for them and they never had to turn the heating down or off if they didn't want to. They also got a computer so the children would not feel different. He never wanted a bloody computer. What good was that? He was working on Social Services to get them a car too so he could take the children out. Charlie's plan was that him and his mate Jimmy could go to any race track they fancy, anywhere in the country, if they had a car. His last conversations with Social Services said they were thinking about a car for the family but no decision had been made yet. As far as he was concerned, they could take Tracy away for all he cared, she was a scrawny, ugly bitch, but they could never take his children away from him. He had never touched the children. He could always find another woman to keep him company and look after the children.

Social Services saw him as a loving father. They had expressed some concern regarding his drinking and his violence towards Tracy, but they never doubted his devotion to his children. As he told them, his bad leg and bad back stopped him going out with his children, but they did watch television together. He never mentioned it was the racing programmes he watched with them. The kids knew all about the odds on a horse and how to place a bet before they knew how to read.

So here he was again, Charlie Shaw, in police custody. They had to be professional and treat him correctly. He would complain if they breached his rights. The police were well aware of his knowledge of his rights; he told them often. He very much enjoyed the look of frustration on the officer's face. If he was in the mood, he would bate them and push them. Many had been close to hitting him but that would have suited him too much. He would have sued for compensation, made a fuss, rung the newspapers. He was hated and reviled by all who knew him in the community.

Charlie Shaw was right. Tracey Shaw had been into the Police station and made a withdrawal statement. She had been let out of hospital and she had gone straight to the police station. She looked a mess. A policewoman sat with her to check how she was. Tracy, in pain, but stiffly upright in her anger, told the policewoman, in no uncertain terms, "You let my Charlie go now. I love him and I want to go home with him." The policewoman checked that Tracey knew what she was doing; next time Charlie could cause her more injuries, it was even conceivable that he could kill her next time. The WPC had introduced herself as Rebecca and asked her kindly and with care to seriously reconsider her decision. Tracy was having none of it. Shouting loud enough to be heard in the next room, she spat at the policewoman, "Mind your own fucking business, he is my man and I want him with me now." At this point, WPC Rebecca Reid, the policewoman who had sat so patiently with Tracy, gave up.

Jazz was called out of the interview room to be told a withdrawal statement had been made and signed by Tracey Shaw and therefore Charlie Shaw could be released. As Jazz walked back into the interview room, Charlie knew he was free, but before he left, he wanted to make sure this bastard of a Paki DS knew his place. Charlie got up out of his chair and told Jazz to be more respectful next time. He told a barely contained Jazz, whose eyes were flashing and his cheeks had gone a bright red, that he didn't like his attitude and he was gonna report him for his lack of respect for a member of the community.

Jazz, tired, fed up and riled beyond belief by this scum, forgot himself and with one fist clenched he pulled Charlie close to him with the other hand and punched him hard. There were no muscles in Charlie's bulging, fat stomach, and the punch knocked all the wind out of him and he fell to the floor. After a few wheezing moments where he tried to gulp in as much air as possible, Charlie told Jazz he was going to get him. Jazz laughed and said, "Prove it! You fell over, I saw it." He shouldn't have given in to his hot anger but enough was enough and Charlie needed to be taught a lesson. Jazz felt good. It was the start of behaviour found unacceptable by the police and the beginning of the breakdown that would take him out of the force for six months.

If Charlie Shaw had known he was responsible for the final straw that caused the breakdown of Jazz Singh he would have been very proud!

It was three months after his mother died that Jazz sought counselling. He never would have touched it with a barge pole before. Along with many officers, he had thought only wimps needed the police counsellor, but the anger that rose in a second to a height of uncontrolled rage had begun to frighten him.

He had always been a bit of a loose canon, in fact, he took pride in being just a tad off the wall and bucking the system he spent his working life protecting. Jazz was a good officer who 20 years ago would have been perfect, but in today's politically correct society, he was a concern to all who worked with him. It would be true to say, and Jazz knew it, that he had been fast-tracked through the system. 30 years old was young to have been made a DS. To have an officer from an ethnic minority rise so quickly through the ranks ticked the Metropolitan Police's diversity boxes. The added bonus was that Jazz was good at his job and deserved his meteoric rise in the police service; it was certainly not a token promotion which was a good result for the Met Police officials.

The breakdown, when it came, answered a lot of questions about his behaviour over the past few years. Manchester Police officials had wondered why he was seconded to them. They knew of the event that happened in Ilford, but he was such a feather in the cap of the Met Police that to let him go seemed strange. The Manchester Police saw him through his two marriages, his mother's death and now his breakdown. He recovered quickly with professional help and they seemed to have a good DS back on track. Now the Met Police were claiming him back. There were complaints from the Manchester Police and letters and phone calls flew back and forth for a short while stating that Manchester Police wanted Jazz to stay with them. The Metropolitan Police exerted its mighty muscle and there was no argument. The Met were reclaiming a DS who at last was fit for purpose. Neither force knew the drink problem would stay and grow.

CHAPTER SIX
London again

He didn't know how he felt about returning to the Met. It raked up memories and events he wasn't sure he was ready to handle. On the positive side, at least he would be able to watch the Hammers playing live. It had been five years since he had worked in London. He wondered if his contacts would still be there. With a rueful smile, he knew they would be pleased to see him again. He had learned a lot in Manchester and if they thought he was tough back then, they were in for a surprise. He was leaner, meaner and deceptively calmer these days. He had given up women, partying and playing the fool but what occupied a lot of his thoughts was when he could take his next shot of whisky, or have a beer. He woke up thinking about drink and ensuring he was never without a supply; he needed a drink. It was a curse, and he hated the dependence but he needed it to stop the shakes and to get him through the day.

He had no one now and that didn't bother him too much. People drag you down and hold you back. He was good at his job and the Met wanted him back. He laughed contemptuously at the thought. They had got rid of him quick enough when everything went tits up and now he was back on form, they wanted a bit of him. He was 40 years old and looking good. He had lost a lot of weight and it was just a bit of a pot belly that showed he drunk too much beer. He shaved his head and it suited him. He had good bone structure with high cheek bones that were highlighted by the dark stubble that never disappeared, however close the shave. He was a handsome devil and he knew it! The sunken dark eyes only seemed to make him more interesting and women were intrigued by him. Jazz was everyone's friend but actually no one got that close to him. He preferred it that way. Whatever hurt him, whatever he missed in life, no one knew, he kept his own counsel. He was Jazz, full of life, a character, a laugh. He was very astute and sharp and certainly no man's fool, but this was hidden behind a playful manner that could change in a slight of hand to a menacing demon if you got on the wrong side of him. Villains in Manchester knew him well and his history ensured they never messed with him. London was to find out the same after a few consultations.

Jazz had to move the same day, which he thought was fucking stupid. It was a hassle, but the guesthouse was easy to leave and it took him 20 minutes to pack his clothes and put them in the car. He lost his home with his last divorce and he walked away with nothing. All he had in the world was his car, a BMW Series 3 Coupe, his pride and joy, and of course the money from the sale of his parents' house. Jazz tried not to think of that money, it was in a savings account for a time when he was more settled and knew what he was going to do with his life. The Met had arranged for accommodation in Ilford for him and he was expected to report to Ilford Police Station on Tuesday morning at 8 a.m. sharp.

He had mixed feelings about London. He couldn't think about that event all those years ago, he wasn't ready yet. Five years ago, the Met Police were a different kettle of fish from today. He smirked when he remembered that anything that happened that had a slightly ethnic background caused a panic in the Chief Supers office and he, Jaswinder Singh, was wheeled in as the ethnic expert.

When the Commissioner for Bombay, now called Mumbai, arrived in East London, no one at Chief Super level knew what to do with him. The knock on his door made Jazz look up from his desk and he saw in front of him a pristinely dressed Indian Commissioner of Police and Jazz's Chief Superintendant. He knew the look in his Chief Super's eyes; he was not best pleased at the mess before him. Jazz absentmindedly apologised for the mess and quickly pushed away the Mcdonald's cartons containing a half eaten burger and cold chips, and threw the polysterene cups of cold coffee into the bin. There was two days worth of food and cups on his desk he hadn't got round to moving. He wiped his hands down his trousers and stood with hand outstretched to welcome the Indian Commissioner of Police. The introductions were strange and the only inkling Jazz had of what was expected of him.

"Yes, well, Commissioner." The Chief Super was trying to make the best of a bad job. "This is our rising star, DS Jaswinder Singh, who will be most happy to help you with any information you may require." The awkwardness of the introduction was only paled into insignificance by the bluster and speed with which the Chief Superintendant left the room.

Jazz smiled and cleared a chair of files for the Commissioner to sit down. A cup of tea was offered and accepted and this allowed Jazz to leave the room to think. In the tea room, he told a DC who was minding his own business and hoping for a few minutes peace that "yet again I am a fucking patsy for the Met Police. This Commissioner hasn't been offered any courtesy car, driver or special attention. All he gets is an overworked DS who is expected to babysit this poor guy. It isn't fucking fair on him or me." The DC nodded but offered no words of consolation. The tea was made and a few biscuits were found. Feeling a bit better, Jazz went back to his office to see what he could do with this man.

Whilst drinking the tea, the Commissioner broke the silence. "What is in that box?" the Commissioner asked, pointing to an over spilling box of cards which looked in some sort of order.

Jazz, glad to have something to say, told the Commissioner, "They are Prominent Nominals."

The Commissioner, nonplussed, asked, "What does that mean?"

Jazz was surprised at his lack of knowledge but with good will stated, "They are people who are prolific in committing crime and come to our attention. Dev Noms (Developing Nominals) they are people who are just starting out in crime and have just come to our attention." Well into his stride now, Jazz went on to say,

"And of course, there are Agency Nominals; they are people who are of interest to this borough as well as of interest to other boroughs. Of course, this is coupled with the repeat offenders." He noticed that the Commissioner looked very confused by all of this and wondered how on earth they worked in India. This man knew nothing of policing.

The Commissioner put down his tea cup and thanked Jazz. He said he had needed a decent cup of tea. Wondering what on earth to do with this man now, Jazz asked if perhaps he would like to look in the custody suite. He could see the look of relief on the Commissioner's face. The poor bastard was bored rigid. Bob was the Custody Sergeant and was introduced to the Commissioner as the most experienced Custody Sergeant in London. Bob could see he was being soft-soaped and realised he was expected to escort the Commissioner and Jazz around his custody suite.

"Luckily, Sir, we are not too busy at the moment so it will be a pleasure to show you around," was Bob's gracious response. What was not heard by the Commissioner was Bob's urgent whisper to Jazz of "You fucking owe me for this, I'm not your bloody errand boy."

Jazz laughed and said, "No darling, you are far, far more special than that." With a kiss blown in Bob's direction, Jazz walked up to the Commissioner, who was studying a list of dos and donts on the wall. "Bob is ready to show us his domain, Sir, if you are ready." Bob walked them both through the procedure of when a prisoner is brought into custody by the door from the yard. They looked through the grill and could see a few police cars parked there. He showed them the custody desk and the cameras which were constantly monitoring the custody suite. They walked and looked into various interview rooms with tape recording equipment and cameras; one was in use so they looked through the spy hole. Then there was the room where fingerprints and pictures of suspects were taken. The cells, of which there were eight, were shown to the Commissioner and he was told how each cell with a suspect in was monitored regularly by camera and by the custody officer who would inspect each cell personally. The bank of screens for all the cameras sat behind the custody suite desk. It was noted that four cells were in use at the moment and Bob expected to have another cell in use when a paedophile living in north Ilford was arrested and brought in. After the inspection, Jazz thanked Bob and suggested to the Commissioner that they retire back to his office.

The Commissioner was not ready to go; he had a further question. "Where is your beating room?" Jazz begged his pardon and asked what he meant. Bob tried to look busy but was intrigued by the question and although his hands were working hard to look like he was organising a list of something or the other, his interest was fully on the Commissioner. The Commissioner, surprised by such a response, licked his lips and slowly said, "The beating room, of course, is where you beat your prisoner."

Jazz shook his head. "No, we don't have beating rooms in England."

The Commissioner breathed in deeply and, with eyes to the ceiling as if registering this comment, tapped his chin in thought and, nodding knowingly, said, "Aah, that answers my question."

"What question is that?" asked Jazz tentatively.

The Commissioner explained, "I couldn't understand why you had so many repeat offenders. We don't have such people in my country." Jazz laughed. He liked this man very much. Bob turned his back and opened the filing cabinet behind the custody desk and laughed. Jazz thought for the moment that perhaps India had the right idea. A beating room at Ilford? No, he wasn't going to let that thought take hold. It made him smile to think of it, especially when Ricky Daniels, a prolific shoplifter who was the bane of all shops that sold alcohol in Ilford, was brought in struggling, effing and blinding, and causing his usual commotion when he was caught.

On the way back to his office, Jazz asked, "Do you think I could get a job as a police officer in India?"

The Commissioner looked at him for a moment and then shook his head. With a smile, he replied, "No, you would never make a police officer in India, you wouldn't have a clue about how to take bribes." Jazz liked him even more. This man had pulled him along, allowing him to think he was stupid. The Commissioner of Police for Bombay was a very shrewd chap and had quite a tongue in cheek sense of humour. They now understood each other.

"Ok no more bollocks, what would you like to do, Sir?"

The Commissioner, who now introduced himself as

Omar, said he was dying for something to eat. No one had offered him any food for hours. Jazz offered the Indian restaurant across the road but Omar asked, "Can we go to McDonald's? I don't have it often and I am particularly fond of a big mac and fries." Laughing, they left Ilford Police Station for the McDonald's across the road.

Jazz added, "Good choice, the curry would have been shit."

Jazz built a good friendship with Omar. When he next came to England, times had changed and he was treated like the distinguished person he was. He had a driver and a car at his disposal. Jazz was in Manchester by then but Omar kept in contact and they spoke on the phone.

Jazz wondered if the same people would be still at Ilford. He hoped Bob, the Custody Sergeant, was still there. He had a great time with him and they worked well together. He laughed to himself as he remembered that time with the burglaries. He was hot then and an ace crime solver.

There had been a spate of burglaries in pubs in the East End. They had seen the chap on CCTV in one of the pubs but no one knew who he was. The bugger was fleecing the pubs of their takings after a busy night and he was getting away with it. There were at least eight burglaries that were thought to be him. Most pubs didn't have him on CCTV but a couple of pubs had a grainy picture of the same man. Jazz had looked at his MO and realised that the burglar had to do a recce of the pubs to see if the takings were worth having. Jazz had sat in a few pubs over the weeks, just waiting and looking and hoping to see this guy walk in. The Unicorn was having one of its quiz nights and there was usually a big turnout for it. Jazz sat in the corner watching and in walked a chap who looked very much like the picture Jazz was carrying from the CCTV footage. He watched him walk in, get a beer and survey the pub. He was sure it was him.

He wasn't going to let him get away this time. He walked up to the chap and arrested him. He was handcuffed and a police car was called to take them both to Ilford Police Station. The chap was shouting and protesting and struggling but Jazz knew it was him, ok, the picture was not that good but it was good enough.

At the police station he was read his rights and Jazz asked Bob to put him in a cell. An initial interview with him was a *no comment* interview and he gave no details of his name or where he lived. Jazz could see he was a drug addict. The eyes and the gaunt, grey skin were dead giveaways. This cocky guy, who said the police had nothing on him and he was being *fitted up*, could just sit and wait as far as Jazz was concerned. He had other things to do and first he was off to find a bag of VHS videos; there were stacks of them waiting to be used as and when necessary. He asked the jailor to tell the prisoner he would be back in 10 minutes and then after an hour, to go back in and tell him he would be back in another 10 minutes. Bob said the prisoner was getting fidgety. Jazz reckoned he would be climbing the walls after three hours, by which time he would need a fix badly.

Jazz had the highlights of the cricket tour to catch up on. It was on the sports programme, so he went off and got a kebab and settled down for two hours of cricket in his office.

Bob knew how Jazz worked and just waited. The PACE clock had many hours to go so that wasn't a problem.

The Inspector came down to do a review of who was in custody. On hearing all the commotion coming from the drug addict's cell, he asked Bob what all the hollering was about.

"That is Jazz's prisoner, Sir."

The Inspector was none too impressed. "Why hasn't Jazz interviewed him yet, why the fuck is he still in custody? Where is Jazz?" By now, the Inspector was shouting and he realised he needed to calm down. Jazz always had this effect on him. Tomorrow, he would call him before him for explanations on his procedures.

Bob tried to calm the situation and lied, "He is out on enquiries, Sir."

The Inspector was having none of that and said quietly to Bob, "If I find out there is cricket on the TV tonight, there is going to be trouble. You can pass that on." He left the custody suite and his final words were, "I will be back in an hour or so and I expect to see that prisoner dealt with."

Jazz always sailed too close to the wind, but Bob covered his back. His timing was immaculate and Jazz walked into the custody suite just after the Inspector left. "Is he cooking nicely my man?

Bob smiled, "Mate he is well done. Any more and he

will tell you where Lord Lucan is. He is crawling up the wall for drugs." The time was right.

"OK, offer him a cup of tea and put half a cup of sugar in it. I reckon it's going to be a full hands up, don't you, skip?" Jazz was flying now. He knew the sugar would give the prisoner a high which would allow him to concentrate and talk about all the burglaries.

The gaoler had been listening and after Jazz went off to interview the prisoner, he asked, "What is a full hands up, Serg?"

"It's a confession" was Bob's response.

This young gaoler was perplexed. "But he won't even tell us his name, so why would he confess?" He was now carried away with righteousness. "Is Jazz going to beat it out of him? I know they do things differently in his country. I have to tell you, Serg, that if he does, I will have to report him to the DPS."

Bob was already fed up with this young whippersnapper who was doing everything by the rule book and messing up his tidy custody suite.

"It's not Jazz to you, its Detective Sergeant Singh to you. Go make the tea and wash out all the cups and give me a break!" The gaoler was just about to add something when Bob stopped him in his tracks and said, "While you are about it, I want you to give me an inventory of what is in the stores and don't forget to count all the pens. I need to know how many red pens and how many black pens. This is an important task; according to the manual for working in a custody suite, we must have a good supply of pens." The gaoler, excited by the importance of the role, thanked Bob and disappeared.

Bob watched him disappear and in despair at the stupidity of the man, said under his breath, "Fucking graduates."

The interview went well. Alan Bilter, who lived in Ilford Lane, wanted to get out of the cell as soon as possible. Jazz brought in the bag full of VHS videos and then a small television and VHS player. He made a fuss of setting the television in the right place and rummaging through the bag of videos. With a sigh of *let's sit back and enjoy*, he said to the now very jittery Alan, "Right, we have all night to look at these to see if we can recognise you on them. Now some are from pubs but they got a bit mixed up with some other videos of pubs not relevant but, as I said, we have all night to look at them".

"No Guv, no need, I will tell you every pub I have burgled, just want to get on with it and get out. I ain't going to be no bother, just do it."

He refused a solicitor and said he would sign a statement when it was prepared. In an hour, he admitted 10 burglaries, two of which were outside their area. He also asked for three lots of shoplifting in Asda on the A13 and two in Tescos in Chadwell Heath to be taken into account. He added for good measure that there were also 10 burglaries in private houses to be taken into account. It was a good result and Alan was let go on bail after his address was confirmed.

Jazz had the luck of the devil in those days. The Inspector came down to the custody suite as Alan was being released on bail. He saw a full hands up to 20 burglaries, which made good reading for his statistics. He still wanted Jazz in his office in the morning for a full explanation but Jazz knew he was on safe ground.

Just as Jazz was congratulating himself on a good result and thanking Bob for his backup, the gaoler came back and interrupted their conversation. "Serg, I have counted all the pens; 127 black and 220 red." The Serg listened to this information with full interest and then enquired, "Hang on, how many actually work, do you know?"

The gaoler, quite nonplussed, said, "But you said"

He was interrupted by a sanguine Custody Sergeant. "I know what I said, Grasshopper, but you must use your initiative, that is the only way to get on in this job."

The gaoler nodded far too much and left to go and find the pens. Jazz and Bob looked at each other in disgust. "Fucking graduates."

Life was good at that point but Jazz's downfall was to come at a time when he was flying high. No one would have guessed how his fortunes would change and just how far he would fall.

AN UNWELCOME VISITOR

Alice had her lunch in the garden. She didn't eat much these days. A small sandwich of cheese and tomato with a cup of tea saw her through to teatime. She did have a piece of chocolate cake after her sandwich, a little treat that tasted deliciously naughty. Well it was her birthday after all. The lunchtime sun was pleasant and sitting in her garden was very restful. She couldn't bend down like she used to so most of her plants were bushes and the roses were particularly lovely this year. She loved the yellow roses, they smelt gorgeous and looked so pretty. Watching the birds bathing in the birdbath at the end of her garden gave her a lot of pleasure. Nature was so clever, she thought.

The roses in her front garden needed a little pruning and the hedgerow was small but needed to be trimmed. She would enjoy doing that whilst waiting for the Chinese gentlemen to arrive. Hers was practically the only front garden in the street with flowers in it. Most were paved over and it seemed such a shame to Alice to see so much concrete. Years ago, everyone had a front garden full of flowers and the road looked beautiful in the summer. She sighed; times had changed and she had to get used to it.

It was 2 p.m. when she went out to the front garden. She armed herself with secateurs and a small bin to put the cuttings in and her rubber gloves. Her apron would keep her top and skirt clean. Before she started pruning, she walked to her gate and peered next door to see if she could spot the car that usually parked down the sideway. It was there and she wondered if she should go and speak to the Chinese gentlemen. She hoped they didn't think she was nosey or interfering. The devil was a dreadful being and it was her duty to say something, she told herself.

She hadn't been formally introduced to her neighbours and so she decided she must take her apron off and her gloves and put everything away in her garden shed; she liked to be tidy. She scuttled back indoors and looked in her hall mirror to check she looked OK and her hair was in place. She wanted to make a good first impression. She smiled; what would they think if she knocked on their door looking a mess? They would wonder who they were living next door to. Satisfied she looked tidy, she made her way to the side door of the house next door. She was surprised to see the door ajar. She thought they were very trustworthy, anyone could walk in.

There was no bell to ring on the side door, so Alice tapped tentatively and called out "hellooooo" in a high pitched scratchy voice. No one answered. Alice pushed the door open just a tiny bit more and called again but still there was no answer. For a few moments, she felt quite perplexed as to what to do next. Should she go in without an invitation or should she go away and come back another time or wait for the gentleman to come out later? It was all very confusing. Her manners told her to go away and wait but her curiosity told her to go in. She could feel the heat through the gap in the door. She had her crucifix on so she knew she would be safe.

With a deep breath, she decided she would open the door further and maybe just stand in the hallway. She thought that wouldn't be too presumptuous of her and she could call out again. Pushing the nervous feelings to the back of her mind, she boldly opened the door and stood in the hallway. Now she was there, she wondered what to do next. The heat was oppressive and the brightness made her put her hands to her eyes to shade them from the hurtful light. The smell was strange but not horrible but not nice either. In her confusion she walked towards what was the front room. She forgot to call out and she forgot her manners. What she saw before her was unbelievable and she wondered if she was dreaming. The front room was filled with green plants all hooked up and in water. They weren't the odd plants you had to enjoy, they were dense and took up all the space of the room with thin aisles between the regiments of plants. Her mouth open and her eyes darting she knew this wasn't right. This was a home, not a garden. In that moment, a shiver of fear ran through her body. She had to get out, she didn't know why she was scared but something told her to get out. As she turned, she was confronted by two Chinese gentlemen.

The shock of the front room and now the shock of being caught in their house uninvited caused Alice to hold her heart and catch her breath. She managed a smile and tried to say she was so sorry for intruding before the second man came up behind her and hit her over the head with a heavy ratchet. She died before she hit the floor; the blow smashed into her frail skull and it caved in causing quite a mess on the floor.

Babbling excitedly and fearfully, the two men searched Alice's pockets to find the key to her house and quickly went next door. The back door was opened and her body was carried over the fence and in through the back door of her house. They laid her by the fire grate in the front room in the hope that the police, when they arrived, would think she fell back onto the fire grate and smashed her skull in an accident.

The house was now compromised and the Cannabis factory would have to be dismantled and moved within a week. The plants were about to be cropped for the third time so the full value of the crop would be made. They needed a few days' grace to clear the house of the valuable product before Alice was found. It was decided that her post and her milk would be collected every day so no one would be aware that anything was wrong. It would give them the time they needed to get away. They had to explain to their boss what had happened and they were more frightened of him than the English police.

It would be Friday, when the milkman came to collect his money, that the alarm would be raised.

THE JAZZ SINGER COMETH

Jazz arrived in Ilford at 7 p.m. Most of his possessions were with him in the boot of the car. He had his music collection, his signed cricket bat by the 1990 England team, bought when he had money to spare, and his aftershave collection, which had grown from a meagre selection of two different aftershaves to 15. He could not explain the buzz he got from such a selection but he knew he had to have them with him. Most of his clothes, the odd occasional table and standard light would be sent down by courier. His 32" flat screen television, a present to himself, was in the back of his car. No way would he leave that behind. He had enough clothes with him to see him out for a week.

He was given an address in De Vere Gardens, off The Drive, as the guesthouse he would be staying in. It was the home of a family from Uganda. They were charming and very welcoming and his upstairs room was big and at the front of the house but hell, he didn't want curry morning, noon and night. The police still assumed he would want that, so no change there, and the thought depressed him. Still, he found Mrs Chodda was an excellent cook and the curry was particularly good. The problem was that since his breakdown, his stomach just couldn't take too many curries any more. His favourite food had always been burgers, fish and chips and a full English fry up, so not eating curry for quite some time had given his stomach a rest. It occurred to him, on reflection, that the police had put him with a Sikh family because he was Sikh. Someone somewhere in the force had thought his accommodation out more carefully than usual. He smiled at that. Perhaps one day they might ask him what he wanted instead of assuming.

He unpacked and got himself ready for his meeting at Ilford Police Station at 8 a.m. on Tuesday morning. He still had mixed feelings but hey, he would go with the flow and see how it went. For the time being, he would install his television and make himself comfortable. As he sat down, his thoughts went to Newbury Park and his mother and father. He unpacked his vodka and a glass and sat in this strange room that would be his home for the time being. He half filled the tumbler with vodka and put a small tonic into it. He drank vodka now, no hangover or smell on the breath. As he sipped, he looked around and wondered if this was to be his life. It suddenly felt very lonely. A few more drinks to help him sleep, tomorrow would be a better day he hoped.

At Ilford Police Station the news was already out: The Jazz Singer was back! It wasn't said with pleasure, more with amazement. No one would have bet on his return after everything that had happened. Although there was a turnover of staff, there were still those who would never move from the police station and would always be there to remember Jazz and that day.

At 7.45 a.m he arrived at Ilford Police Station. He looked for Bob but there was a different Custody Sergeant on duty who told Jazz that Bob would be on the late shift. He had to report to Detective Chief Inspector John Radley. He didn't know him, nor had he heard anything about him. He was shown into DCI Radley's office at 8 a.m. precisely.

His office was immaculate. Jazz had never seen such a clean and presentable office. Police were not known for such homely skills. The guy sitting behind the desk, who didn't get up when Jazz walked in, looked familiar. He said nothing; he gestured towards the chair opposite for Jazz to sit down. Jazz couldn't place him, but he knew him from somewhere. About 30 years old and still quite skinny in his suit, the gov looked at ease.

"So, welcome back, Jazz. I know your reputation and I want to make it clear from the outset that I shall be watching you carefully. We do things by the book at Ilford these days and I am particularly keen to ensure our diversity protocols are adhered to and the human rights of our prisoners are observed. Do I make myself clear?" Jazz nodded. The guv looked at Jazz and continued. "I shall need your mobile number so I can get in touch with you whenever necessary and I shall give you my mobile number. Communication is the key to the success of all clear ups of crimes." Jazz searched his pockets for a pen to write the number down but couldn't find one. The guv handed him a pen with the words "How many pens we have in the station is very important. It is also important to ensure they are all working."

Jazz looked up sharply and realised the heavy irony

in the words and knew who his new boss was. It was the fucking graduate! He knew coming back to Ilford was not going to be a walk in the park but with the fucking graduate as his boss as well, gee, how much humiliation was he supposed to carry? He was then summarily dismissed by his DCI, whose eyes shone with pleasure at pulling this cocky DS down a few pegs.

Bob came in early to see Jazz and they went off for a cup of tea in the canteen. At least that was the same. Rotten tea, overcooked dinners and rock cakes that, yes, ok, were as hard as rocks. It felt good and the nearest to home he could get. Milly was still serving behind the counter, telling off any officer who didn't write their tickets out for meals correctly and asking for the right money. Milly was about 65 years old and this was the nearest to commanding the attention of fit young men she would get. She loved their bantering and if they got a bit saucy with her, she would scold them but always added an extra amount of chips on their plates for their cheek. Milly didn't do the job for the money, she had a good pension from her husband, who, as she used to tell everyone, was a *miserable old git*, so working in the canteen was her pleasure. She remembered Jazz and she remembered the incident.

"How are you darlin?" she asked, with more feeling than he had heard for years. Surprisingly, the emotion welled up for a second and caught him in the back of the throat.

"I am fine now thanks." He smiled at her and playfully leaned forward. "Milly you are a diamond and I am glad to see you again. Give me a kiss and I will feel like I am back home." She giggled and blushed but proffered her cheek across the counter. He gave her a big kiss on the cheek and an awkward cuddle across the counter.

"Would you like a nice 999 breakfast darlin?" she asked.

"Only if you cook it and serve it." She liked that and went off to cook it. Jazz laughed and said to Bob, "I am home."

"So you met your guv then?" Bob knew the answer but wondered if Jazz had got the connection.

"Yeah, it's the fucking graduate. He must have been fast-tracked to reach DCI in what is it? In seven years?"

Bob nodded and added, "You think you have it bad, he remembered me well and has made it his mission to check everything I do. He's only been here a short while but in that time I have had to reorganise all my systems to ensure they comply with every protocol he could drag up. Remind me, Jazz, to treat every fucking graduate like a little god in future."

Jazz laughed. "It can't be that bad. We'll see how it goes. I'm off soon to meet my team. Don't know how many DCs I will have under me."

Bob didn't want to tell him that no one who knew of Jazz wanted to work on his team. He had got all the newbies with little or no experience of the job or Jazz and his reputation. Besides, newbies had no say in who they worked with anyway.

The breakfast was magnificent, you couldn't beat a 999, it contained everything imaginable: black pudding, chips, eggs, bacon, sausage, fried bread, beans, tomato and a mug of tea. The lovely Milly brought it to the table herself, something she rarely did. Her dulcet tones calling "Egg on toast and be quick abaat it" would ring out from behind the counter regularly encouraging the recipient to rush to the counter to collect their food.

At 10 a.m. Jazz's team assembled in the CID room upstairs and waited for him to arrive. He was expecting four officers: one woman and three men. There were only two sitting waiting for him. It was bloody depressing to know he hadn't even got a full team. All new DCs, not one of them will have had any experience, he thought. Apparently the other two were going to arrive in a few weeks, after training. The woman and man sat looking expectantly at him. The two had heard all about Jaswinder Singh. They had endured mockery and mickey-taking since their arrival a few days ago. They knew they were working with a skipper who no one else wanted to work with. A police station is like a village, the gossip runs round quicker than a champion sprinter. They were apprehensive about meeting this apparent top DS who had such a bad history that no one wanted to work with him.

Jazz knew they would have all been told the gossip about him. He kept it light and hoped they would work together successfully. The introductions were standard but he had to start somewhere. The only woman on his team was called Sharon Day and she confidently explained she was a new DC after being in the CSU Department for 10 years. They sympathised with the 10 years and privately thought she was mad to have stayed there so long. No one knew her yet. Tony Sepple introduced himself saying very little about himself other than that he always wanted to work in the CID. He had worked in Romford and was pleased to be in the same area. A little quiet, Jazz thought, but he would see how he came through.

Sharon definitely had balls and he could see she was very interested in him, but he would never mix work with pleasure. He was used to women giving him the eye, he was a handsome devil and he knew it! Sharon was quite a looker and in another place and another lifetime he might have taken her up on it. "But it ain't gonna happen girly," he said to himself. No way on his team. Over the years, he had seen others get together. Ok, it was lovely at the beginning, the women would glow and twitter on about real love and the men seemed very happy. But give it a little while and then the break ups started, which could be pretty embarrassing and sometimes very nasty. There had been occasions when, if they worked to closely together and it was a particularly nasty break up, one of them would have to leave the borough to work elsewhere. "How stupid was that?" Jazz asked himself. "With all the women in the world why foul your own door step?" Women were not his priority at the moment, he'd enough of all the troubles they had caused him in the past.

They looked at him and wondered what he had in store for them. Jazz knew the score regarding how they would have faired with the rest of the CID teams there. It was time to put them straight.

"There are four CID teams at this station, each with a DS in charge of approximately four DCs. We are all responsible to the DI or DCI. We are a different team from all the rest based here. Someone was having a laugh when they put us together. No other team comprises solely DCs with no experience. You are the lowest of the low in DC world. You are the shit and you will be laughed at and you will have the mickey taken out of you for two reasons: One, because you know nothing about detection; and two, because you have me as your DS. I have come back from Manchester and I carry a bad reputation so no one but the likes of you would work with me. You had no choice. Now that was the bad news.

The good news is, we are going to show the lot of them that we are good and better than they are. Whatever I am perceived as here, I am a good DS with a shit load of experience. You want to know anything, just ask. I expect, and I know, you are going to work your balls off because together we are a team that's going to be unbeatable and you had better believe it." Bloody hell, he thought. He was thirsty now. They took a break for a coffee and a chance to digest what he had just said and came back into the CID room to continue.

It seemed stupid to run a team with only two DCs but he would give it a go.

"So what's going on in my area?" Jazz asked the two DCs. They had files at the ready to discuss. The cases were boring ones given to newbies only. A few garden sheds had been broken into, there were shoplifting cases as usual and a fight outside the Red Cow pub on Saturday night. Nothing he was interested in. They exchanged mobile numbers and Jazz sent them off to investigate their cases. It was arranged that they would meet up in the briefing room at 3 p.m. with updates. He went off to see what else was going on in his manor.

CID had a whole floor in Ilford Police Station and Jazz took a look around and introduced himself. There were a few who he knew and remembered. He bantered and moved around, joking and chiding and making contact. The welcome from them wasn't exactly warm but they acknowledged him and that was enough. He shook hands with a few who knew more about him than he realised. Ilford was going to take time to settle back into and it made him feel a bit depressed and unwanted. Not a feeling he enjoyed but time would tell; he hoped it would improve. It was too early for a drink, but God, he could do with a swig of something.

He hung around the IBO room (Integration Borough Operations) waiting to see if anything interesting was coming in. It was busy as usual. The East End had a high crime record and something was always going on somewhere. A call came in that caught his attention; someone had been found hanging from a tree in Valentine's Park. He grabbed the details and laid claim to it. Grabbing a CID car, he called to Sharon and Tony, who were chatting by the door, to move their arses quick. The blue light was put on and they drove the mile to Valentine's park in record time.

The male had been cut down and lay on the floor waiting for forensics and the body bag to arrive. The PC who was standing guard until Jazz arrived had shown him to the body.

"Who cut him down?" Jazz asked the small crowd huddled together by the tree.

A park ranger stepped forward. "I did. I couldn't leave him up there, it wasn't right."

Jazz understood but was very put out that the scene was not undisturbed. "Have you moved anything else?"

The park ranger, obviously in shock and finding it hard to think, screwed his face in thought. "No didn't touch anything else. It was horrible to see him, I climbed the tree and cut him down." Near to tears, he continued, "I tried to hold him but he was too heavy and he fell. If he wasn't dead already, the fall would have killed him." Jazz stifled a giggle, this wasn't the time to see humour in this.

Marshalling his thoughts and working with what he saw, he called his two newbies and said, "I know what happened but for your development, tell me what see and what you think happened."

Horrified that he would make them work this scene in public, they both thought.

"Is this a foot fetish thing skip, a sexual pleasure thing?" asked Sharon. Again Jazz stifled a giggle; what are they like he thought, no idea at all. He looked at Tony, Sharon had dug herself a hole, it was time he did the same.

Realising he needed to say something, Tony added, "It looks like one of those sexual gratification things that went wrong. The silk scarf looks like a fetish thing."

Jazz knew he had his work cut out with these two, but he did have more knowledge than they did on the dead man.

"Look and learn," he said. "First of all, see the saffron scarf our man hung himself with? He is a Sikh, and for the uninitiated, a saffron scarf is a Sikh symbol. Look at his shoes, keys, letters, passport neatly placed in a plastic bag by the tree. The passport says he is new into the country with a six month visa. What that means, my little newbies, is he would be used to climbing a tree back home with no shoes on, so he took them off. Not a fetish, just practical. Until I know better, a sexual deviant practice is not on the cards. Why come to a park to get your rocks off when you can do it at home in private and comfort? This man meant to hang himself, we need to find out why. Far be it from me to become Sherlock Holmes," the heavy sarcasm was coming into play now and Sharon and Tony could hear it. "But I suspect this letter is a suicide letter so it should tell us everything we need to know." In that moment he felt sorry for Sharon and Tony and put an arm around each of their shoulders and walked them away from the crowd. "It's all a learning curve for you. We will get this one worked out and solved."

The letter was to this man's wife Surjit . He had come to England to join his wife who he found out was working as a prostitute. He hung himself out of shame. There was an address on the letter and a name, Kalia; this was the man accused of pimping his wife. Jazz found it interesting that a mobile number had been put on the letter saying it was Kalia's mobile number. Jazz figured he wanted this guy caught. There was no answer when he rang the number.

Jazz took Sharon and Tony to the address in Green Lane, Ilford. It was one of the big imposing houses that fronted the busy street. When the door was answered by an Asian man, Jazz introduced himself and went inside. He found that there were at least six men living in the house and no one knew where the wife had gone or who

Kalia was. The six men were sitting drinking and they asked if Jazz wanted a peg*. He said no, he wanted the whole bottle thanks and they laughed. The terrible two sat quietly watching and listening in the corner. It was early to be drinking so intently, they thought.

The Asian man who had answered the door seemed to be the only one wanting to talk to Jazz. He introduced himself as Ravi. He confirmed again he had never heard of Kalia didn't know where the woman was and had never heard of a husband looking for his wife. Jazz asked for Ravi's mobile number in case he needed to contact him again. Ravi hesitated and Jazz, with a reassuring smile, said "Just routine sir." He got the number and after thanking all for their hospitality, Jazz left.

When they got back to the car, he asked Sharon and Tony what they thought. They had watched and said the drinking men were of no consequence but they both thought Ravi was far too talkative and interested in the suicide not to know something. Jazz was impressed. They were right, Ravi was very keen to know what was happening. A thought struck him and he checked the mobile number on the letter and the one Ravi had given him.

"Guess what?" he roared triumphantly to the two of them. "Ravi and Kalia might be the same person."

He wanted to see Ravi alone so the two DCs were sent back to Ilford nick to check out the intelligence on the house, to see if anything was known. They were instructed to ring him with the information when they got it. They

*An alcoholic drink, generally any IMFL, is almost always called a 'peg' in India only

took the car to get back to Ilford nick; he didn't need it.

He badly needed a drink. Across the road was a small pub and he popped in for a beer to give him a chance to think on what he was going to do. Ravi couldn't be charged with anything to do with a suicide although he was partly to blame, along with the wife who had done a runner. He hoped he would eventually find her. For the time being, he had the pimp but what could he do with him? It was something to think through. He stayed in the pub longer than he intended. Two hours had gone by when his mobile rang. Sharon told him they had nothing on the house. No one there had come to the attention of the police. That confirmed there was nothing on Ravi, aka Kalia, so now it was down to Jazz to sort out.

Why he didnt just walk away, he couldn't answer. He could prove nothing and the suicide should just be written off as that, no sinister intentions or malice. So why did he feel a link between him and the Sikh. It seemed personal and he wanted to do right by this man. He had left his country and journeyed to England in the hope of settling down to a good life with his wife. The house was a boozy hole and no self-respecting Sikh would feel comfortable in those circumstances. Life wasn't fair, he knew that, but perhaps he could even up the score a little.

The four pints of beer had made him think very clearly indeed. He knew what he was going to do with this bastard. He went back to the house intent on sorting out the pimp. Ravi answered the door and welcomed Jazz into the house. Ravi was slightly the worse for drink, he had obviously joined the others in the house in the drinking session going on. With a slap on the back, Jazz said it would be good to have a drink with Ravi. The others in the room were not bothered about them; three were asleep and the other three looked close to passing out. After two or three pegs, Jazz took out his mobile phone and rang the number on the suicide letter for Kalia, the pimp's phone. Ravi's phone rang.

"Go on," Jazz nodded encouragingly, "answer it."

Ravi wasn't sure, he thought something was going on but he wasn't fully clued up so he tentatively answered his phone.

"Hello Kalia." The smooth tones came not only from the phone but from across the room. He had been found out but before Ravi, now Kalia, could run out of the room, Jazz made a dive at him and ushered him none too gently into the kitchen.

Jazz grabbed Kalia's left arm and found the metal bangle of truth that all Sikhs wear. He pulled it off and put in on the cooker. Holding Kalia close to him, and with his face inches from Kalia's face, Jazz menacingly stared for a second. The utter contempt he felt for this worm of a man was on full display. Again, he could feel his temper suddenly rising into his throat and nearly making him choke. Unable to keep quiet any longer, he goaded Kalia and shouted that he was a liar and that he had helped cause the death of an honourable man. Kalia had nothing to say, he kept quiet. The drink had made him incapable of thinking straight and he couldn't see what was going to happen.

Jazz had worked himself into a cold fury. He kept pushing Kalia, asking what kind of Sikh was he to wear such a bangle when all he had done was dishonourable and shameful. Jazz was sweating now, the exertion of his consuming rage took every ounce of his energy. There was only one thing to do now and in a flash, before Kalia knew what was happening, Jazz had picked up the bangle from the cooker with a cloth and pushed it over Kalia's wrist and up his arm. It stopped just before the elbow. Almost spitting the words, Jazz, through clenched teeth, told him, "There is your bangle of truth and now you wont ever forget its message." Kalia hadn't noticed Jazz turn on the cooker and the bangle was glowing by the time it went on his arm. It took three seconds for Kalia to feel the red hot bangle burning and searing into his skin and then the screaming started

Jazz ran the cold tap and put the plug in the sink. It took a minute or so to fill and then he plunged Kalia's arm into the blissfully cooling water. As he turned to leave, his parting words stayed with Kalia: "You make me sick! Your Bangle of Truth has paid you back."

He shouldn't have done it, but it was too late for regrets now. There were no witnesses, the other men were pissed out of their heads so no trouble there. The air outside helped cool his temper and his body. He realised his flash temper was raising its ugly head again, but he regretted nothing. The bastard was as good as a killer. He may not have put the noose round the Sikh's neck but he tied the knot with words and deeds that made the Sikh's life intolerable. Kalia deserved everything he got.

Jazz headed back to the station to find out what his team had been up to. He was later than 3 p.m. but it would do them good to sit and wait for him. Tomorrow he would go and find some of his old contacts on the street. He was sure they would be pleased to see him.

The Jazz Singer had only been back in London for one day and already he had gone far too close to the edge of reason. He knew he was going to ruffle quite a few feathers and he would have to watch his back. He didn't want another breakdown, he promised himself he would never to go down that route of demons again. Next time they would put him away in a mad house and that wasn't going to happen.

The day finished on a boring note. He listened to Sharon and Tony relating their shed cases and the shoplifting cases and any other problems they had. With more good grace than he felt, he listened, gave bits of advice when asked and said tomorrow they would tackle the cases and get them cleared up. For now, he wanted out and to go back to his room in De Vere Gardens. He aimed to put his feet up, watch a bit of telly, relax and have a drink. He stood up and in a loud, theatrical voice, wished everyone on the CID floor a good night and he would see them all tomorrow. Not many heads looked up from the desks to acknowledge his fond goodnight. They could all tell by his loose demeanour that he had a few two many that day and it was whispered that it was par for the course.

Jazz looked at the disinterest and just couldn't give a damn; well that is what he told himself. With a disgust that made him feel better, he vowed to himself that he was going to be the top Detective in Ilford and they had better believe it. The last laugh would be on the bastards in the CID room. He swaggered out, making sure everyone in there knew he didn't give a fuck what they thought and took himself off to his new home.

When he got back to his lodgings, Mrs Chodda came immediately out from the kitchen to speak to him. She was most anxious to make him welcome and had prepared a mini feast of curries for him to sample that evening. It transpired that he was their only lodger and they wanted to look after such a distinguished man. The policewoman who had checked out the lodgings for headquarters had said that Jazz was a Detective Sergeant who had come back from Manchester. They were very pleased to have such a person staying with them. Mrs Chodda, during the day, had called her mother, two aunts, her three sisters from Hackney and all her six nieces and they were in the kitchen waiting to meet Mr Singh.

Jazz, tired from the first day at Ilford, wanted to go to his room, put on his TV and have a drink. Manners overcame his annoyance and he followed Mrs Chodda into her big kitchen diner. Buckling under the weight of more curries than a restaurant could offer, sat hot dishes full of everything imaginable from meat, fish, vegetables, samosas, nan breads, rice and goodness knows what else waiting to be sampled. She must have cooked all day and night to prepare these, Jazz thought. He heard a chair scrape beside him and looked over to a straight line of chairs in two rows. He noted the older women sitting at the front and the younger, quite nice looking girls, sitting on the back row. He had worn a good shirt and trousers for his first day at work. Usually he wore a tee shirt and jeans. He was glad he looked fairly smart. The saris in front of him were magnificent in colour and style. It wasn't only the curries that would have taken all day to get ready; these women looked immaculate. He was very flattered by the attention. They sat and stared at him in silence, which was quite unnerving and he sobered up immediately.

For a few seconds, everyone was held in a frozen tableau. No one moved and it was as if everyone was holding their breath. Jazz broke the silence by going up to the oldest woman and, with great deference, introduced himself to her. The women each smiled and nodded their approval at this gesture. They liked his easy and respectful manner. The mother spoke no English but she was pleased when Jazz spoke to her in a dialect she understood. The young girls all blushed and eyed him up closely when he wasn't looking at them. They insisted he eat and he made a big production of choosing a little of everything and praising Mrs Chodda for her cooking skills. She was actually an excellent cook. Everyone was happy and enjoyed the gathering, except Jazz. He knew they were looking at him as a prospective husband for one of the back row girls.

Mr Chodda entered the kitchen about 8 p.m. and brought some light relief. The older women made a fuss of him and brought him food and drink. By 9 p.m. Jazz thought he had been dutiful enough and with a great display of thanks and the pleasure it had been to meet such lovely ladies, etc. etc., he made his escape. He was going to have to move from this guest house. He had a horrible feeling this could be a regular occurrence and that was just not going to happen if he could help it. He needed a drink badly.

RENEWING OLD ACQUAINTANCES

He woke the next morning with a dry mouth. His stomach was growling and he knew he was going to pay dearly for eating so many different types of curries. Yesterday felt good, getting back into the thick of things at Ilford, but he still felt apprehensive about going into the police station. He could feel a sense of animosity there; it hung above his head like a black cloud threatening to drench him with accusations.

Wednesday morning started with meeting his team, all two of them, in the CID room. He had figured out that he had real newbies. Except for him, no one had any experience in CID and the two that were to arrive later had even less than the two he had now. He thought he would have been given at least one experienced DC. He knew no one wanted to work with him and that thought burrowed deep and hurt. Every team always had a mixture of experienced and new in it. It made sense. He looked at the two DCs before him, Sharon and Tony. He thought, bloody hell what was he going to do with them. With a resigning sigh, he told them they were going to work with him today. He wanted to sort out the shed burglaries.

Sharon and Tony had been round to the private houses and spoken to the victims and examined the sheds. Their conclusion was that with a walkway at the back of the gardens, it gave a burglar good access and getaway and all the sheds had been cleared in a night. Six sheds had been tampered with and various lawnmowers and bikes had been stolen. They didn't have fingerprints and there was no CCTV in the area. Nothing much of interest there but Jazz thought it might be good to introduce them to a few old acquaintances of his. He figured they would still be around. Nothing much changed in that part of Barking.

The burglaries happened in Ilford Lane, which goes from Ilford to Barking. The houses were near the Barking end of Ilford Lane. The CID car was in the car park waiting for them. Jazz let Tony drive. He felt under the weather still and hoped his stomach wouldn't let him down during the drive. He said they were off to the Gasgoine Estate in Barking to meet Mad Pete. En route, he explained that Mad Pete was a druggy on methodone to combat the withdrawal from heroin. Pete was addicted to methadone now. His brain had been frazzled and he looked like the walking dead. He had a flat in a high rise and with nothing to do all day he roamed the streets and got to know what was going on out there. The feral kids, as Jazz called the under 18 year olds who roamed the streets – no school, no jobs and homes they would rather be out of than in – were the major criminals in small time crimes like sheds, muggings, street robberies and gang fights. For whatever reason, that made no sense to any adult, Mad Pete was looked on as a god by the feral kids. He was no Fagin, not enough brains to keep that together, but he did lay his hands on cannabis from time to time, which he shared with the ferals. When really pushed, he was good at shoplifting too. With all the CCTV and security around, he managed to get bottles of whisky through without being stopped. He did target smaller shops where it was easier to distract and steal. Over the years, Mad Pete had gained a lot of experience. It would be true to say that most shops in the Barking area now knew him and he had to travel by bus further afield for a shopping spree.

They pulled up outside the high rise. Sharon and Tony understood this area well and made sure the car was locked. Every town had a 'Gascoigne Estate' in it. High rise flats and maisonettes all built close together with the odd sprinkling of a green with signs saying 'No Ball Games'. The graffiti was quite good in places. Jazz turned to Sharon and pointed out the lack of education in the area. "Someone ought to teach these kids something. That's not how you spell *'bolicks'*. The youth of today are going down the pan!"

Jazz suddenly moved forward quickly. He was now in a hurry to get into Mad Pete's flat. He rang at the bell more times than was necessary and Mad Pete could be heard to grumble that he was getting there as fast as he could. He opened the door and Jazz dived in and went straight to the toilet. He left Sharon and Tony to ask if they might come in.

Minutes later, Jazz appeared, obviously suffering. "My God, Pete, the state of your toilet, don't you ever clean it? I need carbolic soap for my bum after sitting on that seat." Pete looked down and smiled an apology.

A bottle of beer was offered but all thanked him and refused. Nothing in this place was clean, including Pete, who stank of sweat. The two DCs looked at him and reckoned he must be about 50 years old at least. His grey thin hair held together by grease hung limply to his shoulders; not a trendy look at all, more a mad look. His jeans had seen better days and hung from the waist with no bum or stomach to give them shape. They looked like whatever he had eaten, touched or been close to over the past year were stained on them. The blue denim had lost its colour to a barrage of grease stains and dirt. He wore a tee shirt with the words, *if a man is alone in the woods is he still wrong*. Tony liked that and smiled.

"So you are back, Mr Singh." Mad Pete opened the conversation in a most respectful way.

Jazz was not in the mood for pleasantries. "It's about these shed burglaries off Ilford Lane; what do you know about them?"

Pete shook his head and before he said anything Jazz reminded him that he could make life very difficult for him, he knew he was fencing stuff, not big time stuff, but enough to get him put before the Magistrates and he knew he didn't want to go down that route. Pete was petrified of going to prison again. The last time he had been badly attacked by other inmates and he said he would rather be dead than go back there. Jazz was guessing. He had only just returned to Ilford, but Pete didn't look like he had made any life changes and small- time fencing had kept him going before so no need to assume it was any different now.

"OK, Mr Singh, I know the Barrow lads from Barking were fencing some bikes and lawnmowers which came from sheds I reckon. Not the stuff I am interested in, Mr Singh, too big for me."

Jazz knew Pete fenced mobiles only. There was a lot of money in it. Every kid had a mobile these days and street robberies were on the increase when he was last in Ilford. Times certainly didn't seem to have changed in the five years he had been away. Even Mad Pete's tee shirt was the same as he wore last time he was here and still not washed by the look of it.

The Barrow boys were new to Jazz; when he got in the car, he asked the two DCs if they knew of them. They did. The week they had been at Ilford had been spent well. Sharon and Tony had looked at persistent offenders lists and those names that had come to the attention of Ilford Police. Tony added that the Barrow boys were well known in the area for petty crime. Both were on referral orders at the age of 13 years for shoplifting. They were obviously not going to learn from it and were about to go up the next rung on the ladder of criminality.

Jazz thought that sounded poncy and said, "They are little thieves who are never going to change. We had better get their address and visit them." The two of them were looking good and, in a moment of warmth, Jazz turned to each of them and promised, "We'll show the bastards on the CID floor who's the daddy! We're going to be the best."

Sharon and Tony hoped he was right. It all looked a bit hit and miss to them. The CID teams had enjoyed more fun at their expense than was fair. The thought of sweet revenge was very appealing and they both vowed to work hard to make it happen. The bonding of the team was well underway.

A call was made to intelligence, who gave an address in Ilford Lane. The Barrow boys lived in a council maisonette with their mother, a single parent who had lots of uncles visiting regularly.

"Is she a tom?" Jazz asked.

He was told that she wasn't a tom, more she liked to have a man around for a little while. They never stayed long and then she got another man. She didn't work and apart from the twins, Brian and David, she had Kayleigh, who was three years, and William, who was one year old. All by different fathers.

"Sounds about normal to me, lets go visit." Said Jazz, anxious to get going. "I would say it was a pleasure, Pete, but it weren't!" Mad Pete smiled. Mr Singh was back and going to be a pain in the neck again.

Mad Pete begrudgingly liked Mr Singh. He had saved him from prison a couple of times. Pete had never done anything too bad and he had always helped Mr Singh when forced to, but sometimes a very ambitious PC or DC would home in on him and try and fix him up. Mr Singh protected him to a certain extent. He was told that if he ever did anything big, he would not protect him and, in fact, Jazz would ensure he went to a prison with particularly big bad bastards who would love to meet him. Pete stayed fairly clean, just making a bit of a living now and again.

"Well, what do you think of Mad Pete?" Jazz asked them.

Tony answered ruefully, "You take us to the best places, skipper, thank you very much." Jazz laughed, he was warming to Tony, who had an ironic sense of humour. "He's mine, I introduced you but he stays mine and you don't touch him, is that clear?"

Both Sharon and Tony understood and got quite excited because this was real Detective work, like on TV. Jazz could see the excitement rising and told them to calm down and focus on the job of getting the shed burglaries sorted.

The maisonette looked good. Sharon Barrow let them in. She kept a very nice home and looked after herself. The two youngest were sitting watching TV. She was asked where her twins were and she said she didn't know. They usually went out and came back at lunch time or teatime; whenever they felt like it. Seeing the look on the DC's face, she pointed out that at 13 years old they were young adults and were growing up. No one except her thought that was the way to bring up teenagers but they weren't social workers so it wasn't their problem. In answer to their question, she thought that they usually hung around Barking Town Centre, near the station.

When they were back in the car, Jazz phoned ahead and asked for pictures of the Barrow boys. They said they would go and collect them straight away. The journey back to the nick involved stopping at two pubs so Jazz could go to the toilet. The curries were hitting him with vengeance. They had a quick drink, Sharon and Tony had orange and Jazz had a couple of brandies for his stomach. He chewed some gum to cover the brandy breath, which was just as well because the *fucking graduate* wanted to see him in his office.

He knocked on the DCI's closed door. He entered when he heard a "Come in".

"You wanted to see me, Sir?" Jazz asked respectfully. The tirade started then and continued for 10 minutes. Kalia had been in to complain about Jazz.

"You have been here less than 24 hours," which was incorrect, it was getting on for 48 hours, but Jazz was not going to argue the point, "and already I have a member of the public accusing you of GBH. What have you to say about this?" His voice was full of anger and the pitch was getting higher and higher. With a cough to adjust his voice, DCI John Radley pushed a picture of Kalia's seared arm towards Jazz. The shock was real. Jeez, his arm was badly burnt in a perfect circle. He was amazed the metal bangle could have done so much damage. "He had to go to the hospital and he is traumatised by the effect." DCI Radley was trying to stay calm but the urge to shout and lose control was there. "He said you did this to him. Is it true, DS Singh!" It was not a question, it was an interrogation.

Jazz, cornered but coming out fighting, had a response ready. "Sir, Kalia lives in a house with six other men. When myself and DCs Day and Sepple attended the house, we found all seven members of the house indulging in a drinking bout. The six men were very drunk indeed. Kalia was also drinking and whilst he was able to hold a conversation with me, he showed signs of being highly intoxicated. DCs Day and Sepple and myself left the house together. We did not return because intelligence gave us no reason to believe any persons in the house had any history of criminal intent."

DCI Radley wanted more.

"Why would I do such a thing, Sir? We found

nothing in our conversations with Kalia to suppose he would be of any further interest in the case of the hanging. If I may suggest, Sir, he was very drunk and has got muddled up with events." This was a polite way of saying to his DCI, *prove it,* which of course he couldn't. DCI Radley had no idea at all why Jazz would do such a thing and it didn't seem feasible. The hospital had said that Kalia was drunk when they looked at his arm and quite honestly a drunk is capable of doing any stupid thing.

DCI Radley said he would deal with this but he warned Jazz he would be keeping an eye on his working procedures and if he found any reason to suppose he was not working within the protocols of the Metropolitan Police, he would come down on him like a ton of bricks! His face had now burned to a bright angry red and feeling ill at ease and not at all reassured, he dismissed Jazz from his office. Jazz knew he had to be careful and watch what he did in future. He couldn't go on this way. He thought himself a good CID Detective and he didn't like what he was becoming. He would do things by the book from now on. No more Jazz justice. But soon something would make that very difficult to follow.

The DCs had the picture of the Barrow Boys, Brian and David. It was thought a quick recce of Barking Town Centre might find them. It was 1 p.m. and there was just enough time to find them and interview them before their shift was over. Raring to go, Sharon and Tony had to wait in the car whilst Jazz made another visit to the toilet.

"My God, those bloody curries are going to kill me,"

he said. They laughed; an Asian man complaining about curries didn't sound right.

The got to Barking Town Centre at 2 p.m., later than they hoped. The picture was a clear one but all the young lads together were hoodies. They got out and walked up to groups of them and showed the picture and asked if they knew them and where they were. They got a lot of ripe answers which Jazz let pass, but no one knew these boys. It was on turning and seeing two young lads walking towards the station that he saw them. They saw him first and turned and ran. Sharon and Tony were on the case and were fit. They steamed after the two lads whilst Jazz tried to keep up. After five minutes, Sharon and Tony, with one boy each, marched back to where Jazz waited. Off came the hoods and the pictures were looked at; it was them. When asked their names and where they lived, they lied; with a bravado they should not have felt, they gave false names and addresses and said they had done 'nuffink' wrong. Handcuffed and put in the back of the car, Jazz said it was over to the two DCs to sort out and interview them. They were taken back to Ilford and put in a cell until it was decided what they were going to do with them.

With no direct ideas coming from the two DCs, and fed up with just speculation, Jazz told them what they were going to do. To begin with, a search needed to be made of the Barrow Boys' home. Jazz would speak to Mad Pete again, it was possible he might know where they fenced the stuff. He told them Mad Pete did not go down on paper, he was his informer and he was to stay out of the limelight. He suggested the boys were interviewed separately to see if they would own up to the shed burglaries. In fact, Jazz announced he would interview the first boy. They were not identical twins so could not play the game other twins had played by saying *You can't prove which one of us was there.*

Brian and David were waiting for an appropriate adult each to turn up. The mother couldn't come because she was looking after the two little ones. Also, a brief was organised for them both. Until it all came together, Jazz went off to speak to Mad Pete. The two DCs went to organise a warrant to search the Barrow Boys' home. Jazz's parting words were "Back here by 6 p.m. latest and we will pool our information." They went off excited to be doing real police work. Give me strength! he thought. This was a stupid little case and it had taken all his day. He hoped the days got better otherwise he was going to be bored out of his brain.

Pete knew it was the Barrow Boys and said they fenced bikes and lawnmowers to Albie Edwards down Beckton Way. Jazz remembered Albie, a careful man who usually only bought what he had orders for. The Barrow Boys must have been stealing to order. Perhaps that was why they left behind tools that could have fetched a few bob. Albie was using younger boys these days. The burglary was a few days ago. Albie would have got rid of the stuff immediately, but he would go and see him anyway, just to let him know he was back. Not a lot seemed to have changed on his patch in the five years he'd been gone.

The DCs returned promptly and looked very pleased with themselves. They told Jazz, well they argued between themselves who was going to tell Jazz, but Sharon won. Good on her, Jazz thought, she was making herself known. They found £60 under the Barrow Boys' mattress. They slept in bunk beds and it was under the bottom bunk's mattress. They also found a set of new screwdrivers in a drawer. One of the people who had been burgled said a new screwdriver set was missing. It looked like they had found it from the description given. That set the boys right in it.

The appropriate adults were about to arrive and the briefs were already there. As soon as they were ready, interviews would start. They were all into overtime now, which pleased them.

Jazz intended for this to be sown up quickly. He wanted to get home and relax. Last night was ruined with the curry evening, tonight he was taking a kebab home and watching any highlights he could find on the test match in India. He felt exhausted by his stomach reacting to the curries. Again he rushed off to find a toilet.

The appropriate adults had arrived. Jazz took Brian and he let Sharon take David. Tony could watch and learn. It took five minutes for the belligerent mumbling idiot to realise he had been banged to rights. His brief advised him to make a no comment interview but solicitors can be more of a pain in the butt than anything else. If he goes hands up to it, Jazz said it would go well in court; if not and he was found guilty, with all the evidence they had and the fact that David said it was his fault, well, he could get something much more serious. The appropriate adult watched but said nothing at this stage. Brian, incensed that his brother might blame him, spilled the beans and told all. Of course, his brother David instigated the burglaries and they fenced it to someone they had met but whose name they did not know. It was all written down and signed. Done and dusted, now for the other one, Jazz thought whimsically. He didn't think Sharon would have got a confession out of him. The no comment interview was standard these days.

He knocked and entered the interview room whilst Sharon was offering a tissue to a very upset David. "Poor lad, this is all too much for him, skip," she lamented.

The appropriate adult asked for a break for David. Jazz thought it better to get it over and done with so the lads could go home as soon as possible. Another confession was signed and the boys were duly bailed and sent on their way. Jazz always shook the hands of the appropriate adult and thanked them for coming. It was good manners, they were volunteers and besides, best to keep them happy otherwise they could make an interview hell by stopping it every few minutes and arguing points for the suspect. Sharon had done well. He thought she had potential.

Sharon and Tony went home feeling very good but Jazz felt listless and hoped things would improve soon. He wanted a meaty job to get his teeth into. For the time being, he would have to settle for a kebab. He opened the front door of his lodgings hoping Mrs Chodda didn't jump out with any other surprises. She did come out of the kitchen but when she saw he had a kebab she just smiled and said she hoped he had a good evening. With relief, he climbed the stairs to his room, turned the TV on and got a glass. He needed to remember to get another bottle of vodka tomorrow, this one wouldn't last another night. He had a good night's sleep. The nightmares were less frequent and it was always a bonus when he slept well. He got up on Thursday morning full of hope that today would be a better day. His stomach, at last, felt fine, much to his relief.

THE FUNERAL

Thursday was the day he would sort out the Sikh man's funeral. There was no one to take charge of it. He didn't know why, but he felt an affinity with this guy. He must have felt so alone and depressed to have taken his own life in that way. OK, Jazz had experienced that feeling and perhaps that was what it was. He would hope someone would officiate at his funeral when it happened. He had no one at present he could ask.

Unfortunately, he needed to speak to the *fucking graduate* about the funeral. Sikhs are cremated and their ashes are thrown into running water. Ken Livingstone, a little while back, as Mayor of London, had organised a part of the Thames where ashes could be scattered on the water. This could only happen as the tide was going out and had to be properly organised. He needed his DCI's permission to go ahead with this.

DCI Radley said to come to his office at 10 a.m; he was in a meeting before then. So at 10 a.m., Jazz knocked on his office door. Again, he entered only when he heard "Come in". DCI Radley didn't look up from the document he was reading. Jazz thought it fucking bad manners to make him sit there and not even acknowledge him. On second thoughts, it looked like one of those power games. It didn't bother him. He sat and looked at the pictures on the wall. They were all of groups of cadets and certificates that the DCI had obtained on his meteoric rise in the Metropolitan Police Force. There was one with him shaking the Commissioner's hand and another standing to attention with the Queen walking past him. This chap had a very great sense of his own importance but so far Jazz wasn't sure he was going to show he had any common sense as a police officer.

After a long two minutes, DCI Radley put down his paper and nodded to Jazz to speak, Jazz presumed. He explained about the hanging and that the man was Sikh. He told him he had no relatives that could be found in this country and he asked, as a Sikh himself, if he could officiate at the temple and organise his funeral. He added the bit about ashes in running water and that Ken Livingstone had allowed the scattering of ashes in the Thames. DCI became quite animated and thought it was an excellent idea. Of course Jazz could go ahead and make arrangements at the temple. He would personally organise the documentation that would allow for the ashes to be scattered in the Thames. Jazz was relieved to hear he would not have to make a song and dance about getting it done.

He thought their conversation was for the time being finished because the DCI was sitting quietly thinking. Jazz was about to get up and go, thinking he was finished with him, when the *fucking graduate* spoilt it by saying, "I will arrange for the Commissioner's launch to be made available to you for scattering the ashes, that seems very appropriate. I will, of course, come with you." DCI Radley was on a roll and could see more and more the benefits of a Sikh funeral. "The press should be told about this charitable act. It will make a good story and show the Metropolitan Police have a multi-cultural heart. Come back and see me on Monday when I shall have all the information and dates and we can then organise a press release. Photographers will of course be there so a suit please, DS Singh. Of course anything the press need to know should come from a senior officer."

Jazz asked, "Would that be you, Guv?"

A little modesty tried to inject itself into DCI's voice. "Well I suppose, yes, that would have to be me."

"OK, Guv, I will come back on Monday with the details," was all Jazz could manage to say as he left the room.

He was now on a mission of speed. From Ilford Police Station he went to the morgue to check if Mr Singh was ready for cremation. He was told he was. From there he went to the temple and organised a service and the cremation service. It was Thursday and they could, at a pinch, organise it for that afternoon provided all the necessary papers were ready. He was told that otherwise it would have to wait until the following week. That was too late for Jazz. He arranged for the cremation to happen at 4 p.m. that afternoon and he would bring all the necessary papers. The ashes would be ready Saturday late afternoon for collection and that was rushing it.

Jazz spent the rest of the morning and early afternoon rushing around and getting all the necessary papers from the coroner's office to the Births and Deaths Department and the undertakers. He went home, put his suit on and was back for the cremation at 4 p.m. As the surrogate son, he was asked to press the button that sent the coffin to the flames. He was invited into a room to watch as the flames consumed the coffin and the body. As a mark of respect, he sat and watched the flames and hoped Mr Singh's soul was at rest. Surprisingly, his duo turned up and sat with him in the main area of the crematorium and waited until he emerged from the private room. He was actually very touched by that. He decided not to return to the temple, which was traditional. He knew the gossiping aunties there who made and served the food would do justice to the feast prepared for after a cremation. He decided he would rather be with his team and he took them all to the pub for a drink.

They exchanged bits about themselves, which was very interesting to all present. Sharon Day started. Jazz thought she had more balls than most men. Sharon, a sturdily built natural blonde, lived in a small flat she had got after her divorce. She was married to a policeman who was based in Kingston. She moved to this side of the water so they wouldn't meet again. She made it clear to Tony and Jazz that the last person on earth she would date would have anything to do with the police force.

What she didn't tell them was she had been based in Bethnal Green Police Station after her divorce. She had been studying for her DC exams but she still had time to date and bed most of the police officers within her area and when she left Bethnal Green Police Station, her reputation was known far and wide and she was called the slag of Bethnal Green. She didn't know why she acted like she did. She just reckoned for two years she went mad and wild and treated every police officer as a sexual adventure. If she had been a man she would have been called a womaniser with grudging respect. Ilford was a new start for her and she hoped information about her wouldn't get to Ilford. When she changed Met areas, she also changed her name back to her maiden name so everything about Ilford was a new start. Bob, the Custody Sergeant, had already told Jazz about her busy past. Bob was the font of all knowledge, but it would appear that he hadn't told anyone else in Ilford Police yet about Sharon.

Tony Sepple was the next. Jazz thought some of Sharon was rubbing off on him, he was getting more confident as the days went on. Tony, a slight built man with short legs which barely allowed him to reach 5'7", lived at home still. He hadn't got a long term girlfriend, and no he wasn't gay, he added. Jazz reckoned he had been asked this before. Tony had been based at Romford Police Station before he was made a DC. Bob told Jazz that he was known unkindly as Nancy by his fellow officers at Romford. Apparently he had a pretty bad time there but he stuck it out and got his DC exams. Jazz thought his perseverance showed he was a strong, motivated character and someone to lean on when under pressure.

What no one knew was there had been a point when Tony had been contemplating suicide. Every day was a difficult day for him. He still hadn't worked out who he was, all he really knew was that he had made DC and he was going to be the best DC in his unit. He told himself he was celibate and that kept all his sexual feelings under control. He knew he was a ticking bomb but that was his secret never to be shared with anyone. This was a new start for him.

They now looked to Jazz for his contribution. He found it quite difficult to know what to say. He told them he was fast-tracked through to DS and that he was seconded to Manchester Police for quite a few years. He bullshitted about how wonderful Manchester was and what he had done whilst there. He concluded with the fact that the Met Police had asked for him back and that was why he was here today.

They both knew there was more to it but he was their skipper so they couldn't ask for more information. Jazz looked at his small team and was happy with what he had. He told them that they might be new but they had proved their enthusiasm and he had all the skills they would need to learn. He raised his glass and predicted that by the end of the year his team would be considered the best at Ilford and they both cheered and raised their glasses in affirmation.

Sharon and Tony looked at their watches and decided enough was enough and left Jazz still drinking after two hours. They had homes to go to. Jazz thought they were a great little team to have. The two DCs left wondering if their skipper had a drink problem.

Now they had gone, Jazz started on double vodkas. As he told the barmaid, his team were the best and he was going to toast their success. He toasted them for a further two hours and five double vodkas before deciding it was time to go home. He rang for a cab to take him home but it was going to be 10 minutes before it arrived so he went into the off licence next door to the pub and bought a bottle of vodka.

The cab arrived on time and it was 10 p.m. when he opened the front door to his lodgings. Mrs Chodda immediately opened the kitchen door to greet him. She said she had curry and rice for him for his tea if he would like to come into the kitchen. Jazz thanked her and asked if he may eat it in his room as he was very tired. Any other time, Mrs Chodda would not have taken no for an answer but looking at him standing there swaying a little, she thought that perhaps he was a bit drunk. Reluctantly she agreed to bring a plate of curry upstairs in five minutes for him. It took him a while to walk up the stairs and he heard a strange female voice in the kitchen. He wondered if she had invited more young female relatives for him to see. He was glad he got out of that meeting, he was not up to socialising tonight.

He was quite right. Mrs Chodda had her niece by her husband's brother's sister-in-law who had come to visit for the day. Mrs Chodda, on seeing Jazz's condition, had decided not to invite him into the kitchen to meet her niece. She would arrange it for another day when hopefully Jazz was less *tired,* as she preferred to call his condition.

He put on his TV, poured a vodka and ate the curry given to him on a tray by Mrs Chodda. Life wasn't so bad. His team were coming along nicely and he reckoned he would surprise all those people who gave him what they thought was a *no-hoper* team. He felt quite comfortable in his room and the curry was very nice and not too hot. Tomorrow was another day and there were people he still needed to visit. He didn't realise that his life would get busier and more involved tomorrow. His team was set for a rollercoaster ride with Jazz.

ANOTHER DAY ANOTHER DOLLAR

Jazz woke the next morning with a dry mouth and a thick headache that made his eyes scream for darkness as soon as he opened them. After a shower and several cans of fanta with a few headache tablets, he thought he could face the day. He noted that the vodka bottle was half empty. He had quite a few yesterday and decided he would watch his drinking a bit more. Drink made him relax and he enjoyed it but it was a little worrying that he needed it so much. Well, today, he told himself, he would prove he didn't need so much of it. He filled his hip flask with vodka just in case. He had no intention of drinking it during the day but he felt better knowing he had it in his inside pocket.

When he got to Ilford Police Station, he found his team sitting in the incident room waiting for him. They had sorted out the cases of shoplifting and had got the files ready for CPS advice. One case had already been sent back to Tony from CPS saying there was not enough evidence for a conviction. After a brief look through the file and talking to Tony, Jazz took himself off to the CPS room to have a word with the Duty Prosecutor. It was Mary Fellows on duty and she was never easy to argue with.

She seemed genuinely pleased to see him. Mary Fellows was a bright young Prosecutor who had been in private practice for the first part of her career. After working as an agent for CPS cases, she was headhunted to join the organisation. She found private practice was a cut-throat business and private firms expected you to work every hour and more in a day to make money for the company. She was fed up with the work involved and, if she was honest, she was fed up of defending clients and getting more not guilty verdicts than most of her clients deserved. The CPS was an honourable organisation and was there to work within the Director of Public Prosecution's code.

She found working in a charging centre in a police station was cutting edge stuff and she saw it as one of the most important roles a DP could have. If you got the charges right at the beginning, it helped ensure a swift walk through the courts and most of the time a guilty plea to start with. If you have someone banged to rights with the correct charge, they had nowhere to go and often pleaded guilty when officially charged by the police. It was her role, as a lawyer independent of the police, to ensure that whatever the police brought to her for charging complied with the code of practice in the CPS. This ensured it would not be thrown out of court for lack of evidence. This caused quite a few heated discussions with police officers who were very involved in their cases. They might know the suspect was guilty but it had to be proved and there lay the division between the police and the CPS. She loved her job and could take on any police officer. The woman was not for turning unless you gave her the evidence she needed for a charge.

Jazz sat down and gave her back the file on O'Brien, which she had sent back to Tony. Jazz knew he was in for a fight but O'Brien was guilty, any fool with half a brain and a ticket in the human race could see that. He was trying his luck with Mary, but it was worth a go. O'Brien was a known shoplifter for Christ's sake! He was obviously guilty. They argued for 30 minutes with Jazz insisting that O'Brien was guilty as hell and Mary saying prove it. There was no CCTV to incriminate him, the bottles of whisky were in the pram of his girlfriend not in his bags as they walked out. The discussion became more heated when Jazz insisted that of course he put them in the pram and Mary again said prove it. He watched her as she went through the lack of evidence and all the evidence she needed to prove his guilt. God she was a beautiful woman. Her cheeks were red with effort and her long black hair hung beautifully and elegantly to her shoulders. As she pushed home her conclusions and told Jazz to go away and do some more work on the case, a breakaway sheath of hair strayed across her forehead and eyes. As she pushed the strands from her eyes and settled them behind her ears, she looked across at Jazz and for a second their eyes met in a moment of recognition of something left unsaid from their past. A blink of an eye and it was gone. Begrudgingly Jazz agreed they needed CCTV to prove O'Brien took the whiskey and he would get one of his team to investigate where it was. He didn't want to leave, but they both had work to get on with. It might have been an argument over work but Jazz had enjoyed the encounter. Mary always made him feel good, even when she was putting him in his place.

As he got up from the chair, Mary hesitated, only for a nano second but the delay was picked up by Jazz, and then she asked if he was OK. He smiled and nodded. Both wanted to say more but it was not appropriate. With an intake of breath, he wished her a good day and as he opened the door to leave, he murmured, with more feeling than he intended, "It's good to see you again, Mary." This wafted towards her and she sat and savoured the comment left hanging in the air as the door closed after him.

He went back to Tony, threw the file on the table in front of him and told him to go and find the relevant CCTV, adding none too quietly that it should have been on file already.

The morning was getting on and Jazz went to the IBO room to see if there was anything interesting happening that he could get his teeth into. He had got the feeling that he and his team were at the bottom of the list for any jobs of interest and would be given the crappy jobs of shoplifting and sheds. He was having none of that. It was a Friday morning and he hoped something good had come in that he could pinch for his team. It was always a busy room but this morning there were voices shouting over each other with emergencies and calls for officers to attend addresses. He discounted most of them, they were petty break-ins or domestics, nothing very meaty.

He had left his team going through their files for the

shoplifting cases to ensure they were fully compliant for CPS advice. The CCTV was paramount and all were working on phoning shops to ensure the CCTV was made available. They had found that half of Ilford's small shops were using CCTV that was not compatible with anything the police had. Some dodgy salesman had done the rounds and sold cheap CCTV equipment; yes, it worked, but no, it was impossible to put onto any system known to any of the services. It would cause them all a headache but it would do them good to work out how to gain evidence useable for CPS and the courts.

Hanging around the IBO room was not Jazz's idea of fun but he needed a decent job to work on. He tried to banter with the operators in the room. He figured they would give him jobs eventually either because they liked him or because they wanted to get rid of him. Either way, he just wanted something meaty to work on.

Tomorrow he would collect Mr Parmiter's ashes and take them to the Thames on Sunday. He found out the tide was going out at 1.30 p.m. and he decided he would scatter the ashes at that time by Tilbury Docks. He knew that on Monday the *fucking graduate* would go ballistic when he knew what he had done, but that was Monday and he would worry about it then. Mr Parmiter was not going to be the vehicle to get DCI Radley in the newspapers for doing Jack shit! He wanted him to have his ashes scattered in a symbolic and respectful manner as befits a Sikh man, not a press frenzy of flash photography and newspaper men with DCI Radley hogging the proceedings. It was the least Jazz could do for this badly-served Sikh.

He had got to know some of the team in the IBO room and by now he was gasping for a fanta; he needed a sugar rush. They promised that if anything good came in they would save it for him. He went off knowing they meant none of it and he hurried to get his drink and return so as not to miss anything interesting. He popped his head in on his team and told them to be on standby. They didn't know what that meant and neither did Jazz, but it was good to keep them on their toes; this thought made him smile and he quickened his step to the IBO room. He had a feeling something good was going to come in soon and he wanted to be there to make sure it was his to deal with.

WHAT HAPPENED TO ALICE

At 10 a.m. the call came in. Jazz nearly missed it. It was only hearing the name Alice Watson and the address in Wards Road, Newbury Park that made him rush to the desk where the information was coming in.

"It's not for you, Jazz, it's a death of an old lady who looks like she has fallen over and bashed her head, not a crime scene." The officer tried to dismiss him and get on with the logistics of arranging for an officer to stay at the house until the ambulance arrived. Jazz didn't care and was having none of it. It was like a bolt had struck him in his back and he hunched his shoulders for comfort. He felt a tightness in his chest and his breathing was laboured with the shock. Poor Alice, that sweet old lady he had known since a child and spent precious evenings with when his mother died was now dead. It was all so unfair. He had to go there to see she was handled respectfully, she had no one else.

He was full of remorse. He remembered he promised to keep in contact with her but he didn't. He could conjure up all the excuses on why he had never rung, but he was too ashamed to bother. The least he could do was to be there at the house.

Feeling muddled and strangely confused, he took

himself off to the CID room to tell Sharon and Tony to get on with the shoplifting cases and he would be back later. He told himself to get a grip; the sadness, and the tears nearly ready to spill, was not how he wanted the CID room to see him. His depression would have to wait until he had time alone to deal with it. It was a sombre drive to Wards Road, Newbury Park. He hadn't been there for years and he expected it to look the same.

When he arrived outside Alice's house, he had to park a little way away. The ambulance had just pulled up and a panda car was sitting outside. Jazz got out quickly and took control. No, he insisted, the body was not to be moved yet. He wanted to look at the scene. He made the officer who attended the call – who was obviously still fairly new to the job – stay by the door and told him not to let anyone in without his say so. The smell as he entered the hallway said it all. Once you have smelt death, it never leaves you, you always know it. He shouted to the officer to send the ambulance men away because a mortuary van was needed. Irrationally, he felt a swell of anger at the police officer for ringing for the ambulance.

"Fucking idiot, she is stiff as a board and smells like she has been here for days. Yeah gods! Where do they find the imbeciles?" He realised he was going over the top and tried to calm down. He stood for a moment, looking around.

The house was as he remembered it. The multicoloured runner in the hall with lino underneath. Her house was from a bygone age of carpet beaters, floor scrubbing and all the things that never got done in this day and age in quite the same way. It didn't smell of lavender polish like he remembered; the pervasive smell of death had taken over the house. He walked into the front room and saw her. She was lying with her head on the tiled surround of the fireplace.

He remembered years ago sitting with his mother in this very front room balancing a cup and saucer in one hand and a matching tea plate in the other hand. She always gave them chocolate digestive biscuits, which were his mother's favourites. Alice was such a kind, genteel lady. It was always her bone china cups with flowers on them, wide rimmed and so very thin that he remembered being scared to hold the cup too tightly in case it broke in his hand. Alice always made a point of getting her best china out when he and his mother called to visit. She would never put a tea bag in a mug and fill it with hot water; he remembered it had to be loose tea leaves, which she kept in a special tea caddy tin that had pictures of what was supposed to be Ceylon on it. She used a special spoon that measured the correct amount of tea leaves to go in the teapot, and she had a stainless steel strainer which sat on a purpose built saucer ready to be used when tea was required. It was a long ritual that was very comforting to watch and he wished she was making him a cup of tea now and asking all the silly questions about his schooling and what he was doing. He smiled at the thought that she had no idea about schooling and everything he told her seemed to go over her head but she would nod and smile and still make him feel very important.

Now here she was lying in an undignified way,

lifeless and not the Alice he remembered. When she was alive, she was always smiling and nodding and moving around doing bits and pieces. Jazz looked at Alice, prone and very dead, and felt a mistiness that could have become tears. The house felt cold and lifeless, like Alice. The front door was flung open wide allowing anyone to walk in and out without the courtesy of knocking. It felt wrong to Jazz; Alice wouldn't have liked it. He shouted, "Close that fucking door" to the officer outside.

Professionalism kicked in and he went into work mode. There would be time for mourning later; for now he would do his job. Something was wrong here, though he didn't for the moment quite know what. It wouldn't take him long to pick up what had first given him a sense of unease. He owed it to Alice to do right by her. He stood still and just looked. He wasn't himself, he knew that, this felt personal, but he was sure he wasn't making more of this. Of course Alice could have fallen and the big gap in the back of her head could have been caused by hitting the fireplace. She was an old lady, these things happen. Again, he wasn't convinced and he didn't know why.

Jazz, now totally in control, looked up when the ambulance men suddenly appeared in the doorway of the front room. Having been called here, they decided to ignore the officer on the door and come in and just check for themselves that she was dead. Jazz said airily that they could check for themselves if they wished. The fact that she was stiff as a board and not smelling particularly nice was evidence enough. They saw for themselves it was not an ambulance job and left to check in to their control and inform them it was not their call. Jazz shouted to the officer on the door to ask if he had called for the mortuary van and where was it.

He wanted to cover her, to give her dignity but something stopped him. The police officer shouted that the mortuary van would take some time, they reckoned about an hour. The officer came into the hall and poked his head round the door into the front room. The smell was getting to him. He wasn't used to dead bodies.

"Skip, the milkman who rang us is sitting in his float outside. I told him to wait. Do you want to see him?"

Jazz nodded, he thought that would be a good idea and made his way out the front. He told the officer to stay put at the front door and not to let anyone in unless he said so. Again, he said to keep the door on the latch but nearly closed. He didn't want the place full of flies.

The milkman had sat patiently for the past hour waiting to be told what to do. Jazz got into the front of the float and sat beside him. He introduced himself as Ernie, adding very quickly that he knew what Jazz was going to say, "Ernie, the fast milkman in the West." Jazz didn't know what he was talking about. Embarrassed, Ernie, babbled on saying it was a Benny Hill song. Again, Jazz looked nonplussed. Ernie lit a cigarette and dragged deeply.

"She was a lovely old dear you know," he said quietly. "I looked through the letter box and called her name and then that smell hit me. I know what that smell means." He looked at Jazz and then away. "I have found a few dead bodies in my time on this round but she was lovely and always had a cup of tea for me on a Friday when I collect the money." That answered Jazz's question of why he had knocked at the door: it was Friday.

"Did you know she had been dead for a few days?" Jazz asked.

"She couldn't have been because I left milk for her and it was gone the next day. She took it in as usual," answered Ernie.

Jazz looked at him and checked to see if he was sure he had left milk every day. Ernie nodded a yes. Now into his stride, he hesitantly added, "You know, something wasn't right yesterday or the day before. I couldn't put my finger on it until now." He looked at Jazz for encouragement.

Jazz looked directly at him and said, "Go on, what wasn't right?"

Infuriatingly, Ernie sat smoking and looking ahead, deep in thought. Jazz wanted to shake him but held back. They both had this feeling that something wasn't right, they both knew Alice and he needed to know what Ernie was thinking.

After smoking the cigarette down to the filter tip. Ernie threw it out into the street. He turned to Jazz and said, "I have figured out what it was. She always took her milk in early. I deliver about 7.30 a.m. each morning and she used to take it in about 8 a.m., or that is what she told me. She told me often that she liked a cup of tea when she sat to watch Jeremy Kyle on the TV in the morning and fresh milk always made it taste better. She was a sweet old dear." He smiled at the thought. Jazz was getting impatient. He wanted to know what he had figured out. "She always made me a cuppa on a Friday you know. Always a nice biscuit with it too," he added conversationally. He looked at Jazz and saw that look in his eyes and thought he had better get to the point. "Well, when I finished my round, which was about 10.a.m, I had to come down this road to get back to the dairy and when I went past Alice's house, the milk was still on the door step. It wasn't there the next morning so I never thought anything about it. Still," he hesitated for a moment, "you know, it was strange. Never happened before."

Ernie tried to brighten up and smiled wistfully. "She had a good innings," was the best he could come up with.

"So, what time did you knock on the door today?" Jazz wanted to get this sorted and bring it back to a more businesslike style. It was getting all too personal for him.

"It was exactly 9.30 a.m., Sir."

Jazz thanked him and asked him to call into Ilford Police Station just to make a statement after work, which Ernie said he was happy to do.

He went back into the house and thought he would take a look in the kitchen to see if the milk was there. It could have been stolen off the door step, he supposed. On the worktop he saw three bottles of milk. Two of them looked like they had gone off. The cream at the top had that separated look that milk gets when it turns sour. The third bottle looked OK. There was also a pile of letters and leaflets that had been slung in a corner. It was not right. Who would have put the milk and post in the kitchen with a dead woman in the front room and not call the police.

It was then that he realised what he felt uneasy about. He went back into the front room and looked at Alice. There were two things here that were not right: firstly, the back of her head was caved in but there was hardly any blood around, that wasn't right; and secondly, Alice was a woman from the generation that always wore vests, hairnets in bed and had something on their feet at all times – slippers in the house and shoes when going out. Alice always wore slippers in the house. Jazz could see she had nothing on her feet. She had been killed elsewhere and put in the front room to look make it like an accident. Again, he asked himself if he was making a mountain out of a molehill.

He started a search for her slippers. She always wore the sturdy ones that often had a pom pom-like bobble on the top, the ones that always seemed to be in a boring tartan brown. He never understood why such unattractive slippers were sought after in the shops by old ladies. He started to be careful about what he touched. Again, not sure why, but just in case. He pulled rubber gloves out of his pocket. A standard procedure, he told himself. He always carried a couple of pairs of the thin plastic gloves with him. He found what he was looking for under the stairs. A pair of the pom pommed tartan slippers were found neatly together just inside the understairs cupboard. Another thing he noticed, Alice did not have her pinny on. It was her badge of honour. Alice always wore a pinny indoors and in the garden. She had a large array of aprons. She always referred to them as pinnys. Again, he felt a well of emotion threatening to rise up from his chest and into his throat, so he told himself to buck up and be professional. Alice must have been going out. If she was going out, where was her pinny? He looked behind the kitchen door and there it was, in the place it would always be when she took it off to go out. It was hanging on the hook on the kitchen side of the door.

Again, he looked at Alice to see what she was wearing. She was wearing a thick smart cardigan, possibly something she would put on if she was stepping outside. She would have put on a coat if she was going to the shops. Alice looked after everything she had, he remembered, so he supposed she hadn't bought any new coats, it would have been the beige macintosh as usual. The cardigan made him presume she hadn't been going far. Where would she be going, he asked himself. To visit a neighbour perhaps. He asked the police officer if any neighbour had called to see what had happened. The answer was no. Someone was discreetly looking from behind curtains, but no one as yet had said anything to him.

So where are her shoes, he wondered. Perhaps by the front door in readiness for going out, he told himself, but on searching, he found nothing. He looked in the kitchen but there was nothing there. He did see that the back door was unlocked and he thought that strange. Alice's bag was in the back room and he checked it for keys but could find none. Where were her keys? They were not in the kitchen or upstairs, he checked. It was all very strange and worrying. He stood looking at Alice again and softly asked, "Alice what has happened to you? Did you fall or did something else happen here?"

Of course there was no answer but Jazz, in that moment, decided there was more to this than a fall. He took his hip flask from his pocket and unscrewed the top. He took a good swig and waited as the clear liquid slid down his throat creating a stinging warmth that made him close his eyes as he savoured the feeling. He felt better for it and took another illicit swig before putting the screw top back on and hiding it quickly inside his jacket pocket. He could think clearer now. He popped a peppermint into his mouth and walked purposefully to the front door.

The police officer turned to see Jazz on the phone calling for a SOCO team to be sent immediately to this address. When he had finished, Jazz briskly addressed the Officer and, now in full control, barked, "Don't touch a fucking thing in the house, SOCO are coming. Don't let anyone in and the mortuary van will have to wait. No one touches the old lady until SOCO have finished. Do you understand?"

The officer nodded and wondered what on earth was going on. It was boring standing outside the house and this looked as if it would get interesting. "I will have to call into the station sir to inform my sergeant." Jazz nodded, not interested in those minor details. "Just make sure no one except SOCO come into the house, comprende?" The officer nodded. For a moment Jazz felt for the officer, who was going to have to stand outside for a lot longer than first thought. "See if someone from the station is passing and can bring us a cup of tea. Bet you could do with one?" And as an after thought he added, "See if they can get a cake or something to eat, its going to be a long day" The officer was grateful for the thought and said he would ring through to Ilford and see who was about.

Jazz went through the house to the back door. He wanted to know why it was unlocked and where the keys were. He also wanted to now where Alice's shoes were, and then there was the milk. It was all stacking up into something and made Jazz think there was a lot more to this than a fatal fall. His phone rang and when he looked at his mobile, DCI Radley's name flashed on the screen. At that moment he couldn't fully explain his reasoning and he knew he would be asked to account for his actions. He decided to ignore the call.

He didn't know what he was looking for when he went into the garden. Any clue would do. To be honest, he was glad to be outside. The house felt cold and disturbingly empty and the smell of death was choking him. He stood outside and bathed in the warm sun and breathed in some decent air. By the back door were some gardening implements and a bucket. Alice was an extremely tidy person and he wondered why they were not in the shed at the back of the garden. Perhaps she was going to do some gardening and she went indoors and fell. That would account for the back door being unlocked. But it still didn't account for the milk getting into the kitchen or the fact that Alice had nothing on her feet or the keys being missing and the lack of blood around her head. He needed to think clearly.

He needed to find her shoes, they had to be close by because she had taken her slippers off and placed them neatly under the stairs. Anyone else would say that perhaps she wasn't wearing her slippers that day. Not everyone wears slippers in a house, he wasn't stupid, but he knew Alice. She always wore her slippers in the house. Thinking back, he seemed to remember something about keeping feet warm and stopping getting rheumatism or something like that. He knew she did it for a reason. He took his flask out of his pocket and quickly took a small swig, just to help him think clearly.

The garden was lovely and just as he remembered it. How she kept it so nice at her age, he didn't know. The grass was cut and the flower borders around the lawn were full of flowering bushes and roses. He saw she still had the strawberry patch on the left. He remembered sitting in her garden as a child eating strawberry sandwiches on what were always warm sunny days. He told himself to stop doing that; he was thinking about the past again. There was no room for emotion at the moment, he needed pure logic. He walked down the path that went through the middle of the garden to the table and two chairs that sat three quarters of the way down. The garden shed was tucked neatly on the right-hand side next to the fence. The table and chairs were so old. He fingered the table top and smiled; did nothing ever wear out in her house? He walked past the bird table, which was now empty. With more sentiment than he should have felt, he wanted to go back into the kitchen and look for some bread for the bird table. He needed to stay professional, the bread would wait. He opened the shed door and looked in. There was nothing extraordinary in there that he could see. Again, it was neatly arranged with all the garden bits and pieces in their proper places. They don't make women like Alice anymore, he thought. He could have eaten off the floor in her shed, it was so clean.

He went back to the kitchen door and looked to see if there was any sign of a forced entry but there was nothing he could see. Perplexed, his eyes examined the ground around the back of the house and he moved towards a shrub by the fence. He thought he spotted something. There, nestling between the fence and the shrub, was a woman's shoe. He didn't remember what shoes Alice wore but this one was an old lady's shoe with those sturdy little heels and heavy rounded fronts that younger women wouldn't be seen dead wearing. He searched the undergrowth of shrubs, looking for the other shoe, but it wasn't to be seen.

For some reason that didn't make any sense to him at the time he looked over the fence to next door and scanned the garden. It was a mess of weeds, long grass and bits of wood and rubbish. A much neglected garden indeed. At least the 5 foot fence hid the mess from Alice, he thought. He looked close to the fence and there in the next garden was what looked like the other shoe. He hadn't moved either shoe and made a mental note to get the SOCO to check it out when they arrived.

He looked at his watch. He had been out in the garden for over 30 minutes and he wanted to know where everyone was. He went to the officer on the front door and asked if anyone had arrived yet. He was told no, but a passing police car had stopped with their teas and a couple of buns. A cigarette and a cup of tea sounded good and they both sat outside in the sun, enjoying a few minutes' rest. The curtains across the road were twitching regularly and Jazz put his hand up in a wave to acknowledge he had seen them. He laughed inwardly as the curtains stopped moving and he envisaged someone mortified at being found out. He balanced the tea on the garden wall and the cigarette in his mouth while he called Sharon and Tony. Tony answered and said that both he and Sharon were available for anything he wanted, so Jazz called them to Wards Road. He needed them to knock on doors and talk to the neighbours. He asked the officer, whose name turned out to be Mike, if he fancied a McDonald's for lunch. He told Tony to make sure they brought big macs and chips for two and coffees when they arrived. Mike liked this DS, he didn't know him but he did know that most were not as amenable as this one.

"So where are the fucking SOCO then," asked Jazz, almost talking to himself, but Mike answered that he didn't know.

Jazz, on the phone again, told whoever was on the other end at Ilford Police Station to move their arses and get a SOCO here now. "If this turns out to be a murder and the clues are spoilt, it will be on your fucking head!" He wasn't sure it was a murder at this stage, but Ilford Station didn't need to know that.

Jazz wanted to know who was next door. He walked out the front and round to the house next door. After knocking for some time, he opened the letterbox and called, "Police, open up." There was no response. There was a smell that was very familiar and he noticed there had been something covering the back of the front door but it had come away. He couldn't see in through the letterbox as whatever had been put there was still obstructing the view but when pushed, it moved. This allowed the smell to come out through the letterbox. He knew exactly what that smell was.

He went down the sideway and out the back to see if he could see anything through the kitchen window. The front windows offered nothing. Net curtains maintained a look of normality on the outside but closer inspection showed that it wasn't the curtains that kept anyone from seeing inside. He was on his mobile again to Ilford, who were getting fed up with his abusive rantings of where was this and where was that. This time he asked for an electrician to be sent to Wards Road immediately. He explained briefly why and he was promised one in 10 minutes.

He knew he should have waited, he needed a search warrant to gain access, but he also knew that time was important. He shouldered the back door and it gave way more easily than he expected. He would be in trouble for this; his DCI would take great delight in quoting police procedure at him later, but he told himself he was doing his job and time was of the essence.

With extreme caution he looked inside; he was reluctant to venture in without closely looking at what could hurt or maim him. There was nothing metal ahead of him that could electrocute him. He looked at the floor to see if there was a booby trap. No carpet hid a spike-filled hole he could fall into. Cautiously he put one foot inside and then the other, constantly checking where he walked and what he touched. He looked above him to ensure there were no spikes ready to drop down on him and spear him. All looked reasonably safe.

The place had been emptied in a hurry. It was a mess of broken plastic bits and wires and, yes, he could see cannabis leaves, not much but enough to see what the house had been used for. He looked in the cupboard under the stairs. The mains electric had been butchered. Jazz could tell they had gone straight for the mains so the electric companies would not know the vast amount of electric that had been used in this house and of course it wasn't paid for either.

The smell was strong now and he looked inside the front room and saw a few plants in pots. He thought it was skunk; that always smelt stronger and it was worth more money. He asked himself why any plants had been left, it was very odd. He could only assume they were in a hurry, perhaps they were disturbed and just got out. The rest of the room was empty.

His footsteps echoed as he walked carefully from room to room. A cannabis factory in a house always depressed Jazz. It looked sordid and nasty. There was wallpaper on the walls and bits of furniture stacked up in the hallway. Everywhere was filthy. A bit of curtain hung precariously from a rail in the front room. It looked like a house that had been raped and defiled with such cruelty that it seemed impossible for it to recover. The ceilings had many wires hanging down for the lights.

Jazz knew they had cleared as much of the factory as they could. The lights to keep the cannabis warm and growing had gone, but the big air vent that went up into the roof through the ceilings of both the front room and the bedroom upstairs was still there. The house had that forlorn echo as he walked around. The bath upstairs was filled with water and nutriments that had to be fed to the plants. He supposed someone lived here to guard and feed the plants. The settee in the hall looked like the bed with a thin dirty duvet crumpled up in a corner. That made him feel better. No booby traps if someone had lived here.

The few plants that were still in the room looked ready for a crop, the heads were big enough to pick. The smell sickened him. It was a herbal smell with an underlying stench of something like mould which offended his senses. He never understood why anyone wanted to smoke the stuff. If the house was full of plants, as the wiring and dirt on the ground implied, then it would have been worth up to £100,000 per crop and in these conditions the plants would have cropped three times in a year before being replaced. Something made them clear out quickly. It was quite dark and difficult to see. All the windows had blackout cloth nailed to the window frames. The silver-coloured side of the cloth faced inwards to reflect the heat back onto the plants. He opened the front door for some light. He knew he was taking a risk, the lock could have been rigged to electrocute him, it was quite a common thing. Cannabis factories had to be protected from thieves trying to steal the plants and there were all sorts of gruesome and nasty tricks to kill, maim and resist intruders. Jazz reckoned he was OK because it looked like they had someone living here. Most probably a Vietnamese illegal immigrant brought in to do the work. That seemed the usual way of working. They earned good money too. It was reckoned they could earn something up to £1,000 per month for guarding and looking after the plants. Not bad money but to live with the smell and intoxication was either a bonus or a curse, depending on if you used the stuff.

Now the door was open, the light streamed into the hall. Jazz wanted to see if there was anything around that might give a clue to who these people were. It was highly unlikely, these factories were well organised, but someone sometimes slipped up. His attention was taken by a glistening by the stairs outside the front room door. He went over and looked closely. He thought it was blood but it was dry; he thought it might be bits of bone and gristle. It had splayed up the side of the stairs and was sprinkled over quite an area of the stairs in little droplets. As if someone has been smashed across the head, he thought. Could there be a connection, he wondered. He needed to get out of the house. SOCO needed to get in after the electrician and sort this out.

God he needed some fresh air, a cigarette and a drink. He took a good swig of his flask. He needed it today to relax and calm down. What started off as a fatal accident was becoming more of a riddle and getting bigger by the minute. He wanted a meaty job but this felt very close to home. He needed some fresh insight and the SOCO team should provide that.

SOCO would work out whose blood, brains and bone was splattered in the hall. He needed the bloody

SOCO team here now and God help anyone who didn't move themselves in this case. He was getting angry now. It was 1 p.m. and this was not moving fast enough for him. He got on the phone to blast someone at the station and told them to put a rocket under the arse of the sodding SOCO team; and where was the bloody doctor! The response from Ilford Station was just as ripe in reply and he was told in no uncertain terms to open his eyes and look. The SOCO team was there.

He left and went back to Alice's house and found that the two SOCOs had arrived and were talking to Mike at the door. They looked up as Jazz, still walking towards them, was shouting instructions.

"First of all, deal with Alice and take prints off the milk bottles and all around."

When the electrician had made safe next door, the work would begin in there. Glad that someone had arrived, Jazz cheered up and patted a surprised Mike on the back for doing a sterling job. About the same time, Tony and Sharon arrived with the much needed McDonald's.

Jazz, Sharon and Tony sat in the front garden on the garden wall and Mike sat on the front step eating the warm McDonald's and soggy chips.

"How long have you had these in your car," asked Jazz, a connoisseur of McDonald's. "They have to be hot to taste of anything otherwise it's cardboard."

No one answered and for five minutes all was silent as the four of them ploughed through the meal.

With still a mouthful to finish, Jazz began filling Sharon and Tony in about Alice and next door and asking if they thought it could be linked in any way. He wanted them to make house to house calls to find out if anyone saw anything at all, starting with the curtain-twitcher across the road. The doctor arrived just as Tony and Sharon took themselves off to start the house to house questioning.

Jazz showed the doctor into the house, but the SOCO team shouted for them to wait for five minutes so they could finish what they were doing in the front room. Jazz took the doctor outside and offered him a cigarette. They knew each other well and they took to discussing what Jazz had been up to over the years and the latest update on the test match in India. Just as they started to argue over the bowler in the second test match, they got a call from the SOCO team. Jenny and John were their names.

Jenny had been around for many years and was near retirement but John was new and had never met Jazz before. Jenny was a short stocky woman with a large mole on her chin. The pony tail was scraped up on her head as a tired nuisance to be kept out of her way. She hadn't changed at all, still a mess and still lacking any charm, but she knew her job. He liked her. She had known Jazz many years. She heard he had returned and had looked forward to seeing him again. He would never know that of course. She gave him a grunt instead of hello and proceeded to tell him they had dusted for fingerprints on the milk bottles. Jenny told him that most were smudged but she had got one good one and she hoped it wasn't his! She berated his way of working and said she had more fingerprints for Jazz at murder and crime scenes than anyone else. Jazz laughed, this was typical Jenny, not here for five minutes before the moaning started.

"I wore gloves, Jenny. See, still on." He waved his hands in front of her.

She collected up her stuff, still moaning under her breath that she bet the gloves went on as a second thought after he touched everything. She was actually right, he needed to be more careful but he wasn't going to tell her that.

The doctor went in to take a look at Alice. He thought she had been dead for at least three days, if not longer. Jazz could have told him that but the doctor was always cautious about diagnosis until the post mortem. The flies had started gathering in the front room and Jazz found it all too much. The front door had been left open for much of today and it was getting nasty in there. It wouldn't be long before Alice got maggots and he didn't want her to have that indignity. The doctor pronounced the body could now be moved and the mortuary van was sent for.

"I am going to cover her with a blanket now, she has lain here too long without a cover." The doctor looked at Jazz inquisitively. He never talked like this. "Do you know this woman?" he asked.

Jazz lied. He couldn't admit to knowing her because he would have been taken off the case. "She's an old dear and deserves some respect," was all he said.

The flies were shooed away. He would get a blanket soon, but he had heard the electrician had arrived and he needed to see him.

Everyone was outside. The smell was not pleasant. The electrician had gone into the house next door to make sure it was safe for the SOCOs to do their job. Everyone waited outside. It took about 20 minutes. They wiled away the time chatting and Jazz, on good form, was joking and telling whoever was listening about cases he had in Manchester, the scraps he had got into there and how he got out of them.

The electrician left after telling Jazz that the house was now safe.

"Bloody hell! Wasn't it safe before?"

The electrician, feeling quite chatty, told Jazz, "If you had touched anything under those stairs you would have become crispy fried duck before you could have said *whats this wire for?* All the wiring was live." With more faith in Jazz's professionalism than he deserved, he added, "Don't suppose you would have been stupid enough to go in until I arrived anyway." He was thanked for his help and sent on his way.

"So, where to next?" was Jenny's question as she picked up her bag.

Jazz took her next door and asked her to start in the hall. He showed her the splashes of blood and bone and gristle. She looked in all the rooms upstairs. Jazz said he wanted everywhere fingerprinted.

"I suppose I am going to find your fingerprints over everything as well," she lamented.

"Darling, I have been a good boy and you will find nothing of me in here."

Her colleague, John, followed on behind as the playful banter continued around the house. Jazz pointed out various areas he wanted looked at. She gave him one of her *I do know what needs to be done around here* looks. He asked her to check outside in the back garden. He needed pictures taken of where the shoes were as well. He ignored her moaning that she was just one woman and could only do so much in a day. She instructed John to go and measure the cannabis plants; they would need cataloguing before they were taken away. She was going to get samples of the splattered blood and remains before anyone contaminated the scene. That comment was directed straight at Jazz.

He left them both to get on with their job. He wanted to go back to Alice and make sure she was covered. He went upstairs and took the quilt off her bed. He looked at her bed and wondered if people nowadays still used sheets and blankets on beds with a quilt on top. He hadn't seen a bed made like this for years. She had crisp white cotton sheets and two blankets, one green and the other a gruesome orange, both in that thick wool material. The quilt was a silky material and had small flowers all over it with a cream background. It was quite flat; obviously the plumpness had been lost after so many years of use.

He gently covered her with the quilt Her feet protruded out of the end but her face and body were covered. Everyone was busy for the moment and Jazz kneeled alongside the body and took the last swig out of the flask.

"Here's to you, Alice. If this turns out to be anything to do with next door, I promise you I will get the bastards."

Again, the emotion welled up and he wiped the tear ready to spill down his cheek. It started an onslaught of tears he couldn't stop. Alice, his mum and his dad all came to mind and the grief he had not allowed himself to feel over the years just crept up on him and overtook him. It didn't last long. God this was not the place to break down. He made sure he calmed down and sorted himself out quickly. What he didn't know was that Tony had been watching for a few seconds through the gap in the door. He beat a hasty retreat and allowed Jazz a few moments of privacy.

The mortuary van arrived and took Alice away. Jazz, with a deep breath, looked at his watch. It was nearly fucking 4 p.m. and there was still so much to do. He went looking for Sharon and Tony to find out what was happening. Tony was outside talking to Mike. Apparently the curtain-twitcher was not well and had the day off work. It seemed that most of the people in the street were working. The twitcher didn't even know Alice because she was away most weekends and she worked in the week. Tony asked if they could have overtime and work the evening when people came home. This was agreed. Sharon was in deep conversation with some woman down the road who saw nothing and knew nothing but she was telling Sharon about the noise at night from cars that had their radios on very loud. Sharon was finding it hard to get away. Jazz smirked. Perhaps she was not as tough as he thought.

Jenny was still moaning when he visited next door but she had got samples of the blood and bone. He asked if it could be sent for analysis immediately. He needed to know if it could have been Alice who was in the house. It seemed too much of a coincidence, but he knew that coincidences did happen so didn't want to jump to conclusions yet. John was outside photographing the shoes and measuring where they were in relation to the fence, as instructed by Jenny. She got up from dusting for fingerprints and went out to the front garden where Jazz stood. She needed a cigarette. He offered her one and again asked about sending off the samples and gave her his best smile. Ruefully, she said she would make a phone call. It was agreed that the samples would be collected within half an hour and he would know in the morning. He thanked her and kissed her hand. She screamed at him that he was a bloody idiot and she would have to change her plastic gloves now. He pretended to spit out and choke and cough at the thought of what he had kissed. She thought, as he walked away, what a bloody pain in the neck he was, but she liked him and he was good to look at too. With a resigned sigh, she went back to work. The light would be good for another hour or so and there was still lots to do. She walked back into the house shouting for John to move himself and give her a hand.

Jazz got a lift back to the station with Sharon and Tony. They wanted to get something to eat and some notebooks and pens for the evening work. Tony was giving him a curious look and Jazz wondered what that was all about. As soon as Jazz put a foot on the stairs up to the CID floor, he was stopped by a Sergeant who said that DCI Radley was looking for him. The Sergeant added that he looked none too pleased. Weary from the day, Jazz really didn't want a fight tonight. He walked heavily up the stairs; each foot felt like it weighed 20lbs. He knocked on the door and entered after a crisp "Come in" was heard through the door. He was berated for not answering his call and quoted every rule and regulation that must exist in the Met Police for contacting DCIs and communication etc. After expelling lots of hot air, DCI Radley calmed down a fraction and told Jazz to fill him in on all the details.

Jazz told him everything from pick up of call to finding the cannabis factory. DCI Radley was actually very pleased with how the day had gone. That was until Jazz said he had entered the house next door to Alice's without a warrant. The rules and regulations were again quoted and the fact that no warrant had been issued by him. Jazz convinced the DCI that he had needed to get in urgently in case there was someone in there or they would have had time to escape. He added that he thought he heard a voice inside and needed to investigate immediately. As it happened, it was an abandoned cannabis factory but he didn't know that until he looked. He hoped his DCI bought this lie. He reassured him that everything else had been complied with, the electrician the SOCO team etc. His punishment was that a full report needed to be on the DCI's desk at 8 a.m. the next morning.

Jazz realised his evening was now ruined. A few drinks in the pub, fish and chips and a spot of cricket on the TV was how he hoped his evening would go. He needed to just pop to Sainsbury's down the road to get some more vodka. The flask didn't hold much, he told himself. Then, if he pushed himself, he could finish the report in two hours and still get home with fish and chips for a bit of cricket. The pub would have to wait but there would be a drink at home. He bought three bottles of vodka in Sainsbury's. It would last him a good while.

The report was finished by 8.30 p.m. He was pleased with it. He would walk, it would only take him 20 minutes maximum and he could get fish and chips nearer home. The evening air was a little sharp but June was a funny month. It could be glorious one minute and freezing the next. He seemed to have been standing around for a lot of the day and he liked walking off the stiffness in his legs. The air was as fresh as it could be in busy Ilford. He took a deep breath and felt invigorated and calm for the first time that day; he felt good walking home.

The fish shop was not busy. It had been very busy until 7 p.m., the owner told him. This was his quiet time. He cooked a fresh piece of cod for Jazz. They chatted for a while and Jazz found out that this man had come over from Uganda not many years after Jazz arrived. They swapped information about families to see if they knew of each other but nothing was known. Jazz told him he was staying with Mr and Mrs Chodda. Now they had something in common. This man was the brother of Mrs Chodda's aunt's husband in Hackney. Always a small world in the Sikh World, Jazz thought. He got an extra amount of chips on the back of this information and a wally too.

He arrived at the door in De Vere Gardens and fumbled for his keys. With fish and chips in one hand

and a Sainsbury's bag clinking in the other, he had to swap bags to get his keys out. Mrs Chodda, on hearing the clinking and tutting, opened the door for him. He hoped to hell there was no more visits to deal with and currys. Mrs Chodda was learning and didn't stop Jazz from going up to his room with his fish and chips. She smiled politely and wished him a pleasant evening. He gave her a big smile and thanked her. He didn't know if the good wishes were from relief of no more family or pleasure at seeing her. Mrs Chodda was a lovely landlady and he sensed the warmth in her. He was actually very comfortable here and his room was big. When his other bits and piece arrived, he would be settled for a bit.

He should have known Mrs Chodda would have more plans in store for him and her single female relatives. Mrs Chodda had a long term plan for Jazz. First of all, she would make him welcome in her kitchen. Her motherly instincts told her he needed looking after. She was also aware that he would make a very fine husband for one of her relatives. For now she would just see how things developed but an invitation to join her in her kitchen would be hard to refuse and she knew it. Sikh manners and social interaction would ensure Jazz could not refuse.

He opened the door to his room and busied himself getting a plate and glass. He wanted to eat his fish and chips reasonably hot and he needed a drink badly. It had been a shit day and he needed to blot out Alice for a little while; he would have all night to think about her. He looked at his watch and saw he was in time for a bit of cricket on the television. He sat back with his fish and chips, his glass nicely topped up and cricket on the television; he felt relaxed and at home.

He woke the next morning tired with a mouth that was dry and tasted like he had licked someone's sweaty armpit. The headache was intense and deep and he felt sick. He hadn't slept much and when he did, it turned into nightmares of violence and fear, nothing specific but enough to wake him in a cold sweat. He looked over and saw that the bottle of vodka was three quarters empty. That was impossible, he told himself. He must have spilt a lot of it. The hot shower made him feel revived and calm. He drank a fanta from the fridge and the sugar rush gave him a good edge. He popped a couple of paracetamol and knew in an hour he would feel fine and dandy. He filled his flask with the remainder of the vodka for emergencies during the day and took himself off to Ilford Police Station. It was 9.30 a.m. and he was the last to arrive.

Sharon and Tony were waiting for him. As he walked in, he heard the cat calls and snide comments. So he was late; they could all go and fuck themselves for all he cared. It looked like Sharon and Tony had borne the brunt of their comments for some time. Sharon was fed up and Tony was red with embarrassment or anger, he couldn't tell.

Jazz walked round the CID floor with an air of unbridled ease. There were six CID officers busy on the phone or looking at paperwork. He spotted Peter Young, the DS whose team were making the most noise. He slapped Peter on the back in a friendly gesture and asked what they were up to these days. Peter looked at the cocky man in front of him and sneered that they were dealing with many crimes and his team knew what they were doing and their clear up rate was exceptionally high. As he dismissed Jazz with the comment that time was money and was about to walk off, Jazz pulled him by the arm and squared up to him with his face inches from the DS. Through clenched teeth, he said, "My team are dealing with a huge case which we are going to solve in days. My team are half the size of yours with a quarter of the experience of yours but you know what? They have more balls and more sense in their little fingers than your lot of fat-arsed, not worthy of a blow job bastards. Now let's have a bit of respect for the team, DS Young."

With a smile and another pat on the back, Jazz walked over to his team. Everyone had watched in frozen silence and now that the two men had walked away from each other, everyone resumed what they were doing and the noise of people working started again.

Shocked at how he had flared up, it took Jazz a few moments to collect himself as he walked back to Sharon and Tony. He was quite scared at the level of hate and fury he felt and how it had risen and exploded into the room so quickly. He had just meant to give Peter a verbal slap but the demon inside him rose up and beat the crap out of the DS. He thought his demon had been squashed and overpowered and caged in the deepest part of him. He had had enough counselling to deal with it. The fear of not being in control and the fear of another breakdown took his breath away for a moment. He didn't want anyone to see that darker side of him and it was a great shame and embarrassment to him that now everyone had seen him lose control. He was the friendly, disarming Jazz, that was how he wanted to be known. He kept his demons to himself and he would deal with them later. He had work to do and he needed a clear head.

Sharon and Tony wanted to say something but Jazz was having none of it.

"Come on, newbies, lets go find out what forensic have come up with on the blood and bones."

With a smile and a furtive look at the others in the CID room, they both got up and followed Jazz.

As promised, Jenny, the SOCO, had crosschecked the DNA of the blood and bone found in the cannabis factory with the DNA of Alice. It was, without a doubt, Alice's blood and bone. Jazz, to be fair, had thought this was a strong possibility, but he had been in denial, he had hoped it wasn't Alice. He would have preferred that she died in her own house from natural causes.

On hearing the result, the blood drained from his face. So it was true; sweet, kindly, naive Alice had been murdered. If he had time, he would have just sat and cried. He felt inconsolable. What had she gone through in the last moments of her life? The fear, the pain, he just couldn't bear to think of it. It felt like he had lost his grandmother in the most vile way.

Irrationally, for a few moments, Jazz was full of guilt and asked himself if he had let Alice down. He should have contacted her as he had promised. Could he have saved her? He was in the process of beating himself up about this. He went to the gents to splash his face with cold water. He could feel the sweat dripping off his face. He took a swig of his flask and felt better. It was early but he needed it. He kept saying as a mantra "Get a grip, get a grip." He stopped when an officer came into the toilet and looked questioningly at him. Enough, he told himself. He could ring his counsellor if this feeling didn't stop. He hadn't felt the need to call him for many months and he sure as hell didn't want to start now. He could do this, he told himself. He went out to join his team.

They all went to the canteen for a cup of tea and breakfast. Now the work would begin. Jazz, quieter than they were used to, sat with a faraway look. He was thinking of his next step. He was going to get the bastard who did this and avenge Alice. This was his case and he didn't care who he trampled on to find out who murdered her. A tap on the shoulder brought his thoughts back to the here and now and he looked up at an officer who said DCI Radley wanted to see him in his office now. He knew he was going to be taken off the case if it turned out to be a murder. A more experienced team would be given it. Jazz was having none of that. By hook or by crook, he was going to keep this case and get the bastard who did this to Alice.

IT'S MY PARTY

DCI Radley was, as usual, sitting at his desk. Jazz for a moment wondered if he ever left his desk. Where did he pee during the day and did he eat? He told himself this was not the time for such thoughts. He needed this man to be on his side.

He was about to say that Jazz and his team were off the case. He had been told it was murder. Jenny had left a message for DCI Radley as well. Before he was told this, Jazz jumped in with his four point plan; he knew strategic planning was something the DCI loved. Of course this concept appealed to the DCI, and he listened a tad reluctantly to the animated DS in front of him. Point one: Jazz stated that he had been the first on the scene and had identified immediately that there was more to the case than an unfortunate accident. He had identified the cannabis factory next door. The DCI interjected here and forcefully noted that Jazz had flagrantly abuse Metropolitan Police protocol and entered a house without the necessary warrant. He reminded Jazz that the public would be distressed and the press would be angry to know this had happened.

Jazz anticipated this and answered soothingly that of course he would never abuse such a protocol and he only did this because he thought he heard someone inside the house. He added that if said person had been caught, it would have been a feather in DCI Radley's cap. As it was, it had now been proved that the cannabis factory and the death of Alice were linked. His team had spent the evening interviewing neighbours to find out what they knew. He explained that he was about to debrief his team regarding this.

Point two: He had extensive experience in murder investigations. He quoted four murders he had solved in Manchester. He quoted the commendations he had received. Somewhere in a box was a certificate to prove this. He had a lot of experience of murder (this was actually true).

Point three: He had tremendous experience in dealing with cannabis factories. In Manchester this was what he had done for quite a few of the five years he was there. He added that he had good contacts in Ilford, who he could use to find out who were the main players. In answer to a comment, he agreed that yes, he had been away for five years, but his contacts were still there and they still owed him. He could tie the two together. This would be such a major coup for the DCI. The press love a success story and Jazz promised to deliver a success story in a week. Jazz thought he was pushing his luck but he could tag on extra time after a week if necessary.

"And what is point four?" asked DCI Radley.

Jazz was struggling now. He had picked the number four out of the air and not thought about it.

"Point four: To prove to you that I am a good DS and I will work every hour it takes to solve this murder and to find out who was running the cannabis factory. No one else will work as hard as me. I used to live in Newbury Park and I have contacts; it is a personal thing. I want to solve this and as my DCI, I will keep you informed at every step along the way." Christ, he thought. He would give this man his soul if he kept the case but he didn't want to go that far yet.

"There is a point five, Guv." DCI Radley looked interested. "This is a big case and will do your career the world of good if it is solved expeditiously and it will be my honour to ensure you do well from this." Jazz felt sick at such smarminess but it had to be done.

The DCI rolled these thoughts around and coyly said, "I would only do it for the good of the station." Jazz readily agreed. "I am your man, Guv. Let me and my team carry on working this case. We are already discussing the next stage and I expect to have a name within a day." This sounded very good to the DCI. He hesitated for a moment and Jazz, again, wouldn't let it go. "I can do this, Guv, and because of the seriousness, I will keep you informed for your many interviews with the press and give you good updates. If the murder squad get this, Ilford Police Station, your station, Sir, will be out of the loop."

This seemed to be the clincher and Jazz left the DCI's office walking on air but knowing he needed to come down to earth very soon. Stroking naked ambition and telling exaggerated porkies were the order of the day. He smiled, he still had it, the charm and the quick turnabout; he could think on his feet. He was the man! Nothing had changed, he was the person he used to be before the incident in Ilford. It had all come back to him as easily as spitting in the wind.

But he had promised more than he could deliver at the moment so enough of the patting on the back. He was about to mess with the alliances in Ilford. Ilford was run by gangs that had an uneasy alliance with each other. They all understood where they were in the scheme of things. Years ago, parameters had been set after some pushing and shoving, with the inevitable deaths on each side. Everyone worked hard to keep the peace, it was more profitable that way. Jazz was about to poke a stick into the hornets' nest. If DCI Radley knew that he had agreed to the murder of two Vietnamese men, some tit-for-tat arson and a gang war that would finish off at least six more men, he may have reconsidered his decision to let Jazz and his team handle the case.

Jazz went back to the canteen buzzing with adrenalin and stress. With a mug of strong tea from the lovely Milly, he got down to business with his team. He was under immense pressure to solve this, but he told himself he worked better that way.

First things first, he asked how they had got on with the house to house last night. They had reams of paperwork but nothing much to say that would be of any help. It seemed that most of the neighbours worked and no one saw anything. One person said they noticed some Chinese people going into the house on occasions. They thought they owned the house, but they didn't seem to live there; they just visited every week or so. No one had taken much notice and couldn't be more specific about times. It was enough for Jazz, he knew where he was going now and who he would contact. He had a contact who was one of the biggest criminals in the East End of London and he owed Jazz big time. Jazz was about to collect the favour with interest. It would be the start of the killings in Ilford.

ASHES TO ASHES

It was Saturday and he had to collect Mr Singh's ashes from the crematorium. He rang to check they were ready and he was told to come at 3 p.m. It had been a rushed job but they had done it as a favour to the temple.

Jazz had told Sharon and Tony to write up their notes regarding their house to house and he would see them Monday morning bright and early for the next stage in the investigation. He had made a call to his contact and arranged a meeting on Monday morning at 8 a.m. at the temple.

Now, he figured he would get some lunch at the local pub across the road and think out what his next moves would be. A few beers and four cigarettes later, he had got it organised in his head. First things first, he needed to do right by Mr Singh. It was going to be quite dodgy now. He had promised DCI Radley the earth to keep this job but he was about to do the dirty on him regarding Mr Singh's ashes.

DCI Radley would miss out on the press coverage and his photo in the national papers. Jazz was going to have to tread very carefully over the next few days but Mr Singh deserved a solemn and respectful scattering of his ashes as was his right as a Sikh .

He squirmed at the thought of the spectacle. There would be the police launch duly borrowed with the ashes, DCI Radley and himself on board. The press would be taking pictures and there would be the usual scrabble and the shouts of 'Over here, Sir' for a good photograph for the paper. The ashes would be scattered in a most unceremonious way. He didn't dare think what sort of speech DCI Radley would have made to the press given the chance. Jazz laughed at the thought. No, it was going to be quiet affair; just him. He still didn't know why he felt so strongly for this stranger but he did.

The ashes were handed to him in quite a solemn fashion. It didn't look very much for a whole man. The small box was put in a Sainsbury's bag so it didn't scare anyone when he went outside. He would take it home ready for tomorrow. He thought he would have a Chinese tonight. It was good to have a varied selection of food, he thought. First a drink. He found that the nearest pub to De Vere Gardens was the Cranbrook Public House, just 10 minutes from home. It wasn't a particularly nice pub. Built about 1960, it was worn out. There was no particular style and it certainly had no class, which he thought sounded about right for him. The landlord was a good guy and Jazz enjoyed the banter. He put the Sainsbury's bag under the table by the window and drank deeply on his pint of Stella.

No smoking in pubs was a bind but he had a bag of crisps and then went out the back of the pub to the yard area where most of the customers were drinking and smoking. They were a good bunch, mainly Irish by the sounds of it. They joked and ribbed Jazz for being so cockney and took bets on whether he was a Paki or an Italian. After much shouting and comments of "Paki, Italian, not much difference between the two", Jazz shouted back that he was neither. He was a Sikh. He was very light of skin and was often mistaken for someone fom the Mediterranean. He left the smoking area to go home, to the sounds of Irish voices shouting, "They Sikh him here and they Sikh him there, they Sikh the fucker everywhere." He laughed; he had had a great time and would go back tomorrow. He had now made the Cranbrook his local pub.

With four pints of Stella inside him, Jazz was feeling very good. It wasn't until he had passed Valentine's Park that he remembered the ashes. He turned and rushed back to the pub to retrieve them from under the table. As he got there, the landlord picked up the bag and was about to open it. He didn't want to explain about the ashes, so he grabbed the bag from the landlord with many thanks for keeping it for him. He turned, a tad unsteadily, and went home.

He phoned for some Chinese from a leaflet he had found at the police station. They always had lots of take away leaflets for night duty officers. The canteen closed at 5 p.m., which was mad considering the station was manned 24/7. He ordered far too much but thought it would last him two days. The order arrived one hour later, just as Jazz was finishing his third tumbler of vodka and tonic. He paid the man and stumbled up the stairs. Mrs Chodda wasn't far away and watched the big bag of food go up the stairs. He didn't hear her tutting from behind the door.

Jazz woke on Sunday morning at 8 a.m. with a massive headache. It was becoming a regular morning event. He squinted at the remains of the Chinese still on his table. Shit, he thought, he had meant to put it all in his fridge last night so he could eat the rest tonight. He got a fanta out of the fridge and popped a couple of paracetamol. The shower revived him. When dressed, he set about clearing up the Chinese and trying to save the good bits for tonight. He ended up with four cartons, each containing rice, noodles, beef in oyster sauce and prawn balls together with a sticky carton of sweet orange sauce. At this moment, he didn't think he could face anymore Chinese. He felt sick.

Still not quite with it and feeling distinctly remote, he wondered what he had done with the ashes. He looked around his room and couldn't see the distinctive Sainsbury's bag the box of ashes were in. He had a glass of water, he was so thirsty. When his head cleared a little, he looked again. The panic didn't start until he had searched his room three times. He looked everywhere but no box of ashes in a Sainsbury's bag. Thinking back, he remembered taking the bag from the landlord at the pub and coming home. He had it, he remembered fairly clearly walking up the stairs with a bag. He couldn't remember if he looked in the bag to check he had the right Sainsbury's bag. The panic now flooded through him. What if he took the wrong Sainsbury's bag from the pub and someone else had the ashes. He searched the room again using the mantra of "fuck, fuck, fuck" to concentrate his mind on the task.

It wasn't in the room. He would have to go back to

the pub and see if it was still there. He was mightily pissed off that this could have happened. He didn't feel good, he didn't want to have to explain. He went to the fridge for another fanta; he figured a sugar rush would help him think. It took a few seconds to register but in the fridge was a Sainsbury's bag with something in it. He pulled it out and there was the box of ashes. He said sorry to Mr Singh. He figured he would have caught pneumonia if he had been alive. One minute he was in a hot oven burning up and the next he was freezing cold and cooling down. This tickled Jazz and he held his head which hurt as he shook from a massive giggling attack. He put the carrier bag with the box of ashes by the door so he didn't forget to take it with him.

By 10 a.m. Jazz was as right and sober as he was ever going to be today. He dressed smartly in a pair of dark trousers with a shirt and tie. Only his leather jacket gave any hint of being dressed casually. He liked the outfit and thought it suitable for scattering the ashes. He wasn't sure if he was safe to drive but he felt fine and he wanted to get to Tilbury by noon, which was when the tide turned and was going out to sea.

He arrived in Tilbury and found his way to the front. It was a nice day with lots of people around. He walked a way past the busy end and found an area that was quiet. This was the first time he had scattered ashes for anyone. He remembered a film he had watched in his dim and distant past which showed someone scattering ashes and the wind blew up and the ashes went all over the person standing there. He was adamant it wasn't going to happen to him. He had a swift look around and all seemed quite empty. He knelt down. He couldn't get too close to the sea, he didn't want to wet his shoes as the water gently lapped back and forth over the stones. He carefully tipped the ashes onto the water.

He was considering saying something meaningful to send them on their way but he noticed the ashes were not moving as they should have. To his horror, they seemed to stay where they were on the water's edge and they covered the surface of the water like a thick blanket. A twinge of panic was rising.

"Bloody hell. What do I do now?" he said to himself.

He didn't want to put his hand in the ashes to stir them up to get them to move. He was too squeamish to do such a god-awful thing, the thought made him shudder. He knew as the water receded the ashes might just sink onto the pebbles and not go out to sea. That wouldn't do. He looked around for a stick or something to prod the ashes further out into the sea. He spotted a lolly stick and he used this tiny object to stir the ashes but this had no effect. The damn stuff was just sitting and bobbing as the water moved in and out. Panicking, he watched and noted that, bloody, sodding hell, the ashes stayed put. He fidgeted and shuffled his feet as the water dared to encompass his shoes and for a second he thought the sleeve of his jacket might have touched the water and the ashes, which freaked him out. The panic was going and was now replaced by anger.

"How bloody stupid is this?" he asked himself. He had done his best to be true to tradition for Mr Singh but now he was on his own. "Bollocks to this, I'm off," he told no one in particular and left.

This event was disappointingly not the majestic moment he had hoped for but technically he had done the deed for Mr Singh. He didn't allow himself to think that perhaps the scattering of the ashes on a police launch, even with all the press there, may have been more fitting.

He went back to Ilford and parked his car in De Vere Gardens. He didn't go indoors but walked to the Cranbrook Pub for a pint of Stella to help clear his head and raise a glass to the memory of Mr Singh. It was mid-afternoon but still lunchtime and Sunday roasts were on the menu. He ordered roast beef and all the trimmings. He was partial to a roast dinner and roast beef was his favourite. He would wash it down with another glass of Stella before returning home to watch some cricket. He needed to take it easy today and get his energy levels back up. He wanted revenge for Alice. Tomorrow was going to be the start of finding out who murdered Alice and dealing with them.

ONCE UPON A TIME

Bam Bam Bamra was a Sikh gang leader. He covered Ilford, Barking, Dagenham, Plaistow and all parts this side of the Thames up to Stratford. He controlled and kept in order a huge area. He vied for top position with the Triad and Snakehead groups, they all had their own areas of business and worked hard not to encroach on each other's working arrangements. Along with them were all the little people who also vied for work, information and a bit of power. It was not easy to be a top dog, it involved teaching lessons to various people over the years. It was not a problem for Bam Bam, he commanded a fearful respect. There had been quite a few dissidents holding up flyovers through the years, not to mention those minced up and fed to pigs in Essex. Whether these stories were true or not was not the problem, the myth was laid in stone and never challenged. His fingers were in many pies: money laundering, pimping, bodyguards, protection rackets and drugs but never cannabis or cocaine, more Es, crystal meth and amphetamines. The Triads and Snakeheads were the cannabis, cocaine and heroin dealers. He also ran a business providing bouncers for clubs and pubs. It was more that the clubs and pubs could only use his bouncers if they didn't use him, something nasty happened on their Saturday nights, which was not good for business. Bam Bam had been in the area for many years. Another product of Uganda's exodus to Britain, Bam Bam came to Ilford and took over a pretty feeble criminal element; it was easy pickings for him.

A few years ago, Jazz, as a new Detective Sergeant, had formed a fleeting and confidential alliance with Bam Bam Bamra. Jazz knew all the important people on his patch and they knew him. One day, when Jazz was getting his usual early morning newspaper, a lad stopped him as he was about to get in his car and handed him a mobile phone. On the other end of the phone was Bam Bam who said he wanted a quiet word, in private, with him. Bam Bam was a cocky individual and his tone was far too sweet and accommodating for Jazz not to be curious so he agreed to meet him. They arranged to meet in the Sikh temple at 6 p.m. that evening. It was a safe place to meet, no CCTV, no microphones and a quiet corner to talk could always be found. Bam Bam was already in the temple when Jazz arrived at 5.40 p.m. He had hoped to just ease himself in and look around before Bam Bam arrived. He figured it must be important for Bam Bam to already be there. Handkerchief on head and shoes removed, Jazz sat down next to him. Jazz watched as Bam Bam, unaccustomed to being on the wrong foot, tried to find a way of starting the conversation. It was quite fascinating to see *Mr Confidence* so uncomfortable.

"I asked to see you, Jazz, because I know your

reputation." He was looking down at his shoes but his eyes flickered in Jazz's direction as he spoke. He licked his lips and paused for a moment, staring at his shoes, trying to think how to carry on. Jazz looked at this big man who, by the look of his stomach, had eaten far too many samosas for his own good. He was a big man, at least 5'9" and nearly as wide. He was dressed as usual in a well cut suit which helped cover his multitude of sins. He always appeared immaculate as if he was a real business man. His standards never dropped. He had other men to do the dirty work for him so his hands were always clean. He was wrestling with what to say next and decided that he would just say it. With a deep breath, he looked up and blurted out, "I need your help." Jazz looked, he couldn't believe it, was he wringing his hands together? He glanced around wondering who else could see this spectacle. He saw three of Bam Bam's men all with their backs to them watching the entrance doors and ensuring no one got too close.

Bam Bam, having asked for help, now seemed to be more at ease and got on with what he wanted to ask Jazz. "I have a 20 year old daughter, Sandeep Kaur, she has been away at university. A very clever and beautiful young lady." Jazz could see the pride in his face as he talked about her. "She was at Canterbury University studying History. I never wanted her to be so far away but its modern times and, well, I agreed she could go." Bam Bam looked at Jazz and said, "She means the world to me, I want her safe."

Jazz was intrigued. Bam Bam was asking for help

when he was the king of contacts in the area. If Bam Bam couldn't fix it, what did he think Jazz could do? Jazz was getting seriously worried now. He hoped Bam Bam wasn't going to ask him to do anything illegal. He would only consider that in extreme emergencies.

Bam Bam continued, "She has been kidnapped by a sect down in Dover. She has left the university and set up with them. She is asking for money from me to fund them. They won' let her out to see me and they won't let her use the telephone. She is brainwashed and thinks I am pure evil." Jazz nearly laughed; they were right about that. "I have no contacts down in Dover and don't know what to do. I can't jeopardise her safety by going in there and getting her. Besides, she would never forgive me and I couldn't bear that." Jazz thought Bam Bam looked nearly human as he mopped his brow and brushed away tears. "Her mother is beside herself and will never forgive me if anything happens to her." Bam Bam was confessing more than he ever should.

The emotion in front of Jazz was making him quite uncomfortable. This was a side of the man Jazz had never seen before and was not likely to ever see again. He hoped, in the future, when Bam Bam had calmed down, that he wouldn't hold it against him that he had seen the great Mr Bamra so vulnerable.

THE SAVING OF SANDEEP KAUR BAMRA

Jazz hated the fucking sects. He had contacts and after getting all the details possible from Bam Bam, he had left promising to have news in a few days. It had been tricky but his contact John Smith, well maybe that wasn't his real name but it was the one he used, had done this many times before. Sandeep was found; after a week of surveillance, she was kidnapped from the sect's big manor house just outside Dover and taken to a safe house.

Jazz kept Bam Bam informed and said he couldn't see his daughter until she had been cleaned mentally. It was to take nearly eight months before a dutiful, compliant and loving daughter could be returned to Bam Bam's home in Chigwell. When Bam Bam was told she had been rescued from the sect and was safe with people who specialised in returning sect slaves to normal lives, overcome with emotion, he forgot himself and clasped Jazz to him and thanked him. This was certainly not the Bam Bam everyone knew. Bam Bam owed Jazz and promised him that if there ever was anything he could do for him, he was just to ask. It felt good to have one of the top gang leaders owing him a favour. Shortly after,

Jazz was seconded to Manchester and the favour had to wait. It was unfinished business that would be remembered by Jazz.

Bam Bam would never renege on the deal. There was, of course, much more to the story than anyone knew. Bam Bam never mentioned the real truth. To say such things would make it too real and that couldn't happen. It was unsaid knowledge between them and that made the debt a matter of honour. Jazz and Sandeep developed a closeness; they shared a life changing secret that could never be told to anyone else.

John Smith knew of this sect, if you could call it that. It wasn't one of the religious sects as such although its clarion call to the young and stupid, which were Jazz's words, not John Smith's, was, "Make a difference in the world."

The kidnap of Sandeep had gone well. John Smith was an expert at such things. He carried out surveillance on the house where she lived and watched the comings and goings for a few days. There was a routine to the lives of the young women. He noted it was all young women there, no young men.

Jazz visited every week for an update on how Sandeep was doing. It would be three months of treatment before Jazz had a face-to-face meeting with Sandeep at the safe house. She was in a bad way and not fit for visitors. John made it clear that she would see no one except his team who were there to help her.

After the first week, Jazz met John at the safe house. Sandeep was kept upstairs in a large locked room. His team of a nurse, minder and psychologist were there and would stay and get her back to as near normal as possible. It was always going to be expensive but Jazz knew Bam Bam could afford it so the cost was never an issue. In muted tones, John explained that it would take a long time to get Sandeep fit enough to re-enter polite society. Examinations found she had been sexually abused; her body would heal but the mental scars would take longer. She had been brainwashed into believing what she was doing was right and just. She was addicted to crack cocaine and it would take time for her to come off it. The sect had introduced her to crack cocaine, it made her totally dependent on them. It was a sombre thought, and there was a moment's silence as the horror of coming off crack cocaine dawned on Jazz. They both knew how addictive the drug was and that she was in for a rough ride. John Smith added, almost as an afterthought, that she was two months pregnant.

Jazz gasped, this was even worse; a Sikh girl would not be marriageable with a child. John jumped in and said not a problem, she would have an abortion. He added that this had been organised already and a private clinic close by had been booked. For Jazz's benefit he said that the abortion needed to be dealt with as soon as possible before the full treatment and de-programming started. It was all said in a very matter of fact tone. John had done this many times before. It left Jazz knowing he could not and would not tell Bam Bam the full extent of what had happened to Sandeep.

After three months, Jazz was told he could visit Sandeep and talk to her but to be careful what he said. She looked rough and if her father had seen her, he would never believe she could make a good marriage. Bam Bam had given him a picture of Sandeep and the girl before him bore no resemblance to the beautifully made-up girl with the big smile and sparkling eyes in the picture. Her face had broken out in big spots that bordered on boils, her hair was thick with grease and her eyes were dull. She wouldn't shower and she stunk.

The process of de-programming her was not pleasant for anyone. She hated everyone and wanted to go back to the sect. She wanted her stuff to make her feel better and she wanted to be with the people who loved her. She hated her family and she hated John and everyone in his team. She spat at Linda the nurse, she tried to kick the minder and the psychologist, who sat with her and talked to her calmly, she hated the most. One day, he sat too close and she scratched his face and would have stabbed him to death if only she had a knife. To see her so full of hate would have been frightening to anyone other than the team who had seen it all before. Jazz admired them all so much for the work that they did. They said they just wanted to make a difference. Their modesty put Jazz to shame, he wasn't sure he could be so altruistic. Again, he thought, they earned every penny they were paid to do this.

After three months of treatment, Jazz, having seen her for the first time, wondered where the improvement was; he couldn't see anything good about her. All he was told was that it would take time. Sandeep saw Jazz as an outsider and she cried and pleaded with him to take her away and back to all the people who loved her in the sect. It broke Jazz's heart to see her like this. She kept offering her body to him in return for his help to escape. She told him how she would do things to him that would make him scream with pleasure. She talked about sexual acts that no young girl should know about. He kept telling her that her mother and father loved her and were worried about her. She usually put her hands over her ears and screamed at that point. Jazz had to make up some stories to take back to a worried and waiting Bam Bam after each visit.

Every week he visited there seemed to be more dramas and incidents but John said this was normal. She defecated in her bed and the room stunk of urine and faeces. This went on for a week. She tried to kill herself a few times but this was handled. The medication helped her craving, but crack cocaine was highly addictive and nothing would take away all the pain of coming off it. She wouldn't eat. She wouldn't talk. Other times she paced up and down and screamed and screamed until she was hoarse. It was torture to watch on the weekends Jazz visited. He thought she would never return to normality. She seemed to be becoming more insane every week.

By the fifth month, he saw the first glimmer of an improvement. She was calmer and cleaner. She had showered and her hair was brushed and pinned back off her face. She didn't talk but sat quietly as Jazz talked of her father and her mother and how they missed her and how much they loved her. He wondered if the team had got fed up and doped her to keep her quiet. John said no doping up was allowed. She had enough of that in her system and they had worked to clear it out so no popping of pills to keep her quiet. She was in the next phase, which was good. Now she was accepting and listening. Of course all the crack cocaine was out of her system but it was still there mentally. It was a powerful drug that burned bridges of hope and sanity in the brain. Poetically John said they were rebuilding bridges of hope and goodness for her.

Sandeep looked forward to Jazz's visits. She told John that he was her shining light in all the gloom. He was a Sikh and he accepted her and what she had been through. John warned Jazz to be careful, she was falling in love with him. It was explained that he was her knight on a white steed there to save her and take her away from all the pain and misery. Perplexed, Jazz said that the team had done everything for her, they were the ones she should respond to. With a laugh, John said they had inflicted pain and torment and made her do things she didn't want to do. In her mind, they would always be her tormentors. Jazz brought only kindness and wanted nothing from her.

He began to look forward to his visits every weekend. The grounds of the house were beautiful and the setting reminded him of a Capability Brown garden he had seen in a book. There were lines of beautiful oak trees and the lawns stretched on for what seemed like miles. They found a pathway that led to a pebbly beach. Sandeep would hold his arm as they walked and slipped on the wet stones. The days he was with her were bright and full of chatting and laughter. She looked forward to the weekends when he arrived. He shared a dreadful secret with her. Her family must never know what had happened to her. Jazz was the only person to know of her degradation and also her rise out of the cess pit she had fallen into. This made him very special and trusted. They developed a bond that was never to be broken. Months later, she would send him a Sikh bangle to remember her by.

They talked about all sorts of things. He loved the way she looked deeply into his eyes when talking to him. She was a clever girl and he still didn't understand how she had got herself into such a mess and believed all the shit handed out by the sect. It wasn't the time to ask her though, she was still very raw.

What she did share with Jazz was her utter humiliation at what she had done. She didn't think she could ever forgive herself or get over it. How could she live with such a dreadful secret? Her family and her religion would never allow her to live if she was in India. With a sombre face, she told Jazz that in the olden days her family would have stoned her to death for what she had done. Just as she looked about to cry, she was startled by what sounded like a giggle that turned into a full blown laugh. He asked her what on earth she sounded like. He told her that in the old days she would have been married to an old man and when he died she would have had to commit Sati. This was a Hindu custom where the widow was put on the funeral pyre alive with the body of her dead husband to burn to death. He said she lived in the 20th century and in England. He asked her what the hell the olden days had to do with today. Gently he reminded her that her parents loved her and that her secret was safe. No one outside of the house would ever know what had happened to her. She instinctively hugged him for his kindness.

Still, she had blackened her family name and the dishonour she had brought on them made her think that all she could do was to kill herself. OK, he knew she had counselling but she was saying this to him and he would have none of it. He was a Sikh and he told her it was not her fault. He could see how the sect worked and how they ruin lives for their own selfish ends and greed. He emphasised again that no one would ever know. She could cut it out of her life and throw it away. It never happened. She would marry a good man and have a happy life. She looked at him intently to see if he meant the words and he did. She smiled at him and thanked him. It meant a lot to her that a Sikh could say that. She adored Jazz and wished he was the man she was to marry, but of course he wouldn't be the chosen husband. Her father had someone in mind for her and she would comply with whatever he arranged for her.

It was difficult for Jazz to be close to Sandeep. He had become very fond of this girl. He had seen her at her very worst and now he could see her becoming the most beautiful woman he had ever met. He could never allow himself to get emotionally involved with her. The knowledge of what had happened brought them together in a bubble of shared closeness. He could have easily fallen for her; she was beautiful, intelligent and brave and she adored him. It was the horrendous thought of Bam Bam as his father-in-law that kept his hormones focussed and distant.

She knew what was expected of her when she got

back home. The de-programming had finally got through to her and she remembered her father and her mother as loving, giving parents and she missed them. She wanted to be part of the family again. She was nearly ready to return home.

By the seventh month, Bam Bam was getting very fidgety and wanted to know where his daughter was. He vacillated between losing his temper and crying for her. Flushed with temper, he would ask Jazz if he was being taken for a mug. He shouted that no one takes this long to be de-programmed. The next minute he would be near to tears, asking how she was coping, was his little girl OK and could he see her. Mrs Bam Bam was beginning to ask questions about where her daughter was. Bam Bam had told her some story about going to India to see his family but it didn't ring true after so long. She was getting suspicious. All in all, Jazz was finding it hard to manage the situation.

He asked John on the next visit when the hell it would all be over and she could go home. John said soon. It was agreed that in two weeks Sandeep should be ready to go home. Just a little longer to ensure she was ready to cope with life outside of the house. Jazz was allowed to take her out for a meal that evening. They found a restaurant with a small band that played light jazz all evening. They ate and danced until they were the last people in the restaurant. It was a magical evening and each knew it would be their last time together in this way. When he dropped her back at the house, she turned and gently kissed him goodnight. It made him shiver with the expectation of something he couldn't have. She held him longer than she should have and whispered that she would always remember him and she would never forget their time together. With that, she tripped up the stairs to her room.

He sat downstairs with a beer thinking of her, knowing it had to end here and now. It had been a long journey for both of them. John and the team were working on closing down the house and preparing for Sandeep to return home. He toasted them with a beer and thanked them for their work. Tired, they clinked bottles and downed the beer. They would each go their own way. John was the leader and when he next needed their services he would ring them and they would start again in another house in another county. They had earned every penny they got.

On a Friday evening, Jazz took a beautifully made-up Sandeep, wearing an emerald-green sari, to an office in Ilford that Bam Bam called his headquarters. Sandeep was very nervous and worried her father would know and disown her. Jazz asked how her father would know anything. No one would tell him. Sandeep said he would only have to look in her eyes to see what had happened. Jazz laughed and said that was just her imagination. He would be over the moon to see her again. He reminded her that every week her father had asked how she was and how he had nearly cried at the thought that she was in any pain. He shouldn't have done it but Jazz had bought her a Sikh bangle to remind her of who she was. Perhaps he also wanted her to remember him, but he wasn't going to admit that to himself. She said she would never take it off, no matter where she was or who she was with. The bangle would always remain on her arm as a memory of Jazz. The last look full of meaning was all he remembered of Sandeep. He was to hand her over to her father and go on his way. He didn't realise it would hurt so much to leave her.

A phone call the day before had alerted Bam Bam to her arrival. He opened the door expectantly and was not disappointed. Jazz left them with a promise to call Bam Bam the next day. They met in the temple two days later. Bam Bam said he wanted to spend time with his daughter and he and his wife had stayed at home to make her comfortable and welcome her back. They talked on a superficial level about how good she looked and how the de-programming had worked so well. Jazz thought Bam Bam didn't have a clue what had really gone on.

Then there was a look between them that said it all. No words were needed; Bam Bam hugged Jazz and his eyes told him he knew exactly what had gone on and what the team had done for his daughter. It would never be mentioned, the words would never come into the world, but Bam Bam knew and that was why their bond would never be broken.

Jazz had saved his daughter from a public and private shame which would have encompassed the whole family. Her life would have been over, she would have been buried away somewhere in India, living with distant family, possibly married off to a lower caste. She was the cherished only child of Bam Bam and neither mother or father could cope with her life being ruined and away from them. The fact that Bam Bam had done in his lifetime some filthy, evil, tortuous and murderous deeds did not compare with the unforgiveable shame his daughter would have brought to the family. She had to marry well and now this was behind her, plans could be made.

It was not headline news but it was reported extensively about two weeks after Sandeep's return to Bam Bam that a house in Kent which was reported to belong to a religious sect had mysteriously burnt down. It was thought everyone had escaped from the building but the next day the fire brigade found 10 bodies in the cellar. It was thought that the boiler for the central heating, which was housed in the cellar, had exploded and unfortunately 10 members of the sect had been working there and been killed. Identification would take some time because the bodies were unrecognisable but it was hoped that with the aid of dental records this could be reported to the coroner's office within a month. Only Bam Bam and Jazz knew this was no accident. Revenge was swift and sweet.

PAYBACK TIME

It was now time to call in that favour. Bam Bam knew everything that happened in East London. Jazz was on a mission to avenge Alice and get the bastards responsible. Of course no one was talking.

The Triads were not to be messed with; their punishment was brutal and slow, which ensured no one squealed on them. The Chinese were the top of the ladder and next came the Snakeheads. The Triads covered the whole of East London, mainly from Ilford through to Central London. They dealt with huge supplies of cocaine, heroin, some cannabis and whatever was the latest recreational drug. At that moment, methylamphetamine, or crystal meth, ice, glass, Tina, Christine or Yaba as it is known on the street, was very popular and a big money earner.

The Snakeheads, who were all Vietnamese, never spoke to anyone other than their own kind. Everything was kept in-house. No one knew how they thought or what they did. They had quite a hold on Barking and Dagenham. Their cannabis factories were slick and ran like clockwork. They earned them shed loads of money and no one interfered. More and more, cannabis factories were growing skunk. The Snakeheads dealt only in cannabis. They sat uneasily in the area with the Triads.

Bam Bam didn't touch anything that the Triads and Snakeheads dealt in. He offered poppers and other types of tablets to ravers, which the Triads and Snakeheads didn't bother with. His other interests paid him enough money and caused him enough trouble keeping the police off his back as it was.

There had been meetings between the Triads and the Snakeheads and Bam Bam over the years but each knew each other's area of business. They kept their distance. Each were wary of the others, they were all mindful of the police and ensuring everything was low-key enough to keep them from sniffing around. The odd cannabis factory was raided and closed down but all in all there were so many in the East End of London that it was written off as overheads when one went down. What each and every one of the gangs didn't like were interlopers thinking they could work their areas. When this happened, they all united to get rid of them. The Triads, Snakeheads and Bam Bam were known as the Holy Trinity (Father, Son and Holy Ghost), a name given to them by the police and villains. This was an odd name because they were all either Taoists, worshippers of Chinese gods, Buddhists or Sikhs; certainly none of them were Christians.

Jazz woke Monday morning feeling better than usual. He realised he hadn't drunk quite as much last night. He had been tired and fallen asleep early evening. Today he had a meeting with Bam Bam but before then he had to dodge DCI Radley at the station. In actual fact, DCI

Radley never moved from his office, he would send an officer to look for him. He didn't want to get into a discussion about Mr Singh's ashes. He couldn't piss off DCI Radley at this stage, he might take him off the case.

He decided to walk to the police station. It was a bright, sunny morning and the early morning warmth promised much more later in the day. He took his jacket just in case.

As he came down the stairs, Mrs Chodda popped her head out of the kitchen and asked him to come and see her tonight when he got back. She had cooked something very special for him to have with a cup of coffee. She mentioned that she had made some of her very special pakoras for him. He was going to make an excuse but that would have been very bad manners so he smiled and thanked her. He thought he should be back about 6 p.m. She nodded and disappeared into the kitchen. He sighed and wondered what she had got in store for him. He didn't need any hassle at the moment, there was enough going on to keep him busy without Mrs Chodda trying to arrange meetings for him with eligible young women. He walked down the road and thought, Oh bugger it! He missed the company of Sikh society and it was good to be sociable. He spent a lot of evenings alone and sometimes company was a good thing. Plus, it had been many years since he had tasted homemade pakoras. His Mother made the finest, tastiest pakoras in the whole of England. Perhaps Mrs Chodda's pakoras would be too. On that optimistic note, he walked with a spring in his step.

BUSINESS AND PLEASURE

It was 7.45 a.m. and Jazz was feeling good. As he passed The Black Stallion pub near the high road, he looked up as Tracey tripped up to him and said in the high pitched tones of a cockney tinkerbell, "Mr Mr, do you want some business?" Jazz looked at her. It was bloody early and she was wearing a top that barely covered her big breasts and a skirt that was far too short for a 35 year old overweight short woman who had seen better days.

At 5'1" tall, the high heels still made her have to crane her neck to look up at Jazz. With a resigned look, Jazz said, "Tracey I don't have the time and I don't have the inclination. I am on my way to work. She looked up at him and squeaked "You know me Mr?" Of course he knew her. Five years ago and looking a lot better than she did now, Tracey was one of the well known prostitutes who worked around Ilford. He noted Carl was still her pimp and boyfriend from what he remembered. Fed up but feeling kindly Jazz said "You don't remember who I am do you?" A light seemed to turn on in her head and she gasped "Oh gawd, you're police ain't you?" came the shrill response. Jazz nodded his head and Tracey gave him an apologetic smile and coyly asked, "You ain't gonna arrest me are you sweetheart?" Jazz assured her he had better things to do at the moment and finished the conversation by moving on. As he walked past her, he heard her shout to the pimp sloppily smoking a cigarette by the pub door. "'Ear Carl, I told you 'e was the filth, didn't I?" Jazz smiled and thought what style she had; not!

The police station was buzzing with the change of duties, officers going off after night duty and the new shift coming on. Jazz looked around for signs of anyone interested in him. All looked OK and he went to find Sharon and Tony. They looked up and he whispered that they should all retire to the canteen so he could tell them his news.

They had the murder case, which excited them. They huddled closer around the table as Jazz told them he had a meeting with one of the Holy Trinity that morning, which might help and give them a lead. Their job was to speak to intelligence and find out what was happening in the area regarding cannabis factories and how they were working; they would also find out who the main dealers in the area were and look up CRIS reports on them. He knew most of the answers, times don't change much, but it was good to see information coming from a different angle. They arranged to meet at 3 p.m. in the canteen for an update. In answer to their question, he didn't want to meet in the CID office, there were too many ears listening and there would be jealousy that they had the murder case. They could sit in a corner of the canteen and not be overheard.

Again, he asked that they talk to residents in Wards

Road to see if anyone knew anything, however small, that might help in this investigation. Sharon said she was going to talk to the dustmen that came every Thursday, just in case they had seen anything. Tony was going to talk to the postman. They were also going to re-interview the milkman as he was in the street every day. Tony thought that it might be helpful to find out if there were school children around. If so, he was going to interview them. Kids poke their noses into things they shouldn't and hopefully they might get some information that way. Jazz was pleased, they were thinking outside the box. At last it didn't feel like he was doing this alone. As he left the building, he ignored his name being shouted out and quickened his pace until he was past St Peter & Paul Catholic church. He was on his way to the temple just five minutes further down the road.

Bam Bam wanted an early meeting, he had things to do. Jazz knew he was just keeping him in his place and that was OK. As long as he helped him find the murderers of Alice, he didn't give a shit if he wanted to look the big, benevolent man to Jazz. It was 9 a.m. and Bam Bam said he wanted a 9.10 a.m. meeting. Why he was so fucking picky about 10 minutes Jazz didn't know, but he wasn't going to upset the man who was going to help him solve this murder. Bam Bam should never be underestimated. Whatever Jazz had done for him, he still expected to be treated with the respect due him. They were never going to be bosom buddies, business was business in his mind and Bam Bam was the Managing Director.

It was busy in the temple for 9 a.m. The gossiping aunties, as the Sikh women who regularly cooked and cleaned and just met to chat were called, were there getting ready for a funeral feast. Jazz put a hankie on his head and took his shoes off. He made his way to a corner of the temple that was empty and waited. At 9.10 precisely, two of Bam Bam's men came in and looked around. They spotted him in the corner and a minute later, Bam Bam entered and was escorted to where Jazz was seated. It was quietly done but caused quite a spectacle. Most people entered a temple in a humble fashion. Although there was no announcement that he had arrived, his heavies walking him across the temple floor made everyone discreetly look. Bam Bam was known to everyone and no one would have the bad manners or the nerve to stand and stare.

After much huffing and puffing as he arranged his immense self onto a corner seat, Bam Bam mopped his beaded brow and, when fully settled, looked expectantly at Jazz.

"So, how is Sandeep?" was the best Jazz could say as an opener. He thought about her every now and then and genuinely wanted to know if she was alright. Bam Bam smiled, he knew why Jazz mentioned Sandeep. Both knew what they were there for.

The preamble last half an hour. Sandeep was now married to an Italian who owned a private hospital for cosmetic surgery. In answer to the question, Bam Bam said of course the man was a Sikh, but he was born in Italy. She was, according to Bam Bam, very happy indeed. Apparently there were no children yet. It was a worry because they had been married for four years now. Jazz thought that Sandeep must have been married off very quickly after the sect affair. He wondered also if no babies had anything to do with the abortion. Still, as long as she was happy. At least she would grow old beautifully. A lot of women would love to have a husband who could keep their looks with facelifts and face peels, whiten their teeth and make their boobs bigger. No dieting needed if you had liposuction. It sounded like a marriage made in heaven for a woman.

They got one of the women who was a regular at the temple to make a cup of tea for them both. The women took it in turns to be there to cook and clean. It was their job to volunteer for these roles. It was also a good opportunity to meet with other women to talk and discuss everything that was going on in the community. None of the women there wanted to know what Bam Bam was doing though. They were scared of him and knew better than to mention his name. He had a reputation as a benevolent Sikh but when crossed, his fury knew no bounds and his influence in the surrounding area was enormous.

Once he had been served a cup of tea and homemade cake, Jazz started at the beginning and told Bam Bam about Alice. He watched as Bam Bam demolished the six coconut cakes they had between them. Jazz was not hungry and didn't want his. Jabba the Hut came into his mind but he got rid of such a thought quickly. He needed Bam Bam to help him and he wasn't going to sit and ridicule him, even if it was just a thought in his head. He told Bam Bam about the cannabis factory and how it had been cleared quickly. Alice had died in there and was then carried into her house. Did Bam Bam know about this and who had done it? He told him it was personal, that he needed to find the killers to avenge Alice. He told him that he had the murder case but only for a short while. It was going to be handed over to the murder squad fairly soon. The look showed he was serious, he was almost pleading with Bam Bam to help him catch the persons who did this.

Bam Bam wanted to know who Alice was. She was a westerner and for the life of him he couldn't understand why it was so personal for Jazz. It took another hour for Jazz to tell the story of living close to Alice all his young life. He could have just brushed over the details but Alice deserved to be recognised for the person she was. She was important to his mother and she was more important to Jazz than he ever realised in his youth. It was only now that he was talking about her and the things she used to do with him and for him that he realised she had quite an effect on his upbringing. When his father died, Alice helped his mother get over it and in doing so, helped his mother keep in touch with Jazz, who had left home by then.

His visits, rare as they were, were whirlwind visits that caused a commotion and an upset in routine and an upset in emotions when he left as quickly as he arrived. Alice was there to sit with his mother. He felt guilty at the thought and now couldn't believe how selfish and how much of a bloody bastard he had been. He put it down to the ego of youth. His life had seemed so full and busy and his visits were annoying interruptions to his daily life. He loved his mother and he cared deeply for Alice but they were old women who he knew loved him so he never worked at pleasing them. In those heady days, he always thought his mother was happy just sitting and waiting for him. He laughed now at such an absurd way of thinking and how incredibly egotistical he was. All he could do now was find Alice's killers and put them away. In some way, he told himself, this might make amends for any disrespect he might have shown to Alice and his mother.

Sitting there in the temple, he thought he should beg forgiveness, but on the other hand, he thought, he should just get on with doing his job and catching the bastards who had done this. He turned to Bam Bam and said he needed the information as soon as possible. Bam Bam said he would do what he could and see him in the temple at the same time tomorrow.

FRIEDA'S PROBLEM

Jazz went back to the police station to find that Sharon had been told to interview Frieda Clarke. She had been arrested that morning and Sharon was seconded to interview her. Frieda was a well known drunk who, when she went on a walkabout fuelled by too much cheap cider, would annoy and bother pedestrians and cyclists in her path. She was often arrested and was so well known in the magistrates' court she had her own chair. Actually they put a chair in a corner to keep her away from people.

Frieda had a problem brought on by bad diet and too much drink. Her stomach was revolting in more ways than one! She had the most terrible wind and every minute would pass a smell that could make strong men cry. There was no subtlety in our Frieda, when she passed wind, the bellowing noise made flocks of startled birds take flight and neighbours would bang on the walls. Frieda was oblivious to the fuss she caused and was very put out by the way people acted around her.

Jazz made his way down to the interview rooms and peered through the one-way glass. He watched Sharon struggling to interview this woman, who regularly interrupted the proceedings with a slight move to the right of the chair as she ripped forth with a bellowing burst of trumpeting followed quickly by a stench that begged the question that something had died and rotted in the depths of her bowels.

Nothing changes in Ilford, he thought. He remembered Frieda when he was here before. She was about 55 years old now and looking pretty ropey but still feisty and fed up with being arrested. He thought she looked a bit more ragged and thinner than the last time he saw her. Her clothes looked more worn and he suspected that buying drink won over buying essentials in life, like clothes and proper food. Last time he saw her she had more teeth, he thought. That was over five years ago, just before he was sent to Manchester.

Some bright spark had put Sharon in the small interview room with Frieda. The poor girl would be nearly dead by now. He laughed at the thought and went to bale out Sharon. No one interviewed Farting Frieda in a small room. Times had not changed in all the years he had been away. It felt like he had never left Ilford.

Sharon had some news. Whilst interviewing Frieda about her trying to stop a cyclist by kicking his wheels as he past her and scaring the hell out of him, Sharon asked if Frieda ever went into Wards Road. It turned out she had and Farting Frieda had seen something in Wards Road. The council owned a house in Meads Lane which was converted into flats and Frieda had a one bedroom ground floor flat. Frieda often walked the length of Wards Road to get to Ley Street and her favourite off licence. She was telling Sharon about a car she had seen quite often in the sideway of the house. It took painstaking questions to find out it was the house next to Alice she was talking about. She said the car was one of those big cars that presidents have. After questioning her about what it looked like and what badge it had on the back, it turned out to be a Mercedes. There were lots of Mercedes in Ilford and Sharon was about to give up when Frieda started to giggle and said that the number plate always made her laugh. Apparently it said PISS and she thought that was really funny for a number plate. Sharon was going to check it out and get back to Jazz. This was a bloody good break and he slapped her on the back for her brilliance.

She thanked him for rescuing her and said the stench was appalling and now she was going to burn all her clothes and have a long shower. Jazz laughed and said everyone new in the station was given an interview with Farting Frieda as an initiation. She had passed. Sharon walked off muttering that she hadn't passed half as much as Frieda had and in a loud voice advised Jazz not to light a match in the vicinity. He liked Sharon, she had the makings of a good Detective.

He found Tony in the CID office phoning the post office; he was still trying to get through to someone who could tell him who delivered in Wards Road. They were in Ilford so Jazz suggested they walk round to the post office and ask in person. They couldn't be ignored if they stood close enough to a post office manager.

He should have known he had been in the police station too long not to be noticed. He wasn't quick enough to get out of the CID room and was trapped. In the doorway of the CID room stood DCI Radley. Jazz was amazed, he had left his room. He was pointing his hand in the direction of Jazz and was telling him to move himself now into his office. Again he had a tirade of complaints that Jazz was not making himself available, answering his mobile phone and turning deaf when it suited him. This was a reference to his being called earlier that morning and just walking out of the police station.

The troubled DCI was incredulous that Jazz could act in this way and that as his superior he was being ignored. He was about to suggest something unacceptable to Jazz, like taking him off the case, asking for his DS to be downgraded to a DC or putting him on gardening leave whilst his cases were investigated. Jazz couldn't let this happen.

As the DCI took a breath to put Jazz firmly in a place he didn't want to go, Jazz jumped in. "Sir, we are making immense progress. Within 24 hours I have the car identified, I have contacts who are putting out feelers for me and I will have solid information to give you tomorrow afternoon, that is a promise! I am so focussed on this case that I am afraid I don't hear outside influences and I haven't answered my phone but that is because I am in the middle of getting this case and near to an arrest"

The DCI opened his mouth to say something and then, resting his chin on his chest, thought for a few moments. "You have one more day to come up with something substantial otherwise it goes to the murder squad as it should."

Jazz relaxed inwardly and added, "You will have something to tell the press tomorrow, Sir, I promise."

With a nod and with "2 p.m. in my office tomorrow" ringing in the air, the DCI dismissed Jazz to carry on. As Jazz walked away, DCI Radley shouted to him, "And by the way, update me on Mr Singh and the scattering of his ashes." Without turning, Jazz raised his hand to acknowledge he had heard.

Bloody hell, he thought, I need something from Bam Bam and from Sharon and Tony that is going to keep this case with me. He also needed a sweetener when he broke the news to his DCI about the ashes. He grabbed Tony, who was banging the vending machine to get out the crisps he had paid for. Jazz clenched his fist and gave one swift punch to the side of the machine and the crisps fell down. He smiled. Nothing changes, he thought as he nodded to Tony to follow him. They went to the post office which was in Clements Road, off Ilford High Street. It would only take them five minutes to walk there if they didn't fanny around, as Jazz would say.

They found an officious manager who really couldn't be asked to help them. After trying the friendly approach, Jazz lost patience and flashed his badge and proceeded to tell the jumped-up little shit that if he didn't help the police, he could be looking at being taken to the police station and they could keep him there for hours. Then, of course, he added that he could also decide to give him a chance to think about it and knock on his door at 3 a.m. in the morning and march him down to the police station. The manager blushed at the thought and suddenly decided he would very much like to help in any way he could. It took about five minutes to find out who the postman for that round was. They had timed it right, he would be around somewhere because he finished his round at about 11 a.m. Jazz went off to find him.

Tony had wandered off and was talking to staff who were sorting letters and parcels out the back in a large warehouse area. It was bright and noisy and full of people. There was music playing in the background; it was Capital Radio they were listening to as the jingle told listeners regularly. Tony went to the parcel section and got talking to a man named Lenny, who seemed to know everything there was to know about parcels and the area they covered. Lenny, as he told Tony, had worked there as a man and boy. He knew Wards Road, he said that they delivered there many times in the week. Apparently Royal Mail delivered Littlewoods or Great Universal books to a few houses and they were always ordering stuff from them. When asked about who lived there, he said something that made Tony very animated and rush to find Jazz.

Jazz was waiting to see the postman when Tony grabbed him and said he had to listen to Lenny. Lenny was feeling quite good and important. He had said something that got the attention of the two policemen and now he was going to repeat it all but in his very best voice. With encouragement from Tony, Lenny cleared his voice and stood straight and tall.

"It's like this, I took the van on Wednesday to Wards Road. No 51 had ordered a package which I have to say weighed a ton. I nearly did my back in. All that bleedin health and safety stuff about carrying doesn't help if yer knees ain't any good." He caught an impatient look from Jazz and returned to the story. He cleared his throat and got back on track. "So, I was proceeding down Wards Road and I espied two Chinese gentlemen going into the old lady's house. They seemed to have a key and everything. Never thought a lot about it only I knew she lived there because she often was in her front garden in the good weather. I had seen her put out her milk bottle on Monday that week. I have spoken to her in the past because she took in a package for across the road once. A very nice old dear she was." Lenny thought for a moment and added hesitantly, "It did seem strange, now you come to mention it, that two Chinese men should be going into her house."

He was asked if he could recognise them again and Lenny said that they were Chinese and they all looked the same to him. On being pushed a little further, he did say that one of them was quite small with an unusual hair cut. The sides were shaved so he looked bald except for a strip of hair through the middle of his head going down to a short pony tail. He was well-built and looked like he worked out. He reckoned this one was about 40 years old. The other one was quite young, about 25 years old. Jazz could feel the hairs on his arms standing up. This was getting really good. Lenny was a brilliant witness to have. He would be asked to go down to the station at some point to look at some mug shots to see if he could identify these men.

The postman who delivered regularly to Wards Road appeared. He was eating his breakfast, which appeared to be a baguette with cheese and tomatoes in it. It was huge and he took big mouthfuls before speaking to them both. It took a few attempts to get an answer they understood out of him. In the end enough was enough and Jazz told him to put the fucking bread roll down and talk to them. He said he had noticed nothing. He delivered about 8 a.m. every morning and never saw anyone. He had seen Alice sometimes but not often. He had never delivered next door to Alice and said he heard nothing because he wore his iPod and played music on his round. He proudly told them his wife had bought it for him for Christmas. The best present he had ever had, he told them. Jazz and Tony were not impressed.

When he had gone, Jazz turned to Tony and said, "He was as useful as a condom in a maternity clinic." Still, they were excited about Lenny and went back to the station to put together what they had already. A storyboard was being erected for them and they would see what they had got.

Jazz was bubbling, this is what he was good at. Give him a murder and he would solve it. He was going to do this for Alice. The few people in the CID room were interested too and stood looking at the board, with the bits of information Jazz and his team had collated already on there.

Graciously he surveyed them and said, "Gentlemen, if you wish to assist, please do not let me stop you. All information gratefully received." They muttered something inaudible and shuffled back to their desks.

Sharon came into the CID room with a number plate belonging to a Mercedes. The registration was WP15 SCO.

Jazz and Tony looked at it full on and then squinted and stared with their heads to one side. They agreed that yes, I suppose, P15S might look like piss but it was a long shot. Sharon suggested dryly that perhaps they needed to be drunk to see it properly. The clincher, as far as Sharon was concerned, was the fact that it was registered to a company called Tiger Holdings; that had oriental style to it. She had more work to do to find out where Tiger Holdings worked from but she had enlisted the help of a detective who dealt with POCA cases and was used to delving into corporate areas. Jazz needed the information now, time was of the essence and he needed answers by tomorrow. Sharon said the Detective, Stephen Paine, had promised her results by tomorrow. Jazz knew Stephen Paine, he was a miserable bastard who didn't do favours for anyone.

"So how did you get that bastard to help you?" Jazz asked.

Sharon smiled and looked at the floor. "I have my ways, skip."

I bet you have, darling, he thought dryly.

Sharon and Tony didn't know that Jazz had the lowdown on both of them. Sharon had the reputation of an ace slag at Bethnal Green Police Station. To Jazz, it looked like leopards didn't change their spots. He would watch her, he liked her and life wouldn't be easy if her previous reputation became local news. He knew men could be two-faced. They never turned down the offer of an easy lay but then suddenly became all holier than thou and sneered at them, calling them slags and slappers when it suited them. It was not fair; it made promotion difficult and cooperation at work difficult too, for women especially, but those with reputations as slags and slappers would find promotion even harder. Equality and diversity had got much better, he thought, but it was always a man's club in the police force. Women officers had a fairer chance these days of a good career in the police force but networking was still a men only thing which always helped with promotion and working together. If you weren't liked, life could be difficult. She was a clever girl, hadn't she worked that one out, he asked himself. Bloody hell, he thought, I've got a murder investigation that can be taken away from me if I'm not careful, a DC who looks like she's happy to hand it out on a plate and I've got to watch and stop her from getting a reputation as a slapper again! And I ain't even got as far as Tony and what he might be doing to arse up this investigation. Jazz felt tired and wanted to go home and sit with a few drinks. He wanted a break from everything just for the evening. Tomorrow was going to be a big day so he said his farewells and went home.

THE FOOD OF THE GODS

Mrs Chodda was waiting for him. He had forgotten about having a cup of tea with her. He inwardly sighed. He was tired and just wanted to sit and watch TV with a drink in one hand and a cigarette in the other. God that sounded bliss but now he would have to be well-mannered and polite and drink bloody tea. He remembered Mrs Chodda had told him she was making homemade pakoras for him to have with a cup of tea. Homemade pakoras were nothing like the ones bought in shops or, in fact, the ones in Indian restaurants. That now put a different slant on things, and he followed her into the kitchen expectantly. She waved for him to sit down at the table whilst she busied herself at the stove. There was no conversation, just a smile from Mrs Chodda; she saw he looked tired and stressed.

A large plateful of pakoras was put in front of him. She knew he would love them. He took a mouthful and closed his eyes. They reminded him of his mother and his youth. They tasted magnificent. They felt soft in his mouth but with a resistance that made the chewing exciting. The undercurrent of mild chilli and spices caused his senses to explode with delight. It felt sensual and sinful and he enjoyed every mouthful. The potato, onion, and yes he savoured, sweetcorn perfectly cooked and held together with a secret recipe of the lightest batter that all the best cooks shared only with their successor and no one else. He felt like he had died and gone to heaven. Mrs Chodda watched this spectacle of pleasure and smiled. This was what he needed, homemade good Indian food to remind him of who he was. She said nothing while he ate all on the plate. It took him 20 minutes of indulgence and she could see the calming effect it had on him. He had two cups of tea whilst eating the pakoras. He was full but sad that he had finished the "food of the gods" as his mother called pakoras.

He licked his fingers as Mrs Chodda filled his cup again from the big teapot she kept warm by the cooker. He hadn't realised before how comfortable and Indian her kitchen was; the jars of dried spices on a shelf and all the saucepans battered with age and darkened with use were stacked up on another shelf. Her kitchen was warm and smelt of curry and it so reminded him of his mother's kitchen and the time he spent sitting with her as she busied herself cooking yet another dish for the family. It had been a happy time when his father had been alive, his mother seemed to cook all the time. She didn't seem to bother so much when he had gone. He never went without but it wasn't the same.

Mrs Chodda caught sight of his faraway sad look and she put on the table the coconut sweetmeats for him to finish his tea with. She started to talk about her family and how they were all in the Punjab, except for those in England, of course. She asked him where his family were. They talked together about the Punjab. It would have seemed a strange conversation to an outsider. Neither of them had been born in India. They were both born in Uganda, but home would always be India and the Punjab. They both had relatives in the Punjab. Mrs Chodda said she had relatives everywhere, including America.

Their conversation was gossipy and warm and easy. With the warmth of the kitchen and the food in his belly, Jazz was feeling more and more tired and keeping his eyes open would soon be a problem. Mrs Chodda saw this and said that he must come and sit with her more often and she would make sure she had pakoras and other home cooked food for him. He told her he got an upset stomach if he ate too much curry. He actually felt quite ashamed to tell her that but he didn't want a gippy stomach again, especially now when there was so much going on. He felt he could be honest with her. She was a nice woman.

He had sat with her for nearly two hours and all he wanted to do now was go to sleep. He thanked her very much for a wonderful time and left to climb the stairs to his room. He had actually really enjoyed his time in Mrs Chodda's kitchen. She was a lovely cook and a really homely woman; it made him realise that he had missed being made a fuss of and mothered in that way. It was also a bonus that she hadn't tried to palm him off with any female relatives.

That night he had one drink and went to bed. He slept through until 7 a.m. The nightmares hadn't visited him and he awoke feeling refreshed and raring to go. It wasn't until he had showered and brushed his teeth that he realised he didn't have a headache and his mouth felt OK, not that disgusting taste he usually endured in the morning. He felt fresh, rested and raring to go. Then he thought about Alice.

Today was the day and didn't he just know it! The tension was in the knot in his stomach. He could feel the adrenalin bubbling but as yet there was nowhere to project it. It all had to come together before lunch. He set off for the police station on foot. He liked the walk, it calmed him and gave him thinking time. As he walked, he took his mobile phone out and began to work. He phoned Sharon, who said she would have the information for him by 9 a.m. Tony was arranging the mug shots for Lenny from the post office and he was coming in at 10 a.m. He rang Bam Bam and was told to meet him at the temple at 9 a.m. He arranged to meet Sharon and Tony in the CID office at 11 a.m. and pool all their information. He hoped it was good. At 2 p.m. he had to face DCI Radley and keep this case. He told himself he lived on pressure and it always brought the best out in him. But the pressure was about to rise to unacceptable levels.

He checked in at Ilford Police Station. He nodded to the other CID teams who had taken a sudden interest in what he was doing. Tony was busy in the ID suite getting pictures together. Sharon hadn't appeared yet. He grabbed a cup of tea from the marvellous Milly in the canteen and downed it quickly; the hot water scalded his tongue. He left the station and headed towards the temple. He wanted to be early and wait in peace and quiet until Bam Bam arrived. He prayed he had something of use for him. The other leads were fantastic but Bam Bam was the key to getting this finished quickly and making an arrest. If Bam Bam couldn't find out who had done this, then there was no hope for anyone. With that thought in his mind, he walked with a determination and optimism that today was going to be his day.

He arrived at the Temple early. The gossiping aunties, as the ladies who cooked were affectionately known, were there already. He put a hanky on his head and took his shoes off at the door. He found a corner away from all the women talking above each other and making quite a din this morning. The temple echoed with their talking and calling to each other. They looked as if they were cooking a feast today. Feeling depressed for a moment, Jazz hoped it wasn't another funeral. There was too much going on at the moment. He had to think about Alice and her funeral. Who else would bother, he asked himself. He would contact the morgue this afternoon and find out what was happening.

At 9 a.m. precisely Bam Bam's entourage entered the temple. The two front men looked around and saw Jazz in the corner and turned and nodded, which was obviously a sign for Bam Bam to enter. He was followed by two more men. Who the hell does this bugger think he is? Jazz asked himself. He was acting like the President of the United States. Jazz knew Bam Bam's entourage would be tooled up but he wasn't going there. He rose respectfully as Bam Bam walked over to him.

Again, the ladies were summoned to make tea and

bring cakes, which they did respectfully and quickly. After a few minutes of settling into his seat and waiting for his tea, Bam Bam nodded to Jazz and said he had news. Patience wasn't one of Jazz's virtues but it was tested to boiling point as Bam Bam graciously accepted the tea from one of the ladies and proceeded to drink it slowly. The cakes arrived a few seconds later and he availed himself of the selection. He looked as if he was going to make a day of it and Jazz was doing his best to keep still and keep his cool. He picked up his tea and tried to drink it. Every sip of tea caused a stifling heartburn in his chest. He couldn't eat a cake, it would have stuck in his throat. The entourage were positioned around them, looking outwards towards the door. After what seemed like an hour, Bam Bam put down his cup, wiped his mouth with a paper serviette thoughtfully provided by the ladies and looked about to speak. Jazz looked at him expectantly and held his breath.

"This is a difficult matter, Jazz," was the first response he heard. Bam Bam shifted awkwardly in his seat. He looked up and smiled. "I wont be a moment," he said and left to be escorted to the toilet in the temple.

Jazz thought he would burst with tension. This would never happen in a movie, he told himself. You have the meeting and you get told things and then the film moves towards its conclusion. In real life the bloody villain goes to the toilet. How bloody fucking pathetic is that! He could feel the stabbing pain above his left eye and he knew it would spread into a god-awful migraine if he didn't calm down. He sat and tried to breathe calmly whilst rubbing his forehead. He felt hot and his shirt was sticking to him. He waited silently until Bam Bam returned.

Bam Bam arranged his huge self on the chair and leaned back.

"So, Jazz, I have that information for you."

Again, Jazz sat up straight and looked expectantly. The story was long but fascinatingly compelling. Bam Bam had to go back nearly a year to explain what had happened in the East London area. He told Jazz most of it but he wasn't going to give him blow by blow accounts of his working life. He might owe Jazz but he was still a police officer and Bam Bam Bamra never told anyone everything. He was alive today because of his cunning and his intelligence and no favour would change that.

A year ago, the Holy Trinity that ran the east side of London and the Thames became aware of an intruder on their territory. It wasn't something Bam Bam worried about. Apparently it was a Vietnamese gang who were opening up cannabis factories like they had gone out of fashion in houses dotted around Dagenham, Barking and Romford. Most of the cannabis factories run by the other arms of the Holy Trinity were more inner East London but they dealt drugs in all the areas.

Bam Bam expanded this bit of information by saying that he wasn't that worried about the infiltrators because he didn't deal in these drugs; his business was elsewhere. Of course infiltrators could not be tolerated so he watched how the Triad and Snakeheads were dealing with the situation because they would sort it out eventually. There had been a lot of drugs pushed in the area lately, which had knocked the price down on the streets. That was never going to be tolerated for long. There were moves about to be made to stop them but then the bastards killed an old lady, which threw the spotlight onto them all. Everyone had retreated.

What he didn't tell Jazz was that the Triads and Snakeheads had formed an alliance that was going to take all the working cannabis factories for themselves. There was a lot of money out there and they wanted it. They had sat back and watched the Vietnamese develop all the cannabis factories; it took money and time to set each one up. They watched to see how secure and functional each factory was. They watched the police to see if they had any idea of the number of factories there were in the area. Then they were going to orchestrate a mass take over. They were spitting blood that the old lady had been killed and the Police were now swarming around and asking questions they didn't want asked.

Jazz asked where that left him in finding the killers. Bam Bam laughed. "You have more helpers than you need with all of us. We want this finished so we can get on with our business."

Bam Bam put his hand up and waved for another cup of tea and cakes. They were duly brought over by the ladies, who seemed to be just waiting to attend to him when he called. Jazz could see the power Bam Bam Bamra had in the community. Whilst he was occupied getting his tea and cakes, Jazz looked at the bling on the man. He had huge gold rings and signet rings on three fingers on each hand. The watch had to be gold, Rolex of course. Around his neck were three thick gold chains.

He also wore two Sikh bangles on his left wrist. Jazz suddenly realised how noisy it was when Bam Bam moved, all the bling clashing and rattling.

He went on to tell Jazz the names of the two men who had killed Alice. They were Vietnamese and their names were Giang Nguyen and Tho Luong.

"You can take the names to your DCI Radley this afternoon at 2 p.m. for your meeting and this should keep him happy. Soon I will be able to tell you where to find them."

Jazz was going to ask how the hell he knew he had a meeting with his DCI that afternoon but Bam Bam was having no questions asked. He rose and said he would see him again tomorrow with more news. He left, sandwiched between his minders. Jazz watched, along with everyone else in the temple, as the stately procession left.

Jazz sat for a minute wondering what on earth had happened there. He had the names he needed but how did Bam Bam know about his meeting? He looked at his watch and saw that, with all the messing around, it was already 11 a.m. and he needed to get to the station quickly for his catch up meeting. Having waited so long for the information, which was then given quite casually in the conversation, he now had two names. He knew Alice's killers! It took a few moments but it was finally dawning on him and he sat back to let the fact sink in. He had two names to take to the DCI and that was just brilliant, more than brilliant, it was fantastic. He forgot for the moment that Bam Bam seemed to know what his movements were and he forgot to question how and why. He got up and raced back to the station buzzing with a thrill and determination he hadn't felt for a long time. He had names to give to his DCI, the case had to stay with him now. Life was getting good but the dark clouds were not far away.

As he entered the busy front office of Ilford Police station, Bob called out to him and asked if all was OK. Jazz shouted that he was in a hurry and he would catch him later. Bob smiled and shrugged. Jazz instantly regretted his throw away comment. Bob was the only real friend he had in the police and he didn't want to lose his friendship. Jazz shouted that he'd meet him in the Cranbrook at 6 p.m. Bob was going to shout back OK but all he could see was Jazz's back as he ran up the stairs, taking the steps two at a time. He smiled, this was typical Jazz when he was all fired up on a hot case. He would wait for him in the Cranbrook and see if he turned up at 6 p.m.

Sharon and Tony were waiting for him. It was 11.30 a.m. and time was ticking on. He had requested and got a side office to set up for his enquiries. He had explained that all his enquiries were highly confidential and certain names had to be protected. He had alluded to his undercover contacts and how they needed to be protected. DCI Radley was giving him what he needed for the time being. He hoped his 2 p.m. meeting with him ensured he kept the case.

The storyboard was looking more interesting. There were pictures on there and he sat back and let Sharon and Tony explain what they had found out. He would keep the names he was given until last.

Sharon started. She said she had found out that Tiger Holdings was owned by a shipping company but when Stephen Paine searched the records it appeared that Tiger Holdings was nothing to do with shipping, and the details started to get quite fuzzy. The most that could be found out was that it was based in the Far East with a head office in Taiwan and the link to the shipping company was quite tenuous. Tiger Holdings was an import/export company that on the face of it bought and sold silk. But there were no records of any silk having been bought and sold and searching through all the information didn't show what else it bought and sold, if anything. There was a reference in an obscure sub-subsidiary company of Tiger Holdings, called Eastern End Company, to a Mr Tran Tan Giap. He appeared to be the owner of the car.

It all sounded very confusing and strange. Sharon said that Stephen could investigate more if necessary. He said it would take a long time to unravel the company. In his experience, they had something to hide. No legitimate company, even those trying to find legitimate ways of saving tax, would go to all this trouble. There was more to this than he could find in under 24 hours. Jazz asked him to continue to look. In summary, he asked Sharon to check out Mr Tran Tan Giap and see what she could find.

Tony pointed to the pictures on the storyboard. He told Jazz that these were the two identified by Lenny the postman. They were illegal immigrants who had been missing for over a year. Apparently, they had come to the notice of the police 18 months ago for handling drugs and there was a warrant out for them for failing to appear at court. Their names were Giang Nguyen and Tho Luong. To Sharon and Tony's astonishment, Jazz jumped up and punched the air, shouting yes! More excited than he had felt for a long time and breathless with adrenalin, he told Sharon and Tony that his informer had given him these names as the two men he was looking for and tomorrow he would know where they were. The case was theirs and sorted. He asked Tony to follow up with SOCO to find out if these two men's prints were found in Alice's house and the house next door. This would nail them. He asked Sharon to go and see Stephen and ask him to continue looking through the Tiger Holding Companies to see where that led.

It was 1 p.m. by the time they finished and he wanted some downtime before his meeting with DCI Radley. He had to get his story straight regarding Mr Singh and the ashes. He said that lunch was on him and he led both off to the canteen. Milly welcomed them with her best smile. She had a soft spot for Jazz; he always treated her with respect and made her laugh. She would blush to admit it, but she thought he had a thing for her and that made her feel very girly. Not bad for an older woman, she told herself.

As they sat eating, a few DCs came over to ask how they were getting on with the murder. Jazz was flattered they bothered. He knew he wasn't their favourite DS and he knew the rumours about the incident were rushing around the place like wild fire. Gossip in a police station was breathtakingly fast in the speed it got round and soul destroying in its bitchiness. Sharon and Tony had been told to watch their backs with Jazz. It was intimated by some and blatantly told by others that Jazz wouldn't be there for them if they got into serious trouble. He hadn't heard exactly what had been said but he could guess. Things hadn't changed much over the years at Ilford Police Station, he told himself. They had all agreed in the incident room that the answer to any questions regarding the murder was to be 'Everything is coming together and we should have something worth telling you within a day or so.' "You just don't know who to trust and what could be said within earshot of a villain. Police stations are full of villains," is what he told Sharon and Tony. "That is, after all, what police are paid to do; catch the bastards!"

Sharon wished him luck with DCI Radley and Tony chipped in and said they would wait outside to hear the verdict. They both wanted to keep this case and they could feel that they were getting close to nailing it. The adrenalin around the table could have powered a lighthouse for a week. Tomorrow would challenge their stamina, their skills and their nerve.

Lunch was good, steak and kidney pie with mashed potatoes and baked beans. Just what the doctor ordered, Jazz told his team. He didn't exactly tell them how Mr Singh's ashes had irreverently sat on the stones at Tilbury instead of wafting out to sea in a poetic fashion, but he did tell them he was in trouble. They sat discussing possible reasons why he had already scattered Mr Singh's ashes and it was interesting to see what weird and wonderful ideas came up. Sharon suggested aliens came down from a spaceship and took the urn full of ashes. Jazz discounted her idea. He suggested he could say something about the time of the month and when the moon was full the ashes had to be scattered. All thought that sounded complicated because no one knew what the moon was doing anyway. Another suggestion was that the crematorium had lost the ashes. They suggested Jazz dropped the urn as he left the crematorium and the ashes blew away. It was getting silly now and Jazz looked to them for something credible he could use.

Tony was the most imaginative. "Okay," he began, leaning back in his chair. He looked at each of them and, seeing he had their full attention, continued. "Relatives of Mr Singh came from India, unbeknown to you, and took the ashes back with them. When you went to collect the ashes, they had gone."

It was a fantastic answer to his problem. Jazz grasped his idea with both hands. Simple and easy and very believable. He patted Tony on the back and promised him a drink later. It was bloody brilliant. It shouldn't upset DCI Radley and with a bit of luck and the wind in the right direction they would get to keep the case too. He went to his meeting feeling much more confident than he had earlier in the day. DCI Radley was, as usual, behind his desk waiting for Jazz.

THE BOND AND THE PROMISE

It was strange, they had worked together for a few weeks before Jazz came on the scene. They coped alone with the newness of the job and the brutal teasing newbies got in a police station. It wasn't until Jazz arrived that they looked on each other as work partners. Jazz was like a blender, when he arrived, everything got stirred up and whisked together. They had both bonded with Jazz and were in the process of bonding with each other. His way of working was unique and it worked. In the short time Jazz had been around, both Sharon and Tony felt invincible as part of his team. They could see he was a winner. It was a good feeling, if somewhat dangerous. There was always someone ready to poke a stick at complacency.

Sharon and Tony waited in their investigation office with their fingers crossed. They knew the case shouldn't have been given to them. They also knew that Jazz seemed to have nine lives and they reckoned he would talk the DCI into giving them more time. They had names, the car registration, and they were close to getting the killers.

Sharon was on the phone to Stephen, sweet-talking him into taking on the job of delving into the affairs of

Tiger Holdings and giving it his full attention. Stephen moaned that he had enough to do but Sharon was adamant that this was a very sexy case with murder, drugs and goodness knows what else. Much better than the dry cases he usually dealt with. She said she would help him and she would do anything he wanted her to do. Tony listened and wondered what she was going to help him with. Her voice was suggesting more than paperwork. When she came off the phone, Tony murmured that perhaps she was offering too much. Sharon laughed and told him to bog off. She knew what she was doing and hadn't offered anything other than help with the files.

Tony phoned the Fingerprint Department. After a few minutes' discussion, he was put on to the head of the department and it was agreed he was to email through the fingerprints of the two men picked out by Lenny. These would be looked at and compared with the fingerprints found in the murder victim's house and the cannabis factory next door. He was promised results by the next morning. It was understood how urgent this was because it was a murder enquiry. The paperwork was up to date; they had built two files of papers so far. They had set the wheels in motion and now all they could do was sit and wait for Jazz to return and hopefully tell them they still had the case.

Doors certainly opened when you mentioned you were working on a murder enquiry. If it had been one of their small-time thefts, they would have had to join the queue along with other officers waiting to have fingerprints examined. The murder enquiry gave them a heady sense of superiority, prestige and deference. The two of them said how fantastic it was to be involved in this case and they could get used to the treatment you got from everyone involved when on a murder investigation and they didn't want to lose the case, not when they were getting somewhere. They couldn't believe their luck. Two rookie Detective Constables working on a murder case had never been heard of before. They were beginning to think that Jazz was either a saint or the devil to have this luck. They hoped his luck would last. If he had made a pact with the devil, they didn't care, they just wanted to keep this case.

They chatted whilst waiting. Sharon realised she knew nothing about Tony. They had been so busy getting to know the station and how it worked, and then all hell was let loose when Jazz arrived, that they just hadn't had time to properly get to know each other. She asked where he lived and he told her he lived with his parents. That sounded odd to her, but then, she thought, she was very independent and had left home as soon as she could. She wasn't that old before she got married to the bastard. She asked Tony many questions about who he went out with, what sort of girl was he looking for but stopped for a moment when she noticed he was looking a bit uncomfortable. Tony was a nice looking chap. Nothing special, but also nothing out of place, no big nose or horrible teeth and he had all his hair. He didn't smoke and he didn't drink much. She wondered what he did do. Her questions got more and more personal and he told her to stop. After a pause, she asked quite blatantly if he was gay. He was mortified by such a question and answered that he was celibate and not gay. She was quite mystified by such an answer and changed the subject completely and asked if he liked modern music or classical. They discovered they both loved blues music and a bit of classical. Sharon reckoned Tony would make a good friend with no strings attached. She had always wanted a gay man as a friend; all the pleasure of a man without the sex. She wouldn't raise the issue of whether he was gay or not again, she figured he would tell her in his own time.

There were things that Tony never told anyone. He would never call himself gay. He was ashamed that anyone would think that about him. He was in his teens when he discovered he wasn't interested sexually in girls. They just didn't appeal to him. He tried the usual fumbles with a girl but he wasn't interested and it actually sickened him. He had never done that with a boy; he never would, he told himself. There was a young man called Anthony who lived near him that he was friends with. He was blonde and slightly built. He had an air of grace and moved like a dancer. Tony was entranced and charmed by him. He had hands with the longest and most beautiful of fingers that tapered exquisitely and Tony loved to watch them wrap themselves around a book or hold a pen. For some time he followed Anthony around, just waiting for him to look at him or speak to him.

Eventually it became obvious to everyone that Tony was acting more like a lovesick fool than a schoolboy friend. Anthony was not allowed to hang around with him anymore and Tony's mum banned him from going out after school for quite a while. She never mentioned why but her tight-lipped frown said it all. All she ever said to Tony was "Nice boys don't do things like that." The statement was never explained but he thought he must never ever again think about male friends.

Tony carried the guilt of just looking but not touching into adulthood and even his adult knowledge of life could not shake his mother's statement. He decided to call himself celibate. He pushed all sexual thoughts and needs into the background and refused to let them come out to play. He was fooling only himself.

Tony, wanting to get off the conversation about him, asked Sharon about her life and she gave him the potted version. She left home at 16 years and lived in a house with two other girls and a boy. She worked in retail until she joined the police force. She met her husband, who was also in the job, and was married for quite some time before she found out he was on the job with some other woman. She divorced him and enjoyed her freedom. She didn't mention that her freedom entailed sleeping with as many men as she could. After some time, she got it all out of her system and realised it was all meaningless. Her career was her goal now. She wanted a man she could rely on and yes, she wanted a good sex life, but she wasn't going to take as many lovers as she had at Bethnal Green. She knew she could get any man she set her mind on and for the moment knowing that was enough. Jazz would have done her nicely, she liked him and she liked his attitude, which she found very sexy indeed, but if she had learned nothing else, she had learned not to mix business with pleasure. He was safe for the time being.

Now they had both shared a little about their lives she wanted it sealed with a handshake. She held out her hand to Tony and said, "Let's shake on it. We will be buddies and I am there for you." She was a forceful girl, and Tony was taken aback by such a display. He looked at her and hesitated for a moment. Something must have touched him, for he smiled and shook her hand in agreement. Neither would have picked the other as a friend, they were too different in temperament and style, but they each had things in their past they would rather bury. Perhaps that is why they needed to make this alliance work. They would certainly need a buddy to watch their backs in the next few days.

With Sharon in control and Tony embarrassed by such a display of comradeship, they both sat and waited for Jazz to appear. As they were drinking their third cup of coffee, Jazz breezed into the room. He stood still and they looked for some sign on his face of whether it would be good news or bad. He was having none of it and made them wait. He asked for a cup of coffee and threw himself into a chair.

Whilst Sharon was fetching the requested coffee, Tony enquired, "Well?"

To Tony's dismay, Jazz shook his head. "We will wait for Sharon before I tell you," was the answer. Tony nodded, relieved that the shaking of the head had nothing to do with not having the case and more to do with not saying anything until Sharon came back. The tension was high and they both sat tightly and quietly waiting for Jazz to tell them the news. He blew on his coffee and sipped it tentatively "God this is hot," was all he said. He knew he was being a bastard but they could wait a few more seconds.

"Come on, skip, tell us," was Sharon's whining plea. Both were fidgeting now and enough was enough, they needed to be told.

"We keep the case for a week," was all Jazz said.

The scream from Sharon and the shout of "Yeeessss" from Tony was heard in the CID general office. It didn't need saying but Jazz told them they had to work hard to get this case finished. The paperwork had to be perfect, and DCI Radley wanted to see the prepared papers in the morning to ensure all was up to scratch. They raised their coffee cups and chinked them together, the case was theirs and they were going to solve it! Just then there was a tap on the door and an officer entered saying they needed to get to the CAD room immediately, a couple of bodies had been found in a house in Ilford.

Charteris Avenue was nearer Newbury Park than Ilford. It was a tree-lined road with very pretty terraced houses and small front gardens. The house was on the corner of Charteris Avenue and Benton Road. Jazz had his gloves on this time. Jenny, the SOCO, was already there, moaning as usual.

"Are you the only SOCO ever on duty Jenny?" was Jazz's cheery hello.

She muttered something filthy in his direction and carried on looking at the bodies. He was told to wait outside for 10 minutes and then she should be finished. He had a cigarette and told Sharon and Tony to look around. The flask in his pocket called to him and he turned and took a quick swig. He felt edgy; he wanted to know who these two were. He had been called because it was supposed it was something to do with his case. He needed to find out why.

Jenny joined him for a cigarette. John, her assistant SOCO, was told to get on with his job. She was a tyrant to work for, Jazz thought.

"OK, my darling, what have you got for me?" he asked with the sweetest of smiles.

She looked at him and muttered something about him being too bloody fresh and told him the doctor said they had been electrocuted. He reckoned they had been dead about 24 hours. An anonymous phone call came through to Ilford telling officers to go to this address. They were Vietnamese by the looks of them. She said they were in the process of setting up another cannabis factory. The wiring was in ready for the lamps. She reckoned they tapped into the live mains and got careless. She took fingerprints and yes, she knew what he would say, and yes, she would get him an answer by the morning. He kissed her on the cheek and asked if he could go inside. She protested at his kiss just enough to make him realise she enjoyed it. On her say so he went inside. The mortuary van arrived but before they were taken away, Jazz took a look at the bodies. He called in Tony and got confirmation that they were looking at the bodies of Giang Nguyen and Tho Luong.

Jazz was furious. This pair were expert at setting up cannabis factories, so how come they were electrocuted? It didn't make sense. He wanted to talk to Bam Bam. Just as he was taking his phone out to ring him, a call came through from Ilford Police Station. A house in

Barking had been torched and two bodies had been found inside. It looked like another cannabis factory. Jazz grabbed Sharon and Tony with the words "Bloody Hell, doesn't anyone around here live a normal life? Another cannabis factory and bodies found in Barking."

They put on the blue light and the siren and Tony drove to Barking at break neck speed, while they shouted at drivers ahead of them. Confused by the siren and not knowing what to do, these drivers stayed where they were, causing Tony to screech and mount the pavement to get away. They were all hoarse from shouting at all the fucking stupid drivers who got in their way by the time they arrived at the house in Barking.

While they were travelling, a call came through from Ilford CAD room to tell them a body was floating in Barking Creek. It looked like either a Vietnamese or Chinese man aged between 25 years and 35 years. A doctor said this person had been shot in the back of the head. Jazz asked, "What the hell is going on? This is like *CSI Criminal Intent* on the television. Who the fuck is doing this?" None of them could contain their excitement. Never before in the history of East London, well not since the Krays, had so much be going on; within a space of an hour, five men had been killed. There had to be a turf war being organised was all Jazz could think. It had to be contained because he wouldn't be allowed to keep such a huge case. "The drug bastards should rot in hell for doing this now. They are gonna get my case taken away from me," was all he could say.

The fire was smouldering when they arrived in

Barking. The bodies had been taken to the local mortuary. The fire chief said it looked like the fire had been started deliberately but wouldn't confirm this just yet. The bodies were found trussed up in the bedroom upstairs and it looked like the fire had been started around and on the bed where the bodies were found. Jazz left knowing he would get a full report tomorrow.

They went to the mortuary in King George's Hospital. Luckily they had also brought the body from Barking Creek there. It was confirmed all were Vietnamese or Chinese. Again, there was a promise that there would be a post mortem and report within the next couple of days but off the record all had been killed and the body in Barking Creek had a gun wound in the back of the head that looked like it had been inflicted at close range and very much like a contract killing. The two burnt bodies had been tied up with chains. The fire would have taken some time to become a furnace and they would have burned slowly. In answer to Jazz's question, the pathologist said, "Yes, it looked like they had been burnt alive." The pathologist stated this in quite a matter of fact way and was surprised to see the three of them in such distress. The colour had drained out of Jazz's face at this bit of information, Sharon looked close to passing out and was holding onto the wall to steady herself. and Tony was open-mouthed in shock. They were in the police force but this sort of thing never happened on their shift. The brutality and the pain of these killings took their breath away. The pathologist got on with his work, he was used to such things. He was used to dealing with inanimate bodies and never gave a thought to what they were or how they felt before death. To him, their deaths were a puzzle to be solved.

Jazz told Sharon and Tony to do all the necessary paperwork to tally up all the victims and to get systems operating so everything was sent to their office as soon as possible. He would see them in the morning but he told them to ring him if anything cropped up. It was a waiting game with forensics again. This was getting stupid. He was off to talk to Bam Bam to find out what the fucking hell had been going on. He needed a drink and once outside, he took a good long swig from his flask and had a cigarette. He needed time to think. He drove to Bam Bam's office for some answers.

THE BEGINNING OF THE END

He arrived unannounced which, on reflection, was stupid. What if Bam Bam wasn't there? He would be stuffed for answers. He needed to know what was going on. He saw in the road Bam Bam's Mercedes, registration BBB1. He had to be in the office. The minder on the door was very obstructive and wouldn't let him pass. Jazz showed his police badge but that didn't help. It took a bit of shouting and swearing before the oaf on the door called up on his radio to another oaf inside. Bam Bam could see Jazz on the CCTV. He was almost jumping up and down with frustration at being kept waiting. Bam Bam decided to make him wait a bit longer. He didn't allow anyone to come barging into his office when they felt like it. They had to be invited and Jazz needed to learn a lesson. He sat drinking tea and eating a cake whilst he watched what was going on outside.

After thirty minutes, Bam Bam nodded to his bodyguard beside him and he went and fetched Jazz, who had now calmed down and was waiting patiently. He finished his cigarette and walked in when beckoned by the bodyguard. Bam Bam was sitting behind his desk; he waved Jazz to sit on the chair in front of the desk. He beckoned for more tea and cakes and the bodyguard nodded to someone waiting at the office door. They scurried away quietly to collect a tray and serve Bam Bam and his guest. This was done within a minute. Jazz reckoned they permanently had a tray of fresh tea and cakes ready for Bam Bam whenever he called. It was a good service and Jazz reckoned even royalty wouldn't get served this quick. It showed how powerful Bam Bam was in every area of his work, people jumped to attention when he looked at them.

Bam Bam knew why Jazz was here but he would wait until asked before he said anything. The phone on his desk rang and he picked it up and listened. Jazz could vaguely hear a voice on the other end; Bam Bam grunted once and after a minute he put the phone down. He looked up at Jazz and said there had been another house fire and a body had been found in Newham. Jazz knew Bam Bam was either involved in all of the killings or was very aware who was. There had been two fires and six bodies, all within 24 hours. It was all getting out of hand.

Jazz asked who had killed Giang Nguyen and Tho Luong. Bam Bam couldn't answer directly. He hinted that perhaps one of the Holy Trinity were just paying them back for killing the old lady and bringing the business to the attention of the police. The first fire and the two killed in the house in Barking was retaliation by the Triads. The victim in Barking Creek was also the interlopers' man and the latest fire was a Snakehead house so the interlopers were retaliating. Bam Bam said that his business was on red alert for any trouble. Jazz asked for the name of the head of the interlopers and he said Tran Tan Giap was the boss. Jazz knew that name, he was the owner of the Mercedes seen next door to Alice. God, it was all coming together. He needed to find this Tran Tan Giap. Bam Bam laughed, he said what the frig did he think they were all doing? Everybody wanted to find this Tran Tan Giap. Nerves were getting frayed and the killings had to stop.

Bam Bam was waiting to go home. He said his wife had been sent to his daughter's home in Spain for a few weeks until this all died down. Jazz asked how Sandeep was these days. Bam Bam relaxed a little and his face shone. She was pregnant and doing well. He hoped she would have a son. Apparently she was due in the next four months and with a bit of luck Mrs Bam Bam might stay out there for longer than a few weeks. He thought she would be safer there. His home was not as safe as it could be and some of his men were working on securing it from the interlopers, he was waiting for their call to say he could go home.

Sandeep was pregnant, now that was great, Jazz told himself. A little of him felt quite jealous though. He liked Sandeep a lot and hoped her husband was kind to her. He would have waited on her hand and foot if he had married her. She was very special. He saw the latest picture of her on Bam Bam's desk. She looked older but finer. She was a very serene and beautiful woman, no wonder Bam Bam was so proud. He unconsciously felt the bangle she had given him. He had never taken it off.

Getting back to the situation in hand, Jazz asked what the next step was in finding Tran Tan Giap. Bam Bam said his men were working with Snakehead and

Triad men to find where he might be hiding. It was thought he was somewhere in Central London. Jazz asked if anyone had a picture of this man but no one had seen him. Jazz would get someone to check the police systems to see if the name meant anything to anyone. He looked at his watch and saw it was nearly 6 p.m. and he was meeting Bob in the Cranbrook. He left Bam Bam with the news that if Tran Tan Giap was found, Jazz must be the first person to be told. Everyone was holding their breath and hoping the killings had stopped.

As he left Bam Bam's office, he phoned Sharon and asked her to check out the name of Tran Tan Giap and see what she could find. He said he was on the end of the phone if she needed him. Tony had taken himself off to check out an address he found written on a piece of paper found in the burnt-out house. Again, it was a waiting game. He wished it worked like on the films, where information was got instantly. Tomorrow should bring forth some news.

He checked his phone and saw he had four missed calls from DCI Radley. "Yea gods, that man is stalking me," was all he could say. In reality he knew his time was limited, the case would have to be handed over to the murder squad now. He realised they would already be at Ilford Police Station setting up. Still, he reckoned, there was time to get this Tran Tan man and avenge Alice, placate DCI Radley, solve the gang murders and keep his reputation for always catching his man. He smiled ruefully and thought, who the hell did he think he was, superman?

FRIENDS

He got to the Cranbrook pub about 6.30 p.m. and saw Bob sitting there with a pint of Stella. By now Jazz was exhausted. All the adrenalin that had kept him buzzing and on his toes had vanished and been replaced by cement in his legs. He could hardly walk, he was so tired. He didn't intent to stay long, just long enough to have a chat and a drink with Bob and then he was off home to sleep. Tomorrow was going to be tough.

Bob smiled when Jazz sat down. He got up and ordered a pint of Stella for him, he knew what he would drink. They had a comfortable friendship that went back years and it was only Bob who stayed a good friend after the incident all those years ago. Everyone else had turned their back on him and life was bad. Bob had taken him out for a drink regularly and checked if he was OK. Jazz would never forget that.

When Bob asked how things were going, Jazz outlined what was happening. The killings had got all officers running around the boroughs; Bob warned that Jazz needed to keep a low profile because the murder squad were now in place and would have him for breakfast if they knew what he knew. Jazz said tomorrow would be the day he landed the big fish.

Sharon was working with Steve and Tony was off to an address in Forest Gate, which he hoped will give out some clues. Bob asked where in Forest Gate because he knew that area himself. Clinton Road close to Forest Gate Station was all Jazz could remember. He didn't think it would amount to much but it was good that Tony was on the case and trying. Sharon and Tony would ring him later and update him. Bob thought that, as usual, Jazz had everything under control and he wouldn't tell anyone at the station where Jazz was tonight. He slapped Bob on the back and thanked him for being a good friend and got up to leave. It was 8 p.m. and, after three pints of Stella, it was time to go. It would be a very early start tomorrow and he needed to sleep and think.

MRS CHODDA'S HELPER

He let himself in and looked up to see Mrs Chodda at her kitchen door. If she saw his face drop, she didn't show it. Instead, she gave him her brightest smile and said she had a hot cup of tea and samosas for him. She could tell he was searching for an excuse to not enter her kitchen but she pre-empted him and said it would be for 10 minutes only and then he could leave. With a reluctant smile and more good grace than he felt, he followed her into her kitchen.

She stood there a vision of loveliness, a young woman in a bright blue sari, black hair falling to her shoulders and shining with health. She had a minimal amount of jewellery on, as befits an unmarried woman. Her eyes were looking to the ground in modesty and grace. He groaned inwardly. Not tonight, please, he begged to himself. With a sweep of her hand, Mrs Chodda bade him sit at her table in the kitchen. She went to the stove and called the vision of loveliness to her. The tea and samosas were brought serenely to him and he thanked her. He asked her name and she whispered Sandeep. This struck a deep chord with him. It was a common name but seeing another Sandeep today felt strange. He smiled at her and said how lovely she looked.

With Mrs Chodda ensconced by her stove, Sandeep looked quickly to ensure she was not looking or listening and then whispered urgently to Jazz, "Look, you're OK but you are too old for me. So don't think for one minute I am interested in you. You know and I know we are being set up. Let's just play the game and be pleasant, but bollocks to all of this, I am not fucking agreeing, OK?"

He nearly dropped the cup. Gee, the vision of loveliness had turned into a demon. He stammered to say something and then, choking on his tea, he laughed. He couldn't stop. This was the funniest ever. There was him thinking he was being set up and she didn't want him anyway. He tried to look sad at such a comment but it didn't work. Mrs Chodda was looking now and thinking they were getting on very well. She was pleased. She would invite Sandeep again to her house to see Mr Singh. She would give them a few more minutes to chat.

Jazz contained himself and looked up at a perplexed vision of loveliness and said, "Although I am distraught, I agree with you. I am far too old for you. But I suggest you are careful how you talk to future prospective husbands, don't get yourself in trouble with your family."

She smiled and said she was studying law and had no intention of marrying anyone she didn't want to. Jazz knew all about the problems with old traditions and modern Sikh women. Times were changing. She was feisty enough to get her way, he thought.

Mrs Chodda was very happy indeed. She made Jazz

eat some more samosas and got Sandeep to pour him another cup of tea.

"By the most merciful god, Mrs Chodda, these are the best samosas I have ever tasted." Jazz gratefully sang her praises.

Mrs Chodda beamed with pleasure. She looked at him and then at Sandeep and her smile got broader. After some aimless chit chat and a potted history of how wonderful Sandeep's family were and how she was a good girl studying hard at law school, Jazz was allowed to leave. He thanked Mrs Chodda graciously and said goodbye to Sandeep, who had resumed her modest look. As he climbed the stairs he smiled but thought wearily, what a day he had had. Murders, marriage, arson, drugs, gang warfare and samosas, what a mixture.

He got a large vodka and sipped it urgently as he sat down and rang Sharon. She was working late with Steve and said it was getting complicated. He tried to ring Tony but there was no reply, it went to answerphone. He figured Tony would have rung him if there was anything to report. He left a message and said to meet him and Sharon in McDonald's at 7.30 a.m. tomorrow morning. He didn't want to go into the police station before they had a chance to swap information. He would ring Bam Bam in the morning for an update. He looked at the clock and saw it was getting on for 10 p.m. so time for another cigarette and a large vodka and he would then go to bed. He slept soundly until 6 a.m.

CONFESSIONS OF A SMACK HEAD

He had six voicemail messages from DCI Radley on his phone. The first one was tense but reasonable. By the sixth voicemail he was shouting and ranting and promising to see Jazz stripped of his rank and frogmarched out of the Met Police. Jazz could tell he was not best pleased with him. He sent a text message to his DCI just saying he would see him by lunchtime and explain all then. God, he hoped he would have something worth handing over by then. He got washed and dressed, drank a fanta and felt better for the sugar rush. He had left his room by 6.30 a.m. and started to walk towards Ilford town centre. He wanted to get to McDonald's before Sharon and Tony arrived. A few minutes to think and a few minutes of peace before the storm. It was going to be one hell of a day and he didn't want the murder squad to take all his thunder. This was his case and he wanted to finish it his way. If that sounded arrogant then bollocks, he didn't care.

McDonald's was about two minutes from Ilford Police Station but he hoped no one from the station would see him in there. He was about to go in when he felt a hard tap on his shoulder. Before he turned around, he knew who it was, the smell gave him away.

"Hello, Pete, what are you doing up so early and what the fuck are you doing here?" He turned to see Mad Pete looking worse than ever, something Jazz didn't think possible, and in a state of extreme tension and panic.

"They're gonna do 'im in, Mr Singh. They're gonna come and get me and do me in too. You is gotta help me." That was a long sentence for Mad Pete and Jazz changed his mind about commenting on the state of him and pulled him into McDonald's.

They found a table in the corner. It wasn't too busy yet so no one else had to suffer the smell. He got two coffees and lots of sugar. Mad Pete loved lots of sugar. He ordered a McMuffin breakfast for two with some chips. Mad Pete was trying to control himself but failing miserably. His hands shook and it took a few minutes for him to lift the cardboard coffee mug and sip it. Jazz looked at his hands and nails, there was enough dirt on them and under the nails to grow potatoes. Why would anyone live like that by choice, he asked himself. The council had given him a flat which if kept clean would be very nice. Jazz seemed to remember they also paid for new furniture and a TV and kitchen equipment. He did bloody well and then spent the rest of the time making sure it all got filthy and misused and broken.

Mad Pete had a drug problem that went back more years than Jazz remembered. He had been in prison, in rehab and eventually seemed reasonably clean of drugs. The methadone became a habit but it was a legal habit and so overlooked. He was rehabilitated to Barking and Social Services bent over backwards to make him comfortable. Looking at him now, Jazz wondered if they should have just left him in prison and thrown away the key. He was the most useless article in the cosmos. Something had spooked him, and Jazz waited patiently to find out what.

After eating the McMuffin and chips and slurping the coffee loudly, Mad Pete looked ready to talk.

"I ain't eaten for days, Mr Singh, there 'as been stuff going on."

Jazz leaned forward and started to get a bit interested. "Like what, Pete?" Pete squirmed in his seat and considered what he was going to say. Jazz looked at his watch; Sharon and Tony would be there in 20 minutes and he wanted Pete out of the way, he stunk.

Getting impatient, Jazz said, "Come on, Pete, spit it out." Seeing chips still rolling around Pete's mouth, he quickly added with disgust, "Not literally."

He goaded him a bit more and told him to get on with it. Pete was not going to be hurried, he thought about how to start. He felt for the moment warm and fed and safer than he had for the last 10 hours. He told Jazz that he had done some stuff over the years but he would never be party to murder.

Jazz sat up and took notice. "Murder? What the fuck do you mean? What murder?"

Pete was trying to stay calm, but Jazz was spooking him again. The enormity of what he was going to tell him was making him more frightened by the minute. He started to tell Jazz about the murders that had happened in the last few days. Jazz interrupted him and said he knew of these. He wanted to know what this was all about. He told him to fucking sort himself out and start from the beginning and no excuses.

Mad Pete looked at him and said slyly, "You don't know nuffink, Mr Singh. I know everyfink." Jazz looked and couldn't believe Mad Pete was talking to him like this. Where did this low life get so much confidence? The look on Jazz's face made Pete concentrate and tell all. He needed his help, he didn't want to antagonise him.

He told him that a few years ago someone else had come into town. They sold drugs cheaper than the usual crowd. They were setting up shop in most parts of the East End. He watched his step with the Triads and the Snakeheads. No one in their right mind would mess with them but this new lot were very accommodating and generous. They gave him stuff for free. He looked at Jazz with a certain amount of pride and said that all the young lads in Barking and around looked up to him and he gave them bits and pieces from time to time. The heroin was so easily available that he was now back on the stuff. Jazz looked at him, shocked that he had gone back down that path. He spluttered that it was given to him for nothing, they just wanted to have him on their side and this was his reward. He said it wasn't a problem and he felt good on it. Jazz gave him a look of *you have got to be kidding yourself, sunshine.*

In answer to a question from an incredulous Jazz, he said no, he hadn't worried if it upset the Triads or Snakeheads. He reckoned he was just a small cog and they wouldn't notice. Again Jazz gave him a look of *you are definitely kidding yourself.* So when, he asked, did the Triads or Snakeheads get heavy with him? Mad Pete looked down and rather sheepishly said the last few days had been a nightmare.

He told Jazz that since he left Ilford all those years ago, the place had changed. It had been comfortable and he knew who was who and who to avoid. The new lot jiggled things up, he told Jazz. He went on and explained as best he could the set up as he saw it.

"They pushed a bit and I didn't understand why there was no trouble. The Triads and Snakeheads are not to be messed with. I sort of figured they weren't bothered anymore. The Viets started to give me stuff and I figured it was OK. It was good stuff, Mr Singh. I would have been mad to pass it up." He fidgeted in his chair and gave Jazz a look that passed for embarrassment. "I was stupid, Mr Singh. I didn't read the signs."

Pete pulled himself together and, feeling comfortable, took a slurp of coffee and continued. "It all changed a few days ago when that old bird got killed in Newbury Park." He saw Jazz shift and move forward, now very interested indeed. "It was the Viets who killed her and it seemed to start everyone off." He looked pained and for a moment very frightened indeed. "I 'ad visits from the Triads, who knocked me about wanting to know who my contact was. I told them everything I knew but it was nothing much, just a street level thug. It was 'orrible, Mr Singh, I was very scared they were gonna kill me. Then I got a visit from the Snakeheads and they put a gun to my head. Well, I fair nearly dropped the contents of my belly there and then. I told them everything again but they hit me across the back of my head with the gun and left." He took off his cap and lowered his head for Jazz to see the mess of hair towards the back of his head where the blood had congealed. Jazz winced at the sight of it. Pete stopped for a second and the silence was heavy with apprehension and disbelief.

"What did they think you knew, Pete?" Jazz asked gently, he didn't want to spook him. He knew that when spooked, Pete would go into a panic that bordered on a drug-induced madness and he would never get all the information from him.

"Don't know, Mr Singh," was the truthful answer. "Think they just wanted a contact. They knew all the ground level Viets but they wanted to find out how to get to the top guys I suppose. Really odd, isn't it, Mr Singh? Thought they would have sussed all that out before, wouldn't you?"

Jazz sat for a few seconds and thought. He wondered what the hell was going on. It all sounded far-fetched and stupid. He understood from Bam Bam that the Triads and Snakeheads were just biding their time to take over. If that was the case, they would have sussed out the top people running it by now.

Sharon appeared; he looked at his watch and realised time had flown and he hadn't got anything out of Pete worth having yet. He waved to Sharon and told her to get some breakfast and a coffee for Pete and himself. She looked at Pete and remembered him and wondered what he was doing here. She was about to find out. It took a few minutes for Sharon to come back with the food and the coffees. She sat near Jazz and quietly listened and watched.

Pete looked at Sharon and clammed up. Jazz spent a few minutes reassuring him that Sharon was with him and he could trust her. Pete still looked uncertain and Jazz, fed up with him getting all poncy and pathetic on him, said through gritted teeth that he had better just get on with it otherwise he would be in serious trouble.

Pete looked up at him and said, "I'm in serious trouble now, Mr Singh, and it's all your fault!" It was getting really silly now and Jazz calmed Pete down and told him to drink his coffee.

Pete decided to continue and said that it started the day after Jazz and the other two had come to his flat. "The Viets think I am some sort of grass and wanted to know what I told you." Pete hugged himself for comfort. "Everyone is having a go at me, Mr Singh, and the Viets made me go to their place in Forest Gate. It was 'orrible; they ain't nice at all, Mr Singh."

Jazz tried to look sympathetic but he needed more information. Pete was not telling him everything. Kindly, Jazz told him that it made sense to just tell him everything. He promised he wouldn't judge him but if it was important he needed to know.

Taking a deep breath, Pete nodded and just said it out loud, to the shock and disbelief of the pair of them. "Well, Mr Singh, they are gonna kill the poof you have with you."

After a sharp intake of breath, Jazz asked him to repeat what he had just said. By now, Pete was settling, he had got their full attention and he was getting comfortable; he repeated that the man who was on Jazz's team, yes, the one called Tony, was going to be killed soon. He added that he thought they would have killed him too but he got away last night. Pete continued to bemoan the fact that everyone was out to get him and he had no where to go that was safe. He scratched his left armpit and looked up, surprised to see that the attention was not on him. Jazz was on the phone and so was Sharon.

"There is no answer from his phone, skip," was all Sharon could say. She looked at her phone as if she expected it to tell her where Tony was.

Sharon then rang Tony's home number to see if he was there. Tony's mother answered the phone. When asked if Tony was there, she took a deep breath and started a mournful rant about always being the last to be told anything; that Tony hadn't come home last night and he hadn't bothered to ring and tell her and how she had had a very fitful night worrying about him. She finished by saying children were so ungrateful and how she had done everything for him. Sharon thanked her and said when she saw him she would get Tony to ring her. As she was about to say goodbye, Tony's mum added, as an urgent afterthought, "Why are you asking? Wasn't he on duty with you?"

Sharon said that he wasn't but she felt sure he was somewhere and had just forgotten to tell anyone. They each knew this was highly unlikely. Even Sharon, who had known him only a short time, knew Tony would never go off all night without telling his mother. After further promises of contacting her as soon as Tony was found, a subdued Mrs Sepple said goodbye but was left with a nagging fear that her Tony was in some sort of trouble.

Having heard the conversation Sharon was having with Tony's mother and knowing Tony was not tucked up nice and snug in bed and having a duvet day, Jazz was on the phone to the office. It was out of his hands now, he needed help. Bob answered and said he would organise the SO19 team for him but he needed an address. In all the panic he had forgotten to ask Pete where in Forest Gate this house was. Pete didn't want to go back there, he never wanted to go anywhere near it again, but when questioned further, he said he didn't know the number of the house or the street name. He said he would recognise it if he was there but he wasn't going anywhere near it.

"I ain't going near that place, even if you got a van full of police and guns," he protested loudly.

Jazz grabbed him by the arm and pulled him at speed towards the police station and the car that was waiting for them there.

THE WRONG PLACE AT THE WRONG TIME

It had been one hell of a day. Tony was tired but he wanted to make his mark. Sharon found it all so easy and he just never seemed to get a look in. The bit of paper he found was more than he had told them. It was a small book with figures in it; some sort of accounts, he reckoned. Inside he found an address in Forest Gate and he wondered, nay hoped, it would make him the hero of the day.

It was all a bit much to ask for, and he knew that he was most probably chasing a wild idea but wouldn't it be great if he came across something useful? He should have passed this to Jazz, he knew that. But for once, why shouldn't he have a bit of stardust? He was always second best. This was the first time he had gone against standard police procedures and he felt a bit nervous. He shouldn't be on any sort of stakeout without backup or at least phone backup. Heck, he thought, if was nothing then no one would be any the wiser and if it was a good lead then they would forgive him and call him a hero. All the murders discovered today had made East London very unsettled. Every police officer on the beat was looking over his or her shoulder, not knowing what was going to happen next. All the small-time hoodlums were keeping quiet and watching what was going to happen next. It felt very surreal.

He picked up some Kentucky fried chicken and a Coke and sat outside the house. He had time, he was just going to sit and watch for a while. It was a dark road with trees that reached up and encompassed the sky and houses that seemed too tall for the narrow road. All the houses were bunched together, which made Tony feel a little claustrophobic .

Now he was here he wasn't sure what he was going to do. He hoped he would look inconspicuous in his Ford Fiesta, it wasn't an outstanding car. He loved his little Ford Fiesta. He felt comfortable in his car, it was his domain. Not even his mother would say anything about his car and she rarely went in it, preferring to take the bus to do her shopping. She said she enjoyed meeting her friends and going on the bus with them. On dark days Tony thought she enjoyed moaning about him and suspected she told her friends he never helped her with the shopping. She could be a bit of a martyr sometimes, he conceded. He couldn't remember his dad ever saying nice things to his mother. His dad died a few years ago and left him with the responsibility of looking after her. She was a wonderful woman in many ways and he sort of understood why she did some not very nice things; it was to get some attention.

Although she loved him, he knew he was a disappointment to her. She always said she wanted a daughter-in-law to talk to and she wanted grandchildren. Again, on dark days he thought she would hate another woman around her, although she could bitch happily about her, which might give her pleasure. As for grandchildren, she had never seemed that maternal to him. He lived uneasily with her disappointment. The least he could do was try and understand her and at the same time forgive her.

He ate the Kentucky fried chicken carefully. He hated the thought of dripping fat down his suit or on his tie. He only bought good quality suits, he knew it made him look good and younger, accentuating his lean and athletic look. His hair was the short spiky trendy look worn by a lot of young men and it suited him.

She would be ringing him soon to check where he was and he didn't want that tonight. This was his time. On that note, he took out his mobile phone and switched it to silent and tucked it in his inside pocket. It was one of the slimline phones that wouldn't make a bulge in his jacket.

He was enjoying just a little peace and quiet and time for himself. Life had been very busy of late and when he got home his mother never left him alone, always wanting to know what he had done during the day and who he had spoken to. He often thought that she was checking up on him, wanting to know if he had been a 'good boy'. She disapproved of his manicured nails and all the hand cream and face cream he used. He had taken to hiding it all in a locked cupboard in his room. He was a little fed up with all the funny looks she gave him. He loved his mother but sometimes, and he licked his lips to think of the right words, well, sometimes she was too interested in what he was doing. He knew she loved him and most of the time that was enough for him to forgive her intrusions. She would be worried for him if she could see him now, he thought. This made him smile. This was real police work.

He must have sat there for quite some time. He wasn't sure what he was going to do. It was getting very dark and the street lights were almost hidden by the branches of the trees. The shadows lengthened and made him feel the road was not a friendly place to be. Most of the houses had drawn curtains at their windows so no friendly house lights brightened the road, making the darkness more sinister and contained. The house he was watching had a glimmer of light which seemed to emanate from somewhere towards the back of what was the hallway; this boded well, he thought. He felt full and warm and comfortable sitting there. He felt so relaxed that when a car pulled up across the road, it made him jump. He slumped down in the seat and watched.

The car was a Mercedes and the man who got out with the aid of two henchmen was a big chap. Tony watched as he struggled to get out of the car. The man briefly looked around and his two henchmen went ahead into the house that Tony was watching. He waited until they had gone inside and shut the door behind them.

He realised he had to do something now. He couldn't just sit there. He didn't know if the tremor in his hands were caused by excitement or fear; he had never been in a situation like this before. He quietly got out of his car. By the look of the man and his two henchmen, this was not a family visit. He thought for a moment that he should ring into the station to tell them where he was, as protocol expected, but on reflection he rejected that idea. If it amounted to nothing, he would just look stupid. He told himself he would call them if it looked interesting and that made him feel better.

The houses had the smallest of front gardens. He noted that it would only take one step from the pavement and he would be up to the front door. He wasn't sure what to do. The light had been switched on in the front room. He could see light shining through the window even with curtains drawn. There was a small gap in the curtains and he carefully positioned himself so he could see through the gap but whoever was in there wouldn't see him. He peered in but he couldn't see much at all. The room was depressingly dim, he reckoned they had a 40 watt bulb for light. He couldn't make out anyone in the room. There was only a portion of the room he could see and no one was standing or sitting there. It was very frustrating and he nearly overbalanced and had to put his hand up on the window to stop him falling. He turned to go back to the car and ring the station for moral support. He suddenly felt spooked and ill at ease.

He never made it to the car. As he crossed the road to his Ford Fiesta, two men came up from behind him and, one on each side, they grabbed his arms and held him in a vice-like grip. One whispered in his ear, "You wanted to see what's inside, well this is your chance." He was hauled into the house and taken to the back room. He looked from one to the other to see what they were going to do. He told them that he was a police officer and he wasn't alone, but they just smirked at him and told him to sit down and shut up. He did as he was told and watched to see what their mood was. He was scared and had no idea what to do. One of the men had gone off and left him with a bored thug. He was well-dressed in a black suit. He looked like either a chauffeur or a funeral director. Tony shuddered at the thought. They knew he was a policeman and were most probably just trying to frighten him. That thought calmed him and the whirlwind of panic that was building abated. He was a professional and doing his job. He looked intently at the face of the thug in front of him. He would remember him in an identity line-up. They were not that clever. He would get them.

He could hear footfalls across the ceiling and voices coming from upstairs. It sounded like an argument. Someone was rushing down the stairs making a tremendous noise, each foot thumping the steps. Suddenly the door opened and in rushed Mad Pete. "What the bloody hell are you doing here?" was the breathless greeting from Mad Pete. Tony just shrugged, not knowing what was going on. The next moment, two Vietnamese people came rushing in and grabbed Pete. Something had upset Pete and he was going into one of his druggy hysteria sessions. The Vietnamese men looked perplexed by him and ushered him out of the room. The invasion knocked Tony out of his complacency and again he felt that panicky swell rising from his stomach. There was too much going on here and common sense kicked in. Why on earth would they keep him here and let him go? He could recognise everyone. No one had bothered to hide their face. They were going to kill him.

The thug looked at him and saw the panic. He walked over to Tony and put a hand on his shoulder. "Come on mate, its going to be OK. They will let you go soon, trust me. I know whats going on here." Tony looked at the smiling face and heard the soothing words but felt no better. Oddly, he thought being called 'mate' by this Indian guy sounded really strange. He asked when he could leave and the Indian guy said he would find out and left the room. Tony heard the key turn in the door. He was locked in and in an urgent panic looked around to see if there was an escape route. The window looked over the unkempt garden. It was pitch black outside; he looked at his watch and saw it was just past midnight. Time was passing so quickly and he had to get away. He thought of smashing the window and climbing out but saw a man standing in the garden smoking a cigarette. He wouldn't get far. He tried the door just in case but, as he feared, it was locked.

Just as he was about to descend into that feeling of hopeless panic, the door was unlocked. As he heard the key turn in the lock, time stood still for a few moments. He held his breath with fearful trepidation. What was going to happen to him and why had they kept him here? He was not a brave man, he knew that, but even a brave man would be frightened by the knowledge that he was alone and powerless and no one would come to his aid. He knew his weakness, which gave them all the trump cards and put him at their mercy.

The two men entered and saw before them a frightened man about to panic and become uncontrollable. They had seen such fear before. They were full of apologetic smiles and soft voices. The familiar one said, "Look, we are really sorry, but until we checked you out, we had no idea whether you were police or someone we have been having problems with." Tony relaxed for a second. "We are going to take you immediately to the police station and explain everything to your boss." The other thug walked around Tony and with a goodwill gesture brushed imaginary fluff off his shoulder.

Tony tried to say it was not necessary, he had his car outside and thank you anyway but he had to get going. They were having none of it and firmly stated that it was the police station they were taking him to and that was the least they could do. Their insistence made arguing futile so Tony allowed himself to be led out to a waiting car. He noted it was not the Mercedes that had arrived earlier but a Range Rover. It certainly wasn't there before. The three of them got in the back with Tony sandwiched in the middle. Tony asked where the other guy was that they arrived with. The thug he knew just grimaced, shrugged his shoulders and said, "He was no one in particular and left a while ago." Tony knew that was a lie. He had seen them arrive earlier and he had seen the way the two thugs had acted. Only bodyguards jump out of a car like they did. They ensured the man in the back of the Mercedes was safe and escorted him with deference into the house. He was most certainly an important man. Tony wished he knew who he was.

The car took off sedately. They took the road to the A12 and were coming up to the Redbridge roundabout, but instead of continuing along the A12, they shot off by the Redhouse pub towards Woodford. By the time they arrived at Charlie Brown's roundabout and were proceeding towards the Waterworks roundabout, Tony was feeling worried. "Why are we going this way?" he asked. "It's nowhere near Ilford Police Station." They looked at him and smiled. One said, apologetically, "We forgot to say we have just got to pick up someone who is coming to the police station with us. We need our brief cos we know there will be things to explain and he can do it better than us. He lives in Epping, which is just up the road from here." Tony wasn't sure he believed them but he preferred to give them the benefit of the doubt. The alternative didn't bear thinking about.

The road to Epping was long and dark. On either side of the road, the view was of the impenetrable forest. The branches of the trees seemed to spill onto the road and hover above them. In the darkness the trees took on frightening forms and gave Tony a sense of foreboding. The big leaf-bearing branches looked like triffids hunched over the car ready to envelope them. It was a very lonely and disturbing journey for Tony. The disquiet he felt was being quelled and held deep down in his bowels. The Range Rover took a right turn down a track into the forest. Tony sat up sharply and, panicking, asked why they were going this way. That disquiet was rising in his stomach and had reached his throat. The soothing answers were not helping him anymore. He didn't believe that the brief lived down this sort of track. It wouldn't be somewhere a man would live. Tony, in a panic, grappled to get over to the door to open it, but the thug just slapped him back. The soothing tones had gone and they told him to shut the fuck up and keep still.

He kept asking why they were doing this. He hadn't done anything to them. They ignored him. It took only a few minutes to reach the turn-off which led to a small glade The Range Rover came to a halt. Tony didn't want to get out; he held on and he pleaded again that he hadn't done anything to them and for them to let him go home to his mum. Everything was moving slowly and noises and voices were pitched so high that he could hear with a clarity he had never experienced before. They dragged him out onto the brambled ground. It was all so unbelievable, he must be asleep and this must be a nightmare. He could see them clearly standing above him. One reached into his coat and took out what looked like a gun. It couldn't be a gun. There was no reason to do this to him, he didn't want to die. He pleaded again loudly and tearfully that he would be a good boy, he promised. He tried to scrabble away but he had lost the power to move, his muscles all felt like pap. He held his breath and closed his eyes for the last time; they would never open again. The loud shot made the trees rustle; the second shot to his head seemed to echo around the glade.

They took his body into the wood and buried it; they had done this before. The conversation on the way back was far more jolly. They were going to a club that they knew stayed open all night. They deserved a drink. One was on the phone to the boss. All he said was "It's done." He was told the other one had got away but they would get him in the morning. They knew where he lived so no problem.

Tony's life had been lacklustre but in death he would

have been proud. He may have been surprised to know that his mother, on hearing of his death, would go into deep mourning and die from a broken heart one year later. His skipper, Jazz, broken with guilt and convinced it was his fault, would be back in counselling. Sharon, unnerved by his death, would weep tears for him and would also be wracked with guilt and believe it was her fault. His death had spectacular repercussions and made him a hero in police and public legends, which over the years grew far bigger than Tony could ever have achieved if he were alive. He would have been proud of the medal he received posthumously.

A DATE WITH FATE

To sit in a car with Mad Pete on a warm day with all the windows open was not something you would wish on your enemy. He was whining and moaning about not going back to that house. Sharon sat in the front and Jazz sat uncomfortably in the back next to Mad Pete. Jazz wanted to know more about when and where he saw Tony and who was with him.

Pete told him he was going to a house in Upney but the Viets took him to Forest Gate. He said he hadn't figured out why they took him there. He said they babbled excitedly in their own language to each other and he never knew what the fuck they were talking about. He was a bit scared to be taken to Forest Gate because he had never been there and everyone was edgy with all the tit for tat murders taking place. Someone wanted to know what had been said to him by the Triads and Snakeheads when they visited him. He turned to Jazz at this point and said, "Everyone seems to know what everyone else is doing. Everyone wants to know who I am talking to." He turned back and looked at his hands. "I don't want to be this important, Mr Singh. I just want to get back to my life. I liked my life before all this."

"So what happened when you got to Forest Gate?" Jazz wanted to move this conversation on a bit faster. "Well, I was taken into the back room and a Mr Tin Pan alley man, something like that anyway –"

Jazz interrupted. "Do you mean Mr Tran Tan Giap?"

Mad Pete nodded. "That sounds about right, Mr Singh. Do you know him?" Jazz shook his head and told him to get on with it. "Well, Mr Singh, this Mr Tin Pan wanted to know precisely who I had spoken to and when and what I had said. I told him it wasn't much. He asked if I knew any names but I didn't. I don't want to know nuffink, Mr Singh. It's too dangerous out there."

"So when did Tony come into this?" asked Jazz, trying to get this rambling man to move on. "Well, it wasn't long before some man comes in the door, he wasn't a chink, he was Asian and they told me to get upstairs and pushed me up there and into one of the rooms. I could hear someone come in downstairs. I was fed up now and wanted to go home. I had two of them talking ten to the dozen to each other in Viet language. They were getting very excited and I felt like a spare part, they didn't need me there. I was hungry by now, I wanted some dinner. I had been out all day, Mr Singh, with nothing to eat." Jazz told him to stop whining and get on with the story.

"After about 20 minutes I got really fed up and told them I wanted to go now." They said I had to stay up in the room until someone downstairs had gone, he was very important and if I valued my life I had better do what I was told." He looked at Jazz again. "I got into a

224

strop, Mr Singh, I don't know what came over me. I just pushed them out of the way and went downstairs. I must have been mad to do it. I ran into the back room and there was the poof sitting all comfortable with the Asian minder watching him. I could tell I wasn't supposed to see him and the two Viets came in and grabbed me and took me back upstairs." He looked sideways at Jazz; he had tears in his eyes, glistening in the corner. "I knew it was bad, Mr Singh. There was someone else in the front room and when I came out a minder was guarding the door to the front room and looked ready to top me. It was all wrong, Mr Singh, I knew it was really bad; something was going to happen and I was in the wrong place at the wrong time. I had to get away."

Jazz egged him on to tell him more. "Well, I was up in this room for ages and then there was movement downstairs. The two Viets had locked me in the room upstairs and I heard them go downstairs. I can pick any lock, Mr Singh, you know that, so was just biding my time. I heard the front door open and voices and I think I heard the poof's voice. It all sounded OK though, there was no shouting or screaming, just the odd word as they went out the door. When the door closed, I heard a conversation in English for the first time. Someone was on a phone in the hall I think and they said *He would be dealt with* and I thought that sounded bloody dodgy. They then said *Him too* and I thought they meant me. I was so scared, Mr Singh, I was shitting myself. It took me at least two minutes to pick the lock on the door, I was shaking so much. As luck would have it, the landing upstairs was empty. I climbed out of the window in the toilet onto the gabled roof and walked along a few roofs until I was away from that house. I climbed down a drainpipe and got away. I never knew I had it in me to do the climbing but I think it saved my life."

Jazz asked if he knew who was downstairs in the front room and he said he didn't know. He didn't think it was just Mr Tin Pan because he heard Mr Tin Pan's voice and another man's voice and they were deep in conversation.

"So you didn't know they were going to kill Tony, and you didn't know they were going to kill you?" Jazz asked.

"I heard the way they said *he was going to be dealt with,* Mr Singh, and it sounded really bad."

Pete was getting agitated now. They were close to Forest Gate Station and the road must be nearby. Jazz was not sure if Pete was on a drug-induced fantasy or whether there was something to worry about. Nevertheless, Tony was still not answering his mobile and they hadn't heard from him. It was not good. Sharon had sat quietly listening during the journey. She tried Tony's mobile number again, just in case. He still wasn't answering and she swore under her breath.

She looked up as a row started in the back of the car. Mad Pete was getting all panicky and Jazz was losing his temper. The police car had to stop until Mad Pete showed them which way to go. With a lot of shouting and arm waving, Mad Pete took them over the hill past Forest Gate Station and towards Wanstead Flats. Just as they came up to a road on the right, he shouted for the car to turn. They were in Carlton Road and the house they wanted was just over the road; he pointed, waving a dirty hand in the direction of number 29.

Within minutes, six police cars arrived; three were unmarked cars, two were standard police cars and one was a police van. Armed police jumped out of the van and positioned themselves around the house. It was done quietly and quickly. If Tony was in the house, they didn't want to spook the Viets into doing something they might regret. Neighbours watching had never seen so many police crammed into one small area. It was a hive of activity and above them was a police helicopter watching the surrounding area. A police car was parked in the next road and the officers were making their way into the rear gardens that backed on to 29 Carlton Road. No one was going to get away.

Jazz dragged Mad Pete from the car. He was struggling and shouting, "No, Mr Singh, don't make me go in there again."

Jazz told him through clenched teeth, "Shut the fuck up you bastard. The place is full of armed police, what more do you want?"

Mad Pete looked around and for the first time took in the swarm of armed police and uniformed officers. "Bloody hell, Mr Singh, they mean business alright." He was going to enjoy this. It wasn't often he was on the right side of the law and now he realised he was the important person who knew the house and could identify someone. The sight of the guns made him feel brave and fearless. "Come on, Mr Singh, let's get going."

Jazz let him go and watched, amazed, as this usually

sloppy and slow person walked across the road with a spring in his step. The sound of the door being knocked open stopped him for a second in his tracks but, on realising what they were doing, he happily continued up to the house. Jazz followed quickly and under his breath kept repeating, "Please God, let Tony be in there and OK, please God, please God." Sharon was not far behind, praying for the same.

Jazz waited whilst the armed police went in and scanned the house room by room. He listened to the voices shouting "Clear" when each room had been entered. As the dust was settling and it appeared no one was in the house, there was an eye of the storm calmness which was abruptly broken by a voice he knew. Jenny the SOCO had arrived. The usual moaning of "Yea Gods! Doesn't anyone leave a scene clear for me to examine?" reached him before she did. He turned to say hello and got out of her way. As she busied herself getting past him and dragging her box of tricks with her, he asked how the hell she got here so quick. She replied that Tom Black had called her and told her to get there pronto. She looked at Jazz and said somberly, "Of course I would come quickly, he said it was to do with the disappearance of a police officer. That gets top priority in my book!" He touched her arm in gratitude. What made Tom Black assume a SOCO was needed so quickly, he asked himself. The feeling of foreboding had gripped Jazz and it took his breath away.

He had to pull himself together, Tony was his Detective Constable and he was the one who would find him, not Tom Black from the murder squad. He put on a pair of rubber gloves he kept in his pocket and entered the house. He had to see for himself that Tony wasn't there. At least, he told himself, they hadn't found a body. He gave Mad Pete a pair of gloves and told him to put them on and not to touch anything. Mad Pete started to moan, so Jazz pushed him and told him to get a move on. Jazz was anxious, scared and fed up with so much time wasting, he wanted to see what was in the house and if there were any clues as to where Tony might be.

Looking at Mad Pete still moaning, he wondered if the man ever kept quiet. Jenny was in the front room taking fingerprints. He asked if they touched nothing, could they look in the back room. Mad Pete had told Jazz that was where they had kept Tony. Jenny looked up and said she was coming with him. No way was she going to let him corrupt any of the crime scene.

Mad Pete was poking the air with his finger in the direction of the only chair in the middle of the room. "There, there, Mr Singh. He sat on that chair there."

Jazz walked over to the barren chair. He sighed with disappointment. There was nothing at all around the chair. If only Tony had dropped something or left a clue; anything that would help them find him. "Are you absolutely sure he was here?" It occurred to Jazz that it might have been a drug-fuelled nightmare and instead of seeing little green men, Pete saw Tony.

Pete nodded insistently. "He was here, on that chair, Mr Singh, honest." Jazz's frustration was sobvious.

"Enough!" said Jenny. "Get out of my way and let me do my job here." She went and got her bag of tricks and they listened as she told anyone in her way or near the rooms to "fuck off and don't touch anything."

In a moment, she was back and dusting for fingerprints. She got out her magnifying glass, which was her way of working; not many used such a thing but Jenny was from the old school and Jazz suspected her eyesight wasn't quite as keen as the foul language she used and she needed this bit of help. Bent over the chair and peering intensely, she asked in a distracted voice, "Does anyone know what he was wearing?" Jazz hadn't a clue but Sharon told Jenny he was wearing a particularly nice light woollen suit in a charcoal grey with a sharp crease in the trouser to die for (she blushed at having made such a superficial comment at this time). She continued, saying that he was wearing a beautifully pressed white cotton shirt and a pink silk tie. Jazz looked at Sharon, amazed she remembered so much. He supposed it was because she was a woman and took an interest in such things. He just remembered that Tony always looked dapper, which was quite unusual for a Detective unless they were going to court.

Jenny smiled and thanked Sharon and with a pair of tweezers picked up the tiniest of threads caught on the smallest sliver of wood on the back of the chair. It was barely visible to the naked eye. Jenny exhaled, bit her lip and, with a smack of her lips, said "Aha" with deep satisfaction. She dropped it into a plastic bag and sealed it immediately. She caught Jazz's look of *well*? and said she wasn't certain but it could be a relevant piece of wool. The lab would tell them more. She continued to search and dust the chair. She took fingerprints, especially those around the rim of the seat of the chair. If Tony had been here, that is where his fingerprints would most probably be found. Jazz was so glad he had Jenny here. If there was anything to find, however small, she would find it.

They left her to get on with her job and went upstairs to see where Mad Pete had been kept that night and exactly what he did and who he saw when he left the room in a panic. It wasn't much help and Jazz came down the stairs as Mad Pete was showing him how he ran into the back room. He stopped and looked at the front room. He wondered who had been in there. It seemed as if Mad Pete could run around and had seen many faces but he wasn't allowed in the front room and the door was being guarded. It begged the question *why?*

Jenny would be in the back room for at least another hour, she was very thorough. He made sure no one entered the front room. He hoped she would find something of interest in there. He looked outside and saw a woman talking to a police officer so he went to see what was being said. Her name was Flora and she lived across the road. She was telling the officer what she saw last night. It was about midnight and she was pretty mad at the noise outside. She told them everyone had cats down the street and she was woken by cats fighting and mewing. She got up to look out of her window onto the street below to see where they were. It was then that she saw three men coming out of the house across the road. She didn't think much of it other than that she didn't know who they were. She didn't have double glazing so she heard the men saying hello to the driver and something about a journey and the slamming of doors. She said the engine revved for a while and then took off. When she had seen all the police arrive earlier, she wondered if it was connected.

Jazz asked if she would recognise any of the men but she said no because it was dark, though she did say she thought they were all wearing suits. She said she couldn't see much but it looked like one of the men was being escorted to the car. When asked what that meant, she said they had his arm. It was distracting out in the street and Jazz suggested she came down to the station with him where it would be quieter to make a statement. She was happy to do that. He instructed the officers to knock on all doors and see if anyone else saw anything. Cases were always solved better when memories were still fresh. He thanked Flora for coming forward and sat her in one of the unmarked cars ready to go back to Ilford. If anyone else was spoken to, he told officers to bring them down to Ilford Police Station immediately. Flora was his for the moment.

He went back inside and asked Jenny to keep in touch with him and she promised to have everything analysed immediately; hopefully by the afternoon she would have some useful information. He went looking for Mad Pete, who was sitting round the back of the house giving himself a shot of heroin. Jazz overlooked what was happening for the moment. He couldn't have Mad Pete going through DTs and screaming all over the place at such a crucial time.

He took a spaced out Mad Pete back to Ilford along

with Flora, who seemed to find the smell a bit difficult so Jazz opened all the windows of the car. The journey back was interesting. Flora seemed quite an eagle-eyed person, which was fantastic. He was hoping if she saw a picture of Tony she might recognise him. Unfortunately she had watched television in the back room of her house but she slept in the front bedroom upstairs. Therefore she saw nothing all evening and it was only the noise of cats fighting that woke her up and made her look out of her window. He hadn't forgotten she said they got into a Land Rover; they would look further into that at Ilford Police Station. For the first time today he felt like he was getting a bit of a break; Flora was going to help make his day, he hoped. He felt sick in his stomach and badly wanted a drink. He just couldn't think of anything else other than where was Tony and was he alright and the unbearable thought that something bad might have happened and ultimately it was all his fault.

Sharon stayed behind to talk to neighbours and take anyone who saw or heard anything to Ilford Police Station for interviews. She wanted to ensure that no neighbour was overlooked and the right questions were put to them. From experience she knew people often started a conversation with *I saw nothing* but after careful questioning it could turn out that they saw something significant to the case. It felt dark and hopeless and unimaginable that anything could possibly have happened to Tony. Before the guilt of not watching Tony's back overtook her, she got on with knocking on doors.

Jazz found a room for Flora to sit in. He got a young police officer who was just sitting in the canteen minding his own business to babysit Mad Pete. He didn't want him sidling off anywhere. He was going to get Flora a nice cup of tea and organise pictures for her to look at. He knew he would have to face DCI Radley and he was prepared for that.

From across the canteen, a booming voice shattered the hum of muted voices. "There you are you fucking bastard. I've been waiting for you to get back." Jazz didn't have to look round, it was Tom Black, DS for the murder squad. Tom was big in every way. Big body, big voice and a big problem if you got on the wrong side of him. He was 6' 5" of rippling fat. If he hadn't been so tall he would have needed wheels under his belly to get him around.

Jazz turned round and smiled. "Hello, Boomer, long time no see."

The big man strode with an intention that would have frightened someone who didn't know him. On reaching Jazz, he grabbed him with a strength that pressed him to the protruding stomach, taking Jazz's breath away, and then he felt the huge hands affectionately patting his back . Jazz wasn't sure if he was going to pass out with all the pressure on his chest and back. Just as the stars were appearing in his eyes and he thought he might black out from lack of oxygen, the hold was released by a shaking of his shoulders.

"It's good to see you," Boomer shouted affectionately. This was a rare sight; Boomer didn't give most people the time of day. He was viewed at best warily and at worst with fear. He was a loose cannon and no one quite knew what he would do next. Some would say that Jazz and Boomer had that in common.

"How long have you been back you mad fucker?" That wasn't a question, more a statement. He went on: "Back five minutes and there have been seven murders and we have lost a Police Detective. Bloody hell, that's some going even for you, you bastard." Although not entirely serious with these comments, Boomer shook his head in dismay and uttered "I have never known such a fucking, bloody, shitty time in the Met in all the long years I have been here." He stared long and hard at Jazz. And as if by mutual understanding they both walked to DS Tom Black's office and closed the door behind them. The big and brash act had fallen to the wayside and Tom sat heavily in his chair and sighed deeply. He looked up and, in a subdued, quiet voice, he asked, "Do you know what this is all about Jazz?"

Jazz sat hunched on a chair holding his head with both hands. His calm act disappeared and here in private he let the fear and worry that had been suppressed rise to the surface. Boomer and he went back many, many years. They understood each other and Boomer was one of the very few who knew the truth about the incident that happened all those years ago. He would never give out details, the incident was Jazz's call to handle as he wanted.

Boomer should have been a country squire. He lived in Dorset and went home and lead a different life. He grew vegetables and fruit. He hunted and fished and had two huge freezers to keep his harvests in. Boomer was a very intelligent man but his view on life was quite simplistic. If it flew, shoot it and if it swam, hook it and eat it. He worked in a similar way in the Met.

He knew Jazz and when he brushed aside all the splinters of cockiness, drinking and taking chances where prudence would be better, he would rather have Jazz watching his back than many fellow officers he worked with. No other officer would condone that view but to Boomer's simple view of life, Jazz was just an honest fisherman doing his job. He had no other agenda. If you started Boomer on those who wanted to rise in the ranks quickly in the Met and didn't mind treading on the heads, faces and hands of colleagues to get there, the shouting and swearing would go on for hours.

They would work together on this case; they decided between them that nothing would stop them until the murders were solved and Tony was found. Now Jazz had the full force of the murder squad behind him and between them, he and Tom Boomer Black would catch the bastards. They agreed Tony wasn't dead until they found him dead. They were looking for a living man. Both knew this was unlikely based on what Mad Pete had said and where would they take him anyway and why would they bother? It was looking dire. The question they both kept asking themselves was why would anyone want to kill Tony, a police officer, a raw Detective Constable with no known contacts with the Viets; and above all a man who had done nothing wrong that they knew of? None of it made sense at all. Boomer set about sending his team to look into Tony's personal life to see if there was anything there that could give clues to his abduction. They both thought this unlikely but had to go through the motions.

The questions started: Why had he gone to the house in Forest Gate that evening and why would he leave his car? His car was locked up and if he had been hauled out of his car, it was unlikely the thugs responsible would think to lock the car afterwards. They found the wrappings of food he had eaten in the car and they were sent away to forensics to see if they contained any clues. The wrappings had been neatly folded up and placed on the floor of the passenger seat. They could find no disturbance in the car itself to suggest he had been hauled out.

Jazz said solemnly, "It's all going to be down to good old fashioned police work." With that, he asked if he could borrow one of Boomer's team to make some enquiries. Boomer readily agreed and an officer was called in. Jazz told him to check and find out what mobile Tony had and the number. "I think it is one of those fancy candy assed buggers that does everything," he told the officer. "If so we could ping it and find out where it is."

The officer, a youngish man and keen to help, said, "If it is a GSP signal, Sir, we have a good chance of finding it. I will work on it now and get back to you as soon as I have any information, Sir." With a nod from Jazz, he went off. There was a police officer missing and everyone would work long and hard to find him.

Jazz told Boomer that Sharon was looking at the CCTV cameras in the area to see if they could track the Land Rover. "Thank God for CCTV," he murmured to no one in particular.

Boomer, lifting the depressed atmosphere, said wryly, "I see it's old-fashioned policing we are doing."

Jazz looked up and realised what he had said and smiled. "OK, old-fashioned policing and new technology. I'm off to interview Flora and see what she can add." With grim smiles, they both left Boomer's office to go and gather everything they could to find Tony.

Jazz found Flora chatting to a policewoman who had got her a cup of tea and biscuits . She looked at ease and comfortable. Hopefully, she would be ready to go over every detail again and please God come up with something they could use. Time was getting on and if there was any chance of finding Tony it would have to be soon. Flora was a good witness. She had spent the time thinking back and trying to remember something significant in that casual glance out of the window last night.

She told Jazz that all the men had suits on; it appeared that the one in the middle of the other two men was being held by his arms. She said that three men in total got into the Land Rover and there was a driver sitting in the Range Rover so all together there were four men. She wasn't sure but she thought they might be Asian; she couldn't explain why she thought that. It was dark outside and she could only see their outlines. Jazz reckoned they were the Vietnamese. She confirmed the time was 12:10 a.m. because she looked at her clock when she woke up. This gave Sharon a more accurate time to look on the CCTVs. She had a job and a half co-ordinating all the CCTV in the area and getting the bits she wanted to see downloaded. Jazz had no worries about her, she would get it done.

He rang Sharon to tell her the precise time, according to Flora, that Tony was seen getting into the Land Rover. She told him she had six officers using six different machines going through the CCTV. Everyone was anxious to do their bit to find a fellow officer. Now the time was pinpointed, they could easily spot the Land Rover and that would be the start of a CCTV jigsaw which would piece together the journey Tony was on and hopefully find him. There were lots of CCTV cameras in Forest Gate.

Meanwhile, Jazz wanted some time with Sharon. She was the last person to speak to Tony before he went off to Forest Gate. They would talk through it over the phone. He didn't want her to leave the CCTV unit and he wanted to stay close to the station for the time being. He wanted every detail from her now. He called in Boomer to listen over the speaker so he was aware of what exactly happened when Sharon left Tony last night.

Sharon was prepared for this meeting. She had thought long and hard about what was said and what was going to happen when Tony left. On reflection, she thought he seemed a bit cagey about what he was going to do. She said at the time she didn't give it a second thought. He was just going to take a look at the outside of the house. She presumed, wrongly, she conceded, that he would get on to Intelligence to find out who lived in the house and if any of them had a police record. It was the correct procedure and she never assumed that Tony would stray away from correct procedure. Sharon was now making excuses for not checking what Tony was doing and Jazz stopped her there.

"This is not a witch hunt, I'm not looking to blame anyone for what Tony did. If anyone is to blame, it's me."

Sharon wanted to argue but Jazz was having none of it. She confirmed that Tony went off to take a look at Clinton Road about 7 p.m. She said he had paperwork to tidy up and then he got her a coffee just before he left. He didn't share any information with her. As far as she was concerned, he was taking a look at the road and house on his way home. She wasn't aware of any phone calls he made and said he seemed quite relaxed when he left her. Jazz thanked her and told her to get on with sorting out the CCTV.

Now he had to go and find DCI Radley and make his peace with him. Boomer was continuing with his enquiries regarding the murders. So far it looked like tit for tat. Some Vietnamese, some Chinese. Intelligence said two were from the Triads, three from the Snakeheads and two were Vietnamese. There was going to be a round up of gang leaders in a short while. It would take some organisation to ensure the right people were arrested before they went underground. They would be taken to Dagenham Police Station for questioning. The cells were kept empty for their use later in the day.

The station was a hive of activity. With all the hustle and bustle, Jazz still noticed the looks he was getting from those standing still long enough to watch him move through the station. He knew that look. It had happened again and although hatred was a strong word to use, to Jazz it felt like he was the most detested person in the country. The thing was, he agreed with them, he felt like he was jinxed and anyone working with him was in serious trouble. He knew he had to get a grip and keep going until Tony was found. He dodged into the gents toilet for a long swig from his hip flask and to splash his face with water to freshen up. He popped a mint in his mouth and made his way to DCI Radley's office. What could be worse, he thought; he was hated and reviled by his fellow officers, DCI Radley couldn't do much more to him except, of course, pull him off the case. He couldn't let that happen. He owed it to Alice and he owed it to Tony to finish this case. It felt like he had worked a whole day already and it was only 12 noon.

The day, so far, had whizzed by and now it felt like the whole Met force was working on this case. Jazz had never seen so many officers in the building, all vying for desk space and brushing past each other as they rushed here, there and everywhere. Everyone seemed to have a purpose and that purpose was to find Tony and do it quickly. For a moment he felt like a lone person in a bubble as he watched everyone around him move; they were on a mission and none of them wanted to acknowledge him as part of it. He knew that feeling and he had to keep a grip on himself. This was not the time to crack; he would address that later. He was part of everything and he would make sure everyone knew that.

As he passed the door to the custody suite, he saw Bob. The friendly face was good to see. He asked that Bob keep Mad Pete quiet and ready for him when he had finished. Bob just nodded and patted Jazz on the back; he knew what he was going through and said whatever Jazz needed to just ask him. Jazz gave him a grateful smile and carried on to his DCI's office.

He knocked quietly on DCI Radley's office door and waited respectfully for the "Come in" that was shouted crisply from inside. With a deep breath, Jazz opened the door and entered, knowing it was going to be bad.

The shouting could be heard down the corridor. All knew DCI Radley was having a massive fit. They thought Jazz deserved whatever he got and no one cared what happened to him. It was all happening again and those officers who were not around during the first incident were told in no uncertain terms what had happened before. All reckoned Jazz should just jump off the roof and be done with it. He was a Jonah who no one wanted to be near.

I told you so was going around the station. An old PC who was now the Case Progression Officer had a reputation as a *right old woman* but they now listened intently to what he was saying. He was proclaiming loudly and often that he knew this would happen, that Jazz was nothing but trouble. He told everyone that Jazz never listened to advice and always went off and did his own thing and now look what has happened again! It had to be said that PC Iain Blain was having a very self-righteous time and enjoying every minute of the attention he was getting. The young PCs, fired up by PC Iain Blain, were up for sorting Jazz out there and then. It wasn't going to be long before there would be calls for Jazz to be banged up, sacked or just taken off the case and sent home out of harm's way. Rumours about Jazz, his past and the present spread like wildfire around the police station and became wildly exaggerated. Tony was missing after all, he had not been found yet, and he certainly hadn't been confirmed dead, but all levels of staff, from police officers to cleaners, had started to use the word murderer when mentioning Jazz's name. The murmurings had escalated from lousy skipper to murderer and once the rumour started, his name became synonymous with Jack the Ripper.

DCI Radley had calmed down. Jazz was struck dumb by the torrent of abuse and truth he listened to. He had been far too cocky, and yes he had flouted rules and regulations. He had promised to keep in touch and he hadn't. Everything that was being said was true and it felt like with each statement he was being hammered further into the ground. He had no excuse or ability to stand up for himself. Tony was missing and it was his fault. What he did want more than anything else was to stay on the case. He wanted to find Tony. He owed it to him.

The self-confident DS that had strode into his office under one week ago was now a humbled man who just wanted to do the right thing and bring whoever had done this to justice. John Radley found this aspect of Jazz quite difficult to handle. He admired Jazz. He had a job to do and that was to keep him in check, to make him accountable, but he had seen how hard he worked and how he motivated his very small team to work hard and to work smart. He didn't think for one moment that it was Jazz's fault that Tony was in this predicament. No one would have guessed that Tony, a mummy's boy, would have gone off on his own and got into trouble. No one would have thought he had the balls to do it. He also knew Jazz would pay dearly for this. Already the murmuring had started and soon no one would work with him.

DCI John Radley had a lot to contend with. Seven gang murders and one missing DC, a station full of officers baying for Jazz's blood and the press waiting for a statement from him. He sat back and thought, Yea Gods! What have I done to deserve such a shambles? Jazz interpreted this look of resignation as quite promising for him. A bit of him perked up and he tentatively asked if he could work with DS Tom Black. He went on to explain that Tom was happy with this arrangement and added that one of Tom Black's team was working with him this morning.

He explained there were many leads being worked on to find Tony. His mobile phone was being tracked and it was hoped this would lead them to him. Sharon was working on the CCTV and trying to follow the journey of the Land Rover that was seen outside Carlton Road by a witness. He now had DCI Radley's full attention and continued, "I have Mad Pete downstairs and he was the last person to see Tony. I'm going to interview him again. Flora, the neighbour, is making a statement as we speak; she has described the men leaving the house in Carlton Road and one fits the description of Tony. I've been working with a gangland contact who is assisting me with any information that comes to light. I have the name of the top Vietnamese gang leader, Tran tan Giap, and I expect to find him shortly. I got the names of the men who killed Alice Watson and they were found dead from electrocution and the first two of the seven men killed over the past 48 hours. My contact is close to all of what is going on and he owes me big time. I will pursue this today for more leads." Jazz sat back, took a deep breath and looked hopefully at his DCI.

DCI Radley smiled, a touch ruefully, but a smile none the less. Jazz was surprised at this reaction but took it as a good sign. It made him sit up and lean forward. "I know I have said it before, Sir, but I promise to keep in touch. I feel so close to getting this solved. I will find Tony. I have found the killers of Alice Watson. I will find out what the hell is going on in Ilford to cause all these murders. This is my town, Sir, and it has gone mad. I want the chance to help put things right."

DCI Radley leaned back in his chair and surveyed the DS in front of him, who was still fired up. The humble person didn't last long, he thought. He had to admit that he was getting results and though he was going to have a rough time with his colleagues, he was a good officer. He worried, however, that he wouldn't get the support necessary to get the job done. But there again, Tom Black would ensure that happened. In fact, Jazz and Tom seemed a good team. There would be an enquiry when Tony was found and he was well aware that as DCI for Ilford Police Station, he might not come out of it very well. To hell with it, he thought, perhaps some of Jazz is rubbing off on me too. He shifted in his seat and broke the silence. "One more chance, Jaswinder Singh, but only if you work with DS Tom Black." With a dismissive wave of his hand, he added, "Back here, the pair of you, at 4 p.m. for an update."

Jazz left the room, quickly stuttering his thanks. He couldn't believe his luck. Perhaps DCI Radley wasn't such a bad sort after all. In fact, he reckoned he was fucking brilliant. He went to find DS Tom Black to tell him they were partners. The euphoric feeling left him quite quickly as he passed a group of officers standing to one side of the corridor just staring at him in silence. He was about to say hi as he passed when one hissed, "Murderer" at him. Unprepared and beaten by such a name, Jazz reflected for a second on what to do and decided now was not the time to retaliate. He put his head down and moved quickly on to find DS Black. Shocked and sickened by what had happened, Jazz found him and just sat still for a moment. Tom Black prodded his shoulder and asked what the hell was up with him. Internally Jazz was reciting the mantra of *keep calm, not now, keep calm, not now*. He couldn't and wouldn't let this get to him. He had to find Tony and help find the gangland murderers. If he was going to have a breakdown, it would have to wait.

Jazz gave Tom the potted version of the meeting with DCI Radley. They both set their lines of enquiries out and said they would meet up at 3 p.m. with an update. It was 2 p.m. now so not much time today for results. Jazz went off to the gents for a long, long swig from his hip flask. He needed it badly.

He got on the phone to contact Bam Bam. He reckoned he had time for a quick meeting with him if there were any updates. Bam Bam said he might have something in the morning, but nothing today. It was back to Sharon to see where she had got to with the

CCTV. Sharon was moving at a snail's pace. The CCTV was controlled by different areas. It was difficult enough just coordinating the CCTV footage in the same area but now they were into the Wanstead area, they had even more managers to contact. She sounded tired but resolute and said she would stay all night to collate it. Jazz thanked her.

The officer dealing with the phone, whose name turned out to be Miles Sweeney, said it would take a while and he had been promised a result by some time tonight if they were lucky. Patience was not a virtue Jazz had much of and his was being sorely tested. In the meantime, he could at least interview Mad Pete.

Someone was kicking the cell door and shouting to be let out. Jazz knew those dulcet tones. Mad Pete was having a massive panic attack. Of course he needed a fix. How on earth was he going to square it so that he could shoot heroin in a police station? He took him out of the cell and told him urgently and quietly through clenched teeth to "shut the fuck up. I am taking you somewhere so you can get your fix, OK?" Mad Pete nodded continuously and Jazz could see him shaking. He hated fucking heroin addicts, they were so needy and useless until they had their fix and then they went all sleepy and relaxed until it had kicked in fully. Mad Pete was not going to be any use for an hour or so.

Jazz took Mad Pete into a police car, telling the Custody Officer he wanted to drive him around so he could point out relevant places he had been to with the Vietnamese men. He wasn't going to bring anything new to the meeting at 3 p.m. or 4 p.m. but hopefully by tomorrow morning there might be something new. He was going to get some fish and chips to eat while Mad Pete got his fix. He would need sustenance to get him through the night. Soon he would be closer to the truth. It would take a miracle for Tony to still be alive in the morning.

For now, he had to let Mad Pete have his fix. He was in the back of the police car without a care in the world as Jazz drove around. He took the car back to the station in time for his 3 p.m. meeting with Tom. Nothing much had come forward in such a short time. They both knew it wasn't realistic to expect anything else but DCI Radley had to be kept sweet. Their meeting at 4 p.m. was short and sweet and it was agreed a meeting the following day at 4 p.m. should have more updates. Of course, in the meantime, if there were any major developments, DCI Radley would be the first to be told.

The raids on gang members was organised for 5 a.m. the next morning. Tom would be in on that. Jazz would go and help Sharon with the CCTV after his interview with Mad Pete. Jazz took a police car and went to Sainsbury's for a bottle of vodka. He wasn't going to get home until late tonight and he could do with a top up. He told himself he hadn't had much today. A hip flask doesn't hold much, just a few decent swigs and he was going to need something to keep him going.

On his return, he went and found Mad Pete, who was quietly sitting in a cell. He was told he wasn't a prisoner, but he said he felt safer in the cell. He was still spooked by everything and kept saying that *they* were going to get him too. He took a bit of convincing but Jazz wanted to go out in an unmarked car and travel around the area to see the places Mad Pete went with the Viets. After 10 minutes of hysteria, with Mad Pete saying he was never going anywhere near where they were, he calmed down. As Jazz told him, an unmarked police car it might be but it had the police siren if needed, as well as the police radio. He added quietly that the one he was borrowing had toughened glass windows which couldn't be smashed in. That was a lie but Mad Pete didn't have to know that.

It was getting on for 7 p.m. before they left in the unmarked car. Jazz had to speak to Sharon first and see how she was getting on. She said the car was now travelling towards Charlie Brown's roundabout near Woodford so they were making progress. She said she was getting stills of some of the pictures because a few showed the driver quite clearly and so if blown up, might show who was in the back of the car. He said well done and when this was over, he would take her and Tony out for a celebratory meal. Both thought this sounded a bit too optimistic but, nevertheless, a bit of optimism and faith that Tony would be found alive perked them both up.

"So where shall we go?" was the question Jazz put to Mad Pete.

It took a few minutes for Mad Pete to gather his thoughts; he looked nonplussed. Then something turned on in his brain and his face lit up. "I know Mr Singh. They had a place in Barking they took me to. I don't know the address but I know the way there." Jazz nodded and drove down the one-way system behind the library to Ilford Lane, which would take them to Barking.

Ilford Lane was still the same as he remembered. The Bangladeshi families had moved there many years ago. The shops were full of brightly-coloured saris and lots of Indian restaurants. The butchers were, of course, all Halal. The specialist food shops, which supplied wholesale sacks of rice, onions and chick peas together with all the other necessary ingredients required by a good Indian household, were still open. It was quite late now so the pavements, which were usually bustling with mainly Indian men and women, were quieter. Jazz remembered the time he came here with his mother to buy food. As was the Indian way, she bought in bulk. There was only two of them but rice was always bought by the sack. As she would say, it keeps and is cheaper that way.

Indian people were very proud and received guests with platefuls of food. He remembered when he lived in Manchester and visited his relatives. Sometimes he just arrived without notice and before he knew it, the women of the house had wafted into the kitchen and before he could say chicken tikka with rice, little titbits would be brought to him freshly cooked. The samosas were a favourite of his along with pakoras and poppadoms, then a steaming meal with an assortment of meats and fish together with rice would be put in front of him. He would eat like a king though he only popped in to say hello.

When he was married, his family would visit him and his new wife would get in such a state trying to cook a huge meal for his family. He noted she had never helped in the kitchen in Pakistan; her parents had servants to do this. He arranged with her that they would cook curries together and freeze them down so when visitors came she could just defrost the curry and serve it as fresh. He had enjoyed cooking with her. In the early part of their marriage they had tried to make it work but, he sighed in memory, they had nothing to keep them together. She wanted her life back and he wanted something else, what that was he didn't know and he still wasn't sure.

His core was Sikh but his life was as a cockney East Ender. He didn't know who he was but at the moment he just wanted to be left alone to get on with his job. He needed to find Tony very badly. It was getting on for 24 hours since he was last seen and there was no word from anyone about him or his whereabouts. It was like he had vanished off the face of the earth. That was not good and Jazz went cold at the thought.

"So come on, Pete, where abouts in Barking am I heading?"

Mad Pete shifted in his seat, he didn't like this at all. "Gascoigne Estate, Mr Singh, I'll show you where when we get closer."

Of course it would be the Gascoigne Estate, Jazz thought, it was often the place where the trouble happened. Old timers had told him that years ago the Gascoigne Estate was a nice place to live but over the years it had got shabby and trouble makers were moved on from area to area and eventually ended up living on the Gascoigne Estate. It was true to say that if you had a persistent offender, especially the ones under 21 years old, they usually came from the Gascoigne Estate. Mad Pete lived on the Gascoigne Estate so he should have known the name of the road.

"What are you playing at, Pete? You know this area very well." Mad Pete shifted nervously, not wanting to say anything.

Jazz stopped the car by the side of the road and turned to Mad Pete. "OK, what's going on? There is something very strange happening in this area and your playing silly buggers isn't helping one bit." Mad Pete shifted uncomfortably and tried to look away. Jazz was losing his temper. He had no time for this fucking stupid coyness. He had very little time to play with and he needed answers now. "What is going on in my town and why?" he shouted at Mad Pete. This was followed by a few moments of threats and promises of keeping him safe; *we have known each other for years and you know I will look after you.* Jazz added quietly, "Without me you are dead meat and you know it, Pete."

Jazz could see that the nice treatment wasn't working; Mad Pete was still hesitating. Enough was enough and Jazz told him that they were going on a trip. He knew the place the Triads hung out. He was going to drive up to the front of the restaurant they used for meetings and screech to a halt; that should get their attention he reckoned and then he would throw Mad Pete out of the car and make off to Ilford Police Station. He had Mad Pete's attention now. "I don't care what they do to you, they can have you for fish bait." That thought turned Mad Pete chalk white with fear. He spluttered and stuttered and whined that they would kill him slowly if they got him. Jazz promised to protect him which caused a *yeah right* look from Mad Pete. He knew Tony was dead and didn't think much of Jazz as a protector. "Well you're dead if you don't help me that's for sure and I don't know if I care anymore. You want my help then you help me." Jazz was losing patience with this dirtbag, he needed the information now.

Mad Pete knew he had no choice now; he had to trust Jazz. With a resigned sigh and shrug, he gave in and said he would tell him everything he knew. Before he started, he made Jazz promise to take him wherever he was going. He didn't want to be alone. He could feel the drug-induced madness creeping up ready to engulf him. He wished things were different. All he wanted was to be left somewhere safe and warm and with a stash of heroin to keep him going, but that wasn't going to happen. He wanted to shoot up again, to feel that warm and comfortable feeling that made him float and smile, but Jazz wouldn't have that until he knew everything. He promised Mad Pete he could have what he needed afterwards.

REALITY CHECK

It transpired that not long after Jazz left Ilford, the Viets moved in. Mad Pete always had his nose to the ground and knew when *things* were afoot. He explained he had to be careful and one step ahead of the Holy Trinity. "They could get pretty nasty, Mr Singh, if you put a foot wrong. I have had a few beatings to put me in my place when I stepped out of line. I hated the lot of them. The bastards didn't let anyone else work their area. I had to make a living, Mr Singh, and they weren't having it."

"When the Viets arrived, they came in small and quiet like. I saw them set up a place on Gascoigne and I said nuffink. I ain't grassing on no one. They had a nice little cocaine factory set up and I got talking to one of their keepers. I used to do a bit of running for him, nothing big. First of all it was just getting him some milk or whatever he needed cos he couldn't leave the house. He got to trust me and I'd do other little jobs like taking just a bit of spliff to Edmonton. He looked after me and they treated me right. Over the time I got to speak to one of the bosses, who gave me some heroin. I missed the stuff. I did odd little jobs for them. It was very hush hush so as the Holy Trinity never found out." Jazz was speechless, who would employ this pathetic excuse of a man to run drugs for them? The Vietnamese, obviously, but were they that desperate? Mad Pete saw the look and added defiantly, "I am honest, Mr Singh, and trustworthy. They looked after me and I was valuable to them."

Jazz, incredulous by now, just asked, "Why, in the name of God and all that is good in the world, would anyone think you were valuable?"

Mad Pete didn't like that and Jazz could see he was getting red under his filthy collar. "You know nuffink, Mr Singh. You've been away a long time." It was the sly look Mad Pete gave him that made Jazz slap him. He shouldn't have done it but it wasn't the time to play games. A man's life might depend on what happened today.

"I've got contacts all over the place, Mr Singh, and I sold stuff for them on the streets. Never where anyone knew me, but it earned me money and respect. I did little jobs for them. I couriered stuff between houses for them. No one looked at me twice. They were feeding me heroin, and I had just a baby* habit to start with , but the habit got to be a bit king kong*1 and I needed to buy the stuff from the man*2. They paid me good money for not too much work."

"So how come they got this far and the Triads and Snakeheads didn't stop them? It doesn't make sense."

Mad Pete didn't know the answer to that. "It's been kinda strange for the past few years. I didn't feel scared until now. Things just sort of happened and no one stopped it. They had got I reckon up to 20 cannabis factories set up, scattered throughout Ilford, Barking and parts of East London."

*baby means minor heroin habit – *1King Kong means big habit –
*2 The Man – Dealer

It seemed unreal and too fantastic to be happening. Jazz knew the Triads and Snakeheads had the area sown up. He knew from Bam Bam that the Viets were being watched and a takeover was due but to allow them to grow so big seemed unimaginable. It had to be they had no idea how big the Viets were getting. Mad Pete had started and he was mumbling on so Jazz turned to catch what he was saying.

"And then that old lady got killed and all hell was let loose. They seemed to know I was involved and they are going to kill me, Mr Singh, I know it. You have got to protect me." He was getting hysterical now and Jazz knew he needed a fix otherwise he would be totally unmanageable.

"Take me to the place you wanted to show me and then you can have a fix. I presume you have the stuff with you?" Mad Pete nodded. God I would be in trouble if my boss heard me now, Jazz thought. Aiding and abetting a known drug offender was not in the Met Police rule books. "Where are you taking me by the way?" Jazz asked as he realised he hadn't a clue what was going on in Mad Pete's brain.

"To their headquarters, Mr Singh. I ain't going in, but if Tony is anywhere I reckon he would be there. But he is dead, trust me, Mr Singh, he ain't breathing no more." Jazz told Mad Pete to shut it." He pushed that thought to the back of his mind. Tony had to be alive, he couldn't die just like that for nothing.

The journey didn't take much longer, but in that time Jazz had a moment to realise that Ilford had changed beyond belief. It had its problems in the past, but not on this scale. Mad Pete was a small-time low life who dabbled in anything easy, and always illegal, that could make him money. Now he was telling him that he was involved in what appeared to be a growing drug syndicate and he was in the middle, helping them. It didn't make sense. He wanted his old Ilford back. Poor Alice, how did she come to be killed for just being a sweet, dear old lady? He knew the men who had killed Alice and they were dead and good riddance. Now he had to find who had taken Tony. It was gobsmackingly gruesome that any gang in Ilford had the nerve to take a police officer and create the mayhem this would cause. That they felt powerful enough to take on the Met Police defied belief. This had to be sorted and soon.

Following further instructions from Mad Pete, they arrived at what looked like an empty warehouse on the edge of the Gascoigne Estate. It was on an industrial estate that was in decline. Funnily enough, the police were considering building a police station not far from the building they were outside.

"I ain't going in, Mr Singh. They are all out to kill me now." Mad Pete was getting agitated again. He was told he could stay put and lock the doors. Jazz was glad to get out of the car. Mad Pete stunk and as he got more agitated, the smell got worse. As he got out of the car, Jazz smelt the sleeve of his jacket; it stunk of Mad Pete. God, he thought, they will smell me before they see me.

Now he was here, standing in front of what on first glance looked like a derelict warehouse, he didn't know what to do. For a few seconds, he stood there. He couldn't see any cars or life around to assume anyone was inside. He turned to Mad Pete in the car and through the open car window said, "If you don't hear from me after 20 minutes, ring 999 and get the police here." He walked off as Mad Pete started whining, "Mr Singh, don't leave me here, I ain't safe, they will kill us both."

MAD PETE

What possessed Jazz to think Mad Pete would stay in the car would remain a mystery. As soon as Jazz walked around the back and he couldn't see him anymore, Mad Pete got out of the car and ran. He knew if he was quick he could get to his flat in 10 minutes. He had enough bolts and locks on the door to stop anyone getting in. He would be safe there. He reckoned there were would be more killings before the gangs were done. He knew that if they didn't think twice about killing a policeman and the fuss that would cause then they would kill anyone. Mr Singh was on his own.

He was a liar, he knew that. He smiled at the thought. He was a damn good liar at that! So he *bigged it up* to Mr Singh about his involvement with the Viets, it was about time he showed him some respect. The truth was, he toadied up to the Viets when they started up. They treated him like their lapdog and threw him a few scraps. He did a few minor jobs for them, nothing much, and he bought heroin from them. He knew he shouldn't have started on the stuff again but he felt good now. He gave them street information. If there was one thing he was good at, it was hearing what was happening on the streets. He told the Viets when the Triads were unhappy and looking for dealers on their grounds who hadn't bought from them. He told them where the Snakeheads hung out and who would be there. They knew that Bam Bam was no worries to them because he didn't deal in their shit. The Holy Trinity as a group was a worry though and they kept their heads down and laid low so as not to antagonise them. He was useful sometimes to them.

Life had been OK for Mad Pete until the Viets arrived. He got by with his disability pension and his flat paid for by the council. He was on methadone and although he was addicted to it, it was at least legal and he got it for free on the NHS. He bought stolen phones and sold them on and he dealt a bit in cocaine. When the Viets arrived and fed him free heroin, life was oh so warm and happy at the beginning, he felt good. But they started to charge him after a while and he needed more money to survive. He was under pressure to pay for his stuff.

He needed the Viets to earn enough for the heroin. Fencing phones didn't pay enough to feed his habit. The more he needed the Viets, the more he worried about the trinity. He kept his head down and invested in more locks and chains until his house was nearly as secure as the Bank of England vault. He knew one day they might come looking for him. Today was that day and he was going to hide until it had all blown over. The tit for tat killings were good for him; he hoped that by the weekend they would have killed each other and would all be dead, then he wouldn't have to worry anymore. He knew he was dead meat if they caught him.

What he chose to forget to tell Jazz was that he had played them all off against each other. He had taken money from them all and ratted on them all too. He knew names and he knew what was happening. He was like a rat in a basement, unseen but all knowing. The Viets, Snakeheads and Triads had realised the common denominator, and Mad Pete was it. He didn't care who did what to whom, he just wanted money. No integrity, no long-term plan and no sense, he had run into trouble and it was true, everyone did want to kill him now. Everyone thought Mad Pete was low life scum and that he only had the intelligence to do as he was told. He had the temperament of a rat. He was crafty, cunning and clever, without the morals of honour, integrity and loyalty and certainly no hygiene; you could smell him coming a mile off.

He stopped on the way home at the local Spar shop to pick up some bread, milk and a couple of frozen dinners. He checked his change and he had enough for some tobacco and fag papers as well. He had no intention of shifting out of his flat for a few days. He looked around to check no one was lurking who might be trouble for him. The shopkeeper served him quickly, glad to see him leave. The air freshener was out and sprayed quickly once the door closed.

He had spent the night avoiding his flat, convinced they would come and find him and kill him. He hadn't thought he would be safe at his address but now he realised it was the only place he might be safe. Once he had locked all the doors he would sit down, shoot up and relax. He had enough stuff to keep him going for the next few days and by then he hoped the gang fights would be finished and everyone who was after him would be dead.

"COME INTO MY PARLOUR," SAID THE SPIDER
TO THE FLY

Jazz walked slowly round to the back of the old building. It was never going to win any prizes. A pile of old brick defiantly held together in a box shape. The windows were high and glazed in places with the odd broken pane, it looked like what glass had survived was held together with dirt and pidgeons' droppings. He would have said the place was abandoned but he passed the loading bays and the newness of the shuttered doors stood out. The shutters that would be pulled up to open and accept a container lorry full of goods sparkled with a newness that showed up the shabbiness of the rest of the building. He supposed years ago it was used as a storage depot for goods en route to London. It was close to the canal and in those days goods were ferried up the canal from ships moored at docks near Tilbury. The new doors made Jazz realise it was in use again, but by who, he wondered. This old industrial estate was in a state of disrepair and due for demolition in the next few years, but someone was working here.

As he turned the corner towards the back of the building, a chilling wind seemed to stir up and blow his jacket open. He shuddered with discomfort. Looking around, he realised no one could see him. The thought crossed his mind that this would be a good place to kill someone, they wouldn't be found for years. He pulled his jacket close to his chest and tried to shake off the feeling that he shouldn't be here alone. Impetuous they called him, and he conceded that perhaps they were right; 'they' being his colleagues and his bosses. He was here now and he needed to do something to find Tony. This looked an ideal place to set up business and if Mad Pete was right, the Viets had this place. He stopped by the corner of the building and took out his hip flask. He needed a drink. He took a long slug and felt so much better. It was long overdue with everything that had been going on today. He could think clearer now.

The day was drawing to a close and the air had that nip in it that made you want to go inside. It had a muted feel, the birds were settling down and the traffic didn't sound quite so loud, even the breeze had quietened down. He had to get into the warehouse before it got really dark. Of course he didn't have a torch with him and he cursed himself at the thought. With everything that had been going on, it was only now that he realised this might be dangerous and that possibly he was a prize idiot for being here with only a heroin addict for backup.

There was a small door at the back and he tried the handle; it moved and gently he pulled on the door. It was opening. He waited a second and pulled it just enough to see through the crack. He checked if there was anyone standing in front of the door; it looked empty. He listened for a moment and thought he could hear voices but they were muffled and seemed a little way away. With a deep breath, he opened the door enough to squeeze in quickly and close the door behind him. His breath was urgent and far too loud. He saw a box and squatted behind it to give himself a chance to gain control of the trembling feeling, get his breathing under control and become more calm. He looked around, his eyes darting from one side to the other. He knew this was stupid and he felt a fear that was not going to be helpful. He needed to get a grip. To be impetuous you need to be brave as well and Jazz wasn't feeling very brave at all at this moment. To creep out again quickly and go and get help seemed the best option and he was considering doing just that. He had no radio, no weapon, he was alone, no one knew he was here and this gang appeared to have no respect for the lives of police officers. He was stark staringly bonkers to be here and he realised he was the biggest fucking idiot in the whole of the Met Police Force. He was scared out of his head and had to think what to do next.

The gunfire should have sent him scurrying for the door but it had the opposite effect. Galvanised like a runner after hearing the starting pistol, Jazz ran to an area further into the warehouse and hid behind some boxes stacked carefully in the middle of the huge cavern like interior. He couldn't see anything yet. There was a lot of noise with tables overturning and chairs scraping the floor. The shouts were in another language, some sounded Punjabi and he understood they were instructions to look round; he picked up the words *get him*. Then there was a medley of what he thought were

Vietnamese words shouted excitedly and urgently. In the end, he couldn't understand anything. The sound level had risen to deafening heights that echoed around the warehouse. The gunfire started again with a vengeance and Jazz just ducked and held his breath for it to stop. He really should have got out and ran for backup, but he didn't. He stayed where he was and prayed to all the gods in heaven to make it stop.

The silence was loud. It felt like everyone had died and he wondered if that was possible. Perhaps they had shot each other and they were all dead but that was wishful thinking on his part. After a moment of silence, he moved cautiously along the line of boxes that were stacked high enough to conceal a six foot man. When he reached the last box, he stood pressed against the stack of boxes and fought a momentary panic rising from his stomach. With two or three deep breaths, he got down on all fours and cautiously looked around the box to see who was still alive and who had a gun.

In front of Jazz was a perverted pageant of bodies lying at obscene angles with more blood on the floor than a blood bank would hold on a good day. Jazz quickly counted eight men; there may have been more, but he was more concerned about the three living men holding guns standing to the right of the blood fest. They were talking in low, quiet terms in a dialect that sounded familiar but not one he knew personally. He couldn't understand what they were saying but he hoped they would not hang around for long. Having killed so many people it seemed prudent to get the fuck away, he thought. He felt overwhelmed by the sight and smell of what was before him. The coppery smell of the blood invaded his senses and the cordite from the guns tickled his nose, making him want to sneeze. He felt sick at the sight.

He watched the three men intently. They were not arguing but there was a strong discussion going on. He thought they looked more South Asian than Chinese and wondered where they came from. In a flicker of an eye, one of them caught sight of something moving by the boxes and ran towards Jazz. With nowhere to go and in a state of blind panic, Jazz watched in slow motion one of the men running towards him with his gun ready to fire. "Oh shit and bollocks and fuck everything, I'm a gonna." He cursed under his breath. Any thoughts of action were wasted as the gunman was on him before he could think. His body had gone stone cold and he felt like he weighed a ton. He was dragged into the arena of death and kicked in the back to make him move. In English one of them asked who he was and he told them he was a police officer and his backup was on the way. The third one had gone outside and seen his car, empty. They frisked him and there was no radio on him. He hadn't used his mobile, they checked calls made. Jazz double cursed himself. Why the hell hadn't he rung the station? They smiled at his threats.

No one was coming to save him, they told him and they laughed. One went outside whilst the others tied him up and sat him on a bloodied chair they had retrieved from the floor. They goaded him and prodded him. They laughed scornfully and told him they liked killing police officers and they liked to hear them pleading for their lives. One stuck the gun in his ear and said that would be too quick. They pushed it into his stomach and said that would be much more painful and a slower death. They said they would toss for it, to see who would be the one to kill him. They pushed their faces into his and told him with curried breath that they hated the fucking police.

He asked them if they had killed Tony. They laughed and said if he meant the poof then yes they had. They told him how he begged them to let him live and how he had promised to be a good boy. He had cried and cowered and was a big Jessie they were glad to shut up. They shot him in the head. Jazz's breathing was rapid and he was going into shock. Tony was dead. Oh God, he thought and he asked, "Why kill him? He was a nobody." They smiled and said that it was for them to know and him to find out. They promised he could ask Tony himself because it was going to be his turn to die very soon.

They left him for a moment. The third one who had gone outside was gesturing to them to follow him. He knew they were going to kill him. In the two minutes before they returned, he went to hell and back in a tormented fog of pain, recriminations and prayer. He didn't want to die like this, alone and forgotten. One of them came back and told him he was very, very lucky that he had a guardian angel. His senses were heightened and the panic was bubbling through his body. It felt like a reprieve and it made him swoon. They seemed to all have left him. In the silence, amidst the carnage around him, Jazz just sat in shock, suddenly not knowing what they meant and if they were coming back to kill him.

He was dizzy with the panic and fear and knowledge of Tony's death. He knew they were telling him the truth. He looked at the carnage around him. A table was overturned and on the floor were scales and all the paraphernalia of a drug factory. There were small plastic bags scattered everywhere. He counted the bodies he could see again and there were 10 in his sight; he didn't know if there was any more. He had never seen so many murdered people in one place before and it stung his senses to look at them. He tried to free himself but nothing moved. They had tied him so tight he could feel the rope cutting into his wrists and the rope holding his arms felt like his blood was being cut off and his fingers tingled with numbness.

REPRIEVE AND RETRIBUTION

It felt like he had been there alone with all the dead bodies splayed around him for hours but it was, in fact, 40 minutes before the door was violently opened and in charged the SO19 team. They scared the hell out of him and he was one of the good guys, so anyone else in there would have run at the sight of them. The fifteen burly men holding guns and wearing protective gear that made them all look like Mr Universe spread out and searched the area. Tom Black followed up at the rear and Jazz could hear him coming as he boomed out, "What the fuck are you doing here, you bastard? I thought you were doing some real detective work not swanning around here." He stopped when he saw the carnage in front of Jazz and under his breath Jazz heard him say the nearest thing to a prayer Tom Black would ever say: "Jesus Christ in heaven save us all!"

His ropes were undone and it was then that the shaking started. Someone found a blanket from somewhere and wrapped it around Jazz. He was in shock and as his hip flask was found on him, he drank the last gulp in it. They took him outside to the waiting police car. Someone would drive the undercover car back to the station for him. An ambulance arrived and

Jenny the SOCO appeared with her henpecked partner to check out the scene and look at the bodies.

"Bloody hell, Jenny, are you always on duty?" Jazz shouted from the open door of the car.

With a half smoked cigarette in hand, she walked over to him. "I might have bloody known you would be involved somewhere. Your sodding fingerprints had better not be all over the evidence, young man." She saw he looked shaken and noted the blanket around his shoulders so offered him a cigarette and lit it for him. He smiled with gratitude and she nodded back. He looked like shit and she wondered what on earth had happened. With a sigh, she stubbed out her cigarette and picked up her bag. She looked around and spotted her lacky, John. She shouted to him to "bloody hurry up and get moving, I haven't got all day." Muttering something about him being a lazy bugger and that it was always her that had the sodding work to do, she trundled off to look at the carnage in the warehouse. Jazz could hear her in the distance shouting at some poor officer to "bloody get your sodding hands off that door before I report you to your Superintendant." Everyone in the vicinity visibly relaxed when she had gone.

Tom Black strode up to the car and was irritated by everything going on; he wanted to get things moving and find out what had happened here. He asked for SO19 to stand down and got the place covered by police to ensure no one entered the area. Now he wanted to talk to Jazz and find out what the hell had happened here. He took a look at Jazz and figured he was fine and didn't need a doctor. He needed answers now. Tom

Boomer Black shouted to all around to keep an eye out and to let him know as soon as the SOCO had finished her work, he was off with Jazz to the station to get his statement.

They went to the canteen where a hot mug of strong tea was put in front of Jazz by a worried Milly, who fussed and asked, "Can I get you anything else, dear?" as she tucked the blanket round him in a motherly gesture. He looked up and smiled at her and shook his head. She took no notice of the refusal, she knew better. With a gentle pat on his shoulder, she went back to the kitchen to cook him something tasty. A good meal would make him feel better.

Boomer was busy shouting at officers in the canteen, making them move to the other side of the room. He wanted an area around Jazz that was people-free so he could spread out and talk in private. They could, of course, have gone to an interview room but that wasn't necessary or comfortable. A cup of tea, something to eat and room to move was all that was needed as far as Boomer was concerned. A formal statement would have to be made soon but for now he wanted facts to work on.

While this was going on, Jazz found another flask in his other pocket with some vodka still in it. He turned his back to Boomer and the others and, facing the wall, took a quick swig. That stopped the shaking for a while and he was now ready to sit and talk. He was in more shock than he realised and for a moment he pulled the blanket closer to him for comfort. Milly brought out a plate of sausage and chips which he didn't want. With her encouragement though he took a chip and realised this was the first thing he had eaten for many hours. Using his fingers, he picked up the sausages and ate them with the chips; they tasted good.

Boomer and Jazz sat for an hour going over events. A photo ident would be set up for Jazz to look through to see if any of the faces belonged to the killers. That was being organised. He was in big trouble, he should never have gone to the warehouse alone, he knew that. Boomer said he would do his best to help him but he had to admit Jazz was a silly bugger to even think of going there alone. What amazed them both was that Jazz was not killed. They went over the conversation and it appeared conclusive that Tony was dead. Boomer thumped the table and swore to the heavens above that he would get the killer of a police officer. Jazz solemnly stated that was his job and he wouldn't rest until he found Tony's body and his killers. Boomer, in a moment of unbridled passion, grabbed Jazz's hand and shook it with a force that nearly knocked him off his chair and vowed to help him. Overcome by such comradeship, the tears rolled and after a few salty snotty minutes, Jazz felt better and pulled himself together. There was work to be done and killers to find.

He sat in a formal setting and gave his statement, which was meticulously taken down by another officer. Boomer was too busy for such things, he was off looking for the photo idents to see if they had anyone who looked like the killers. They spent another hour looking through photos but none were recognised by Jazz. It was all a mystery. It was thought every one of the gang members in the Holy Trinity was in the picture idents. Surely there couldn't be another gang out there? That would be too much for one small town. Someone had brought them in especially for the job. This led to the thought that perhaps this was all intended to happen. Perhaps it wasn't to do with Alice's death as first thought. Perhaps that was a smoke screen for a take over. With all these thoughts in mind, Boomer and Jazz took off for the warehouse to see what was happening and if Jenny had found anything interesting for them to use.

The mortuary vans had arrived and were waiting. The photographer had been allowed in by Jenny to take photos of the bodies before they were moved. Boomer let Jazz approach the formidable Jenny. He had noticed that she was kinder to him than other officers. Jazz shouted to her from the door and asked if he could come in. She had been working there for the past four hours and it was getting late now, just past 11 p.m. She looked tired. With so much to do, she had called in extra help and there were two additional experienced SOCOs working throughout the warehouse collecting samples and cataloguing what they found. Jazz shouted hello to them and they both raised a hand in response.

Jenny told them to not move far yet because although the work was nearly finished, she was going to check the area again to make sure. She told them there were twelve bodies, most within the area seen but two were found dead in a corner. All were shot but until the autopsies had been done, she couldn't confirm what type of gun was used. All she would say was they were shot many times and there was more blood around than she had seen before.

Jazz took her outside for a cigarette, he could see she hadn't had a break. He got one of the policemen standing guard to go and find a place for some cups of tea. Jenny shouted out, "And no bloody sugar this time." The officer nodded and went to find a late night cafe.

Jazz let her smoke her cigarette for a few moments and then asked, "So, off the record, Jenny, what do you think?"

She looked up at him and frowned. He was taking liberties but she reckoned it was his job to ask. She lit another cigarette with the end of the one she was smoking and threw the old stub onto the floor and trod on it. She took a fresh drag of the new cigarette, closing her eyes as she inhaled. "Well, they all looked Vietnamese to me and they were not very old, I would say mid-twenties to mid-thirties all of them. They were shot with a pretty mean gun, can't say at the moment until I get an ident on the bullets but if I had to guess I would say a Glock, the preferred gun for law enforcement agencies around the world. They are pretty accessible for your gangster type. Expensive, yes, but very effective and easy to get hold of these days. The way the bullets hit the bodies, the firing would have been instant to have caught them so quickly and covered them all in the same area of the body. A Glock can do that. Anything larger and heavier without a quick-fire action wouldn't have hit the bodies in the same way." She stubbed out her cigarette and told him, "And don't bloody quote me on any of this. I'll know in the morning." With that, she went back inside to carry on working.

He shouted after her, "Thank you, darling." She grunted something obscene and went inside the warehouse.

He could hear Boomer getting a mouthful from Jenny as he followed her into the warehouse. Boomer had been looking around and Jenny had caught him looking inside one of the boxes. It's not often you saw Boomer looking sorry and lost for words but Jenny had that effect on everyone. She was damn good at her job and she was admired and always the preferred SOCO for any job on their patch.

It was late and there was nothing else they could do tonight. Boomer had a 5 a.m. raid the next morning to round up the gang members. Cells had been booked at Ilford, Dagenham, Barking and Forest Gate Police Stations to contain them all. Jenny had promised them some information by mid-morning and the autopsies would be carried out tomorrow as well. Boomer and Jazz each picked up a burger from a late night stall in Ilford and then they each went their own way home. Jazz wasn't part of the raid so he would have a lie in until 6 a.m. It was going to be a busy day tomorrow.

On the way home, he rang Sharon for any news. She said it was a long time coming but she was hopeful that by the morning there would be some news. She sounded tired. The CCTV had been slow going but they had finally got on camera the car at Charlie Brown's roundabout going towards Woodford at the moment.

She hoped they would be getting somewhere soon. She was off for some sleep and had left an officer carrying on the work. In answer to his question, she told him that she hadn't had anything to eat yet. She was going to pick up a curry from some place on the way home. She had heard what had happened to him and checked he was OK. He promised to update her tomorrow and told her not to be concerned because he had a guardian angel, the killers had told him that. He would tell her in the morning about what was said about Tony. They agreed to meet at Ilford at 7 a.m. and decide what they were going to do.

He needed a drink and was glad to get home and into his room uninterrupted. It was nearly midnight and the Chodda family were asleep. The facts were terrible and hard to comprehend. Tony was dead but they still had no idea where his body was. Alice was dead, a sweet old lady who deserved to die in her sleep, not at the hands of a murderer. He should be dead and for the life of him he didn't know why he was spared. It would haunt him for the next few months. At the last count there were 17 bodies and when Tony's body was found the count would be 18. The murder squad from Scotland Yard would be There soon. There haD never been so many murders in such a short time on any pitch in London. It rivalled Chicago at its worst and the press would be making mincemeat of the Police force. He sat with a drink thinking life was a mess. But if he thought it was bad now, tomorrow was going to be worse. He would need all his stamina to survive the day.

THE BEST LAID PLANS OF MICE AND MEN

He met Sharon at 7 a.m. He hadn't slept well and was at the station by 6. a.m. He waited to see if any of the gang members had been brought in yet. Boomer had some that were being processed in the custody suite. Fingerprints were being taken, photos taken and when all the entries into logs had been made, they would be put in a cell ready for interview. The noise in the custody suite would have woken up anyone in the vicinity. Bob was on duty and he said hello but there was no time for chit chat, he had his hands full. Jazz wasn't needed for this operation so he took himself off to wait in the canteen for Sharon.

She arrived looking dreadful. She said she had only got four hours sleep by the time she got back, had something to eat and showered. He commiserated but got her back on track to talk about the job in hand. He went through the details of the previous night and his finding the warehouse, the bodies and how he was caught and he thought he was a gonna. Sharon looked pale at the description but when Jazz told her what they said about Tony, she went chalk-white. He was glad he hadn't told her last night.

When asked about Tony's phone, she said she had a

phone call to make. She said she had an expert looking into it for her and it all depended on whether the phone was used or not, which was depressing to hear. The good thing was that at some point in the evening Sharon had rung him and so had Jazz and his mother. Even if he had had his phone off, the signal would have got through to the phone and would show them where he was when he was called. Sharon confirmed that she had spoken to Mrs Sepple, Tony's mother, yesterday evening and confirmed the number she had rung Tony's mobile on and at what time. It would seem she was the last one to have rung him. So far, she added, his phone was at Forest Gate when both she and Jazz tried to ring him. They crossed their fingers that Mrs Sepple had rung him late enough for him to be wherever he finally arrived at so they could find him.

She told Jazz that her conversation with Mrs Sepple went from utter panic and hysteria to full blown cold, murderous anger at her boy being missing and she was looking for someone to blame. Sharon said it might be best for Jazz not to contact her until there was further evidence. The air between them felt heavy and a deep depression fell like a soggy blanket over them as they both knew the news would not be good.

Before they left, it was decided that today was the day that all the evidence must come together. Sharon would finish the CCTV, which should take them to the vicinity of where Tony was. The phone expert had until lunchtime before she would get angry and demand some evidence. By 1 p.m. at the latest, Sharon hoped to have her information at the ready.

Jazz was off to see Bam Bam to see what on earth was happening with the Holy Trinity and to see his reaction to the early morning raids on his men as well as all the others in the Holy Trinity. He would then seek out Jenny, who by lunchtime should have lots to tell him.

He checked with Boomer and said he would meet him at 2 p.m. so they could update each other on what they had found. Boomer was in his element and had before him all the nasty pieces of work he had longed to pull in before. This was his opportunity to wring as much information out of them all as was possible within the PACE clock time. They had been pulled in for a legitimate reason and they had 24 hours before the police had to make the decision to release or charge.

Boomer, Sharon and Jazz were ready to go off and work in their own areas and come back with information at lunchtime. They were about to say goodbye and go on their way when an officer from the front desk cleared his throat and said that there was a woman in the front office waiting to see DS Singh. When asked her name, the officer said it was Mrs Sepple. They all stopped for a second and looked at Jazz.

"Yea Gods, I don't envy you with Tony's mother," was all Boomer would say as he left to return to the interview room where 'a particularly nasty piece of scrotum' was waiting to be interviewed. Sharon said she would go with Jazz as backup. Jazz told her to go and find a comforting PWC to sit with her. He wiped his face and wondered what on earth he was going to say to this distraught mother.

As soon as she saw him, she rose out of her seat

with a vehemence he had only seen in films. "Where is my boy?" she shouted across the counter, spitting the words in the direction of his face. "I know all about you, you murderer!" she shouted, her face contorted with anger and hatred. "I want my baby back now!" she screamed and walked purposely up to the counter and hit the glass in front of Jazz's astonished face with all the force of a demon. It didn't break but Jazz ducked instinctively at the blow coming towards him. He was then faced with a broken woman who melted back into a chair, bent over and was wracked by deep, loud sobs. Everyone in the front office had been caught in a tableau of stillness whilst they watched, in shock, the tirade before them. Now she was sobbing, all movement returned and each person resumed what they were doing. Sharon had arrived with a PWC ,who took Mrs Sepple to a waiting room and said she would get her a cup of tea.

The accusing looks did not miss Jazz. He could feel them piercing his back. Everyone agreed with what Mrs Sepple had said. He was a murderer. He was responsible for Tony and he let him down. The other incident was brought back with a vengeance. What had only been muttered darkly by those who knew was now spoken of by everyone. Jazz was a Jonah and anyone who worked with him was liable to end up dead, it had happened before and now it had happened again. As he stood there in the middle of the front office, Jazz was shown by his fellow officers that he was no longer considered one of them. They turned their back on him and blamed him along with Mrs Sepple for Tony's disappearance and possible death.

He had to go and see Mrs Sepple. She had come to see him, and he had to speak to her to tell her what they were doing to find Tony. He told Sharon to get on with the CCTV and the mobile phone, he needed to have everything by lunchtime. She would have stayed with him as support if he had asked but she wished him luck and left. Time was of the essence, this needed to be solved and finished quickly, before there were more killings.

He walked into the small interview room and nodded to the PWC to leave. He sat down and faced Mrs Sepple. She looked drawn and dishevelled but she didn't care. "Where is my baby boy?" she implored. For the minute, the fight seemed to have gone out of her. He was relieved at this. She listened intently as he told her everything that was being done and how they were trying to find him. He kept his conversation optimistic, suggesting they would find Tony alive and well. He knew this was not going to be true, but until they knew for sure, he could still be alive.

He asked her when she last tried to ring him and she said she was up all night and tried regularly, about every 30 minutes in the end. She said he would never leave her like this on purpose. He always rang her and told her when he was going to be late. She asked why it was different that night, he hadn't rung her at all.

Jazz, at a loss to know how to answer, went on to say what a dedicated officer he was and that if he found a lead, he was enthusiastic and determined to find out the facts, and he sometimes got carried away with his work. He added what a fine upstanding Detective he was. She liked to hear this and agreed with Jazz.

He said that there were at least 100 officers searching for him as they spoke. This may have been a slight exaggeration but, in fact, those dealing with the gang raid, the CCTV, the phones and everyone in the police stations in the East End were doing what they could to find out where Tony was, and that was a lot of officers. He suggested she went home and waited. They were all getting on with the job of finding him and he wanted to be out there too. Numbed by worry, the fight had gone out of Mrs Sepple and she got up and left. She turned at the door and said she wanted to be kept informed of what was happening. Jazz readily agreed and said she would be the first to know. She hesitated for a second and added chillingly, "If he is hurt or…" she hesitated for a second, not daring to say the word "dead, it will be on your head. You will be to blame and I will take you through every court in the land to get you put away for a long time." With that, she left the room, closing the door quietly behind her. Jazz exhaled. He had been holding his breath and the tension could be cut with a knife. He had to hold on and keep control.

He called for the PWC who was waiting outside the room to arrange for a car to take Mrs Sepple home. He suggested she should stay with Mrs Sepple until there was further news. This was agreed and they left the station. Jazz sighed with relief. How on earth was he going to tell her when they found Tony? He pulled himself together, he had work to do and time was running out. A quick drink from his flask helped. He tried to shrug off the look in Mrs Sepple's eyes; she had spooked him.

He wanted to see Bam Bam. Jenny would be ready for him at about 10 a.m. He had been held up longer than he wanted to by Mrs Sepple but he reckoned he still had time to see Bam Bam first. He knew he was in trouble there as well. Bam Bam's men had been raided and were banged up at some police station in the area. He would be none too pleased to see Jazz. Gee, what a start to the day, was all he could think. Once outside, he took a cigarette and inhaled deeply. It was still a bit early but he had his flask with him and the spare one filled too. He took a small swig, just enough to fire him up. He hadn't had time for breakfast and there had to be some protein in the vodka, he presumed.

It was now nearly 9 a.m. and he wondered if it was a bit early for Bam Bam to have arrived. He saw his car and realised of course he would be early. His men had been rounded up that morning. He was lucky it hadn't been him as well. In fact, he wondered why he hadn't been arrested with the others. On reflection, he knew that everyone was aware that Bam Bam didn't deal in drugs and wasn't anything to do with all that was going on. That's what made him so helpful to Jazz; he might not deal in it but he knew what was going on in his patch. No one knew of their special relationship. They would never be friends but Bam Bam owed Jazz big time and although he would never call himself a grass, he reluctantly threw useful snippets of information to Jazz when pushed.

This meeting would be a test of their special relationship. Bam Bam was not alone, his right-hand man was with him. He was spitting nails in the direction of Jazz. "How dare you arrest my men? How dare you bring them into your gang round-up? Everyone knows it's nothing to do with me." He was getting very red and hot under the collar. His huge belly wobbled with the exertion.

Jazz held up his hands and apologised and tried to say something helpful but failed miserably. "I know you're mad about what's going on. I've just come to check how you are. I was concerned, but I see you're OK here and you have…" He waved a hand at the other man, not knowing his name and not knowing what to call him.

"If you mean Jimmy, then yes, I have Jimmy with me. That would have been too outrageous if he had been taken to the police station as well." Jazz nodded to Jimmy. He would try and remember his name next time.

Jazz tried to calm the situation. "Look, this is all getting out of hand, Bam Bam. Between us we have got to put a stop to this. I've come for your help. Is there anything you can tell me that will get this back on track? 17 murders in a few days is just a bit too much for this town and it's got to stop. My DC is still missing and I understand there is a good chance he was murdered. Killing a police officer is about the worst thing any criminal can do. Everyone is out there looking for him and when he is found, and if he is dead, there will be no peace in this town until the murderer is caught." Jazz sat down. He was feeling worn down by the scale of events and needed some help now.

Bam Bam asked Jimmy to find some tea and cakes for them both. God, this man has a sweet tooth no matter how dire the situation, Jazz thought. Bam Bam wanted a moment to think so Jazz sat and waited. He didn't have much time but Bam Bam was worth the wait.

"I am not certain, Jazz, but I think you are looking at both the Triads and Snakeheads here. They formed some sort of alliance. They were working to take over the cocaine factories, you know that, but something spooked them into action and triggered all these killings." He looked at Jazz and waited for a reaction.

Jazz thought there was something not quite right here. "I saw three of the murderers and they weren't Chinese," Jazz said.

Unruffled, Bam Bam uttered, "Ah, I don't suppose they were." Jazz wondered what that meant.

There was a moment's silence as the tea and cakes were brought in. Tea was given out to Bam Bam first, with the offer of a cake, and then to Jazz, who took the tea and declined the cake. Bam Bam sipped his tea and finished a small cake before he was ready to continue. "You really should try one of these, they are beautifully cooked." Bam Bam said as he proffered a coconut cake. Jazz shook his head and said no thank you. It was infuriating to watch this gross man eat, but Jazz knew he had to sit calmly if he wanted any information.

After wiping his mouth and setting his cup down, Bam Bam turned his attention to Jazz. "Of course they have hired people to do their work for them. It makes sense. This is our town and we are not going to jeopardise our men by getting them to do the dirty work. It would have been planned and everyone would have ensured they had an alibi that night. I am nothing to do with it but my men all have alibis too." Jazz, shocked, asked why the fuck Bam Bam hadn't told him this was happening. Calmly, Bam Bam, eyeing up another cake, said, "There was no time. I only got wind of it about an hour before it happened and I was busy getting everyone together somewhere public. We all went to the Gurdwara and donated money. We were well remembered."

Jazz asked, "If you have nothing to do with the killings, why did you need an alibi?"

Bam Bam looked at him almost with pity. "You think we would have been spared if we didn't have alibis? Don't be naïve, you know as well as I do, if the cap fits…" Jazz looked away, he knew that could be true.

"The gunmen were South Asian not Chinese, explain that."

Bam Bam looked at him again as if he was a stupid cretin. "If you are buying guns for a job, you pick the best. Sikhs are warriors and they were the best and they were available immediately." He shifted in his chair, picked up the cake that he had been eyeing and took a huge mouthful. He continued to talk with difficulty as he chewed through the thickness of the coconut and icing. "I know who they are and they left the country as soon as they had finished. Very professional and slick." He caught a look in Jazz's eyes and quickly added, "Don't even think about getting me to identify them or bringing me into this. It is not my war. I am on the side lines and that's where I am staying. We have a good working relationship, don't screw it up."

Jazz goaded and Bam Bam sidelined him for the next half an hour. There was no more information to be had. Jazz asked again if he knew what had happened to his DC, Tony Sepple. Bam Bam said he had made enquiries but no one was talking. Jazz told him that the gunmen had told him they had killed Tony and they laughed about it. Bam Bam stopped eating for a second and sat in silence, thinking. "I had no idea, Jazz, I wasn't told that. Are you sure?"

Bam Bam said he wanted everything to settle down. The police were making his work difficult and everyone was on edge. The relationship between the Holy Trinity was getting quite strained, the police were interfering and, all in all, the East End was not a nice place to be. To kill a policeman was the height of stupidity and caused everyone to batten down the hatches. He promised Jazz that if he got an inkling of who ordered this, he would tell him. He wanted the police off his back. It was obvious Jazz would get no further with Bam Bam but he asked him to keep making enquiries. They needed to find DC Sepple. Jazz left feeling uneasy but was not sure why.

He phoned Sharon to find out what was happening and she told him they would have more information soon. He made his way to the mortuary, where he was meeting Jenny. Tom Black rang him and said he would meet him there. When Jazz asked how the interviews with the various gang members were going, his reply was simply, "Fucking bollocks." It was beginning to feel like everyone was rushing around chasing their own tail and someone was watching them, laughing at their stupidity and ineffectiveness.

He suddenly felt very alone and out of his depth. For a moment, he missed the blind loyalty of his mother. She never understood his work but she understood her love for him and in her eyes he could never do wrong. He missed having someone who was proud of him. At the moment, he had nothing to be proud of and he took the blame for Tony's disappearance fully on his shoulders. He didn't know how he could face himself let alone Tony's mother or his colleagues if Tony was found dead. His answer was to take another quick swig from his beloved flask. The heat of the vodka as it trickled down his throat, kissing his tonsils as it passed, gave him some strength and purpose to carry on. He knew he was on a route that would lead to them finding Tony dead and then he would be confirmed as a murderer. He would face his demons then.

THE BEAT GOES ON

Jazz arrived at Jenny's office to find Tom and DCI Radley with him. Jenny was off doing something important in the next room; she coulbe heard swearing and slamming cabinet doors. Jazz tentatively walked into what felt like the lion's den. DCI Radley lost no time in asking him what the hell was happening in his manor. Jazz sat down, composed himself and repeated what the Asian gang had told him by about Tony. DCI Radley slumped down and exhaled a wearisome and defeated sigh. "I had heard but wanted to hear your version. I hope it's not true." Tom and Jazz both murmured their agreement. With a slightly lighter tone, he asked, "So what happened this morning? I understand you have a contact in the gangs feeding you information."

Jazz cringed at such an explicit choice of words. "Please, Sir, don't mention out loud that again. He's a very valuable contact and if anyone gets an inkling, he would be dead meat and I would lose a contact." DCI Radley nodded gravely and said it wouldn't be mentioned again. He went on to ask what news he had.

Jazz told him the Asian killers were specially commissioned from outside to do the job. The Snakeheads and Triads combined forces for this one.

They wanted the Viets out and to take over their cannabis factories but didn't want to bloody their own hands. The killers had left the country. In answer to the DCI's question, he nodded and said, "Yes, the same ones that told me they had killed Tony." Again, he was asked why he was spared and Tony was killed. It didn't make sense; why Tony, what did he see? They knew now why they weren't bothered about killing a policeman. It was obviously because they were leaving the country so the problem wasn't theirs. "I bet the Triads and Snakeheads were pissed off though," added Jazz.

DCI Radley told them both that he wanted to follow up the leads from Jenny and the CCTV. He told them he was fed up just waiting for results. He had nothing to tell the press and the raids on the Triads and Snakeheads wasn't getting them anywhere. They all had the same alibi. He added that even Bam Bam had an alibi for his men, which he thought was strange. Everyone had a cast-iron alibi. It was very frustrating. He was going to spend the day seeing what cropped up.

Tom and Jazz hid as best they could the feeling of depression that their boss was going to step on their toes at a crucial time. They wanted to do things their way and not have him poking his nose in. The truth was that the murder squad from the Yard wanted to muscle in on this and DCI Radley was having none of it. He was going to follow Jazz's example and go AWOL. He hoped that something concrete would turn up today to finish the case and give the credit to Ilford Police and not the Yard murder squad, who were always poncing about on the television. It was a depressing thought, but he knew that if nothing was found today, it was likely he would go down with Tom and Jazz as officers who were only fit for school playground watches.

Jenny, unaware of the conversations that had taken place, breezed into the room carrying papers, plastic bags and other objects related to her job. "Well don't bloody stand there! Take some of these from me," was her grumpy welcome. She had in total 40 bags and a sheaf of paperwork. There were bullets in most of the bags.

"Gees, how many bullets were fired?" Tom exclaimed.

"Actually there were in excess of 60 bullets fired. Some are still in the bodies; no time to do an autopsy on all of them yet though. We had a count up as best we could. And these," she pointed to the smaller bags ,"are the bullets retrieved from three bodies and the walls."

This time it was Jazz who whistled and said, "My God! It was meant to be an outright slaughter."

DCI Radley stepped forward and looked at the bullets. "Ah, Glock I see, most probably a Glock 26. Fires up to 33 rounds and with three men that is quite some firepower."

Jenny looked suitably impressed. "Well, actually yes, you are right, DCI Radley."

He smiled. "Oh call me Johnny."

Jenny smiled coyly and nodded.

Jazz, watching this, could only think, For goodness sake, get a room! This is a murder enquiry and I have a pair of losers flirting with each other. He butted in and loudly asked, "So what does this mean?"

Jenny let Johnny answer and he said convincingly, "This means they were hired killers. The Glock 26 is the preferred gun for law enforcement agencies in America and for hired killers. It is the gun that never lets you down; it's light to hold with a smooth firing action and with 33 rounds per magazine, it's going to get you out of any trouble and do the job quickly." He noticed the looks of surprise from Tom and Jazz and explained with a wry smile, "I studied guns and had a Glock 26 for a few years."

The silence made DCI Johnny struggle to carry on the conversation. "I belonged to a Metropolitan Police gun club. I'm quite a good shot but rusty now." He wanted to move this conversation on so with a smile he turned to Jenny and enquired, "Fingerprints?"

She nodded and said the majority were accounted for. Her team had checked with the home office and found most were here on visas, only three were not known and illegal immigrants. There was a dramatic pause and Jenny continued, "The one that will interest you is Tran Tan Giap. He was there; found him slumped in a corner behind some boxes." It made sense, this was a takeover and Tran Tan was the head of the Viets. It fitted in with what Jazz had been told. It looked like the gang war was over, but they still didn't know who had organised this. Was it the Triads, the Snakeheads or both working together.

At this point, the DCI stold them that Interpol was on standby for any information he had. He got on his mobile phone to tell them about the Asian killers that were said to have left the country. He needed any leads they may have as soon as possible. Tran Tan Giap was also mentioned and he wanted to know anything that might help them with this case; where he had travelled and with whom and any associates they knew about. He turned to Tom and told him to check up on his men to find out if any of the interviews had pulled anything in. He spoke to a gatekeeper in the office and checked that officers were out on the beat asking questions. He added that he didn't want *Ippledips** doing this work, he needed experienced officers.

He left Jazz for last and said that now he wanted to see Sharon and what was on the CCTV cameras. The three of them made their way to the door and into the waiting car. Jenny shouted after them that the autopsy results would wing their way to them when completed. Johnny shouted back that he wanted a phone call and the results would be collected immediately then, as an afterthought, he shouted, "And make that today." Jenny's swearing was muffled but the sentiments were understood. They laughed, wheel spun the car and put the blue light on to save time. The air buzzed with action, Jazz felt more animated than he had done for a while and was anxious to get going and find Tony and solve these murders. He was beginning to like this DCI now he was getting his hands dirty instead of sitting in his office.

They moved at speed to Plaistow Police Station, where Sharon had commandeered a fleet of rooms. She was enjoying the power of it all. A police officer was missing and she was getting everything and anything she

*IPLDIPS is a raw recruit uniformed officer- Initial Police Learning Development Programme

wanted. A room for was set up for CCTV with three officers working full time on looking at the footage and another negotiating with out of area command centres for CCTV. In another room was the mobile phone work and in another were interview statements and anything that might help find Tony. Sharon was in her element and proud to say she was making magnificent progress. Her goal was to find Tony alive. If he was found dead, it would be her fault and that just couldn't happen.

She had got everything very much under her control including the officers there. Four mugs of tea and some biscuits were found and Sharon updated them on the CCTV so far. "We have just reached a dead end I am afraid," she told them. "Once you get past Woodford Green, the CCTV stops as you reach Epping Forest. Epping town has CCTV and there is no sight of them. We lost them on the road between Woodford Green and Epping town. It's one hell of a big area." Even the chocolate digestives didn't help, it felt like they were swallowing glass. The depression lasted a few minutes until one officer found a good picture of the men in the car as they waited by traffic lights in Woodford Green. He had blown it up so the occupants could be seen clearly.

They spotted Tony in the back sitting in the middle of two men. The driver was very clear. None of the faces were known and all they could tell was they were Asian. Jazz recognised the driver as one of the men in the warehouse. It felt like a bolt had hit him in his stomach. They had said they had killed Tony and there was one of them as clear as day in the car with him. Everyone present felt charged with an unbelievable need to find their man as quickly as possible. A copy of the picture was sent to facial mapping to see if any one of them was on record there or with Interpol. It would take time but hopefully answers could be found by the evening. Computers made the process much quicker. The picture was emailed to London immediately.

The interesting part of the CCTV that Sharon wanted to show them was that after an hour, the same Land Rover was picked up on CCTV coming back along the Woodford Green road. A good picture was chosen and blown up; although a bit blurred, it showed only three men in the car. It wasn't very clear, but everyone thought that it was Tony who was missing in the picture. The Land Rover was still being tracked by the CCTV operators and it was thought this would take some time. For now, they knew that Tony had disappeared between Woodford Green and Epping town Centre. Everyone was in work mode and their adrenalin was roaring. They needed to find Tony now.

A team of officers was assigned to the road between Woodford Green and Epping town Centre. They now knew they were looking for a Land Rover and they had the number plate. It took only 10 minutes to be told that the number plate was false. Every turning off of the road was to be explored and minutely examined for tyre marks. It was a huge job because there were many off road parking places that cars could take, some were official car parks and some were easy off roads, which many a courting couple would make use of. It was thought that Epping Forest at night might be responsible for at least 10% of babies conceived in the Essex area. DCI Johnny Radley got on the phone again and asked for more officers and a coordinator to make sure any evidence found wasn't fucked up.

Jazz wanted to go out there with the officers to find Tony. Being stuck in this office was very frustrating and maddening. It was still possible that Tony was alive and just held somewhere out there in the forest. He didn't really believe it, but for the time being, he wanted to believe it very much. He was about to ask DCI Radley if he could go with the officers. Sensing such a question, Johnny Radley put his hand up to warn Jazz to not even ask. "We have the mobile phone signal to get now."

A clatter of heels made them turn to see an excited Sharon, barely containing her glee, enter the room. She had the arm of a tall lanky streak of a man with hair that badly needed cutting. "This is Devlin and he has some interesting news for us."

They all sat up straight and looked intently at this 20-something man who was now very embarrassed to have such an audience. He flopped around and brushed his hair out of his eyes. "Get on with it, man," was the abrupt order from DCI Radley.

"Oh yes, of course, please excuse me," was the muddled response as Devlin gathered himself together. Before another, more robust reprimand came his way, Devlin took a deep breath and started. "We have found the phone, well what I actually mean is that we are fairly clear on where the mobile phone might be. That's not to say we know in centimetres where the phone is, more within a radius of half a kilometre."

They looked at each other and Jazz piped up, "What the bloody hell does that mean, Devlin?"

The tension in the room was thick enough to cut and this made Devlin very anxious indeed. He started to trip over his words again, not knowing where to start or where to finish. This was new technology for the Met. Though it had been around for a while, the ability to home in so closely was a new achievement to be pinned to the coat of the Science and Technology Department. Devlin knew his stuff, he was the bright spark who had helped build the department's reputation in the country. To those working in the field, the saying was 'If you need to know, ask Devlin.' Devlin's one big downfall was his inability to explain his genius to anyone else.

He had joined the Met as a lab rat. Before long, it was noticed that he had hidden his immense talent for technology behind an enormous bush. Technology had moved with leaps and bounds, which had caused many experts in the Metropolitan Police Technology and Science Departments to struggle to keep up. It seemed like criminals were always one step ahead, always finding ways to manipulate technology to their advantage. One of the prime examples of this was the Securicor vans.

Theft of the money boxes had stopped when a green dye coated anyone who illegally opened a money box. For a while, a policeman's lot was a very happy one. It didn't take long to find villains who had robbed Securicor vans and opened the money boxes. The green dye was all over them and no amount of washing could get rid of it. It turned villains into Jolly Green Giants, as officers called them. Securicor vans, for some time, were safe. Then a way was found to open the money boxes and not trigger the green dye. Again, it was open season on Securicor vans and other ways of foiling villains had to be found.

Devlin had left university a clever young man with a 2:1 degree but with little idea of how to apply his skills. A chance comment from his father, who worked for the Met police, took him down the route to the Technology and Science Department. It didn't take long for his superiors to notice this young man who regularly could be found doggedly working on a problem, often until late in the evening, and coming up with a solution. After two years, he was given his own office and team who worked on specific problems handed to them. Where others struggled to maintain the huge developments in technology, Devlin embraced each and every challenge and his skills grew at the same time as technology grew. He liaised with his contacts in British Telecom over mobile signals but only through his computer. He rarely met anyone.

Devlin loved his job and had found his goal in life; he embraced technology in all its forms and understood it in a way others couldn't. He devoted his work time and a lot of his personal time to solving any problem the Met threw at him. His reputation soared and he became the darling of his department, but at the same time, his personal development and social life plummeted.

The consequences of such devotion to duty and the pursuit of technological results was that Devlin someone became who seemed to have lost the skill of interacting socially and verbally with other human beings. If he had his way, he would only send reports to be read and never have to actually deal with people. He had got his own way for most of his working career but today the DCI wanted to talk to him in person.

Tracking people using mobile phones was fairly new and for some time had been quite haphazard in just how helpful it was. Devlin had worked in this area for a while, narrowing the margins of error. For a while now a mobile phone could be detected quite easily using a radius of five to ten miles, which was helpful. To be able to detect within 100 metres was very useful. DCI Radley wanted to hear from Devlin what the actual position was regarding the mobile phone that belonged to DC Tony Sepple. Sharon had made sure he came along and explained it to all present.

Phased by being asked to *get on with* it, Devlin went into the only mode he could function clearly in and that was technical mode. After two minutes of oscillations and projections, and more technical jargon that went over the heads of everyone present, the restlessness and frustration was getting loud. Jazz, seeing that the chap in front of them was totally dysfunctional tried to prize answers out of him that might be helpful to them. The only question on everyone's lips was *where is the bloody phone now*? A map had been put on the wall of the area around the road from Woodford Green to Epping. Jazz took him to the map and asked him to pinpoint where the phone could be found.

After much flapping and qualification of data, Devlin

was pushed into reluctantly giving them an answer. If he had seen the frustrated rage only just contained by officers behind him, he would have fled the room. The tension was now at breaking point and, with a deep sigh, Devlin pushed away his technical demons, which under normal circumstances would not have allowed such an unsubstantiated analysis, and put a pin in the map just off the Epping Road. He protested that this was an educated guess and by no means certain due to fluctuations in the satellite being used but by now everyone had left the room and was on the phone to various strategic officers at the scene.

Sniffer dogs highly trained in finding bodies had already been marshalled and were on their way to Epping, the heat-seeking helicopter was making another pass over the area and so far nothing had been found. Jazz, Tom and DCI Johnny Radley were heading for the nearest police car to take them to the site. Sharon was told to stay put and get on with the CCTV. Hurriedly, Jazz added that she was doing a grand job and they couldn't do without her working on this. He shouted as he dashed for the car that she was responsible for getting them this far in finding Tony and she should be proud. She wasn't, she felt it was her fault Tony was in this dangerous, possibly fatal, position. She did appreciate Jazz throwing her a crumb of comfort and worth though.

When their police car halted as near to where the pin had been put as was possible the tyres smelt of burnt rubber and the blue flashing light was still turning in a giddy fashion. The whole area was teeming with police officers and cars. The distant barking told them the sniffer dogs had arrived and seemed to be excitedly working beyond the trees. The press were there in convoy with TV cameras pointed in every direction and flashes from photographers causing Jazz momentary blindness as he got out of the car and saw them all pushing, shouting and calling for them to make comments. The press were just about held back by a thin cordon placed across the road and four policemen. It was bedlam and DCI Johnny Radley told officers in no uncertain terms to push them all back to Woodford. Why the hell they were so far down this road was beyond him and evidence could be lost because of them. A police van arrived packed with TGI men. "Thank God the Trojans have arrived," Jazz muttered to Tom. The beefy men were used to dealing with difficult and dangerous crowds. They all jumped out of the van and began pushing the press back along the Epping Road. The shouts of *freedom of the press* and grumbling and curses could be heard for some time. They all heard the sound of the many car and bike engines starting and then a calm descended as the press were escorted back to Woodford Green.

They had a way to walk. The road block didn't allow any cars beyond the point of a mile past Woodford Green. There was still a mile to walk to the epicentre of where Devlin thought the mobile phone might be located. They could see officers on either side of the road working in formation to ensure any clues they might find would not be overlooked. It was a painstaking task and many off-duty police officers had volunteered to help. It was a huge area to cover and by now there were 200 police officers combing Epping Forest for DC Tony Sepple. They could hear megaphones being used to ensure groups of officers were walking in the right direction. The sweep of officers was tight and well orchestrated. Everyone wanted to do their bit to help and policemen and women from different regions worked alongside local officers.

Jazz, Tom and DCI Radley marched swiftly down the middle of the Epping Road, watching everything going on. They carried a radio and a voice told them that a more intensive search was happening in the next off road track on their right. They hurried to get there, fearful that they might miss something of importance. They knew which track it was by the police officers crowding around the that part of the road.

A call from a dog handler made them run towards a clearing. The three sniffer dogs were all straining on their leads to get close to a tree stump and were barking excitedly. There was something buried under the tree stump lying casually across the ground. The dogs were trained to sniff out dead bodies; Jazz hoped it was a dog or something buried there, the alternative made him feel sick.

Someone got a shovel and two officers were called to move the tree stump and branches attached. Everyone standing in the glade held their breath and waited. Tom interrupted the silence as they watched the branch being shifted and inappropriately whispered to Jazz, "If he is here then that fucker Devlin isn't just bollocks for brains after all." If it had been any other situation, Jazz might have laughed, but now was not a good time and he was intent on willing it not to be Tony's body.

It took ages for the branch to be shifted; it had something to do with the shape. The two men wielded it as best they could but for those watching, the frustration of just wanting to see it off that space was becoming unbearable. The huffs and puffs as the two men exerted themselves to move the weight and the awkwardness of the thinner but longer branches was mirrored by those watching. No one could step in and help because the area around and beneath the huge branch needed to be protected. The idea was that the men should pick up the stump and offending branches. The area underneath was not to be disturbed but the branches were soft and wanted to sweep the area as the stump was lifted. Another officer was brought in to help by holding part of the branches up. No one wanted to walk on the area that might contain a body. The slow process was painful to watch. Eventually, the three men coordinated their holds and on a count of three, hoisted the stump and branches off the floor. They moved quickly to one side and put the stump down well away from the freshly dug area.

The dogs were barking excitedly and straining on their leashes but they were held back from the spot. They all stood around the potential grave in silence and were about to make a decision on what to do next when they heard a female voice shouting from the road. "Don't touch a fucking thing otherwise you will be wearing your bollocks for earrings."

Jazz wondered if that woman was ever off duty. He

shouted, "Hello, Jenny, what's a nice girl like you doing in a place like this?" She gave him a curt wave and told him to fuck off.

She stomped into the glade with her heavy bag. She rested beside Jazz and just looked at the area before her. She whispered to him that she was off duty but when one of her boys was missing, she was on duty all the time. His eyes pricked for a second. This hard-bitten woman who had seen everything filthy and gruesome done to a human being was quite sweet in her earnestness. He wanted to just hug her, more for himself than her. He needed some comfort. Sensing this, she stroked his arm absent-mindedly as she surveyed the scene. With a sigh, she started to shout her orders. Her assistant was close by and he caught the brunt of her threats to do the bloody thing right this time. After a bit of grumbling about too many feet disturbing the area, she told the two officers with spades to bloody get on with it.

They dug for a surprisingly short time. The body wasn't buried deep. If it had been left a day or so longer, the animals would have dug him out. For yes, it was a him, as the suit implied. He had been shot in the head three times and most of his face was missing. Jenny's professionalism never faltered. She looked the body over quickly to estimate what had happened to cause death. It was pretty obvious to anyone looking. One bullet through the eye which came out the back of the head, another in the side of the head which exited by the ear and a third bullet smashed his nose, spread his face all over the place and exited the back of head. Jenny raised her head, looked around and shouted out, "I need someone to clear this area and start to look for the bullets; they should be on the ground somewhere. All bullets exited the head and were fired at close range. If you find one, don't bloody touch it, just call me over." A mortuary van was called for and whilst waiting, a rudimentary search of the victim's pockets was made. It looked like it could be Tony but the face was unrecognisable.

Sharon had arrived and stood in the clearing crying. She knew it was Tony. The suit and the shirt and tie were his. All her professionalism disappeared and she took herself off to the car to sob. A cigarette was hastily lit for her by an officer standing nearby. Jazz, ashen by now, walked into the woods for a few seconds. He needed a drink badly and reached for his flask. He drank deeply without tasting. The after effect left him breathless and warm. He didn't know what to do now. He walked over to Sharon and sat in the car with her. He lit her a cigarette and watched her smoking like it had gone out of fashion. He lit her another cigarette. She threw the stub out of the car and dragged heavily on the new cigarette. Her hands were shaking and she couldn't talk. They both cried in silence.

After a while, the door to the BMW police car was prised open and Boomer stuck his head in. "Ok you two, there is work to do, get a move on and stop fannying about. We have bastards to catch." The words motivated them both to get out of the car and search for DCI Johnny Radley. He was found shouting orders to every officer within the vicinity. He told everyone in no uncertain terms that the area was to be combed and any clues there were to be found were found pronto! The actual track had not been walked on, every officer and person involved in finding Tony's body had walked on the edges so the tyre marks were still evident. There was no doubt they would belong to the Land Rover seen on the CCTV but no stone would be left unturned. The mortuary van had arrived and the body was taken carefully to the van and off for a post mortem. A subdued Jenny promised the results in the morning.

The dogs had been taken away and rewarded and all officers left were in a heightened state of anger and each wanted to be the one to find out who had done this to one of them. Everyone would work 24 hours if necessary to find whatever there was to find in this part of the forest. Sharon said the CCTV had shown the Land Rover back to Ilford Lane and was then lost when it went down some back roads. CCTV was being looked at in the whole region in case it reappeared on a CCTV route.

It was all looking like a murder set up by either the Triads or Snakeheads using the Asian murder squad who appeared to have left the country. Jazz said he would go and talk to his contact in case he had heard anything of interest. Tom was going back to Ilford Police Station to find out if anything interesting had come out of the interviews with the gang members picked up that morning. He knew there was nothing because he would have been sent a message but now was not the time to be negative. Someone somewhere knew what had happened here and why. DCI Johnny Radley would visit Mrs Sepple and give her the bad news about Tony as soon as he was properly identified. Everyone knew it was him; his wallet was on him and contained all his details and police badge. His mobile phone was found turned off in an inside pocket. It was Tony.

Sharon asked Jazz if she could meet him later for a talk and a drink. She just didn't want to be alone. He nodded and said he would meet her in the Valentine Pub at Gants Hill. It was away from work but close to where they both lived. No one knew them there and they could talk in peace. He figured by 8 p.m. he would be free and she nodded that she would see him then.

He looked at his watch, it was 6 p.m. now and he needed to move himself to get to see Bam Bam. He was told to report with Tom and Sharon to DCI Radley's office in the morning at 8 a.m. sharp to consolidate information. Of course, he added, if anything came up that he needed to know urgently, they should call him on his mobile. He said he would be available any time, day or night. Jazz was beginning to like this man more and more. He was a policeman's policeman. He went over to Jenny and thanked her for coming and said he would see her tomorrow. Jenny grabbed his arm and squeezed it. Words were not needed; she tried to smile but neither of them could go that far.

TONY'S LEGACY

Jazz found Bam Bam still at his office. His car was sitting resplendently outside his office. It was beautifully polished and glistening. He rang the bell and waited for the usual response. He could see the security camera move direction slightly so that it pointed directly at his face. Bam Bam would be watching him standing there. He would enjoy it more if Jazz squirmed a little but Jazz stood still and tall and waited. The door was opened by the usual heavy who asked him what he wanted and told him to wait until he found out if Mr Bamra was available. He shut the door and left Jazz on the doorstep waiting. It was all the usual bullshit. Jazz refused to feel irritated by this, he knew it would show in his face. In fact, he lit a cigarette and turned his back on the camera. The bastard can't watch my face now, he thought. After a few minutes, a disconnected voice from the intercom attached to the wall said he could come in and the door was opened by another heavy employed by Bam Bam. He looked like he could stop bullets. The man was so big all he could do was sashay along the corridor towards the room Bam Bam was in. Jazz felt positively skinny behind him. He told himself never to upset the likes of him.

He was welcomed by "I have just heard, they have found your DC Sepple." Jazz was going to ask who told him because it was still under wraps until Mrs Sepple had been told but Bam Bam swiftly carried on the conversation. "I have been making enquiries all day to find out who actually employed the Asian squad. It would seem that the Triads and Snakeheads joined forces on this." Jazz asked why he had not been included in this because he was part of the Holy Trinity. Bam Bam shifted awkwardly in his chair. "I have nothing to do with the drug war and so they haven't bothered to include me in any of it. I have to say, when I found out, I was most put out to be excluded. It doesn't do my business any good to look like I am not part of the Holy Trinity but they are welcome to all the problems they have got now."

"No one is talking, Bam Bam. All the gang members have been interviewed today and they all have alibis. How am I going to break this? All the Viets have been killed including their leader, Tran Tan Giap, in the warehouse. The Viets are finished now, so who can I get for ordering the killings?" Jazz had thrown out the request and waited to see what came back. He should have waited quietly but the anger and frustration welled up and he jumped to his feet and thumped the desk in front of Bam Bam. Jazz shouted "They killed my DC, Tony, they killed a police officer, my officer, for no reason. I want whoever did this, I want them badly, now." Jazz was fed up with being pushed and pulled and having to be respectful to the piece of scum in front of him, enough was enough, it had to stop now. Something wasn't right here, Bam Bam knew more than he was telling and there was no way he would continue to go along with this charade of pretending to be respectful to this lump of shit.

Jazz stood taut with rage and through gritted teeth he was unable to hide the venom in his voice. "The Asian squad would not have killed Tony without orders. Someone ordered them to do it and I want to know who. You know who did this. You owe me, Bam Bam, and I am calling in the debt now. I want a name and I want to know where they are is now." He banged the table again for effect. Now hot with rage and breathless with shouting, Jazz waited for an answer and he wanted a damn good answer.

In the silence, the door opened and the huge ape of a man entered to see if all was alright. Bam Bam waved him away and he left, closing the door quietly. He tried to be placatory; he smiled sweetly at Jazz and said how he understood how difficult and sad this was for him. As he was about to order tea for them both, Jazz again slammed his fist on the table and leaned forward until he was barely a millimetre away from Bam Bam. Their noses almost touched as they stared at each other in a stand off.

Bam Bam sat back, unused to being treated in this disrespectful and unforgiving manner. He looked at Jazz and saw a broken man. He sighed, he would let the disrespect go for now. He said he would have a name and address for Jazz by the morning. Jazz wanted to know if he was being put off but Bam Bam protested loudly that he was almost sure he knew who the man was but it could also be another as well and he needed to find out for sure and where they were. Certain people were in hiding, he confided to Jazz. By now, Jazz was looking as if he could kill him and said, again through gritted teeth, that he wanted the information by 9 a.m. tomorrow morning and not a minute later. He was soothingly assured he would have it by then. Bam Bam pressed the button under his desk; he wanted Jazz out of his office now. The door opened and Jazz was shown to the door by the heavy. He could hear Bam Bam in the distance shouting for someone to get into his office now! He hoped that meant Bam Bam was working straight away on finding the men who ordered Tony's death.

Exhausted, defeated and feeling dreadful, Jazz headed towards the Valentine Public House in Gants Hill. He got there about 7.30 p.m. and decided to buy a bottle of vodka in the small off licence beside the pub. He needed it to help him sleep tonight. Tomorrow was going to be a busy day and he would need all his strength to keep going. The niggles in the back of his head were scratching away and he knew he had to keep a grip. The breakdown last time had started with the niggles in his head. They were just tiresome to start with but eventually they consumed him and took him over. He didn't want to go there again.

He ordered a large vodka tonic and found a seat out the back where he could have a cigarette as well and waited for Sharon. She arrived about 8.30 p.m., just as Jazz was downing his fourth double vodka tonic. She saw his drink and went and ordered a vodka and orange for herself. He muttered he would get it but he looked like he wouldn't move very quickly. She could see he had downed a few and she didn't blame him. She wanted to get rat arsed as well, just for tonight. She wanted to forget everything.

He looked up as she returned with a drink and some crisps. Almost apologising, she said she hadn't had anything to eat for most of the day. He said they could get a takeaway if she wanted. Without looking up from her drink, she told him there had been no progress in finding the Land Rover. It had just gone off the radar. The stuffing had been knocked out of both of them tonight. They had another drink. The silence was broken by Sharon taking a deep breath and suggesting he came back to her place in Chadwell Heath. She said it was just a small flat and they could pick up a takeaway. She added that she didn't want to be alone tonight. He asked if she had any orange juice at her home. She nodded. "In that case," he showed her the bag he had under the table, "it's back to your place and we'll get pissed." The cab rank was just around the corner and they walked unsteadily toward it. They saw a Chinese restaurant on the corner and they went in for some rice and spare ribs. Neither cared what they ate as long as it was something. After 10 minutes, with plastic bag in hand they tottered to the taxi rank. It took all of 15 minutes to get to Sharon's flat. It was one of those new blocks that seemed to spring up quickly just off Chadwell Heath high road.

It was tiny with a kitchen at one end of the lounge. He supposed it was good for one person but with low ceilings and walls close together, he felt claustrophobic. He reckoned his one room off the Drive felt bigger than this. There again, he didn't have a kitchen, just a fridge and kettle and he didn't have a bathroom, he used the one on the landing. Sharon was busy finding glasses and plates and he could hear her rummaging through a cutlery drawer. She was making excuses for the mess. He looked around. He didn't think a cup on a table and a few magazines constituted a mess. He thought she should see his room. He looked around. It was all white and sterile. There were no pictures on the walls and even the settee was white leather. She was no homemaker.

For a moment, he was deep in thought, somewhere between his mother and Alice. They were homemakers, he thought. He was rudely pulled out of his thoughts by Sharon tapping him on the shoulder and telling him to come and sit down to eat. He saw she had laid the table. He thought they were going to sit on the settee and watch TV but no way was that going to happen. The radio had been turned on and was playing something soft as she poured him a drink. He looked down and saw she had taken the bag with the vodka in it. He sat down opposite her and felt good for a moment. It had been a long time since he had played mothers and fathers in this way and it relaxed him. He picked up the paper serviette she had laid by his plate and smiled a thank you. She ruefully smiled back. Nothing was said between them as they ate and drank.

It was an hour later, after a few more large vodkas, that the tears and laughter started. They cried for Tony, they laughed at things he had done and then cried some more. They cursed and swore at the bastards who had killed him and fervently hoped he hadn't suffered too much. They blamed themselves and each protested that they were to blame and not the other. It turned into a snotty argument on whose fault it was and they nearly came to blows as tempers reached a height.

The drink, the emotion and the tiredness overcame them. They staggered to her bedroom. Jazz wasn't thinking clearly and just wanted to lie down and sleep. She told him in slurred syllables that she was knackered and just wanted to sleep. In the dark, they stumbled to the bed and undressed. As they lay together, suddenly naked, the warmth of a caress and the heat of an embrace made them both cry silently. They fell asleep holding each other tightly. It was three hours later that he woke and roused her. They made love quietly and gently.

WITH A LITTLE HELP FROM MY FRIENDS

He opened his eyes, wondering what woke him. Then he heard the snoring beside him. "Jesus Christ!" he whispered to himself through clenched teeth. He looked to the ceiling and asked himself, "What the fuck have I done?" This shouldn't have happened, he broke his golden rule. *Never ever be on the job with a woman in the job.* For a brief second, he agonised about how this was going to be put right. His eyes darted as he thought and landed on the alarm clock. He sat up with such a start that it woke her. The mayhem started.

It was bloody 7.30 a.m. and they had to be in DCI Radley's office at buggeringly 8 a.m. He couldn't find his fucking underpants or his sodding socks. Sharon was rushing around washing and getting dressed. She brushed her hair furiously. In 10 minutes they were both dressed and washed. He would shave later, his 6 o'clock shadow was very dark but it would have to wait. As they gathered bags and he checked his change for a cab, he turned and quietly said, "It was great, but it never happened." She understood and nodded silently. She wished he hadn't said that but she knew she couldn't have him. It had been wonderful and the lovemaking was so sweet and tender it almost made her cry as she remembered. He saw her face contort with tearful embarrassment, and he hugged her and whispered, "It was wonderful, thank you. But we work together, so it can never happen again." He hesitated for a second and added, "I will never forget last night, it was magic." In a second the mood changed and they dashed out the door to hail a cab. She blinked back the tears as they sped towards Ilford Police Station. The booze had held back some of the emotion last night but today it felt like a dam about to burst. She had to keep control.

When they arrived at the police station, he told her to go in first. He would pay the cab and follow in a few minutes. He didn't want everyone to know they arrived together; there would be too much talk. He was kidding himself. Of course they were spotted and the gossip had started before she got to the crime room. He didn't have a hangover but he felt decidedly jaded. The meeting was going to be deeply depressing but it had to be done. He would visit Bam Bam afterwards. He hoped he would give him the names that would get this solved. He wanted to find Tony's killers so badly it hurt.

He could hear the low hum of many voices as he walked along the corridor. A feeling of dread passed through him, he had to face them. As he entered, he could see the room was full. Every Detective Constable and Detective Inspector in the region was there. Normally when teams were called together there were always the jibes and banter of rivalry together with the jokes and raucous laughter. But today was a sombre gathering. One of their own had been killed and no one likes a cop killer. It had become the number one task for everyone in the police station. Nothing else mattered. If the petty crooks had an inkling of this, street robbery and shoplifting and burglary would be rife. There were officers lounging on desks and the chairs were moved to make room for more bodies than were normally together for a briefing. They were all squeezed in with more goodwill than was normal.

The noise level dropped suddenly as Jazz entered the room. He had been here before and knew why and what they had been saying about him and Tony's murder. He understood because he too felt responsible for Tony's death and it was the same the last time. He had hoped he would never again experience the feelings of such hopelessness and despair that dragged his soul into his boots. Again, he took all the blame and again he felt alone. He had to get through this. He would find Tony's killers, if he did nothing else in his life, he would do that. He had never found John's killers and, damn it, for the second time he had shown himself to be a total loser!

He mentally shook himself back to reality and looked around the room with tacit assurance. For now he had to carry on and, with this in mind, he smiled at everyone and said good morning brightly to show he didn't have a problem with the looks of faintly hidden scorn pushed in his direction. The eyes watched him in silence as he walked, shoulders back, head held high and with more dignity than he felt. His eyes searched and found Sharon standing in the corner of the room; he went and joined her. At this moment, she was the only friend he had and he wasn't sure if he had messed that up after last night. Today felt a very black day and he hoped it would get better. Thank God he remembered in the rush this morning to fill his two hip flasks. He knew he would need a few slugs of vodka to keep him going today.

They all waited for DCI Radley to make an appearance. There was no fanfare but a slamming of the door and a stack of files and papers walked into the room. As the table was cleared to make room for the files, which were deposited with a grunt, everyone saw it was Detective Chief Inspector Radley. Now divested of the plethora of files, he raised himself to his optimum height and commanded everyone around him to be quiet and listen.

Tom Black joined him at the front and Jazz was beckoned to come forward by an irritated DCI Radley. "Come on man, don't just stand there." This was not what Jazz wanted at all. He wanted to hide away from the accusing eyes but with more self-assurance than he had thought he could muster, he walked to the front beside Tom Black. It was going to be a very long meeting, going over all the facts and dissecting every bit of information.

They started with Alice and finding her body and progressed to all the Vietnamese bodies they had found and the ones in the canal identified as Snakehead and the Triad men. It was a horrible mess and they had no one to pin this all on. It was noted that the two who murdered Alice had been found dead, electrocuted in a cannabis factory. They ploughed through every bit of evidence and when everyone was up to speed with exactly what had gone on over the last few days, they all settled to discuss Tony. This was why so many officers were here: Tony, who they now knew was killed by a gang of Asian hit men. The Asians had been brought into the country to kill and destroy the Vietnamese who had set up cannabis factories in the East End. It would appear that all the Vietnamese gang had been rounded up and killed in the warehouse. A footnote was added that it was believed they had all been killed and intelligence could find no reason to believe anyone escaped.

Back to Tony; the question was asked why? Why was he killed? What was he doing in Forest Gate and why didn't anyone know he was there?

Tom Black summed up what his team had been doing: Interviewing the Snakehead and Triad gang members. He said all had alibis. Funnily enough, he told everyone present, it would appear the Triads were all together with their local newspaper reporter. "Apparently," and he spat the words out, "Charlie Wong has donated a vast amount of money to fund a drop in centre for the disaffected youth in the East End." He was going red in the face and boiling at the thought "The fucking bastard is only setting up a good place to ply his drugs and the bloody bastard press have given him rave reviews." He pulled himself together and added, "Freddie Chow from the Snakeheads had all his men conveniently in view at the races at Yarmouth. Why the hell the bastards were there I have no idea but they were far enough away for no one to be able to slip away for 10 minutes and shoot the bloody opposition." Tom's voice had risen to a crescendo and he needed to calm down. "Finally, Bam Bam's mob were at the Gurdwara for some religious do and there are lots of witnesses to say they stayed and no one left." He looked around, sighed and added unnecessarily, "So, we are all up shit creek without a fucking paddle on this one."

DCI Radley uncomfortably thanked Tom Black for his, and he searched for the right word, his colourful update. It was his turn now, and he told everyone present that the Asian gang which had been identified as being brought in to assassinate the opposition, which they did, and which was responsible for killing DC Tony Sepple, was thought to be out of the country now. He added that Interpol were on the case and were looking for this group. It was too early yet for an update but he felt sure more information would be available soon. He said he was in constant contact with Interpol. He was waiting for SOCO to come back with anything they had found out. He said something should come forward today.

Jazz was asked to update everyone on his area. He stepped forward with a bravado that hid his shame. He told everyone he had a meeting with his informant this morning and hoped to get some information on what was going on and if anyone knew who could have authorised Tony's death. With more venom in his voice than he meant to show, he added that he would personally avenge Tony's death and catch the mean mother fucker who did this.

Johnny Radley concluded that the killings had to stop. The murderer of Tony Sepple, a DC in his borough, was going to be found. He reminded everyone that time was of the essence and to get going. He wanted everyone interviewed again. He wanted all witnesses checked. He wanted all the neighbours living near the houses marked as cannabis factories and the house in Forest Gate re-interviewed. Everyone present knew what they had to do and where they had to go. He drummed into everyone that *someone somewhere knew something.* He finished by saying all were to be back in the operations room by 4 p.m. for updates.

The signal to get going was given and everyone present was suddenly motivated and up and talking and shouting instructions on where they were going and who they were going with. It was mayhem. Jazz looked at the crowd of dedicated officers in front of him and he felt proud. Everyone in that room was there because they wanted to find Tony's killer and they would do it for free. For once, overtime wasn't an issue. One of their own was dead and that just didn't happen in England. Jazz turned to the table to pick up the scattering of paperwork.

The figure standing in the doorway, ramrod stiff and straight with silent determination, watched the melee of men gathering themselves together to go about their business. She was spotted by a few officers and in a matter of seconds, the cacophony of voices, loud and urgent, all shouting for supremacy, was extinguished. The sudden heavy silence made Jazz turn and look at everyone in the room. They had all stopped and were staring at the person in the doorway. Standing there was Mrs Sepple. With trembling dignity, she walked slowly towards Jazz and his DCI. Her face was frozen in a grimace of pain, the grief barely contained. She was wearing the deepest black. A path was cleared as she moved forward. Like a tide, the officers present stepped back to allow her through and then forward after she had passed. Now everyone was watching Jazz.

DCI Radley stepped forward to greet her and gently took her by the arm to guide her away to somewhere quiet. But she was having none of it. She grunted as she roughly pulled her arm out of his grip. She had eyes only for Jazz. In a voice that seemed to come from the bottom of her soul she whispered vehemently that he was going to pay for what he did. Each word was aimed with a pointed poisoned tip to hit him between the eyes and make him suffer like she was. Only no one could suffer as much as she. She told him her world had been crushed and twisted and rung out and she wanted to die and be with Tony and it was his fault that Tony was dead. That word gave forth an anguished sob but she then became calm. In her calmness she was frightening. From the lowest part of her abdomen came a rumble of sound that forced its way into her throat and fired out of her mouth: "Murderer!" she said. She raised her hand in a flash and struck him across the face. She looked into his eyes and again screamed, "Murderer!" She struck him hard again across his face. DCI Radley, stunned and static by her actions, suddenly found movement and grabbed her arm as gently as he could and, whispering reassurance, spirited her away to his office.

The silence was palpable. Jazz held his stinging cheek. He couldn't lift his eyes to see everyone standing looking at him. He could feel the heat of their scorn and contempt and if he could, he would have just disappeared off the face of the earth. He wasn't sure he could carry on. Sharon, who had been standing in the corner, rushed to his side and turned him from his accusers. She whispered, "She is sick with grief. She doesn't know what she is saying. We will find Tony's murderers and everyone will know who did this." In desperation, she shouted, "It wasn't him!" to everyone standing in the room. They all knew about Jazz and the other incident so she could save her breath. It was him last time and it had happened again on his watch.

Everyone left feeling pretty sick at seeing Tony's mother in such despair but each and every one of them was determined to do their best to find Tony's killers and the man who had ordered his death. The room soon emptied, leaving Jazz and Sharon. Tom Black had left with Radley and Mrs Sepple. There were a few questions he would like to ask her if she was up for it.

On Jazz's instructions, Sharon was off to the Pathology Department to see if anything interesting had come out of the autopsies and there were fingerprints and bullets and whatever else they found to go through. She would report back to Jazz as soon as she knew anything of interest.

Jazz was off to see Bam Bam and he hoped and prayed he had the name of the bastard who ordered Tony's death. He wanted him arrested and in a cell before nightfall. It was early but he needed a drink. He stopped in the gents and sat down in a cubicle and drank deeply. He looked around at the regulation white tiled walls and thought what had he come to? Sitting on the bog drinking vodka and it wasn't 10 a.m. yet. When this was all over, he would sort himself out but for now he needed this.

He had time to spare. The phone call from one of Bam Bam's henchmen told him to be at the Gurdwara at 11 a.m. Again, Bam Bam was playing games. Of course he wouldn't be dictated to by the likes of Jazz. He was never going to see him at 9 a.m. because Jazz had ordered him to be there. There was no point in getting upset and making an issue out of it. Jazz had to calm down. He knew Bam Bam and what he was capable of. It was well known that Bam Bam would have someone badly beaten and the odd limb snapped for any disrespect shown to him.

At least it gave him a couple of hours to get himself straight and ready for the meeting. It was all taking its toll and Mrs Sepple just about finished him off. He splashed his face with cold water and looked in the mirror. He didn't like what he saw. OK he couldn't see horns or vampire teeth but the view was just as horrific. He wasn't a murderer, he knew that, but he didn't stop it happening. Once was bad enough but twice was incomprehensible. He would have to resign. God! He loved his job, he was good at it, he knew that. But why would anyone ever trust him again? At this moment he wouldn't even get a job as a lollypop man let alone as a Detective Sergeant with a team of Detectives under him. The drink helped stave of the deep depression that was trying to descend on him.

He decided he would get a coffee, he had time to kill. "Gees," he said in disgust, why had he used that word. For a second, he closed his eyes and mentally pulled himself together.

As he made his way to the canteen, he heard his name

called out and he turned to see Bob striding along the corridor. "I've come looking for you. Fancy a cuppa?" Jazz smiled and nodded, he could do with the company. Bob had always been there for him when everyone else had turned their back on him. Bob got the teas and they sat in a corner of the canteen. Eyes were on them but Bob told him not to worry, it would pass. "It's just gossip, Jazz, tomorrow it will be someone else. You're a good officer and anyone in their right mind knows you had nothing to do with Tony's death." He hesitated for a moment and his eyes flicked up and met Jazz's gaze full on. "But my God boy! You sure as hell sail close to the wind." He laughed and breezily said, "You need to lighten up boy. You've got work to do. Tony needs your kinda brilliance to find his murderer."

They talked for a while about cricket mostly and then it was time to leave and go to the Gurdwara. Jazz told Bob in confidence that he hoped Bam Bam would have the name he desperately needed to nail the man who ordered Tony's murder. He felt better, stronger. Bob had been around a long time and was good to bounce ideas off. He always made him feel good. The canteen was a hive of gossip and the fact they had sat together as friends would be noted by all present and shared with everyone and anyone. In a show of gratitude for his solidarity, Jazz patted Bob on the back and shook his hand. He promised to let him know how things were going.

Jazz arrived at the Gurdwara with five minutes to spare. He could hear the hum of muted women's voices in a corner of the big hall. The gossiping aunties were cooking again. He hoped this time it was for something more pleasant than a funeral. He looked around and found a corner at the edge of the great hall with a small table and two chairs to wait for Bam Bam to arrive. Everyone who came to eat sat on the mats on the floor and ate but he couldn't see Bam Bam sitting on the floor. It would take a crane to get him up again. He had taken his shoes off and put a hankerchief over his head as was expected and now she sat and waited.

Gurdwara Karamsar was a beautiful domed Gurdwara. The outside was made of sandstone and intricately hand carved by Rajasthani stonemasons. The sweeping staircases took you up to the prayer room. The women went up one staircase and the men up the other. Looking around, Jazz realised that in this day and age you never had to starve. The gossiping aunties cooked all day every day and anyone could come and eat. It made him proud to be a Sikh.

The Gurdwara was built from funds raised in Ilford and the surrounding areas by wealthy Asians. Bam Bam was a notable benefactor to the Gurdwara and was considered highly by everyone. It still amazed Jazz that money could even buy you a place in heaven. Bam Bam was an evil man capable of most acts and it galled Jazz to have to work so closely with him. He would rather be arresting him and getting him and his filth off the streets of the East End.

Sitting quietly for the first time in what seemed days, Jazz thought back on the events that had culminated in so many deaths. He had hardly thought about Alice. He made a mental note that he must find out when her funeral was. It seemed unfair that the gangland killings had upstaged the mourning period and thoughts of Alice. She deserved to be mourned. At least her murderers were found. Unfortunately, they were dead and so no trial, but she had been avenged.

Tony was a different kettle of fish. He was murdered in the execution of his duty and as a young man his life had been ended far too soon. The big difference between the two was that Jazz could have done nothing to save Alice but he could and should have saved Tony. He was tormented by the mother, who spoke the truth. It was his fault. He should have kept a better eye on what Tony was doing. He should never have let him go off on his own. In that moment, he knew he had to find Tony's killers if it was the last thing he ever did. He prayed silently for the first time in quite a while for help in finding Tony's killers.

Bam Bam was late. The bastard knew what was going on in the East End and yet his ego had to be fed. Jazz thought wryly that his ego was as big as his belly.

It was 10.10 a.m. when four of Bam Bam's henchmen walked in and looked around. They spotted Jazz in the corner occupying a table with two chairs and turned and left. A moment later, the melee of bodies moving in through the door showed they had returned. Now there were six henchmen walking two by two with Bam Bam in the middle. His entourage disturbed the peacefulness of the Gurdwara and all eyes watched him walk up to Jazz and sit down. The henchmen, with eyes darting, kept guard at a suitable distance. Bam Bam was getting a bit big for his boots by displaying such a presidential arrival. Did he think he was Mr Big, Jazz thought. Well, he sure was that in size. He could have sworn Bam Bam's stomach had grown since yesterday. The man was huge in size but nothing but a low life in character. Jazz did his best to keep the contempt he felt out of his eyes and face. He needed this bastard.

He waited respectfully as Bam Bam made himself comfortable on a chair that looked too frail to bear his weight. When the positioning and grunting to get comfortable had stopped, Bam Bam nodded to his six men to disperse to the door and just out of listening range. He could see Jazz looking quizzically at so many men in his entourage. "It's dangerous times. That's why I have all six of them here." He nodded towards the door and said, "I have another four looking after the cars outside." He came in a bloody motorcade as well, thought Jazz, so much for confidential information here. Everyone who wanted to know would know who was in the Gurdwara. Jazz could see the smug look on his face and knew the display of power was giving Bam Bam more pleasure than it should and that his security could be compromised. On second thoughts, Jazz thought he couldn't care less about Bam Bam's safety as long as he got the information he needed.

Settled now and with a smile and a nod to the aunties in the corner, two coffees and cakes were brought to the table. Bam Bam thanked them for their kindness. He sat contemplating which cake to start with. He looked quizzically at Jazz, who shook his head. They were all for Bam Bam and he gently picked the one nearest him. Bam Bam grunted with the effort. He didn't have much room for movement with a stomach as big as his and the leaning forward caused him great difficulties. Jazz assisted by lifting the plate closer to him. With a curt nod, Bam Bam proceeded to devour the cake in two bites. Finishing with a sip of coffee, he sat up straight and looked ready to talk. At last, thought Jazz, his patience was at screaming point.

Looking congenial and quite relaxed, Bam Bam beckoned to Jazz to move closer. He gave one swift look around him to ensure no one was listening or looking directly at them and turned back to Jazz. In an alarmingly gentle fashion, he opened the conversation with "By the way, don't you ever come to my office again uninvited." The look on his face didn't marry up with the gentle tones. He looked close to hitting Jazz. Now he had his attention, he carried on. "These are dangerous times and I don't want anyone to think I am a grass. Don't you fucking put me in the shit." In lower, quieter tones, with his face inches from Jazz's, he added, "No one is safe. Anyone can be wasted, remember that." He patted Jazz on the arm in a most friendly way. "Just a little warning, my friend." The tone was upbeat but the underlying meaning was threatening. Bam Bam had flexed his muscles and showed just how menacing and dangerous he was. It took Jazz's breath away and he could feel how terrifying it would be to upset Bam Bam.

This was not how it was supposed to be. Everything felt wrong. Jazz had come here to ask the questions. Bam Bam owed him and he was calling in his dues with interest. What gave Bam Bam the right to turn on him in this way? His growing anger was immediately suffocated by an unsettling fear. He realised for the first time that he was out of his depth. The world felt out of sync. He had never felt fear in Bam Bam's company. He presumed his utter contempt for the man cushioned the vibes. The 'Them and Us' scenario which meant villains kept their hands off police officers seemed to have gone out of the window since Tony was killed. In the present killing spree, it seemed that no one was safe, not even little old ladies who knew nothing about no one. He watched as Bam Bam devoured another cake, oblivious to Jazz for the moment.

Bam Bam knew exactly what his words had done. He had had enough of this jumped-up little shit of a Sikh. OK, he surmised, he had done him a favour in the past but it had been well paid back and enough was enough now. He wanted to get on with his work and not have to pander to this pathetic excuse for a police officer. He knew Jazz's history with his drink problem, two marriages and his counselling. It made him sick to see a grown man, a Sikh man, who should be braver and stronger than most, act like a useless twat! He had decided that today all debts were paid and he would get on with his work. Jazz was becoming like one of those irritating buzzing wasps that annoyed the hell out of him. Today he would swat him and if he didn't take the hint, he would have him stamped on.

Jazz waited patiently and watched Bam Bam totally engrossed in the cake and the coffee. Bam Bam's ego was so huge that he was comfortable in the knowledge that everything and everyone would wait for him and in his world you never presumed to interrupt him or step out of line. You waited until he was ready.

He seemed to have finished the cake and, after wiping his mouth with a brilliantly white handkerchief, he looked up at Jazz. Jazz leaned forward expectantly. "This town is full of police buzzing around and causing all sorts of upsets," was Bam Bam's opening statement. Jazz nodded in agreement, but he kept quiet and waited to hear more. "The gang have gone back to India. Don't know who they are exactly but you might want to ask

Freddie Chow and Charlie Wong. I heard that they had joined forces and called the gang in to get rid of the Viets who had got too greedy on their patch." Jazz knew this much and it wasn't enough. He wanted names of the gang and something to link Freddie and Charlie to the gang.

Bam Bam was frustratingly quiet and calm. He looked disinterested and bored with being there. Now he had finished the cakes, he looked like he wanted to leave. Quietly, Jazz said, "I need something more." Bam Bam looked at him sharply. "I have done more than enough for you, it's dangerous out there and there is only so much I can find out." This wasn't a conversation, it was a statement. Bam Bam rose to leave. "We are quits now. Don't bother me again, this is at an end." With that, his henchmen came forward and walked him out of the Gurdwara.

He had been gone 10 minutes and Jazz was still seated in the Gurdwara. He kept asking himself what the fuck that was all about. He went over each word and came up with nothing. Something had changed but Jazz didn't know what it was. Bam Bam was now not interested in any of this and certainly not interested in helping him. The information was total shit and meant nothing. Any idiot knew the names of Freddy Chow and Charlie Wong. Time was getting on and he needed a lead.

He finished his coffee and decided that he would pay a visit to that low life, filthy, cowardly vermin – Mad Pete. He hadn't forgotten he had left him at the warehouse and just scuttled off like the stinking rat he was. He hadn't finished with him yet. He knew more than he was telling him. He vowed that by the time he had finished, Mad Pete would tell him anything and everything he knew. He got up and made his way to his flat on the Gascoine Estate, Barking. Time was of the essence, he needed something concrete today.

ENOUGH'S ENOUGH

The landings stunk of urine and cabbage. Jazz could never figure out why it stunk of cabbage because to the best of his knowledge no one ever cooked in these stinking flats. All were on benefits and were the dregs of society. The council, in their infinite wisdom, seemed to put all the dregs of humanity in the same place. They used their money for drugs, booze and the bloody 42" plasma screen TVs they all seemed to possess. No wonder Mcdonald's, Kebabish, and chicken takeaways always sprung up on these sorts of estates. He knew of babies who were fed Mcdonald's at a very young age. Mothers would chew it up and then give to their babies. David Attenborough should come and inspect the wildlife of the Gascoigne Estate sometime, he thought.

After banging on Mad Pete's door long enough to make his hand sore, he shouted threats that would make any self-respecting torturer shake in their boots. The noise had woken Pete's neighbours from their comatose sleep, it was only 11 a.m. after all. Raised voices could be heard telling Mad Pete to open the fucking door and let the mad bastard in and give them some peace. This seemed to do the trick and Mad Pete shouted through the door, "Don't touch me, Mr Singh, and I'll open the door. You got to promise not to touch me."

Jazz, riled beyond belief, took a deep breath and tried to calm himself. His hands were shaking with the exertion and the depth of the anger that had risen shocked him. He had to get a grip and yes, if Mad Pete had opened the door earlier he would have punched the lights out of him. Now, he needed to know what Mad Pete was keeping hidden. "I won't touch you unless you provoke me, that's a promise," was the sensible answer shouted through the door.

Jazz took out his hip flask and took a long shot of vodka. He closed his eyes for a second and felt the fire slip down his throat and soothe his senses. It took Mad Pete many minutes to open the door. "How many fucking locks and chains have you got on this door?" shouted Jazz. He could feel himself getting riled again and that wouldn't do. He didn't need Mad Pete to go into one of his druggy hysterics, he would get nothing out of him.

"Only one more, Mr Singh, I promise," was the response.

Mad Pete opened the door with just the door chain on. He wanted to check how Mr Singh looked before he let him in. Jazz gave a grimacing look that wasn't quite a smile but it was the nearest to amenable he could manage. Mad Pete's eyes flicked from his face to his hands, still not sure if he was going to beat him up or not. Jazz whispered, "Look, Pete, are you gonna let me in or not? You don't want to bring to the attention of your neighbours that you are a grass for the police, do you?" He nearly laughed at such a stupid thing to say to

Mad Pete. The whole fucking neighbourhood must have heard the shouting and banging that had just gone on, but it didn't register with Mad Pete.

Hesitantly, Mad Pete unclipped the door chain. As soon as the chain was off, the noise and speed of Jazz kicking the door and barging into the flat stunned Mad Pete and nearly knocked him off his feet. He ran to his kitchen and tried to close the door but Jazz was too fast for him and as he kicked the door open, it caught Mad Pete on the head. The kitchen was small and there was nowhere to hide. Mad Pete stood with his arms across his face and whimpered, he was waiting for the fist to strike him. He flinched and cowered as Jazz grabbed his arms and made him face him. The gash on Mad Pete's forehead had started to bleed and blood was trickling down his face. "You bloody idiot! Have you got a clean cloth?" Mad Pete nodded and opened the kitchen drawer. A tea towel was produced that was supposedly clean but he wouldn't put money on it. Jazz snatched it from Mad Pete's hands and proceeded to pat his forehead. "You took a nasty blow there, Pete. Got a bleeder going here." He patted it until the bleeding stopped.

"Fank you, Mr Singh," was all Mad Pete could say. His eyes were darting, waiting and wondering what was going to come next.

The momentary calm allowed both of them to relax a fraction and start again. "So, Pete, what's with all the locks and bolts on the door?"

Mad Pete gave him a furtive look and then looked down at the floor. "It's dangerous out there, Mr Singh."

Jazz laughed scornfully. "Tell me about it." Mad Pete started to get agitated and was fidgeting and uncomfortable. In a moment of anxiety, he blurted out, "I'm sorry I left you, Mr Singh. It's just that I was really scared, they are bad people and they would kill me if they could." He raised his head a little to look at Jazz and sheepishly added, "I'm sorry you were nearly killed." Jazz looked at him and wondered how he seemed to know what had happened in the warehouse after he left. Where did he get his information from?

His place stunk of everything imaginable. There was sweat, feet, festering mould, smoke and the sickly smell of cannabis, but the overpowering smell was of a toilet that hadn't been flushed for a long time. "How about we go out and get something to eat? We could go across the road to McDonald's." Anything to get out of here, Jazz thought, he was beginning to feel sick. Mad Pete was making noises that eventually came out as him being too frightened to leave his flat in case someone was out there to get him. Jazz reminded him that he was a police officer and he was safe with him. Mad Pete replied by shaking his head and raising his eyes to the sky. Of course Tony's death made that seem a pretty stupid statement to make. Eventually food and a hot drink won. Mad Pete hadn't had anything to eat for the last day, and perhaps Mr Singh was right, no one in their right mind would touch him in public. He left his flat on the understanding that he would be escorted to McDonald's and escorted back to his flat afterwards. With this agreed, they went across the road to get some food.

Most of the food purchased from McDonald's was taken away so the place was fairly empty. Jazz found a table in the corner near the back of the restaurant. He needed a quiet place to sit and talk to Mad Pete. The order of big macs, fries and milkshakes took only minutes to come. In no time they had munched their way through a couple of big macs each and chips. Mad Pete burped his appreciation. Feeling full and comfortable, he sat back and relaxed for the first time in days. It felt safe at the back of McDonald's. Through the massive front windows, they could see who was walking their way and the place was still fairly empty. On this estate, most people didn't get up until lunchtime.

Jazz wanted a cigarette but with Mad Pete so relaxed, it wasn't the time to go off and smoke. He needed some information now. Mad Pete knew more than he was telling and for the life of everyone in the police force, no one knew what the hell was going on or why. Jazz knew it was to do with the Vietnamese but this was a massive takeover with more murders in 24 hours than East London was used to. It didn't make sense. The Holy Trinity knew that it paid not to rock the boat. Now the police were all over them and wouldn't let go, it was just the sort of thing they had avoided for years. Business is never good if you have the Police breathing down your neck the whole time. Even their parking tickets were being looked at and if they put one toe out of line, they would get pulled in. This was all very bad for business.

He needed to keep Mad Pete calm and unspooked to get the answers he needed. "We have worked well together over the years, haven't we?" asked Jazz. Mad Pete nodded. He was about to mention negative things like being kicked and roughly handled at times but Jazz didn't want that to come into the conversation. "So, I help you and you help me?" was the follow up. Before Mad Pete could answer with negative comments, Jazz added, "You can't go on being frightened to open your door. So let's get the bastards who are scaring you and I'll get them put away for a long time." For a second, Mad Pete looked interested but then the panic started to kick in. Jazz could see him getting worked up and into panic mode.

With a voice as smooth as silk, Jazz added, "You know you and I are friends. I've gotta look after you. I want you to feel safe in my town." Just as Mad Pete was going to retort grumpily that it was Jazz who had caused most of his fear by interfering with things he shouldn't have gone near, Jazz added that there might be a reward for information given which helped capture the gang who had caused all of this. He wanted Mad Pete to be the recipient of the money on offer. There had been no mention of a reward yet, but Mad Pete didn't know that.

He sat up and looked very interested and alert. "How much reward?" he asked. Jazz said he wasn't sure yet, but he reckoned it would be a nice little sum for the right person. It seemed to make a difference and Mad Pete asked what he wanted to know. He added hesitantly, "That's if I know anything of interest of course."

This was all a game to be played. Jazz needed to be careful. He didn't want to spook Mad Pete. Once spooked, he would go off on one of his drug-induced frenzies and he would get nothing out of the man. He asked quietly, "Who is at the back of all the killings, Pete?"

Something clicked in Mad Pete's brain and the beginnings of paranoia fuelled the start of the hysterics. "Nuffink, I know nuffink, Mr Singh. Don't ask me. I'm dead meat. I wanna go home." The words were almost a chant and the signs of madness were creeping into the conversation. "Slimey snakes and evil toads. I wanna be left alone. The river of blood is at my door." Jazz was getting concerned now. Mad Pete was certainly living up to his name; he was going mad. What the hell had caused such an outbreak? It was obvious that Mad Pete knew something that had scared the hell out of him.

"OK, Pete, no worries. We will go back to your place." He hoped this would calm him down. Perhaps back in his flat he would feel safer and more sane. He had to find out what Pete knew without making him go off his trolley. The short walk across the road to Pete's flat was fraught, with Mad Pete spooked beyond belief and jumping at his own shadow. A boy on a bike whizzed past them and Mad Pete, in a moment of hysteria, almost climbed over Jazz to get away. If he was frightened that someone was watching him, the noise he made would have alerted anyone within a one mile radius anyway. The whole of Gascoigne Estate knew where Mad Pete was at that moment. Jazz had never heard a man scream like that before. He grabbed Mad Pete by the arm and dragged him to the door of the flat. Shaking and by now almost crying, Mad Pete took a while to open his door, he shook so much he couldn't get the key into the lock. Jazz took it from him and opened the door and pushed Mad Pete into the flat.

From being quite civil and normal, Mad Pete had

turned into a screaming nutter and it had well and truly spooked Jazz, who by now was feeling quite shaky. He asked himself what the hell had gone on there. He had found himself looking around to see if anyone was watching them. He had that feeling that crawls up your backbone when you think someone is behind you and about to stab you in the back. Whilst Mad Pete went to get a fix in his bedroom, Jazz searched his pockets for his flask. God, he needed a drink now. He swigged a mouthful and let it glide down his throat; he closed his eyes and felt the firey golden liquid relax his mouth and throat; it sent soothing signals to his brain. The warmth had spread to his fingertips and he felt calm. All the nerve ends that had been tingling in his body felt stroked and he was at peace. He waited patiently for Mad Pete. He was thankful he didn't have Pete's problem of needing a drug fix to survive.

After what seemed ages but was in fact 15minutes, Mad Pete made an appearance and looked calm. Time was getting on and Jazz tried to hide his impatience. He had to handle this right. A bottle of Becks came out of the cupboard. Mad Pete showed a bottle to Jazz, who shook his head and declined the offer. In silence they sat opposite each other and Jazz waited for Mad Pete to empty the bottle in small swigs. With a deep breath, Jazz uttered, "So!" Mad Pete looked up at him and waited expectantly.

Jazz licked his lips and started. He had thought about it and now was the time to lay out in detail what he wanted and why it was best for Mad Pete to tell him what he needed to know. Mad Pete watched him closely and waited. The drugs had made him feel normal and settled.

"From my point of view," Jazz started, "I need to know what's going on in my town and who is responsible." He saw Mad Pete shift uncomfortably in his seat and quickly went on. Soothingly he said, "And from your point of view, Pete, you need to feel safe and protected." Jazz looked at him and thought that seemed to do the trick for the moment. Mad Pete was calm and listening.

He tried to smile, but smiling at Mad Pete was difficult. The man was a walking municipal tip! The same tee shirt from years ago was still on his back and didn't look as if it had been washed in that time. Most of the historic stains had merged into one shiny black mess. He looked as if he had tried to shave at some point in the last week but the effort wasn't worth much. An undergrowth of hair was fighting with bits of stubble and scabs and jeez, scraps of food were caught up in the hair! Mad Pete was the tramp who always appeared either drunk or drugged, a man you never looked at when you walked down the street. You knew he was there but no one would make eye contact with him or allow their eyes to rest on him for more than a fleeting second.

It occurred to Jazz in that split second that he was looking at a man most people never saw. Mad Pete could walk the town and no one would remember him unless he did something to bring himself to their attention. He had his gang of young followers who seemed to admire him but in that moment, Jazz could see how Mad Pete could know things others wouldn't. Who would notice him in a busy place? Who would care what this no good low life saw? He didn't have the brains to remember anything, he was a druggy with an addled brain. Jazz knew they were wrong on that count. Mad Pete, in his own little world, was doing very nicely. He made money from the mobiles he fenced and the little running jobs he did. Someone had made a big mistake in underestimating his abilities.

"The way I see it, Pete, you're fucked if you do and you're fucked if you don't. You're the fucker who fucked the others, fucked up and are now fucked, am I right?" Mad Pete nodded. He warmed to the fact that Jazz totally understood his position. "So what are we going to do about it?" It wasn't a question Jazz needed Pete to answer. He was going to tell him the answer to that. "You're gonna let me help you, that's what your gonna do."

Mad Pete thought for a moment and then reluctantly nodded. "Yeah, I think I'm gonna have to do that, Mr Singh," was his considered reply. "First, how will you protect me? I ain't got nowhere to hide. They would kill me if they knew." After thinking about it, he added, "They're gonna kill me anyway. They don't know what I know but they will kill me in case I know anything." Sprawled in the chair looking at his feet, Mad Pete was considering his options. He looked up at Jazz and asked what he was going to do for him.

This was going well and Jazz picked his words carefully. "First, I will ensure anything you tell me is kept secret. If it goes to court, I can arrange for closed door talks with the judge so your identity is never known in open court. This is standard stuff, Pete, we do it all the time." It was not that common but he wasn't going to tell Pete that. "As an informant we have ways and means of looking after you. Apart from that, I will look after you. We have history, Pete, and I always look after those who help me, you know that from the past, don't you?" Mad Pete nodded. Jazz had always looked after him. He was a bastard at times but an honest bastard, he acknowledged. He didn't trust anyone else, but he trusted Jazz.

He had a lot to weigh up. He knew they would get him at some point. He knew most of those who had been killed. He knew about the police officer they murdered. He knew everything and they had his name in their pockets and at some point in the not too distant future they would come and get him. He hated the bastards who had done this, it was unnecessary and had caused the East End to now be under the spotlight and Mad Pete lived his life out of the spotlight. He figured that if the gang didn't kill him then the police would arrest him because they would be pissed off and arresting every person they could find who was a little bit out of order just to show the public they were doing their job. Besides, he was scared. More scared than he had ever been. Up until now, no one gave a tart's toss who he was, now his name was blazoned out there and there was most probably a bounty on him. The Indian gang were ruthless and cold-blooded murderers. He stood no chance. He had to get away.

"I'm not staying 'ere if I help you," Mad Pete blurted out.

Jazz looked up sharply. "OK, not a problem. I don't blame you, I wouldn't want to stay here either. The place stinks!"

Mad Pete looked hurt. "Not because of that, Mr Singh. Everyone will be after me if I grass."

Again Jazz promised that a safe place would be found for him. "Now tell me who in the Holy Trinity I should be looking for," asked Jazz. Enough was enough and time was getting on. He had to find someone today and put a stop to all the murders.

"You want Bam Bam," was the answer.

Incredulously Jazz looked at Mad Pete. "You can do better than that, sunshine. Stop messing around. It's the Triads or the Snakeheads and you know it!"

Mad Pete shook his head. "No, Mr Singh, it's Bam Bam. He murdered everyone including that police officer."

Again Jazz looked at him and dismissed this bit of information. "Bam Bam doesn't do drugs. He wouldn't be interested in cannabis factories and the Viets. It's not his bag. I want the truth. If you mess around now, I can't promise you any safety."

"OK, Mr Singh, I'll give it to you from the top. It was about the time the Viets came to town. I did some running for them. They were new to the area and I helped with messages and shopping." Jazz thought he made them sound like respectable families in a new area, not the bloody drug manufacturers and dealers they were. "I do some running jobs for the Holy Trinity from time to time, nothing much and they didn't know I was doing the same for the Viets. I hear things, Mr

Singh. I ain't no grass, I keep quiet. No point in drawing attention to myself. No one was happy with the Viets and the Triads and Snakeheads were watching them to see how they were doing. They were doing good, Mr Singh. Their cannabis crops were top quality. The best skunk you could get. They gave me heroin for nothing to start with and it felt so much better than methadone. I liked them, Mr Singh, they looked after me.

"I do bits of jobs, nothing much, for Bam Bam. I like to be helpful and do the shitty jobs no one else wants to do. I clean stuff for them and take stuff to the dump for them. Nothing exciting but they chuck me a few quid every now and then. I kept on the right side of everyone and never took liberties. I knew something was happening. Heard the odd bit every now and then and just put two and two together. The Triads and Snakeheads were getting jumpy about the Viets about the time you came back. Something riled them. I was doing the odd running job for them but they were getting edgy and it got a bit scary to be around them. No one takes much notice of me, Mr Singh, but I was very careful to give them no reason to be worried about me. I know it was Bam Bam's men who were putting it about that the Viets were getting powerful and thinking of taking over the East End. It had felt a bit tense for a while by the time you came back. Then that old lady got killed by the Viets and all hell let loose."

Jazz listened intently. So far it all made sense.

"I seemed to be working more closely with the Holy Trinity around that time. It might have been that they only used people they could trust and they all seemed to either trust me or think I'm not worth much and not to be worried about. All true, Mr Singh. I tell nobody nuffink. I ain't stupid, I know what these people can do, I just keep my head down and my mouth shut." Jazz knew that to be true and gained a bit of respect for Mad Pete. He certainly wasn't as stupid as he liked people to think.

"I don't know why exactly everything took off like it did and all the killings happened. I could guess and I bet I'm right. It was a good opportunity to start the gang war that has been brewing for ages." Jazz asked what the hell that meant and who he was talking about. "Bam Bam brought in his family from Pakistan to deal with this. Not sure if they're all related to him but they're connected in some way, either relatives or through marriage, he would never trust anyone else. The gang have been living in his house for the past four months. His missus is staying somewhere abroad with the daughter."

Jazz, again, had to stop him and ask why on earth would Bam Bam do such a thing. If he had brought the gang over from Pakistan four months ago, there were some premeditated plans here, he thought. He asked Mad Pete why he was doing this. Mad Pete replied, "I'm not a bleeding psychic, I don't know what's going on in his head." He added for good measure, "I think the Paki gang are still here and staying in Bam Bam's house." When asked why, he pulled a face and said it was just a feeling he had. He thought if they laid low in England while everyone was watching the ports and airports, it would be safer. Jazz was doubly impressed; that Mad

Pete had thought this out was pretty clever stuff.

"The Triads and Snakeheads are very edgy. They don't know what's going on and they are looking for a target. I've always worked for the Holy Trinity and I think they might be after me too." In a plaintive call to the ceiling, Mad Pete asked, "Why the fuck is it me? I ain't told no one nuffink and I aint done nuffink wrong." He looked at Jazz and said "Where are you gonna hide me. I ain't safe here anymore once you start poking your nose into everything."

Jazz's brain was going ten to the dozen. It didn't make sense yet it made complete sense. Bam Bam was a cocky devil but taking a chance in riling the Triads and Snakeheads seemed pretty daring. What on earth gave him the confidence to pick a fight with the Triads and Snakeheads? The Pakistani gang appeared to be just a killing machine and perhaps that had made Bam Bam a bit too confident. English gangs didn't usually like to take too many chances if they didn't have to. No one with any sense wanted to bring themselves to the attention of the police. It looked like the Pakistani Gang didn't care what chances they took, they were going to move out of the country when everything settled down. They didn't have to live with the consequences, which could have made them bolder.

He had to check things out. He understood that Mad Pete thought Bam Bam had started all the killings but he still couldn't get his head around this. Bam Bam had never been interested in the drug world except for the odd few poppers he sold. Taking on the Viets and then causing the internal gang war was a pretty tall order. To cause such mayhem didn't make sense. Bam Bam had always lived comfortably with the police, the Triads and the Snakeheads. To start a turf war just didn't make sense. If someone put it in a book, no one would believe the story line, he reckoned.

Mad Pete got very spooked and nearly went into a druggy fit when Jazz told him he was gonna arrest him.

"Hold on, hold on, Pete, and listen," said Jazz, trying to placate the madness that was rising. "If I arrest you, you will be safe in a cell whilst I go check out Bam Bam. I don't want to leave you here. You'll be good for a few hours before you need another fix and by then I'll be back and release you into my custody." Mad Pete nodded, understanding what he was saying. He got fed and watered in Ilford Police Station and that wasn't a bad thing, he told himself. It was 2 p.m. by now and Jazz needed a result by the end of the day. He got Mad Pete to gather up his stuff and bundled him into the car and drove to Ilford Police Station.

He took Mad Pete into the custody suite and Bob was on duty which was a bit of luck. Another Custody Sergeant would have wanted to have reasons and charges explained to him. Bob was his mate and he knew he would help him. He asked Bob to put Pete in a cell for a few hours whilst he made some enquiries. He said if anyone asked, he was going to interview Mad Pete later. The PACE clock was fine for the next 24 hours and he would be back in a couple of hours. Bob wanted to ask lots of questions but Jazz said he didn't have time now and would tell Bob everything when he got back. Bob was not happy but said he would do what Jazz asked for old times sake. He shouted to Jazz as he led Mad Pete to a cell that he had better not be longer than two hours.

He looked up Bam Bam's address on CRIS and, with the help of a local A-Z, went off to look around. Time was getting on and he badly wanted something concrete by the end of the day. Bam Bam lived in Epping, which was very posh. He had moved there after Jazz had moved up to Manchester. He got in his car and before he set off, he reached into his inside pocket for the flask. He took the last swig of the flask and urgently checked his other pocket. He was relieved to feel the full spare flask; he would need it later.

Jazz looked at the tall solid gates ahead of him. There was an intercom on the wall beside the gates. He couldn't see anything. Business must be good, he thought. He couldn't even see the house. The road to the house was down one of those private roads. He saw one other gate on the opposite side of the road and reckoned there were not many houses down there. It smelt of wads of dishonest money. The East End villains had developed airs and graces and had all moved out to either Epping or Chigwell. Bam Bam used to live in Chigwell in a big house but this looked like it was on land big enough to build a small town.

He had parked a little way away from the house. He suspected CCTV was erected on the top of the gates and he didn't want to announce himself yet. The walled estate seemed to go on for ages before he got to the gates. He got back in his car and drove sedately past the gates to see where the wall ended. It was nice here, the afternoon sun was shining and warm and the air was calm. It seemed a nice place to be, with the birds singing and the bees humming. If it had been any other time, it would have been good to sit propped up under one of the oaks that stood majestically on the green nearby and have a little drink. Even the roadside greenery was enormous. It didn't look like there were many houses down this road. He spotted another set of gates further down on the right but Bam Bam's property still kept going on and on. The wall was 7 foot high at least. At last he came to the end of the road and the wall. The wall did a right angle that was off road and straight ahead was a thick privet. He pushed his hands through the prickly spines of the hawthorn bush and could just make out what looked like farmland.

"Now what?" he asked himself. He had come this far so he had no choice, he had to get over the wall and into the grounds. It had been a long time since he had climbed a 7 foot wall and crept into someone else's property. It wasn't something he did on a daily basis. He knew he was putting off the inevitable. This was the most dangerous thing he had ever done. If Mad Pete was right and the Pakistani gang were here, he was dead meat. If they weren't here and Bam Bam found him abusing his trust by climbing into his property, he was dead meat. It was a no win situation but he had to find out.

The wall wasn't as hard to scramble over as he thought. It was an old wall with aged, crumbling stone that offered him footholds, which helped him climb. There was shrubbery and trees the other side. They were not close enough to the wall to help a potential burglar but far enough away to hide the house and grounds. So far so good. He jumped down onto the ground and ran to the trees and bushes ahead. He looked through the bushes and saw the mansion. It was a good 500 yards in front of him and it was open grassland and road up to the house. He sat and looked around from the safety of the shrubs and trees. He had no idea what he was going to do now. Suddenly the singing of the birds and the hum of the bees felt quite threatening. What the bloody hell was he doing here? He had taken the word of a druggy and had invested his precious time in following up a dodgy lead – a man who had always professed to be uninterested in the drug industry. He should have gone after someone in the Triads or Snakeheads. He was here now though and he had better make the best of it.

With a sigh and the wish that life would be a little bit easier and not such a fucking bummer, he decided he had to bite the bullet and make a move. He would be exposed no matter what he did. He decided not to walk up to the house face on. He would walk along the tree line for a while and then consider walking across the green. He followed the wall for 500 yards until he was at the side of the house. It was still 500 yards, he reckoned, across the grass to reach the house. He kept calling it a house but, seeing the side of it, it was more like an hotel. It looked like it could hide a small army inside.

He could just see another building at the back the house. It looked fairly close to the tree line. He just needed to follow the wall and walk further along the tree line. He hoped the trees would continue to afford him some protection. He felt jittery about walking across the lawns and being so open. It took him another 15 minutes to reach the outer building. The trees and shrubs had got thicker and he found it difficult to walk through them. He presumed that because there were fields the other side of the wall, this area was particularly overgrown to stop anyone trying to get in. It was a struggle to get through the biting bushes of gorse and brambles and blackberry bushes that stood in his way. A startled blackbird flew up from the bush in front of him, shrieking its warning cry. For a second it scared the hell out of him and he felt desperate to get out of the mangle of thorns that were trying to get him. He fought the bushes and crashed and thrashed through them. The sight of his face scratched by brambles and his hands bloodied and sore from pushing away the thorny fronds showed he was the loser in the battle with the undergrowth. The outer building was only 50 yards from the tree line and looked quite secluded. He raised his hands and thanked Niranka for his mercy. He squatted, looking around and catching his breath. Everything looked still and calm, in fact, the place looked empty.

He thought what a prized prat he would feel if Bam Bam was sitting innocently in his home. Again he beat himself up with the thought that he would be the laughing stock of the Met Police and hated by Bam Bam for the intrusion if this turned out to be a wild goose chase. He wondered why sometimes he just didn't stop and look at the bigger picture. Mad Pete was just that, mad! Of course it was all a lot of tosh! Before the self-doubt overwhelmed him, he reasoned that now he was here, he might as well check it out. If someone stopped him, he would think of something to say, or just hold his hands up and come clean. He felt in his pockets for his flask and was comforted by the feel of its shape and hardness in his pocket. He deserved a swig. The warmth and familiarity of the clear liquid sliding down his throat made him feel good. His adrenalin was rising. He ran fast towards the outer building with renewed vigour and a determination to get this done and dusted and go home.

He reached the wall of the outer building and thought so far so good. He wondered where everyone was; he reckoned a house and grounds of this size would need quite a few staff to maintain it. The outer building was a swimming pool. He walked to the side of the building and saw the front was all windows. He couldn't see anyone in the pool house. The distance to the house didn't seem so bad now. He was at the side of the house, which seemed better to him. Again, he could see no movement and proceeded to run to the safety of the house walls ahead of him.

Now he was so close, he stopped to think what on earth he was going to do. Was he going to break into the house? He had no choice, he hoped a back door would be open or something. Smashing a window would certainly ensure he was given a good slap by Bam Bam for the temerity of such an act. No one would dare to do such a thing. He wondered for a moment if he had caught some of Pete's madness. He had the best grass in Bam Bam that any crime fighter could have. How was he paying him back? He was breaking into his house. Again, he wondered if he had a death wish.

He stood still, thinking of his next move. He was at the side of the house and there was a set of French windows that opened onto the patio that seemed to encompass the house. It was raised and he had to climb a set of steps in front of the French windows. He had been lucky so far. No one was looking out of the windows and he scuttled past them to the safety of the brick wall close to the corner of the house. He heard a noise that appeared to come from around the corner at the back of the house and he peered tentatively towards it. A man was standing there smoking and looking out onto the expanse of lawn. The area appeared to be ringed by trees. It must stand on at least 10 acres of land, Jazz thought, and surmised that it was once a house for the landed gentry. It had an early 1800s look about it. Now was not the time to think like an estate agent, he told himself ruefully. What to do now was the question.

At last the man finished his cigarette and disrespectfully threw the stub into the flowerbeds that sat either side of the steps that led down to the lawn . He turned and walked back into the house, closing the door behind him. Suddenly it felt like the world had held its breath. Jazz couldn't hear the birds singing and even the bees had disappeared. He moved quickly and quietly towards the back door. With a little movement on the handle, it opened quietly. He realised he had been holding his breath and exhaled as he opened the door a fraction more to see what was behind it.

It opened to a lobby that appeared to have many doors leading off from it. It was empty and with a deep breath he entered the lobby and shut the door behind him as quietly as he could. He walked to the first door and listened intently but couldn't hear any noise or voices. Again with a deftness he didn't know he had, he opened the door softly and silently. Through the crack he saw no movement and on opening wider saw that it was an empty room. It looked like a tack room of some sort. It had saddles and reins on the wall and boots neatly in a row on the floor. The room led nowhere. He examined the other rooms one by one and they appeared to be sculleries and one led to a big, modern kitchen. It was all empty and he thought that was surprising. The final door led out into a long hallway. He could see that further down the hallway it opened out more so he presumed this end of the hallway was the servants' end. The first door he came across on his right was slightly ajar. He tried to peer in but he could see nothing but a wall. He listened and heard nothing again. It was like the Marie Celeste, lived in but empty and puzzling.

By now he was feeling less cautious and opened the door a bit further than he should have. He saw the feet first and then he felt the stinging blow from the metal bar the man had in his hand. When he came to, his first sensation was pain, deep, thick and bright. They had sat him in a chair and his head lolled as he tried to open his eyes and focus. The muddle of voices he could hear around him stopped as he tried to open his eyes. He groaned as the light hit his eyes. He was surrounded by men, lots of men. He tried to think where he was and why he hadn't heard them in the house. He looked up and screwed his eyes and brow in thought. They looked familiar and for a moment he couldn't remember where he had seen them before.

Slowly, as his eyes adjusted to the light, his mind cleared. His thoughts raced. He recognised them. Fuck!

He remembered them well. They were the gang of killers he met in the warehouse. They were the gang of killers who had caused all the damage and killings in the East End. He had come to find them but now he just couldn't believe what he was seeing. Bam Bam couldn't be behind all of the killings, it didn't make sense. He wondered if the hit on the head had caused some damage and he wasn't thinking straight.

They could see his confusion and they laughed. "Call yourself a policeman," they taunted. "You knew nothing and sadly now you think you know, you won't have anyone to tell." They pushed him about a bit but they were in a relaxed mood, not tight as a bow and on the edge in the way they were when he saw them last time. They were obviously having a relaxing day. The drinks were poured and he could see they had been playing cards. They must be in the pay of Bam Bam. They were not here to do any damage. To think Mad Pete had been right.

Now he had come round, they tied him tight to the chair. He asked what they were going to do with him and they just said "Shut up" and carried on with their game. He asked if they had done the same to Tony, his DC, and they just laughed. In a squeaky voice, one said, "I promise to be a good boy" and they all roared with laughter. Jazz suddenly felt very hot as he realised these were Tony's killers. The hot sweat lasted a few minutes. He again asked why they had killed Tony. He said surely Tony was nothing to them and it was always going to cause big trouble when a police officer was killed.

They looked up from their cards and he thought they were going to answer him but they were looking at Bam Bam, who had just entered the room. Bam Bam strode up to Jazz and looked at him with a coldness in his eyes and a quiet fury on his lips. "What the hell are you doing in my home?"

Jazz could have laughed. He had killed more men in a few days than anyone else had since the IRA bombs and he had the cheek to be indignant that Jazz had trespassed. "What the hell is going on, Bam Bam? This isn't your style. You had a police officer killed and an old woman has died who was nothing to do with any of your filthy plans."

Bam Bam was beside himself with fury. He spat out, "You Bevacoof!" (*you idiot*). Spittle was flying from his mouth and he was shaking from the exertion of trying not to shout. He added in disgust, "You have been protected up to now, but oh no, you just can't leave well alone." He pointed sharply at the men in the room. "One more day and they would have gone back to Pakistan and some sort of normality would have returned. Now you have forced my bloody hand." He shrugged his shoulders and for a milli-second he gave Jazz a loser's look of despondency. "I can't do anything else to protect you. You have used up all I owe you."

The anger, just bubbling under the surface, rose again and Bam Bam went bright red and looked close to punching Jazz. With barely controlled fury, he asked, "Who the hell do you think saved you from being iced in the warehouse? Me! You should have been killed there and then but I saved you, you ungrateful fucker."

Again he pointed at the others in the room and loudly said, "They wanted to kill you many times. But I," the finger came back and he stabbed himself in his chest, "wouldn't let them." For a few seconds, he looked straight into Jazz's eyes and let his words sink in. He was not happy and swiftly turned and walked out of the room for some fresh air in disgust, mumbling something about *ungrateful fucker* and *serves him right*.

There was a bit of Bam Bam that felt some gratitude towards Jazz for saving his daughter but not enough to let him live. If Jazz, all his plans, meticulously worked out, would be for nothing. There was no way he was going to jail, he wouldn't survive the experience. This was the culmination of one year's planning. He intended to own the East End and he intended that the police would boot out the Triads and Snakeheads for him. It was going very well until Jazz put his size 10 shoes all over the area and got in the way. For that alone he deserved to die.

Jazz needed to buy some time. He knew he had not a lot of it left. He was told by Bam Bam that as soon as it was dark, he would be taken into the forest, like Tony was, and shot. As a favour, he was told, he promised it would be as painless as possible. It didn't make Jazz feel any better.

He had gone stone cold and pale at the thought that he would be shot before the end of the day. He was numb with fear and could feel his bowels loosening. His breathing was coming in short bursts that made his head spin. He had to calm down. His brain raced to find some way of stalling the inevitable. He needed to think of a reason for them to keep him alive. It had never occurred to him that he might be in this position. Sitting here tied up and waiting to be killed, it seemed highly stupid and naïve of him not to have thought this could be the outcome. Again, he wondered if he was as good a Detective as he thought he was.

With some time to spare until it got dark, Bam Bam returned to the room and offered Jazz a drink, which was accepted gratefully. A vodka was produced for him and his hands were untied, but his feet were very securely shackled to the chair and he was now watched intently by at least one of the gang. Bam Bam was ruthless and business always came first but Jazz had saved his precious daughter and for that he would make sure he was drunk before they shot him. He knew he had a drink problem and so a few drinks would do the trick. He owed him that.

Bam Bam made his excuses and said he had to make a telephone call and would be back in a while. With time on their hands, one of the gang, a young Asian man, about 28 years old, with cold eyes, taunted Jazz and told him they had watched him crashing through the brambles. He asked him in mock surprise why he didn't realise that CCTV cameras had followed him as soon as he climbed over the wall. In fact, another one of them said, they had taken bets on how long it would tale for him to enter the house. They all thought he was a ponce for taking so long. The laughter was raucous and jeering. They held him in the highest contempt and looked forward to finishing him off. Jazz held his glass with both hands to steady the trembling as he drank his vodka. His hands shook fiercely and he worried he would spill some. He needed every drop of it to calm down.

When Bam Bam returned, he found Jazz quite calm and cocky. He baited him and asked if Bam Bam thought he was stupid enough to come here without a safety net. He asked him to consider that he had a witness ready to tell the police everything he knew about Bam Bam and his operation. He added that his witness knew enough to get him put away. On being asked sarcastically where this witness was, Jazz told him that he was safe in police custody. Bam Bam stood still and digested this bit of information. Jazz felt, for the first time, that he was getting some sort of control. Watching Bam Bam considering his words, he told him he had to be set free, unharmed immediately. Soothingly he added that this would be one less charge against him when the police came to arrest him. He added unnecessarily that he would tell the police he had been treated well.

From the silent form of Bam Bam standing and digesting this bit of alarming information, a hint of laughter escaped. He was struggling not to laugh but failed and the force of the laughter shook his huge stomach. Jazz looked on in amazement. Why the fuck was he laughing? He had just told him he was nicked and there was nothing he could do about it. After a few seconds, Bam Bam controlled himself, blew his nose and mopped his brow. The odd giggle escaped him but he was calming down. The gang of men in the corner were playing cards. Silent and unconcerned, they held their game and watched as Bam Bam struggled to settle himself. He was going to enjoy explaining it all to Jazz.

He started with an insult. He whispered with menace, "You sanctimonious little prick." Disgusted by the lack of respect shown him, he pushed Jazz in the chest and told him, "You don't come to my house and threaten me." Bam Bam walked around Jazz and smiled at his band of men. "You are right, lads, he is an idiot." He was enjoying letting Jazz into his little secrets. "You thought I was your grass, did you?" It wasn't a question that needed answering. "Actually, you were playing into my hands every time. I wanted the Triads and Snakeheads to fight and you helped me do that." He leaned closer to Jazz and added sarcastically, "Thank you."

Jazz watched as he walked slowly and deliberately to and fro past him, finally stopping again in front of him. He leaned forward and said, "So you want to know why your police officer was killed?" He raised his eyebrows and, after a theatrical pause, answered slowly and clearly, "Because he was there." Realising Jazz didn't understand that chilling statement, he added, "I know he didn't see me, or certainly recognise me, but I wasn't going to take the chance. He had to be got rid of, my plans wouldn't be destroyed by a silly little bender pretending to be a police officer." With disgust, he added, "Where do you get your recruits from? The Met Police are going down the pan, you just can't get the staff anymore." They all laughed at that.

"So you killed him for the sake of it," challenged Jazz.

Bam Bam shrugged his shoulders and said, "If that's the way you want to view it, yes. It was a chance I wasn't going to take."

Again Jazz challenged, "How did you know he hadn't

reported where he was to the police station? What the fuck made you think you were invincible?"

Bam Bam had had enough of such disrespect in front of others, he was not used to being spoken to in this manner. He gave Jazz a hard slap for his insolence. All he would say was, "I have contacts. I know what's going on. If a police officer takes a shit in East London, I know about it."

Jazz wondered if that was an exaggeration but it had a ring of truth. It was beginning to make sense to him. There had been times, and Jazz remembered them now, when Bam Bam seemed to know where he should be and what meetings he was attending and at what time. Now he wondered why he hadn't asked questions at the time. Again, he asked himself what sort of detective he was.

Bam Bam lightened up a little and in an off the cuff way said, "Oh by the way, if Mad Pete is your informer, and I have it on good information he is, he is on his way here and I shall be having a conversation with him shortly." Jazz was just about to ask "How? He was in the police station" when Bam Bam, still in a conversational tone, added, "He is being brought here as we speak." With more sarcasm than was necessary, Bam Bam asked, "Were you wondering how I could do this?" Jazz nodded, speechless, his brain racing to work out what the hell was happening and, more to the point, why his safety net appeared to have gone.

With time on his hands and in the sure knowledge that Jazz wasn't going anywhere, Bam Bam wanted to show him just how good he was. The contempt was showing again. "You really are a fucking stupid bastard! I can do anything I like and get away with it. Sure, I have to be a bit sensible but I have the best paid police officer *in my pocket* to assist me. He has helped me for years." He was taunting Jazz now and desperate to tell him something that had been the best kept secret for the last 10 years. He could never tell anyone such valuable information and it gave him much pleasure to share it with someone who would appreciate the treachery and who would be dead in a few hours. To see the expression on Jazz's face when he told him would be worth it. He was going to enjoy this very much.

The goading started again. "What a great detective you are, DS Jaswinder Singh. You never knew your best friend, the helpful and comforting Bob; the officer always there to help you when you needed it. Well it may surprise you to know he is on my payroll and tells me everything." He watched Jazz's face closely and enjoyed the shock he saw developing. He whispered, "Oh yes, he tells me every single detail." He looked into Jazz's eyes and knew the next bit of information would finish him off. "Remember back five years ago when you and DS Bleasdale were on a stakeout?" He saw the sudden realisation of what was to come on Jazz's face. "Indeed, you are beginning to understand now." It was very satisfying to share this information and see the reaction it was getting.

Bam Bam's ego had risen over the years. He knew he was the big man in the East End and it felt good to push this bit of disrespect shown to him back into Jazz's face. All his plans and ideas had been worked on over the past five years. He knew he was far more intelligent than any of the other Holy Trinity. No one knew of his plans except his gang from Pakistan, who only know what was necessary. He had no one with whom to share his triumph and his immense skills in planning such a brave and foolhardy takeover. He had planned that the killings would set off rival gang killings and all the evidence would point to the Triads and Snakeheads. He was going to sit back, look innocent and wait for the police to do his dirty work. He wanted the East End for himself and he was well on the way to achieving his goal. He would be the most powerful man in England and the thought filled him with pride. It felt good to share this information with a police officer who he used to respect. He could tell Jazz everything and anything. He would be dead in a few hours. It felt good to share.

Now, everything felt in jeopardy. Jazz, the stupid fucking idiot, had walked into something he had no idea about and caused his plans to be sidetracked. At no point had Bam Bam considered that he might be found out. That was just not possible. He was far too clever and had thought of all eventualities. Then along came Jazz, pushing doors and asking questions that made Bam Bam feel vulnerable. He had never felt vulnerable and for once he felt afraid. It was a very uncomfortable feeling, which caused him to panic.

He had instructed Bob to bring Mad Pete to his house. A totally irrational and stupid move, that in saner times he would never have considered. Bob tried to argue that the police custody process would not allow that to happen. He was shouted down by Bam Bam and told to fucking do it now or he would ensure Bob would go down with him and anyone else involved in this fiasco.

Jazz asked what had happened that night with DS Bleasdale and what his involvement was. Bam Bam looked at him and shrugged his shoulders. For the moment he couldn't be bothered to reply. Jazz licked his lips. Bam Bam was on edge. He could see he was barely in control and perhaps liable to do something stupid and rash. This was not the Bam Bam of old; this was a very frightening person to be in front of. He looked like one of those mad Italian Caesars who could raise or drop a thumb to extinguish life instantly. The usually rational and calm egotist that Bam Bam was had disappeared. Jazz didn't want to goad him. He knew if he wasn't careful, Bam Bam could have him killed there and then, never mind about in the woods and in the dark, but he needed to know what had happened all those years ago.

With the talk of that night and what happened ringing in his ears, Jazz's body felt shrivelled up and dried out in shock. Bam Bam had something to do with that night and Bob, his hatred of Bob was only just blossoming; couldn't have had anything to do with it, surely? No police officer would be involved in the killing of another officer. Everyone loved John, it didn't make sense. He needed to hang in there, the thoughts of the previous nervous breakdown scared him into pushing his mind to stay calm and clear and find out what happened that night. Jazz cajoled Bam Bam. "I'm dead meat in a few hours, it makes no difference. What happened that night?"

Bam Bam, going from calm to chaotic in a blink of an

eye, decided he was going to enjoy telling Jazz how clever he was. He couldn't talk so freely to anyone else. He reminded Jazz that on the night of the stakeout he had a conversation with Bob on the telephone. Smoothly and with a smirk on his face, Bam Bam told him that he knew Jazz and Bob talked all the time. Jazz remembered the banter. Bob had been a good friend, always watching his back and keeping in contact with him to check he was alright. On the night of the stakeout, it was boring as usual. Bob rang regularly and chatted and joked and it helped pass the hours. He could tell Bob anything and he knew he would cover his back and keep quiet about his working practices that were a little below police standards.

The stakeout was a drug deal organised by Bam Bam. At this stage, the police did not know who was involved and Bam Bam wanted it to stay that way. Bam Bam had given instructions that the meeting was to be called off and was in the process of organising it when he got the message that John Bleasdale was on a walkabout and might see more than he should. Jazz was waiting for a takeaway to be delivered so John Bleasdale was dealt with in the only way that would keep the meeting secure; he was shot dead. Bam Bam added, with that sarcasm again in his voice, "Your good friend Bob kept us informed of what was going on at the stakeout. Very useful man." Jazz, sick to the stomach, thought back on everything he had told Bob that night. He had told him exactly what John Bleasdale was doing and where he was. He had contributed to his death and that hit Jazz harder than anything to date. John Bleasdale was his partner and friend and he had helped the bastard in front of him kill him.

Everything was beginning to make sense now. He had wondered how Bam Bam knew what was going on. Why had he not thought about it more before? He kicked himself mentally for being such a cock sure prick. He had to ask the question: "Was Tony killed because of information you received?" Bam Bam confirmed that he had received nothing about Tony being there. He was spotted by his men. He added that he thought he was a stupid officer who didn't know what the hell he was doing. Like John, he was killed because of what he might see rather than what he did see. It was all so senseless. Two decent men's had been taken for no apparent reason.

The tension in Jazz's chest got sharper and heavier. He thought he was going to have a heart attack but knew it was the stress. "I never thought you were such a cold-blooded killer."

Bam Bam looked at him and considered what he had said. "You do what you have to." He sighed and added "Greatness is not an easy mantle to carry." Jazz wondered at that point if he had gone barking mad. He sounded like a megalomaniac. He again asked himself why he hadn't seen the signs.

The heavy silence was broken by Bam Bam's mobile ringing. For a megalomaniac he had a blousy jaunty tune on his mobile which just didn't ring with greatness. All he said was "They are here." Then he left the room. Jazz reckoned *they* must be Bob and Mad Pete. God he felt bad for Mad Pete. It was his fault he was about to enter the lion's den.

STAKE OUT

DS John William Bleasdale was a great and good man who had a lot to answer for. He was a DS from Ilford Police, and the partnership between him and Jazz was a match made in heaven. He was a bit older, and at 45 years old, John had seen a lot of life and had worked out how to make life work for him. He was reckless, he was brave and he was a bad influence on Jazz.

He was originally a scouser but had left Wallasey in Liverpool for London after a family incident. He talked lots to Jazz about his family but confessed he hadn't seen them for years. The man was very proud of his children and Jazz remembered how he always had that look in his eyes when he talked about them. He remembered the sadness. Jazz had learned all the *cutting corners* techniques from John. DS John Bleasdale was an honest policeman. Jazz admired him and believed John Bleasdale's deduction skills rivalled Sherlock Holmes'. He was the Detective who always got his man and Jazz wanted to be like him. There was a mutual admiration between them and they watched each other's back with a loyalty not often seen in the police force.

That evening had been an utter pain in the neck. The stakeout had not been planned in advance; it was a last minute rush. They were told in no uncertain terms to get their arses over to Ilford Lane and keep watch on a house opposite. There was news of a drugs meeting but no other details had been given. With the address of the flat above a sari shop in their hands, they made their way there. The grumbling got worse when they got there. It was a deserted place with one chair to sit on. They were hungry and thirsty. They had been about to go off duty for a night in the local boozer and instead they were in this godforsaken flat. Jazz had the number of a takeaway pizza place in his phone and they ordered one of the mega feast pizzas and a couple of beers.

John Bleasdale was fidgety and wanted to know what was going on across the road. He was bored with just watching and he told Jazz he would just take a look across the road and be back in time for the pizza. He told Jazz to stay put, he didn't want to miss the pizza, he was starving. Jazz argued that he didn't think it a good idea for him to wander off but John patted him good-naturedly on the shoulder, called him a *wooze* and told him not to worry. He blew him a kiss as he left the room and Jazz heard him laughing all the way down the stairs.

Bob had rung to check he was alright and they moaned together about how the bosses messed them around and why couldn't someone else have done the stakeout. Bob had asked where John was and Jazz said he had got fidgety and had gone to take a look at what was going on. He said he had the important job of waiting for the pizza man to arrive. Bob had laughed and said he would ring again later.

He didn't want to remember it. The events of that

evening caused his eventual breakdown. It was like watching something in slow motion. One minute John was outside the house across the road and the next time he looked he saw him in an upstairs room. The light was bright in the room and he could see John clearly. He was just standing by a chair and the next minute someone in the room, out of Jazz's line of vision, shot him and he fell to the floor out of sight. He remembered he just stood looking for a few seconds, unable to believe what he had seen. He had blinked and looked hard because it couldn't be true. These things just didn't happen . He had hesitated for a while longer, distrusting himself. John was a practical joker, there were often times when he had caught Jazz unawares with some sort of surprise. Perhaps this was a joke too. No one had said this was a dangerous stake out, in fact they had no information other than it was a meeting to do with drugs. He stood and watched, waiting for John to stand up and poke two fingers up at him. It didn't happen. After what must have been a couple of minutes, Jazz galvanised himself into action and phoned the police station and reported in what he had seen. Even then, he kept saying he might be going over the top with this and sorry if it was a waste of time.

It wasn't a waste of time. The body of John William Bleasdale was found upstairs in the room across the road as Jazz had seen. He had been shot three times, two in the chest and one in the head to make sure. It was a bad night for everyone at the station. Jazz had never got over it. The blame was laid squarely at his feet. It was said many times to him that he should not have let John

Bleasdale go out there alone. They were partners and were expected to support each other. He couldn't tell anyone that he was waiting for a pizza and beer to be delivered. It was against police policy and that John had taken such a flippant and dangerous decision to make food more important than safety was not something Jazz would tell. He would keep DS John William Bleasdale's memory as pure as he could, he owed him that. He had lived with the guilt and blame all these years and it had eventually caused him to suffer a mental breakdown. The big hole in the world left by John Bleasdale's death had not been filled. Jazz still missed him and sometimes he could swear he felt his presence around him. He put that down to the nervous breakdown throwing up weird feelings. Still, he remembered that whenever he felt John's presence, it made him feel good for the moment.

Now he knew what had really happened, his hatred for Bob was bubbling nicely. If he ever got free he vowed to pulverise Bob to a lump of blubbering, bloody pulp. Being arrested and sent to prison was too good for him. For a policeman to kill or be part of arranging the death of a fellow police officer was unbelievable. Police officers looked after their own, it was instilled in them in training and practised daily as teams networked and covered each other's backs. It was the most heinous of crimes and Jazz firmly believed that, like those who are traitors to their country, cop killers should be executed.

The shouting alerted the gang playing cards and they jumped up and ran to the door. Jazz could hear Mad Pete having one of his druggy panics; they would have to knock him out to restrain him. He could hear the scuffling and swearing going on outside the room. After a few minutes, there was silence and Mad Pete was dragged in unconscious.

Bam Bam had obviously only overseen the foray because he looked in pristine condition, which was more than could be said for several of the gang members. Some had nasty scratches and one had a ripped shirt. Mad Pete had put up quite some fight until one of the men had punched him on the chin, at which point he had gone out like a light and collapsed in a heap on the floor. Jazz looked around for Bob. He might not be able to touch him but by God he wanted to see the bastard.

Bam Bam looked at Jazz and lightly told him in a voice dripping with sarcasm, "Oh yes, I expect you want to know where your friend Bob is. Bob had to get back to the station. He is on duty after all." Jazz hoped he lived long enough to see Bob in a bloodied heap on the floor after he had given him a good kicking.

Mad Pete stirred and struggled as he felt the rope holding his arms and legs tight. They had left him in a heap on the floor, no courtesy of a chair for him! Bam Bam seemed to know what Jazz was thinking and said it wasn't worth putting him on a chair. In a short while they were both being bundled into the car and taken on a ride. Jazz knew what that meant.

Another drink was passed to him by Bam Bam. He gratefully drank it. His hands were shaking so much, he wasn't sure if the glass could reach his mouth without him spilling most of it. Experience counts, and he managed to down it all and closed his eyes as the soothing nectar slid down his throat and warmed his chest. There was nothing he could do. His ace card was lying on the floor and now they would both die. Mad Pete, quiet now, looked up at Jazz with real fear in his eyes. Jazz tried to think of something calming to say to him but failed.

FINALE

All good things have to come to an end and it was time to move. Bam Bam nodded to the biggest member of the gang. "Jamal, you take this one," he said, pointing to Jazz. He smiled at the young men in the corner. "And you three take Mad Pete. The rest just follow us and make sure everything goes smoothly. See you back here," he hesitated and looked at his watch, "in an hour, so don't waste time. Your flight is at 11 p.m. and I want you all gone."

They scrambled out of their chairs and grabbed Jazz and Mad Pete. Jazz had his arms tied tightly before they moved him (they were taking no chances on him trying to escape). Jazz looked round at Bam Bam and in a tight voice asked him to reconsider what he was doing. He had murdered enough people, he lamely stated. Bam Bam left the room without answering and thern was no one to plead with. The gang were doing their job and couldn't care less why Jazz and Mad Pete should live or die. They wanted to get it over with and get on the flight back home. They had made good money in England and were looking forward to spending it in Pakistan. It all felt hopeless and Jazz felt like a lead weight. He had given up.

They were bundled into a van outside. Even Mad Pete was silent. He was trussed up tightly and the gag harshly tied across his mouth ensured he said nothing coherent. He too seemed to have given up the fight and sat slumped against the side of the van, which was cramped with all eight of them tightly packed in. All Jazz's senses were heightened and it seemed to him that he could hear a pin drop and see everything in the dark. His sense of smell was also heightened and the smell of curry, cigarettes and sweat was overpowering. He shook with the fear, knowing that there was nothing he could do to save himself or Mad Pete.

They waited patiently for the big gates to open to allow the van to move out. They spoke in Punjabi and Jazz listened. The conversation was inane, mainly about home and girlfriends and wives. Normal conversations in an abnormal situation, it was very surreal. One started to discuss another job they had been commissioned to do but the others shouted him down and said they had had enough of work and wanted some relaxation after they got rid of these two. It was chilling to realise that they were already dead meat as far as these men were concerned.

The car started moving as the huge gates opened. They had just turned onto the road that would take them to Epping Forest when a bang could be heard. The driver swore and said it sounded like a tyre had blown. He stopped the car and got out to look.

It all happened in slow motion and was so unbelievable that Jazz would never quite comprehend what happened. It was the dogs, the men, the shouting and the guns. He was punched in the face and kicked in the stampede of bodies trying to get out of the van and those trying to get in.

Eventually he recognised the blue of the Met Police uniforms and almost fainted with relief. He was bundled out of the van and untied and wrapped in a blanket. He was shaking from head to toe. Someone was talking to him but it was as if he was deaf. He heard the voices but not the words. He was taken to hospital and manhandled and checked and given an injection. It was said by the doctors that he was in deep shock. It was the next day that the interviewing started.

He heard DS Tom Black before he reached his room in the hospital. "Where the fuck have you put him?" was the dulcet tones that rose over the sounds of the bustling hospital bustling. After a few moments, Boomer burst into his room shouting joyously, "So there you are, you fucking bastard, skivving on the job as usual."

Jazz smiled and retorted, "Missed you too, darling." Boomer laughed, a loud raucous sound, and plonked himself on the side of the bed, just missing Jazz's legs. After eating the grapes someone had left for Jazz and sampling the bottle of coke left to one side, Boomer got down to work.

What no one except Boomer knew was that Jazz had asked for a microphone to be hidden on his body. Jazz had said that he didn't know if he was making a mountain out of a mole hill, but it was possible Bam Bam was more involved in the gang killings than first thought. Tom Black was a big loud man but Jazz could trust him and when it counted, he was a damn good officer. He asked that it be kept between themselves unless something occurred. They both knew they would never get a search warrant based on the ramblings of Mad Pete.

After he had left Bob and Mad Pete in the custody suite, he had rushed to find Boomer, who he grabbed and took outside to urgently tell him about Mad Pete and what he had told him about Bam Bam. In answer to the question from Boomer, he distractedly confirmed that Mad Pete was safe in custody until he got back. He trusted Boomer to watch his back and knew he would be decisive and game for such unorthodox surveillance. Jazz said he would take all the blame if it went tits up and this was the clincher for Tom Black.

It had been arranged extremely quickly, the microphone had been tested but not for the length of time that was normal. He had to hurry, Mad Pete could only be held in custody for a short while before someone started complaining. They could only find a survelliance kit that had a radius of six miles and that would mean that Boomer would have to be laid up somewhere quite close with the receiver and the tape recorder. It was too short notice to get the more sophisticated kit; it was the best that could be organised in such a short time. Jazz went into the grounds not knowing if he was being received or not. Foolhardy, stupid, unprofessional and dangerous were the words used by DCI Radley at the debrief.

To find out that Bob was an informer for Bam Bam and had been for many years was a shock that no one expected. Boomer had heard everything and got it all down on tape. He had rung DCI Radley immediately and a team of SO19s were assembled ready. It had been decided it would be safer and easier to wait until the van with the gang and Jazz on board left the house to waylay them. A marksman had shot out the tyre to stop the van and the rest was history.

Boomer told Jazz to lie low for a bit. There was going to be trouble with the way he had worked. The hospital were keeping him and Mad Pete in for a day or so just for checks. He added that he thought Jazz had done a fucking grand job in single-handedly capturing the bastards. Jazz thought that was a bit over the top, but he appreciated the sentiment. Boomer was not usually given to compliments.

Jazz, burning with the knowledge of what Bob had done, asked Boomer what had happened to Bob. The response, in true Boomer style, was, "Fuck the fucking fucker's fucked." After that was digested by Jazz, he added he was under arrest and at present was sporting a very black eye where someone had accidently punched him in the face when he was resisting arrest. That would do Jazz for now.

It was a feather in the cap of DCI Radley and DS Tom Black's murder squad. The gang of murderers had been captured and the success of the daring rescue was the main headline on every radio and TV news programme. It was in all the papers with a picture of DCI Radley looking quite regal in his ceremonial uniform on the front page. He had modestly stated that his teams had done all the work and he was very proud of them. There was no mention of DS Jaswinder Singh.

Mad Pete left his room in the hospital and found Jazz alone watching the news. It was the only news worth watching on TV. He stood there looking cleaner than Jazz had ever seen him, with his hairy arse hanging out of a hospital gown; it was not a pretty sight. Mad Pete had strode determinedly into Mr Singh's room and now stood at the end of the bed looking unsettled and aggrieved. He said there was no mention of Mr Singh or himself in anything on the news and he thought that was very bad.

He told Mr Singh he had done a great job and the fuckers would have been nowhere without his information. He wanted to know why no one had interviewed him, Mad Pete, the saviour of the capture and rescue. Jazz just raised his eyebrows and wondered where the ego had come from. He mumbled a few words of what Jazz took to be thanks for saving his life. Mad Pete had heard later about the microphone and officers waiting to rescue them. He added venomously that the fucking pigs could have told him what was going down. He asked incredulously, "Didn't they realise I could have died of a heart attack? I was so scared they were going to kill me." Jazz smiled at the logic of the man but in an unusually polite tone thanked him for his views on the rescue. Mad Pete couldn't hear the sarcasm in the words, which usually accompanied anything remotely civil said to him. He wondered if Mr Singh was right in the head after all the *argy bargying* that had gone on.

As Mad Pete left the room, he turned and hesitated for a moment. Looking straight at Jazz and with much contained emotion, he uttered, "Don't care what the others say; you are the big man in my book, Mr Singh."

Jazz waved his hand in the direction of the door and sent him on his way with a "Fuck off". Mad Pete closed the door and smiled. He was alright, Mr Singh was back to his old self again.

Tomorrow was another day. Jazz had a burgeoning nervous breakdown to tackle, a revenge to organise and a desperate need for a drink to satisfy. He was Jaswinder Singh, the Jazz Singher to his friends and enemies. He had to pick himself up and go on. He would never let anyone get close again. No one could be trusted. He was a loner and that was the safest way to be.